GAL EDGE

SAVAGE WARS

JASON **ANSPACH** NICK **COLE**

Edited by David Gatewood
Published by Galaxy's Edge Press

Cover Art: Tommaso Renieri
Cover Design: Beaulistic Book Services
Formatting: Kevin G. Summers

Website: InTheLegion.com
Facebook: facebook.com/atgalaxysedge
Newsletter (get a free short story): InTheLegion.com

OTHER GALAXY'S EDGE BOOKS

Galaxy's Edge Season One:
- Legionnaire
- Galactic Outlaws
- Kill Team
- Attack of Shadows
- Sword of the Legion
- Prisoners of Darkness
- Turning Point
- Message for the Dead
- Retribution

Galaxy's Edge Season Two:
- Takeover

Tyrus Rechs: Contracts & Terminations:
- Requiem for Medusa
- Chasing the Dragon
- Madame Guillotine

Stand-Alone Books:
- Imperator

Order of the Centurion:
- Order of the Centurion
- Iron Wolves
- Through the Nether
- The Reservist
- Stryker's War

Prologue

The state of play in those heady days before the rise of the Legion and the beginning of a galactic-wide Republic that would last nearly fifteen hundred years was simply fantastic. Citizens of the present age paint that time as a sort of dark ages that had fallen over the early galactic nations. But in truth it was a time of fantastic wonders. The fragile human explorer colonies that had first leapt outward to the advent of the hyperdrive had blossomed into incredible civilizations, and even fledgling empires, all connected by the gossamer of faster-than-light travel. The Age of the Hyperspace Civilization had begun.

Espania ruled over a clutch of dazzling worlds along the Siriusian frontier. From Spilursa came the galaxy's finest technologists, bringing with them their haunting leaps into the world of Theoretical Dark Science. And the Vesper Confederacy, the Rigel Assembly, Britannia, and the old United Worlds were the power players as man first began to unite into the tribes that would form the mighty galaxy-spanning Republic.

But these fragile stellar homes, expanding outward toward the ever-widening frontier, were not without their monsters.

And sometimes the worst monsters are ourselves.

Our savage selves.

All throughout the centuries that passed since the advent of faster-than-light travel, the Savages' massive sub-light colony ships—ships that had left a dying Earth during its darkest hours—had flung themselves outward. Only recently had they begun to heave into the frailer systems along the frontier—systems already inhabited by their human brethren who'd left Earth later but reached the stars much earlier, thanks to the hyperdrive.

These encounters, though rare, were neither merry nor happy. They were outright nightmares. Because the Savages, in their ages-long crawl through the intergalactic dark, marinating in their dystopian science experiments, had slowly but surely began shedding their humanity. They were now something... much different.

Though they were called Savages, and the term stuck and entered the popular lexicon, they viewed themselves as far superior to their un-evolved brethren. And in some cases, especially with regard to technology and weaponry, they were.

Fortunately for the human colonists, the Savages' feeling of superiority extended to the *other* Savages—those who had left Earth in different lighthuggers. Each ship had its own portrait of the divine, of perfection, surpassing all others, and each saw all other Savage visions as blasphemous—and thus all other Savage tribes as blasphemers. Enemies. Targets. Thus those early Savage attacks were isolated incidents performed by isolated ships. And the frontier colonies were able to use their technology to amass boarding parties and naval resistance, driving the larger lighthuggers away and sending the smaller ones burning helplessly into the atmosphere. The fights were costly but localized—and winnable. The sluggish lighthuggers were easy to detect and easy to defend against.

Until the Savages acquired one key piece of technology.

Hyperdrive.

And with that, the Savages found themselves able to assemble. To put aside the rancor they had for one another and focus on the *real* threat to their survival—us. To prepare for war greater than the galaxy had ever seen— at least since the days of the Ancients. The Savages were set to assume their place as rulers of the galaxy. Forgotten kings and lords, returned.

Their ascension would begin at New Vega, the brightest of the new colonies of forgotten Earth's children.

It was there that the Savages would come in from the cold interstellar distances.

It was time.

For the next fifteen hundred years, there would be war between the Savages and the rest of the galaxy. A war for mastery. A war for domination. A war that could end only in total victory, for one side or the other.

There was no other solution. The Savages were gods, and all others owed them worship.

In that first fiery crucible that would become the Battle of New Vega, human men and women—along with the dozen alien races known at that time—answered the call. But death walked among them. Starships clashed, the sky caught fire, and cities burned to molten steel and ash.

Great destructive powers were unleashed. Nightmares were made all too real.

That horrific battle was a mere taste of what was to come in the long years ahead. A taste, and a dire warning.

And hither came Tyrus Rechs...

PART ONE

01

Captain Goss had the helm as the flat sturdy transport fell from hyperspace just beyond the planet's outer atmosphere. There were five assault carrier transports in this flight, and all had come out of hyper in formation, which was no easy feat. But the United Worlds, or UW—pronounced "U-Dub" by busy spacers and soldiers—had the best-trained navy in existence, and as long as they were working with themselves, and not the other unprofessional navies of the Coalition, they could be relied on to execute advanced fleet maneuvers.

It was always the combined ops with other navies where things got a little sketchy.

"Radar," said Goss, setting the deflectors to full forward. They were picking up a lot of chop from the outer atmosphere. The entire ship, fifteen decks and four hundred meters long, was bouncing and tossing as they set up to thread atmospheric reentry. "Get me a ping on *Indomitable*."

He turned and smiled at Colonel Marks, the commander of his passengers. "We're havin' fun now."

Marks made an effort to smile back, but the man was so enigmatically unknowable it was hard to say whether he was having fun or just letting Goss know that he was aware that *he* was having fun. And Goss was just fine with that. He had grown to like the colonel a lot in the flight out; they'd often played chess in the officer's mess in the late ship-time evenings. Marks was an exceptionally quiet man—not much for conversation. Goss was fine with that too. The captain liked doing the talking, and Marks was a perfect complement, content to sit and listen. Listen, and beat him at the game soundly every night.

Goss marveled at that. Colonel Marks wasn't a brilliant player—he lacked the flash and the imagination of someone who saw all the corners of the board and laid elaborate traps—but he was relentless, and he had the ability to see ahead. Goss had once asked just how many moves ahead Marks could see, but the man wasn't able to articulate much.

"I just run my game and have a pretty good idea of what people are going to do at any given moment."

That was about the most conversation Goss had gotten out of him at any one time during the jump.

"*Indom*'s coming through and on our six," said Radar. "But she has no escorts. Didn't make the jump on time."

"Damn," muttered Goss. He dialed in the approach. They were at one-twenty angels and coming in fast. Their atmospheric carrier was supposed to be overwatched by

Rigelian Free Trader corvettes, but as always, inter-navy ops were proving difficult.

"Get me Admiral—"

The shaking began to subside as they entered a new atmospheric layer, but a new problem barged its way into command before Goss could finish his sentence.

"Sir, we got contacts," said Radar. "Multiple bogies coming in from all directions."

"At this altitude?" said the first officer from the co-pilot's chair.

The tac officer chimed in over comm from back in the *Montague*'s tiny Combat Information Center. "Maybe New Vegan Air Force? Some sort of high-altitude fighter we don't know about."

"We better hope," said Goss. "Spin up the PDCs. I don't want to get caught with our pants down."

He switched over to private comm on his headset, selected Colonel Marks from the menu with a flick of thumb on the flight yoke, then turned once more to his chess opponent. No one else could hear over the ambient roar of the *Montague*'s powerful engines and the violence of reentry.

"Colonel?"

Colonel Marks looked up from the battle board.

"Doesn't look good," Goss said. "Tac support carrier came in alone. You better get your men ready. My guess is the LZ is gonna be hot and we're not gonna be holding over New Vega City. With no escorts she'll be coming in blind. She won't be able to deploy cover until we're below ten thousand. That means no air support to take Rio."

"Thanks for the heads-up." Marks unbuckled from his jump seat and made his way aft and below to his unit down on the assault decks.

"Gonna be a long day," sighed Goss as he exchanged a look with his first officer.

"Got that—"

Right was what the first officer was about to say when the point defense cannons opened from the *Montague*'s starboard side. All three at once. Their groan was the sound of thousands of twenty-millimeter depleted uranium balls being flung along plotted intercept trajectories to engage the incoming bogies. The rail gun system was expensive and antiquated, but it did the job better than any modern blaster cannon had ever been able to. Plus, old Earth had the resource base to provide the high-velocity projectiles.

"Bandits!" called out Goss, upgrading the unknown identifier of bogie to bandit. An adversary and not just a contact. "Eleven o'clock."

Matte-gray tiger-striped twin-hulled fighters streaked from left to right in front of the descending tactical assault carrier group.

The defense cannons managed to smoke three bandits, but two enemy fighters unloaded at almost suicidally close range, and the effects were instantly devastating to the flight crew of the *Montague*. These Savage weapons were far more powerful than any blaster technology the crew had ever witnessed on starfighters.

For a moment Goss's mind refused to believe what was happening. He told himself it must just be particularly low-interval blaster fire. But the sudden swarm of dumb rounds that raked the forward bridge sounded just like the *Montague*'s archaic but effective perimeter defense cannons—which, in a very advanced form, were also nothing more than what some had once called "guns."

The bridge was holed in a dozen places, and the entire flight deck turned into a cat-five hurricane as it depressurized. Any crewmembers who hadn't been strapped in were sucked out by rapid decompression into the high atmosphere. Goss turned to see his first officer, riding shotgun, have his head vaporized by a massive round.

The captain could feel himself being sucked out and away, but the restraining harness built into the pilot's chair held fast. His flight helmet saved him too, when his head was violently thrown about and into the various systems too close at hand. But he was blacking out all the same.

As he struggled to connect his oxygen, he monitored the instruments to check what attitude his ship was in. It hadn't heeled over. That was good. But it continued to drop through the atmosphere of New Vega. Warning bells and damage klaxons whoop-whooped for his attention. Crewmembers were screaming or shouting orders.

The radar intercept officer screamed over chat and was sucked out through a gaping hole in the fuselage seconds before pressure equalized.

Goss felt an arctic blast of oxygen wash over his near-frozen face. He gulped it down, deeply. Emergency bulkheads were slamming shut between the bridge and the CIC.

Engine four failed.

He was trying to fly the ship when he saw the *Hernandes*, another assault carrier in the group, go up in a sudden ball of fury off the port side.

Twelve hundred and forty people dead in a flash.

Not important! he screamed at himself as the wind shrieked in through the shattered hull. *Fly your own damn ship, you idiot!*

He could hear comm reports telling him the *Indomitable* was in trouble and requesting help. Engineering reported that number four had gone up like a firecracker and that there were mass casualties on the deck.

But the ship was back under his control. He had power and maneuverability. It wasn't dead stick yet. And his job was to get the infantry down and secure a beachhead around Objective Rio.

He took a calming breath and felt a sharp pain in his lungs. Looking down, he saw that his flight suit was dark and wet. He'd been shot in the gut.

"Not important," he muttered through gritted teeth, and flew the approach to Objective Rio, dipping lower into the atmosphere.

At twenty thousand, the Savages opened up with air defense artillery at their beached whale of a ship.

02

Sergeant Major Andres hovered nearby as Colonel Marks pulled the unit's standard-issue ablative plate carrier over the gray digital camo fatigues the Twenty-Fifth Light wore for urban combat. Marks was early middle age— young to have already made the rank of colonel within the Spilursan army. Andres knew he'd been in Black Watch, Spilursa's Special Forces group, and assumed he must've been a highly motivated super trooper to have ranked so hard so fast, and that it was only because he was so high-speed low-drag that he'd been placed in command at the last second after the last CO had taken suddenly ill.

The sergeant major already had his commanding officer's load-carrying equipment ready when the man stood. The colonel slung himself into the LCE, grabbed his helmet from the locker, and tapped the comm interface to make sure he was connected to the command net. Then he took the unit-issue pulse sidearm, a snub-nosed Mulotti and Garic with tactical grips and fifteen-shot charge pack, and holstered it.

Andres handed him a troop-issue pulse rifle. "Uh, sir!" he shouted, struggling to be heard over the damage control alarms. "I know you Black Watch types like to use all your high-speed toys and all... and I advise you to just carry what you're used to since it seems like this is gonna be lit as can be and everything. You don't have to carry the unit issue."

Just as Marks opened his mouth to yell back, the alarms finally shut off, and the ship—which had seemed out of control for a moment or two, and was probably heavily damaged—was now once more steady and stable, and definitely in some kind of descent profile. He guessed they had lost one of the engines up top.

"No thanks, Sergeant Major," the colonel said. "We all use the same gear."

Nothing more. Nothing less.

The sergeant major was still learning that the new colonel was all business—Marks never gave the impression that he was anything but—and with enemy flak coming in close to the hull and exploding, that didn't seem a bad thing. It looked like things were indeed going to get hot.

Maybe not Kimshana Hoolie Valley hot, but hot enough.

***

The colonel entered the briefing room to find his five company commanders studying their battle boards with their helmets tucked under their arms. All of them were young, high-speed infantry officers. There were no weak links. Marks had made sure of that. And so had Admiral Sulla, the United Worlds liaison who'd been the prime motivator behind the whole operation.

"Gentlemen," began Marks.

The officers turned to face their commander. He'd ordered saluting dispensed with for the duration of the op, and none of them even twitched a muscle. Considering how military courtesy had been drilled into them by the professional Spilursan army, one of the best in the Coalition, Marks was impressed with their ability to quickly adapt.

But he didn't let it show in the least on his stern face.

"Things don't look good." Marks's face didn't show concern over the fact. "Obviously you're watching Fleet CIC. Three transports destroyed already. That leaves us with the Three-Six Armored Cav. We will hold Objective Rio until the fleet arrives in full. You have your sectors; if the situation changes on the ground, be ready to adapt. Join your companies in the MTACs. And be ready for anything. I'll remind you once again: every Savage ship is a different thing. Expect the unexpected, and you won't be surprised."

"Yes, sir," the men boomed in reply.

As the captains departed to join their companies aboard the mobile tactical assault crawlers, Sergeant Major Andres led Marks to the headquarters MTAC, where he joined the HQ command team and plugged into Fleet CIC.

Multiple images showed every Strike Force Warhammer asset in system. There were half as many as there were supposed to be, and most were coming in drips and dribbles. Task Force Wrath would arrive shortly, once the initial insertion LZ was secure, but many of the ships coming through in the first wave were getting shot up by what Fleet CIC was now tagging as Savage interceptors.

"How they have ships the size of our fighters that are both space and atmo-capable is a mystery to me," muttered the S-2 officer, shaking his head over a battle board.

Marks was more concerned with the approach to Objective Rio and the city that surrounded it. It was pre-dawn dark—oh-three-twenty-four local time. Much of the fantastic city was in complete blackout. The feed from the cockpit sensors wasn't good. Lots of disturbance.

"Is that from us, or local effect?" someone asked regarding the quality of the feed.

"Probably us," said the S-2. "Ship got hit pretty hard coming in. But the flies are holding her together on three engines."

"Good for Navy," someone noted dourly.

Then they all saw it.

Some gawped. Others cursed.

The Savage ship was massive. Easily ten kilometers long. It was just a shadowy shape down there on the surface, but that shape revealed a slender bow, a fat and stacked midships, angular decks carved and rotating cylindrically along rising planes, and massive sub-light engines flaring away from the rear. Almost like an old-school rocket made high-tech if your perspective of such things was five hundred years old. And somehow it had managed to set down inside the city. Like it wasn't going anywhere ever again.

"Should just pave this place with nukes. That's what Rechs would've done."

"Yeah, and then we'd be war criminals too."

The lighthugger was a thing as old as space flight itself. Something from the Earth of long ago. They'd called them colony ships back when the world was falling apart. Now the galaxy called them the Savage hulks.

"We dead," noted some NCO.

"Cut that," said Sergeant Major Andres sharply.

"Thirty seconds, Colonel," said Goss over the comm. "Good luck, and it was nice knowin' you." Then the captain coughed, and it didn't sound good.

Marks could tell the captain of the *Montague* was wounded. That much was clear. But he was a hell of a pilot, and he would get them down and into the action. Which was all any infantryman could ever ask for. A chance to show and fight without getting killed on the way.

That, and to be shown where the enemy was so that the shooting could start. After that, it was anybody's game.

"You too," Marks said tersely. And then the comm was cut.

"Thirty seconds!" shouted the loadmaster over the assault bay speakers. "Be advised—"

A massive explosion somewhere along the hull sent the ship lurching violently, but it continued its approach to Objective Rio over the outer suburbs of New Vega City. They were almost there. The LZ was lit by the invisible neon green of the Pathfinder's marking lasers. But the rest of the city was shadowed in blues and grays.

"Strap in!" yelled the sergeant major. "This is the big show!"

Marks did a weapons check on the Twenty-Fifth's issue pulse rifle while he made his way to his crash chair.

The pulse rifle was a good weapon. Forty-shot charge pack. Full auto and semi. Two-hundred-watt pulse. Good weapon. Boxy and workmanlike. Prone to mag dump if not cautious.

But to the colonel, a weapon was a weapon. He'd killed with lots of them. In the end, everything was the same. Point and shoot. Don't miss. Be quick about it. Life and death depended on such basics.

And he would use anything he could get his hands on to kill every Savage there was. Even if he had to reduce the galaxy down to its Stone Age components.

03

It could have been any four of the MTAC crawlers that went up first. But it was the Alpha Company crawler that took the high-speed rail gun round fired from within the city. It cooked off the fuel tanks, immolating two hundred plus men in an instant. And all of this only twenty seconds after being down and clear of the *Montague*.

That was often said to be the official beginning of the Battle of New Vega. Alpha going up in an instant. Or so the moment would be defined by the few who would survive to tell what had happened.

The Twenty-Fifth was experienced. Mostly a lot of brushfire stuff—violent, short, and brutal. They'd fought on Kimshana against guerilla insurgents trying to take the colony for themselves, and they'd done their share of bug-hunting on some outer worlds in the Spilursan sphere. But they'd always had support superiority in the form of tac air and artillery.

Nothing had prepared them to see Alpha get smoked within seconds. Nor to see the wounded *Montague* smoking from several different sections. Its engines were spooling down and its lift repulsors were inactive. It didn't look like the crew was even making an effort to get off the LZ.

And Marks was pretty sure that Goss was dead.

He turned to the operations sergeant in the command team. "Tell them to get off the LZ. Three-Six needs to put down."

Enemy fire was coming at the four surviving crawlers as they moved toward different sections of the massive sports complex designated Objective Rio. The insertion LZ for Strike Force Warhammer. At its center was a stadium capable of seating a million spectators watching up to ten different games at once. This was the only place in New Vega large enough to be a landing zone while also providing cover to the vulnerable ships once they set down.

The *Porter* was circling overhead and taking fire from both within the city and from the Savage hulk beached near the Hilltop District. And even higher up, way above the stadium battlespace, the tac support carrier *Indomitable* was fighting her way down through the cloudscape. She was getting swarmed by those new interceptors, but she had PDC fire to spare. The Rigelian escorts that should have accompanied her in would've been nice, though.

"Drop the ramps and get the men off. Tell the crawlers to keep moving to secure the complex perimeter," Marks ordered. "Fire and move into position. The Savages don't get this stadium!"

Someone aboard the *Montague* must've slaved the bridge to the emergency bridge, because the three huge engines spooled up into an urgent whine and the massive repulsors on the underside thrummed to life. Slowly, amid the spray of grit and dust and incoming fire, the squat snub-nosed assault frigate lifted off.

It had just cleared the rim of the fantastic stadium when a missile hit it amidships. The pilot, or whoever was flying, added power; the engines glowed brighter as they struggled to push upward. But the damage was catastrophic. The ship pitched over and smashed into the residential neighborhoods beyond the stadium. Its reactor exploded, sending shock waves throughout the area that leveled homes and buildings.

"Big bird down!" someone called over the command net.

Colonel Marks disembarked from the crawler with Headquarters Company and followed the four-story, gray-camoed MTAC toward a massive triumphal arch that had been the complex's featured centerpiece for the one-hundredth anniversary of the Galaxy Games just two years earlier.

Search and rescue was trying to get a sitrep and clogging up the command channel. Colonel Marks keyed in a command override, and his voice played over all other traffic. "Get off the net. They're all dead."

Whether that was true or not, now wasn't the time to send in search and rescue ships. The LZ was hot, there were no formal lines or influence or controlled sectors established, and there was effective anti-air in play. Sending in rescue ships would only get more people killed.

"Delta engaging the enemy," came a message over the command net.

Marks and HQ Company reached the mouth of the arch at the stadium's western approach.

First contact.

Marks knew this was the most important moment in the battle. Because they didn't know what they were facing yet. Or how to fight it. He'd fought Savages before and every battle was different, because every Savage ship had evolved along different lines of technological development for close to five hundred years.

He stopped and scanned the dark sports complex. The only source of illumination was Alpha's burning crawler. After battering its way through a stadium exit, away from the LZ, it had been met almost immediately with a direct hit from the rail gun.

At the north end of the complex, Delta's crawler was unloading with her secondary pulse turrets on tangos the colonel was trying to image with his 'nocs. Whatever they were, they moved fast. Like four-legged spiders. But just as Marks thought that, he saw one stand up on two legs. The other legs were suddenly arms, firing some sort of rifle. Then it ran in a crouch off between a massive line of turnstiles that led into the stadium itself.

More and more of them were swarming into the complex, all rushing for the stadium like a rabid throng of seamball hooligans. These Savages could scamper over surfaces fast, as though they had some kind of innate climbing tech. Which meant they'd have no difficulty quickly reaching the tops of the hundred-plus-story super towers that were strung out across the once-incredible jewel of New Vega City. These looked directly down into the stadium, and sniper or ranged fire assets positioned there could easily acquire targets covering within Objective Rio. Like Alpha Crawler.

From above, the *Porter* came in fast, flaring her repulsors hard, her reverse thrusters howling like a squadron of banshees. The Three-Six Cav were also Spilursan regular army units, and having some light armor and scouts moving in would help give a better picture of the battle in the hours to come.

If they made it off the LZ.

Behind Marks, the HQ crawler's turrets dumped copious amounts of pulse fire beyond the arch. The colonel turned and ran toward the MTAC's rear door. Now he would get a better look at what these particular Savages had decided to become out there in the dark.

04

Headquarters Company consisted of three infantry platoons assigned to protecting the staff officers of the Twenty-Fifth. All of them were shooters. As were the staff officers; each had entered an officer candidate program only after serving at least one tour as enlisted and being recommended for promotion by their NCOs. That was standard across the Spilursan military, which had merged old elements of the original Earth militaries with some of the old Martian units and brought them together to form an effective fighting force.

As Marks moved forward, lead elements of Headquarters were already engaged in a heavy firefight with forces beyond the arch. He tapped his comm.

"Platoon leaders, tell your NCOs to watch the flanks. Walls of the stadium and then the seating. Be advised… enemy has the ability to rapidly climb over obstacles."

An anti-armor missile streaked past the crawler and sidewindered off into the night sky. At least the vehicle's ECM algorithms were having some luck scrambling incoming tracking.

Marks linked up with SGM Andres.

"I need the SDMs to move into counter-sniper mode," he told his senior-most NCO. "Watch those three buildings."

He tagged three slender downtown super towers within weapons range of the stadium. All their windows were dark; power was down across large sections of the city.

"Roger, sir." Then Andres was off to pull the squad-designated marksmen back and reorient them to this possible threat.

A fusillade of actual gunfire, a thing Marks hadn't heard in years, resounded off the sides of the stadium and out across the cityscape. It sounded ominous and hollow in that way that only gunfire can. Some type of heavy weapon was moving forward and spitting death.

The wounded were starting to be dragged to the rear. Each platoon had a designated medic, and a casualty collection point was set up at the rear of each MTAC. Marks got sitreps from Delta, Charlie, and Bravo, then moved forward to link up with the Headquarters Company commander, who was supervising an emplaced grenade launcher mech that hurled belt-fed micro-grenades all across the front of their line. Buying time to get the rest of the company into protected firing positions.

The company commander had his helmet's SmartEye flipped down and was scanning the enemy on biometric IR. Marks threw himself down behind a pile of rubble that had been turned into a fighting position and pulled out his battle board. He linked into the CO's SmartEye feed and studied the terrain beyond the stadium.

It was a wide pavilion that opened up into a massive transportation station. Dead Savages lay out there, their bodies illuminated by their fading body heat. Except... not exactly. Marks expanded the image and studied a specific corpse as ghostly rounds and lightning streaks of tracer fire zipped past their heads.

The dead Savage showed fading body heat in its head, fully covered by a helmet. The rest of its body was already well below body temperature, except in those spots where it had been hit by streaking pulse rifle blasts or impaled by hot shrapnel from the GLM.

Interesting.

The grenade-launcher mech positioned forward of the crawler took an RPG round and exploded in a sudden shower of sparks. Thankfully the ammo clamshell that fed grenades to the GLM didn't cook off and blow everyone nearby all to hell.

"Sergeant Baz!" shouted the CO, Captain Forrester. "GLM's down. Send in the secondary." No doubt the platoon sergeant had the platoon's assets at the rear along with the mounting casualties.

Marks watched as a trooper took a hot smoking round right through the helmet and simply fell over. Ricochets and close fire zinged and streaked across the entrance to the arch.

"Leave First Platoon here," Marks ordered Forrester. "Get Second and Third up on the stadium rim, right and left flank. The crawler will hold, along with First."

When the captain didn't reply, Marks looked over. "Steve! Did you—"

Captain Forrester was dead. A round had smashed right through his ablative chest armor. The plate was effective against the blaster and pulse fire most military units found themselves facing in modern warfare, and it was rated to withstand ballistic impacts from most projectile weapons. Which meant the Savages must be hurling some particularly fierce slugs into the lines.

Marks took over.

"Captain Forrester is KIA. This is the colonel. I'm taking command of Headquarters. Second and Third Platoons, pull back and climb up to the stadium rim. Set up firing positions from there. Second on the left, Third on the right. Signal when you're in position."

He got confirms from both platoon leaders before switching over to the platoon sergeant on the company net, who reported that Headquarters had six KIAs and three wounded.

"Medics ain't used to treating this many gunshot wounds, sir."

Marks ignored the comment. It didn't matter. Gunshots were what they would have to deal with. "Send me your reserves forward. Tell them to hug the tunnel and stay away from the crawler."

"Wilco, sir."

The reserve GLM, a tiny little mech that deployed and spat out micro-grenades, was trundling forward when the surge came. When the Savages stormed the arch.

Marks steadied the pulse rifle behind a chunk of concrete and aimed at one of the approaching Savages working its way up behind an abutment that guarded a wide set of stairs. Center mass with the micro-dot scope, and he squeezed the trigger.

The first round nailed the thing in the leg and did nothing.

Marks reentered and fired again, this time nailing the thing in the upper chest. Still nothing. The hot round zipped through the thing's body, but it merely dragged away a spray of metal debris.

Heat signatures in the head, he told himself.

Tougher shot.

Marks had always been a shooter.

He let go of his breath and zeroed a shot right into the thing's helmeted face. Truth be told, the first two shots had slowed it. Like some machine suddenly switching from turbo to cruise.

But the last shot dropped it completely. At less than eighty meters Marks saw the dark silhouette of brain matter and helmet fragments cross the night through his scope.

More were coming.

He turned his aim to a trio of Savages getting close with what looked like a large recoilless rifle. Some sort of anti-armor team, if he had to guess. The leader went down when Marks squeezed off five quick shots to see if enough body damage would do the trick just as well as a headshot. It did. Sparks and explosions erupted from the thing, and it shifted into its spider configuration and tried to scuttle under a dark advertising display, but Marks kept nailing the beast until it went down and didn't move.

Tangos two and three crouched down behind the same abutment, out of sight. Now was the moment they'd be loading some type of rocket to take out the crawler, and at this range, the ECM might not have the time to do its job again.

Marks dumped the pulse rifle's charge all into one shot. Then he waited, scope resting on their last known position. Half a minute later, as the Savage gunfire reached a cacophonic level of chatter and the pulse rifles spat out staccato bursts of barking whines in reply, one of the Savages in the recoilless rifle team surfaced like some ancient submarine.

Just the head.

Spotter, thought Marks. The guy turned his shapeless helmet back and forth across the line. The helmet was dull and mirror-smooth all around, nothing to distinguish the front from the back. Marks watched through the medium-range engagement scope as the Savage inclined his head to the left. Like he was talking to someone. Someone below the abutment.

Some things never change.

No matter how post-human you dream of becoming.

Human communication is hardwired into the DNA.

Marks shifted the scope to that position. To the spotter's left.

Number three popped up with the recoilless launcher, boxy and hexagonal, resting on his shoulder, readying for a firing solution on an identified target.

His shoulder? thought Marks in some distant part of his mind.

Who knew? Could be a her.

It was unimportant. They'd given all that up when they became Savages. To Marks, they were *things* now. Animals.

He pulled the trigger on the pulse rifle, pre-set to dump the whole charge, and vaped the shooter in a spray of blood, brain matter, and armor.

The rest of Fourth Platoon was coming up alongside to join First.

Marks rolled over onto his back and yanked his battle board off his ablative chest plate. He filed an intel report with all leaders on target acquisition. *Head shot is a kill. Use more rounds center mass to take them down. Three at least.*

Send.

He looked at the roster for Headquarters Company. Most of the officers had stuff to do right now. Interfacing with cav coming off the *Porter*, redistributing supply. Getting the intel drones up in the air.

Captain Forrester was KIA.

But the First Platoon leader was still alive.

Colonel Marks activated his comm. "Lieutenant Milker."

Ted Milker was on the far side of the arch, fighting from an alcove with a heavy pulse rife team. Directing fire as the strange-limbed shadows, like spiders or octopuses, then like men running, shifted and moved closer.

"Milker here, sir."

"Promoting you to captain. Headquarters is yours. Do not fall back."

"Can do, sir. Won't forget nothin'."

Which was the old motto of the Martian Light Infantry. Over the long years, it had found a home in far Spilursa.

05

With Headquarters now under control and the first wave of Savages fought off—nothing more than a probe, it seemed—the colonel set off to connect with the other four surviving companies and get their defenses linked up. Sergeant Major Andres accompanied him, as did a young PFC who served as the sergeant major's messenger.

They found Charlie Company first. Charlie had fought off a counterattack on the flank in which the Savages had tried to come through the stadium's lower levels. The flank attack had been easily driven off, but there had been some casualties.

Still, they weren't hurt as badly as Delta. At the north end of the stadium, Delta had been hit hard. Fifty percent of the company had been killed or wounded, and they were already low on charge packs for the pulse rifles.

Bravo was the only company in great shape, with almost no casualties.

The sergeant major went with his aide and an ad hoc recovery team to check on the ruin of Alpha's crawler, and when he returned, the news was not good.

"Hunnert percent casualties, sir. No salvageable assets."

On the field inside the stadium, the massive *Porter* remained down. With anti-air in the area, it was deemed best not to take off until the *Indomitable* could get air cover up.

Marks and the captain of the *Porter*, along with Colonel Dippel of the Three-Six Cavalry, connected via comm with the admiral aboard the *Indomitable*, which had finally been joined by her Rigelian escorts. They were on station at nine thousand feet east of the main metropolis, out to sea, and preparing to commence air operations within the next thirty minutes.

"Less than an hour before daylight," muttered the sergeant major. "Be nice to have a look at the city before we go poking around for a fight."

After the initial Savage outbreak six weeks before, the city had gone dark. Little to no intelligence had been acquired since.

"My job is to get out there and find civvies," said Colonel Dippel matter-of-factly. "My troops are ready to go, but I'd feel much better with drone recon and full daylight."

"What about Angel?"

Everyone looked to Marks. Though he was relatively unknown to them, he knew his introduction into the strike force at the last minute had caused a lot of speculation as to who he really was. He was used to that. He'd been told, many times, that there was something about him that seemed older, wiser. More knowledgeable. Did that. Been there. Stacked the bodies.

Which, of course, he had.

Angel was the next insertion wave of the strike force. A heavy assault carrier would make a low pass and drop the rest of the ground units across the city along designated lines. The idea was to link them up and form a cordon inside the metropolis to commence rescue and assessment operations while engaging the Savages in combat.

Rescue the civilians.

Assess the degree of Savage infection.

Terminate the Savage presence.

Marks switched comm to the Pathfinder captain. He got the platoon sergeant instead.

"This is Bullfrog Two. Bullfrog Actual is KIA, sir."

"Bullfrog," said Marks, "do you have the drop plot for Angel?"

"Negative on plot at this time, sir. We caught it hard with Delta when the Savvies came through over there. Just me and one other left, and I'm hit. Sorry, sir."

Marks cut the comm.

"That'll be a bad insert, sir, if they got no jump markers," cautioned the sergeant major. "We gotta make sure they come down around the stadium at a minimum, otherwise our lines won't hold."

Dippel strapped his helmet on. "That's us then. Recon in force. We'll go out two blocks from the stadium and drop markers."

That was when the next Savage attack came against Delta. They hit hard and fast. Again.

"We'll exit through Headquarters," said Dippel as he ran to link up with his troop.

"Be quick about it, Matthew. You have less than an hour to have those markers in place," warned Colonel Marks.

"Yes, sir," Dippel said, nodding. He continued on, almost sprinting to his objective.

With enough men like that, Marks thought, *I could beat the damn Savages all the way back to the ruins of Earth.*

06

Three-Six Armored Cavalry (Fast Attack)
Attached to Coalition Strike Force Warhammer
New Vega

Staff Sergeant Michael Greenhill was riding in the third vehicle of the lead element of Colonel Dippel's recon when they passed through Headquarters perimeter, squeezing by the big crawler guarding the tunnel. They passed the wounded at the casualty collection point, the dead laid out nearby and covered with their own ponchos. A thing no one had thought to use before the operation, as the weather report said no rain for the next three days. But the senior NCOs had known why you always brought your ponchos.

Now a young sergeant like Greenhill knew why, too.

"Sucks to be them," said the driver. Curts.

Greenhill said nothing from the TC position inside the Leopard ATAV. Above their heads, the gunner swiveled the heavy pulse gun from left to right and watched the streets to the sides. The lead two vehicles were covering forward.

Dawn was in the east and not thirty minutes away when they made their first contact.

Civilians.

They came out of the dark from one of the taller buildings, surging forward and waving. Dirty and bedraggled.

About what the troopers of the Three-Six had been told they would find. Some looked hopeful. Some were crying and dragging dead-eyed children forward as though they were running for their lives.

From the lead vehicle, Colonel Dippel called a halt and directed the second vehicle, carrying the company commander, to move forward and cover the far end of the street. Greenhill's ATAV pulled up short of the surging crowd.

"Stay frosty, Burke," Greenhill reminded the gunner atop the Leopard.

Greenhill had fought on Kimshana. He knew you could never trust crowds. And he knew what to look for. The true believer with the thousand-yard stare mixed in with the desperate rest. The man on a mission. He watched closely as the colonel stepped from the vehicle, covered by his gunner, to interact with the crowd.

"He better jes' tell 'em to walk the hell on back to the stadium, 'cause we on a mission, Sarge," said Curts.

Greenhill said nothing. He was still trying to find the man-on-a-mission guy. Studying the crowd and scanning faces.

And he saw him. Her. The him was a her.

He saw, but he didn't *see*.

Because when the voice, the whisper, tickled at the back of Greenhill's head, he didn't pay attention. Or rather, he had too much to pay attention to in that sudden moment of chaos. And this woman, this pregnant woman who looked like she was going to heave all over the place... she didn't qualify to the sergeant as a man on a mission.

She detonated not five meters from the colonel.

Who knows why?

Greenhill should have keyed in on how fast she was approaching. Practically throwing herself through the crowd. Her face screaming while her body moved like some kind of marionette automaton.

She went off like twenty sticks of dynamite and cratered the street. Everyone was killed. The colonel. His driver and gunner. All the civilians.

The impact glass of Greenhill's ATAV spider-webbed, but it didn't turn into a typhoon of flying fragments. And the vehicle didn't overturn; it jumped once and settled down. Glass blew out in the buildings here in what was probably some New Vega financial district.

Greenhill's bell was rung. For a moment he sat there hearing nothing. Nothing but a dull hiss in his ears that quickly turned into a whine.

"... whole thing is just gone, man!" said Curts. He was apparently referring to Colonel Dippel's vehicle. It was indeed gone.

And the company commander's vehicle was being overrun by more of those black-spider-crawling-and-then-running Savages. They came in so fast the captain's gunner didn't even have a chance to fire before Savages were hauling him and the captain out.

The captain fired his sidearm point-blank. He misted one Savage's helmet.

Two others tore him apart half a second later.

"Light 'em up!" screamed Greenhill at Burke up top.

When Burke didn't fire, Greenhill turned to see nothing but Burke's boots and bloody legs leaning against the side of the turret.

Greenhill moved fast. Talking on the comm and crawling back into the gunner's hatch, never minding the blood and gore of what used to be Specialist Burke. He'd been through worse.

"All units push forward. Ambush. Say again, ambush! Follow my lead!"

And it was true.

Savages were firing from the buildings on both sides. The vehicle behind Greenhill's was frozen. No one was moving. Other vehicles were trying to get around it.

Greenhill opened up on the Savages ahead. Firing a full burst of twenty heavy pulse shots at the Savages—the armored spiders who sometimes walked like men—that were... *feasting* on the bodies of the men from the lead vehicle. Tearing out big chunks and holding their faceless helmets either beatifically skyward or down in some almost prayerful posture before some type of blender in their hands spun and eviscerated the flesh they'd torn free.

The shots from the heavy blaster tore into the once-humans. The heavy pulse cannons atop the ATAVs did significantly more damage than the lower-powered pulse rifles every infantryman carried, even to the armored bodies of the Savages. Shots sizzled straight through their armor, leaving massive gaping holes. In some cases they simply tore the upper torso right off the almost humanoid body.

Greenhill turned and waved for the convoy to move forward.

"Follow the map to the next marker placement!" he shouted at Curts.

There was a slight pause before Curts mashed the pedal and the Leopard jumped forward with an almost ethereal hum.

"We gotta fall back!" yelled one of the other TCs at Greenhill over the comm. "Colonel's dead. Mission is compromised, man!"

As Greenhill worked the barrel across the street, firing into the Savages and cutting them down, he ignored this and all the other horror-struck comm traffic.

"Negative," he barked harshly. "Stay on mission."

With Greenhill on lead, the convoy blasted its way through the ambush, leaving with more than seventy percent of its troops. They reached the next marker objective and deployed a beacon with less than twenty-three minutes to the next drop, designated as Angel.

"Hard left!" yelled Greenhill over the whine of the Leopard's engine. "Pick up the intercept for the next marker. Big park down the street."

The dawn was rising in the east, and the morning air was hot and humid. And despite the forecast for no rain, to Greenhill—who could tell such things from all his years in long-range recon—it smelled like rain was coming.

Beyond the park was the massive hill that topped New Vega City, a place named the Hilltop District by the colonists who first landed here centuries ago. The base of the leviathan Savage starship—designated "The Nest" in operations briefings—lay just below Hilltop, to its left, yet it towered over the spectacular Hilltop super towers at the heights of that neighborhood.

When Three-Six arrived at the large park sprawl, they found that it was on a slope—not entirely free of the hilltop grade. Something the map hadn't been clear about. Greenhill noted it for the marker's packet upload, hoping the loadmaster and the jumpmasters would take the time to interface and give a heads-up to whoever was going to drop on this particular loc. There wasn't much time to do more. Not if all the OBJs were going to get tagged.

"Are you seein' that?" said a sergeant from one of the remaining vehicles.

Greenhill was busy inside his battle board activating the marker, but he looked up. He saw the monster coming down toward them.

Or that was what it looked like.

Moving along one of the broad highways of the seven massive thoroughfares that led down the hill, crushing all manner of buildings as it went, was the largest mech Greenhill had ever seen. None of the Coalition worlds had ever produced anything even remotely close to being as big and ready to fight as the beast that was now coming his way. Even the Sinasians, the mech masters, the ones who had pioneered mech technology, had never built anything that even came close to what the Savages had fielded.

The thing was easily five or six stories tall, and it moved on four massive articulating spider's legs. A central flat command disc rose up from its center, and from this jutted two wicked-looking heavy artillery pieces. And now that Greenhill was paying attention, he realized the ground was rumbling with each strike of its legs.

"No time," said Greenhill. "Moving on to the next marker drop. Spot report it to Fleet Intel. We gotta keep moving before the—"

The sky overhead broke like sudden thunder.

Greenhill had seen streams of such things happening before. Usually pro-military *oorah* patriotic stuff designed to scare the colony worlds into submission. But to be beneath it in real time... that was a whole other thing.

The old United Worlds's most iconic piece of military hardware was indeed something awe-inspiring to behold.

Troopers within the column, parked in the shadows of the park at dawn's last blue, the sun rising red and violent in the east, watched as the massive super-carrier *Hyland G. W. Washington* reentered from jump right into the atmo west of the city, streaking into the dawn on a descent profile. Drop hangars and doors were opening all along her sides and belly.

When you absolutely must scare the living daylights out of the natives, send in the super-carrier.

Successive sonic booms caught up and cracked the skies wide open.

"We can win this!" shouted Curts as he dragged on a smoke.

And Greenhill, who wasn't necessarily a pessimist, more of a realist, wondered if indeed they could get out of this without having to go all Tyrus Rechs on another world.

After all, there were only so many worlds left.

Even that nightmare mech, the massive walking spider heading down into the fray, a definite game-changer, had to pause and watch as the incredible carrier, diamond-shaped from this angle, began dropping units all over the city.

They were awe-inspiring. But they were early.

The timetable wasn't perfect.

Things would be messy.

But it was still an incredible sight to behold.

Heavy armor was dropped by screaming repulsor pods. Drone gliders landed the heavy artillery. Sticks of infantry and light vehicles came down by chute. Other units by fixed-wing cargo literally fell out the back of the super-carrier and then flew on their own. Strike fighters and bombers were shot from catapults off the top of the massive starship.

Instant division on demand.

The UW super-carrier was the workhorse, and hero, of old Earth, and she'd delivered in almost all of the great old battles. I-Day at Centaur. The Breach. The Red Pirate Wars, back in the day.

Within moments, the dawn sky was filled with an army dropped right at the Savages' front door.

"Yeah," said Greenhill to no one. The blood from Burke's body was still as wet as the morning dew atop the ATAV. "We got a chance. Jes' gotta do this the right way."

07

Twenty-Fifth Spilursan Light
North Arch, Objective Rio

Colonel Marks had sent the sergeant major to gather a reaction force to support the defense of Delta's position in case it was overrun. The quickly organized QRF would be staged near the *Porter* and ready to move as soon as possible.

The colonel arrived on scene to find wounded infantry already being dragged back from the heavy fighting at the north gate. Two platoons had been significantly reduced, and the crawler had taken at least three hits from incoming anti-armor fire. Captain Moreaux had been killed, leaving First Sergeant Watt in charge of the defense. The first sergeant himself was bleeding from a shrapnel wound and his arm was in a sling due to a compound fracture.

"Watt," Marks said upon assessing the first sergeant's injuries. "Pull back. In your condition, it's best to organize the mess developing at the rear of the crawler."

"I'm still good to go, sir!" replied the first sergeant. And he kept fighting.

Heavy-duty charge packs lay discarded all alongside the crawler, ejected during the death machine's blazing fury against the Savages that constantly moved and fired in an attempt to take the gate.

"We got this," insisted Watt as the colonel stood and considered whether the man really should remain in the fight. "Our best LT is forward and holding."

Marks nodded at the wounded NCO and moved off at a crouch to link up with the LT. A sniper team, shooter and spotter, signaled the colonel as he moved forward.

"Safest way forward, sir, is through the ticketing entrance inside the wall of the tunnel. Savvies got snipers out there and they're zeroed in on the arch-tunnel itself."

"Thanks," said the colonel.

He moved off into the darkness of ticketing booths that had been blasted open. A labyrinth of booths, barricades, and turnstiles girded both sides of the arch, providing cover from incoming fire.

He checked his watch.

Fifteen minutes until dawn.

All his experiences with the Savages told him that if they could hold until then, things might turn around. But the truth was you never really knew when it came to the Savages. "Expect the unexpected" wasn't just a saying. It was a rule. And the dead had paid to learn it.

Inside the warren beyond the ticketing booths, Marks found the medics, the wounded, the dying, and the dead. Those still drawing breath were being pulled farther back inside the lines. The dead would remain. There was no time to remove them.

"Where's Lieutenant Maydoon?" Marks called out.

"Lieutenant's that way," shouted one of the infantrymen tasked to assist and guard the medics. Pulse fire and incoming hard ammo ricocheted in the tunnel arch and whined on high-pitched, almost-hysterical notes.

The colonel nodded and continued on.

As he came up behind a heavy pulse gun team bleeding charge packs and rocking the enemy with a storm of blaster fire, he saw the problem with the battlefield at this end. This entrance to the stadium had been designed to accommodate traffic from the heavily populated northern portions of New Vega City. What must've seemed like a good defensive position to the Delta CO had turned into a turkey shoot from the various apartment blocks and hotels that girded this end of the complex. He'd made matters worse by digging in too far forward, and as a result had gotten murdered by ranged sniper fire.

Maydoon, the LT now in charge, had pulled back to a series of security barriers that formed a chokepoint. But there was an ample kill zone between the support weapons to the rear and the forward infantry fighting out there in the security barriers.

From the vantage of the support teams, who were raining fire on a staging mass of Savage troops, it was clear that there was a larger Savage attack brewing from an underground tunnel opening—probably an exit from the city's subterranean transportation system.

Marks set up next to a weapons team sergeant, settling into cover against the wall of an alcove as the heavy weapon let loose a histrionic blare that echoed throughout the stadium complex.

"We're runnin' low on charge packs, sir. If they push the LT, we won't be able to sustain fire to keep 'em off," shouted the support weapons team leader.

The colonel peered out at the situation with his 'nocs. The weapons team sergeant was right. It would take no more than a fifty-meter dash for the staging Savage mass to overrun from the left flank. And the infantry fighting from inside the security barrier would never see it coming.

"To make matters worse, I got no comm," said the sergeant as the nearby heavy pulse gun stopped roaring and a charge pack was swapped out amid much cursing from the team.

"C'mon, man!" shouted the gunner like a kid whose fun had just stopped. "I'm lit to go!"

Marks pulled his battle board off his chest plate and tapped his way down through the comm channels to get ahold of Lieutenant Maydoon out in the security barriers.

"You want me to send a man out there to connect?" asked the team leader, seeming impatient for the colonel to make some reply. "He'll probably get killed trying. But..."

"Warmonger Actual to Delta Four-One," said the colonel.

Nothing.

"Warmonger to Delta Four-One, over."

Some static; a high-pitched whine. Perhaps someone saying "Go for Four-One" crackled through. But it was hard to say.

Marks debated what to do next. He could broadcast and hope they got the heads-up that they were about to be overrun. But all he'd be doing for sure to improve the situation was hope...

"Give me all the cover you've got," he ordered the weapons sergeant.

"Roger that, sir. Wait, *what?*"

Colonel Marks vaulted the smashed ticket window the emplacement was firing from and ran for all he was worth down to the security barriers.

For a second, there was nothing but dead silence from the weapons team sergeant. Then the man screamed, "Covering fire, you bastards!"

The entire firing line opened up as the colonel crossed into the kill zone, sprinting as hard as he could through sniper fire to reach the security barriers where the lead element of Delta's infantry was holding out.

08

"Inbound!" came the flash report over the command net. Concrete and glass exploded all around the colonel as he raced the last ten meters and practically threw himself into the wall of the security barrier.

He moved along the wall to a small overwatch building in the center of the stretch of barricade—most likely constructed to spot incoming terrorist attacks—and linked up with the remnants of the platoon fighting from within. The condition of the building reflected the condition of its occupants: it had been shot up in almost every place along its concrete walls, but like the platoon, it was still holding.

The moment he entered, as men fired from the windows at tangos across the plaza, someone shouted, "Incoming RP!"

The building shook as the micro-missile exploded against its outer wall. Across the plaza, Savage weapons teams opened up in earnest. And out there above it all, the colonel heard some ancient, familiar sound, like an electronic game from long ago, signaling out over the Savage masses. A sound so old the young would never recognize it. And the colonel barely did. Or rather didn't at all. Just some old fading to forgotten memory that shouldn't be here in this present madhouse.

That signal meant the Savages were coming now. The rush was on.

"Orient left flank!" Marks shouted. "Prepare to repel!"

He had no idea if a unit trained under the Spilursan military would understand that command. But the old Martian Light would have.

Maydoon started shouting out names and physically repositioning soldiers inside the bunker to meet the threat that wasn't even seen yet.

Then hundreds of fast-moving armored Savages, cartwheeling, running, and firing all at once, came up out of the tunnel entrance and rushed the security barriers.

The colonel raised his pulse rifle, flipped to full auto, and started dumping fire into the swarming mass charging the left flank. The support teams from farther back were pouring in even more fire. And yet for all the firepower being expended, it wasn't enough. Within twenty seconds the first shot-to-hell Savages had reached the barrier.

One of the Delta riflemen was dragged through a window and disappeared. A Savage stuck his weapon through a wide opening and sprayed automatic gunfire that should have killed more than it did. A Spilursan infantryman took a burst across the torso, screamed, and batted the Savage's firing machine gun toward the ceiling, then with his last breath dumped his mag into the faceless enemy.

And still more Savages were coming.

Badly thrown incendiary devices were tossed from the Savage lines and managed to ignite some of their own in sudden streams of liquid lava. Yet incredibly, the Savages, with living fire crawling all over them, continued to shoot into the security barrier from just meters away.

A voice over the comm. "Wizard to Warlord Actual."

The colonel racked a new charge pack, held his rifle out the fractured window, and dumped the entire pack into the surging mass. Thunder ripped the sky above, and the colonel recognized the telltale atmospheric reentry of a UW super-carrier entering the battlespace. A soldier was handing grenades to the LT, who was popping them and tossing them into the Savages. Explosions rocked the barrier, sending debris and fragments everywhere.

One of the infantrymen sat down and began to scream in the middle of it all.

"Go for Warlord," said the colonel as he slapped in another charge pack. Noting there were not a lot of charge packs left.

"Air support on demand," came the terse reply.

The colonel dropped his weapon and ordered an airstrike on his battle board. Not *directly* on the security barrier bunker, but close enough to be a real problem.

He marked it urgent.

A second later he got the confirm from the air boss running strikes with the newly entered interceptors and bombers that had come in with the super-carrier.

"Fast mover inbound, Warlord," said Wizard. "Special delivery in twenty seconds."

Which seemed, to the colonel, to be forever away.

A grenade came through the window, bounced off the far wall and landed near an infantryman whose head had been blown off.

"Grenade!" shouted the platoon sergeant.

The colonel had just put his battle board away and was reaching for his weapon. He was in no position to cover, or to do anything to protect himself.

He and a lot of other soldiers would take the blast full on.

But Lieutenant Maydoon was already moving.

He grabbed the body of the dead headless infantrymen and in one swift motion slammed it down on top of the tomahawk-shaped explosive.

Then he threw his own body on top of the other.

The grenade went off.

Body parts showered the defenders.

Above all this, beyond the automatic gunfire of the Savages, the scream of an inbound Valkyrie close-air-support strike bomber erupted across the sky.

"Heads down on the ground," warned the dry voice of the pilot over comm. Like it was just another day at work for the guy. And not the end of the galaxy for some.

The colonel looked up and saw the four-tailed bomber with forward-swept wings lining up for her run. It came in steep and fast as the wings suddenly swept back, putting it in a slower flight configuration. Then the lethally famous AGM-98 pulse pod system opened up with her intuitive targeting, dumping twenty thousand high-cycle pulse shots across the Savages swarming the security bunker.

Archival footage of the battle, studied from every angle in order to understand the strengths and weaknesses of the new Savage threat, would reveal that over three hundred Savages were killed in that pass. The AGM-98 system's AI targeted and spent at least fifty high-velocity blasts on each target in a sudden blur of fire. It was so much fire that it even slowed the Valkyrie's approach—which in turn only allowed the targeting AI to be even more thorough in its lethal work.

A moment later it was gone. And so was the sound of gunfire from the Savage lines.

The colonel scrambled forward across the bodies inside the barrier. He reached Maydoon's body and pulled him over onto his back, hoping there was some treatable wound that meant the kid was still alive. Or at least had the chance to go on living.

But it wasn't a body.

It was a live young LT with no visible damage. The headless infantryman, whoever he was, had saved his platoon one last time.

09

Dawn broke as the colonel made his way back into the stadium. The once-pristine sports complex, the jewel of the galaxy even just a few years back, looked now like a post-apocalyptic ruin from some destabilized colony world. Or a movie set.

The Three-Six Cav's drone recon detachment was sending back reports that the Savage assault that had begun in the last half hour had broken. The streets surrounding the stadium were mostly clear, and it looked like some of the larger enemy concentrations were pulling back under the cover of the massive Savage ship located near Hilltop.

The jaw-droppingly massive mech that had been spotted coming down the hill toward the park had fired three barrages against the stadium before Coalition bombers off the *Indomitable*, flanked by interceptors, had made a decisive run and knocked it out.

This streak of good news was immediately dampened by casualty reports. The disconnected units that had been dropped almost willy-nilly by the super-carrier all across the battlefield were hurting. To make matters worse, the supreme Coalition commander, appointed as overall leader for this action, had ordered all units to hunker in place for the next two hours until he could assess the situation now that he was on the ground.

"He should pull them back to the stadium," muttered Marks after the operations briefing over the comm net had ended.

"Makes sense to me, sir," said SGM Andres. "But the big dog says we got to hold on to what we got. Like General Ogilvie thinks we got lucky and gained ground with that ate-up drop going bad like it did and all."

The colonel pounded a coffee someone had handed him and studied his battle board. "He just doesn't want to admit he was wrong," he muttered to himself—though the sergeant major and everyone else nearby heard him just the same.

The colonel almost added something else, thought better of it, and drank more coffee instead.

For the next hour, he and the sergeant major checked the lines of their unit, making sure the surviving command teams were linked up with the units on their flanks.

At Delta once again, which was verging on total ruin with now less than twenty-five percent of its original troops, the sergeant major remarked, "They're gonna put us on guard duty in the rear, sir, once they get a look at our numbers."

This made the colonel none too happy.

Another hour later they arrived at the ad hoc Combat Information Center set up on the troop deck of the *Porter*. What had started out as a grand operation to deal with the new, oddly concentrated Savage problem was now looking to the colonel like an absolute and utter failure. And the situation was getting worse by the second.

"Everything is going according to plan," announced Ogilvie to a collection of commanders and staff officers.

General Ogilvie. Supreme Commander of Coalition Forces.

"It may look dire," he continued, shaking his head slightly, but not enough to dislodge a strand of his well-manicured iron-gray hair, "but we couldn't have asked for a better drop on the board. Some of our units have established forward operating spheres within direct striking distance of the Savage Nest. I'm greenlighting offensive..."

He paused as he noticed Colonel Marks and SGM Andres, covered in dust and dried blood, without proper chest armor, carrying rifles inside the TOC. Which had been expressly forbidden by executive correction to the Coalition SOP.

"... operations immediately," finished the general. Then, on a droll note of disapproval: "Colonel Marks, so very glad you could join us. I'll chalk up your heavy casualties to your last-minute appointment of command to your unit. Still, all things considered, you did a commendable job holding the primary insertion point. Though it would seem that we no longer need Objective Rio as a staging base now that we're switching over to the offensive in..."

He murmured to an aide. The aide murmured quietly back after consulting one of three battle boards he was carrying.

"Just under two hours," finished the general as though some expectedly delightful party would commence round about that time.

Instead of the bloodbath and death that would reach industrialized proportions.

The colonel cleared his throat.

Only because it was dry.

"As I was saying," continued the general, having registered his quiet disapproval with the colonel's late arrival to his sacred briefing hour in the way he kept looking the man up and down, "because most of our lead infantry units jumped first and centered around the original markers, we have a unique opportunity"—he said this brightly—"to form an assault force that will pass through our support units, which are now the most forwarding operating elements, and form a combined arms assault team as we drive in on the enemy Nest... and destroy it forthwithly."

Again, the colonel cleared his dry throat.

This irritated General Ogilvie for a brief second, but his calm cool savvy player's professionalism quickly covered. He sensed an opportunity to assert total control over the coalition of factionalized world militaries who'd been distributed to him in an almost pell-mell fashion to deal with the Savage threat once and for all. Pulling this off was sure to put him in good standing to run for United Worlds prime minister in the next election, two years from now.

And then... who knew? Some factions were talking about forming a Galactic Confederacy of all the human worlds. Was it too much that he dare to dream of being the first leader of such an assembly?

"Something wrong, Colonel?" he asked, fixing Marks with a look of cool, contemptuous appraisal from his perfect blue eyes.

The colonel smiled. And it seemed a thing he was not necessarily given to or much practiced at. Then he walked forward through the press of career officers gathering about the task force's supreme commander. Some of the officers looked rather put out at having to make room for this nobody colonel who'd only just been attached to the strike force at the last second.

"Well, sir," began the colonel. He didn't bother to add the customary *no disrespect intended*. "If the Savages push, most of those units located nearest the colony ship are not suited for combat operations, specifically CQB."

He moved toward the tactical display and indicated the forwardmost unit. "This is the Ninety-Third Artillery out of Hayes's World, firing hundred-forty-millimeter counter-battery fire. Or here..."

He swept his hand, dirty and bloodstained, toward another flanking unit resting under the digital shadow of the massive leviathan he'd called the colony ship even though operations SOP had made sure to specifically refer to it as "the Nest." Like it was just a bunch of insects that needed clearing out before the city could return to normal commerce and operation. Nothing more, sorry about the inconvenience of a horde of post-human monsters descending on you en masse with who-knew-what technological voodoo they'd cooked up in their long haul through the stellar darkness to download on the unsuspecting citizens of this world.

And of course, that was always the question. What had they cooked up this time?

"This..." continued the colonel, "is a UW heavy armor regiment. If the Savages come at us again, they won't have infantry support for more than two hours, according to your... timetables. Sir."

No one missed the amount of cold disgust with which the upstart intruder colonel had used the word *timetables*.

Now it was the supreme commander's turn to clear his throat.

"I'm sorry, Colonel."

He wasn't.

"But the Savages have obviously seen our initial display of force and are on the run. Hardly the first time they've fled before our might. I wouldn't be half surprised if they didn't back up into their little ship and scoot off altogether. So far..."

He murmured once more to the aide.

The aide murmured back.

"... we have no active units engaged, and drone recon analysis indicates zero enemy contact on the field at this time. They've either fallen back completely to the Nest or they've gone underground. In which case we can gas the tunnels and deal with them more than effectively in that manner."

"Excuse me, sir..." said one of the staff officers. A small, unassuming man. Major Musahshi. He was running intel for the entire operation. Attached from the Sinasian Worlds Defense Forces. "We're ninety percent sure that the New Vega populace is sheltering in the subway system. From the early days of the colony, it was specifically designed to be used an emergency bunker system. Respectfully, sir, gassing the subways will result in tens of thousands of civilian casualties."

This took the supreme commander back a bit. Enough so that it may have been evident in his expression to the other men in the room. Marks certainly saw it.

Any hope Ogilvie had of being a galactic leader would be torpedoed in light of a genocide of his own making.

Yes, he thought to himself. *Genocide must be avoided at all costs.*

If only for the sake of his political aspirations.

"Thank you, Major, that option must be taken off the table," he announced, as though he alone were the voice of reason restraining them from their eager push for results despite pesky mass civilian casualties. "Our primary objective is to rescue the civilian populace. If we do nothing else here, then we must do that!"

There. That sounded like a quote someone might put on a statue, in light of how well everything was certain to go.

"But the point will be moot once we've eradicated the Nest. We obviously have superior forces," continued Ogilvie, finding his tenor and feet once more, "and once we've breached the old colony ship... er... the Nest... we can certainly expect enemy forces on the ground to go into a defensive posture if standard Savage hierarchical philosophy kicks in like we know it will. Then, why, for all intents and purposes, they'll just clean themselves out of the sewers and subways, attempting to save the ship. As I've stated previously in my papers on this subject, once they feel threatened, it's wheels up for them and they'll clear off. And if the Navy..." Supreme Coalition Commander Ogilvie nodded to the Navy admiral and his small support staff attending the briefing. "If the Navy arrives on station at the appropriate moment, once the ship lifts off and she's fat and slow in low atmo... well then, the game will certainly change. Won't it, lads?"

Lads.

Lads, thought the colonel. *Like this is some weekend vulx-hunting party on Britannia Centauri.*

Lads.

"You're going to get everyone killed," muttered the colonel through gritted teeth.

Several career-minded officers immediately expressed their disgust at such an insubordinate outburst.

"Excuse me..." began Supreme Commander Ogilvie, going florid. "Just who the hell do you think you are exactly, Colonel?"

Marks squared his shoulders and faced his superior.

"Ahem." The impending stare-down was interrupted by the Navy admiral, a man named Sulla who wore the midnight-blue dress trench of the United Worlds Navy. "I'd like to invoke the Commitment Clause established by our respective governments. Clearly, this spat is interplanetary—Earth and Spilursa—and it needs to be tabled. Time is of the essence. If we miss putting the cap over the battlespace and that ship reaches jump, we won't get another shot at this particular group of Savages until they reemerge at a time of their own choosing, causing the same chaos we see before us today."

"That *some* Savages have implemented jump technology is undisputed, but that's hardly confirmed with this batch," Ogilvie said, not removing his gaze from the subordinate colonel. "And if they're without it, we'll easily chase them down, even if they do manage to lift off planet."

"That's true, Commander," said the admiral. "And until we get in and crack the local sensor data net, we can't be sure what their capabilities are. But that ship came in fast, without warning, and set down before the local military could respond. Even before the government could get off a boosted message to her local allies. If not for a damn free trader captain and her crew, who barely got out of here alive, we might not have even known the Savages were here. So I can't say for certain they have jump capability, but I'm not prepared to bet against the possibility, sir."

Admiral Sulla knew he had delved farther into the details than was called for. A tendency of his of late. But of course, all that was an act. He had achieved his purpose: getting the meeting back on track and taking fire off of Colonel Marks.

Ogilvie swept away Sulla's comments. "Regardless of their capability, you are correct about one thing: according to regulations, we need to stay on mission. Though"—he fixed Marks with a steely glare—"I will certainly be pursuing this matter with the arbitrating Coalition body at a later time." He regained his confident, almost haughty bearing. "I am well aware that our assets aren't picture-perfect on the field as of this moment. Once operations commence and we get our marines, Centauri crusaders, and the other infantry units attached to the strike force forward and up in front of the support units, then our positioning will be correct for a final assault on the Nest."

The general turned and murmured once more to his aide-de-camp.

The aide did not murmur and instead set up the tactical display to show Phase Two of Operation Warhammer.

"As you can see... we cross the line of departure here and pick up the flanking support units. By the time we form our line of advance, we'll still be at least four kilometers from the identified Nest entry point TacAn has targeted for breach. While we can't gas the subways, a thing I simply will *not* condone, we can of course nerve-gas the Nest once we set up a control perimeter here."

He pointed with an actual riding crop at the digital schematic of the Savage colony ship. Halfway up the rising district of Hilltop, along a narrow street lined with half-crushed buildings, an outer deck hangar had opened up.

Colonel Marks was about to speak up again, but Admiral Sulla caught his eye and gave a fractional shake of his head. No one noticed what passed between them. They were all staring at the Nest.

The colony ship, the hulk, was truly a relic out of the past. An ancient lighthugger forty decks high at least, it should have burned up in some celestial miscalculation, or come apart in the gravitic tides of one of the super gas giants of some undiscovered system it wandered into years ago, or settled into decay on some lost planet out toward the galaxy's edge.

It had no place here.

And yet here it had arrived, a threat to the human hyperspace colonies, established while it lurched through the outer darkness. And whenever these abortions showed up, there were, historically and inevitably, only two possible outcomes.

Either the planetary defenses destroyed the hulks and their post-human inhabitants...

... or the Savages killed every person in the colony before moving on.

Total kill. One way or another.

10

When the meeting broke up and commanders who'd be working together began to interface, the admiral drifted away from his staff who were busy coordinating naval support for the upcoming operation. He crossed through the crowd in the tactical operations center aboard the troop hangar of the *Porter*, toward Colonel Marks.

The colonel saw him coming and said something to Sergeant Major Andres. The sergeant major nodded and moved off, probably to interface with the supply chains aboard the *Porter*. Now that the *Montague* could no longer resupply the Twenty-Fifth, they'd need to dip into the *Porter*'s combat stores. Charge packs for the standard M73 automatic pulse rifle were chief among the most critical of needs if the barely combat-effective unit were to remain operational. Otherwise they'd be using sidearms, demo packs, and snide remarks.

Never a good combination.

"Colonel Marks," said Admiral Sulla formally, glancing from side to side.

"Admiral," muttered the colonel.

"Okay, you've said your little piece. I know this looks bad, but you've got to give this a chance. Can't do it the old way."

The colonel said nothing.

"He's an idiot. I get that. But the Coalition couldn't form unless they picked the least threatening and least capable person they could find to lead this. They didn't want another Warren turning absolute dictator. So... he's an idiot, but he's our idiot, Colonel."

Marks took a deep breath and continued to stare at the admiral. His eyes were cold casual murder.

But Sulla considered this to be their normal state. More or less. And sometimes he wondered if it was he, Sulla—who'd known the man the longest—who was the only one to see that cold casual murder. Wondered if all the rest of the galaxy saw was just a normal, early middle-aged man, compact, trim, and fit. All business. No mirth. Military.

He wondered if that was all they saw.

And how could there ever be mirth, having seen what he's seen? thought Sulla. *Having done what he's done?*

How?

"I *am* doing it your way," the colonel muttered. "But it sure as hell doesn't seem like anything other than the same old same old. And a lot of these kids are going to get killed today. You and I both know, if the Savages get a stranglehold on a world, they'll spread like a virus."

"We're running out of worlds—"

Sulla caught himself. His voice had been more forceful, more insistent, than he'd wanted it to be. He smoothed his coat and finished without saying what he was going to say.

There was a long silence. Some of the other officers from the breaking-up meeting may have glanced over as the exchange got a little intense. Or so it seemed.

The colonel leaned forward and spoke in a low voice.

"This world is already dead. They..." he said, indicating with a terse nod the staff officers of the supreme Coalition commander, "just don't know it yet."

And then a hubbub that had been rising over near sensors and acquisition grew in volume. Officers were picking up their gear and running for the cargo door of the *Porter*. Running for their waiting units spread out beneath the Hilltop District.

11

Three-Six Cav
Twenty-Sixth and Park

For all intents and purposes, Sergeant Greenhill was in command of Fourth Platoon, Charlie Company, Third Battalion, Sixth Troop. The element Colonel Dippel had selected for the recon-in-force to place the drop markers. The company XO was now the commanding officer.

After handling the wounded—there weren't many; most had died—and getting a blue-sky report, they'd been ordered to hunker in place at the bottom of the long sloping park that led up to the Hilltop District. It was a perfect golden morning with clouds off to the east. In the distance, up the slope, the behemoth walking mech that had come out from the Savage Nest was still burning, sending up oily plumes of dark smoke to drift off to the west.

"Look at that!" someone shouted from farther back along the convoy parked in the shade of a silent office tower. Greenhill had ordered everyone to watch their sectors and to stay vigilant—and to stay inside the MTAVs in case the need to roll out on a react fast came down from higher up.

They were "fast attack, all the way."

Or so they barked out each time they saluted a superior officer.

Someone had been watching the sky. To the south, where the bizarre old dinosaur of a Savage hulk wallowed beside the glittering jewel Hilltop neighborhood that had once been New Vega's boast to the galaxy, the air around the massive ship was beginning to shimmer and sparkle, all along its flat dirty white exterior.

Greenhill grabbed his 'nocs from off his chest plate and dialed in on the enigmatic ship.

His mouth dropped open.

"It's a damn drone strike."

He touched the comm on the side of his helmet and got a message off to the fleet CIC, alerting them of a possible inbound drone strike. Then he turned to his men.

"Seal up the vehicles and switch the mounted guns over to internal remote. Right now!"

Mere seconds later, vicious bat-shaped drones, ceramic white on their tops and shimmering polished metal underneath, slammed into the convoy and filled the skies around the city streets with great dark swarms.

Windows smashed. The automated guns dialed up and engaged the drones as they came whipping down the street firing small bursts of low-caliber ammunition. Sudden violent sprays of lead smashed into the armored vehicles.

The Savage drone fire was ineffective. The MTAVs had been designed for conflicts out along the Spilursan frontier where many of the local indigenous races, like the violent wobanki, possessed antiquated firearms as their highest military tech.

But then the drones began to smash directly into the MTAVs and explode. That was where most of the damage was done. Three vehicles cooked off within the first minute.

Through the smashed safety glass of his MTAV's front windshield, Greenhill tried to observe what the drones were doing. Those that weren't smashing into vehicles were circling, as though waiting their turn to exploit some vulnerability.

And, thought Greenhill to himself, who'd been in a drone strike during the brief Spilursa-Espania Conflict over Tezakan, *they're acquiring more data for a better strike.*

The MTAV, Greenhill knew, had one design flaw. It carried external munitions cases along its rear panels. The containers were bulletproof and blaster-proof and could be deployed outward like shields for the infantry to cover behind when dismounted... but the end of one side of the large box had been left unarmored for some enigmatic design reason. A hit on this panel would cook off all the munitions within, volatile charge packs and demo packs together. Worse, the vehicle's fuel cells were close by, under the thinly armored skin in this section. They were protected from below in case of mines, which meant the resulting explosion was a shaped detonation that blew through the troop compartment to the rear of the vehicle, usually killing everyone.

Greenhill had seen it happen before.

"They tryna figure it out and all," he muttered to himself.

And then, as if on cue, one drone streaked away from its holding pattern and whipped straight in at Sergeant Beachum's vehicle.

Flying debris and fire went in all directions. Greenhill watched as the driver, the guy with the only chance of escaping a cookoff, struggled from the vehicle without his weapon. His fatigues were on fire in a few places, but he could have rolled on the ground and put those out once he got the mind to stop running.

The driver managed five steps before another drone, maybe half a meter across and a meter long, slammed straight through his back and came out the front of his chest, dragging his heart and spine out onto the street before fluttering away.

"All vehicles!" roared Greenhill into the comm. "We are exiting the AO. Follow me!"

"Where we goin', Sarge?" asked Curts.

"Gun it *now*, Private!"

Curts didn't hesitate, and a second later the MTAV was racing away from the park. Half a block down, Greenhill told the driver to cut hard for a narrow side street. The top-heavy MTAV went up on three of its six ceramic wheels and barely threaded the narrow alley.

Greenhill switched on the vehicle's rear camera and tried to make out how much of the unit was following. He could see three other MTAVs before his view was blocked by the rest of the platoon.

"Kill it!" he shouted.

The MTAV idled in place as more of the platoon followed inside the alley. The high buildings on either side would provide a sort of baffle against the drones, forcing them to fly in from fixed entry points—if they pursued at all.

"This can't be it, can it?" Greenhill asked his driver.

"Looks like everyone's dead or hunkered inside the alley," answered Curts. "At least in here, them drones can't maneuver well."

That was true enough. Hitting the right panel would be much more difficult.

"Three-Six," Command announced over the comm. "Proceed three blocks west. The 931st Artillery needs an assist."

"Here we go," Greenhill muttered, resisting the urge to shake his head. Curts was staring at him like he hoped the sergeant would tell him they were staying put in the alley.

But that's not what you did when your brothers needed help.

"You heard 'em, Curts. Let's roll."

12

Colonel Marks linked up with his sergeant major once the impromptu meeting with Admiral Sulla came to an end. The sergeant major's face told Marks that things had gone to hell, all without saying a word.

"Details," Marks ordered.

"It was an anti-personnel strike, sir," replied Andres. "We got mass casualties in Charlie and Bravo. Delta was almost no good after the landing. So that leaves us with most of Headquarters. Here's what we show from the feeds."

Colonel Marks watched as images of the drones came in quickly, swarming away from the old colony ship and striking as many of the exposed as they could find. Those in vehicles, or under cover, had survived for the most part. But those in the open had been torn to pieces by the high-speed deadly drones.

The colonel looked at his unit roster display. The battle board's readouts showed him a lot of needless waste. A lot of dead who'd never needed to die in the first place so that a bad plan could be tested.

He nodded to himself.

He would let them go as far as they could. But he'd brought something along to make sure the job got done in the end.

"We still go to hit the LOD in thirty minutes, sir?" Andres asked.

Marks set his jaw. That idiot Ogilvie still wanted everyone to cross the Line of Departure in thirty minutes. But that wasn't something he could communicate down the chain of command.

"Affirmative, Sergeant Major," said Marks.

"And we're on foot, right?" asked the sergeant major, like that was the worst idea in the world after what had just happened. "No crawlers."

"Roger that. We pick up a company of Espanian Sentinels and follow the right flank in."

Well..." said Andres slowly. Thinking things over. "I don't like it, sir. I mean havin' them big ol' Sentinels and their main guns is nice if we meet some more armor, but another drone strike and we gotta go for cover real quick like. That's fine and all if we in the city itself, but if we get caught out in the open, we're gonna lose a lot of my boys."

"I agree, Sergeant Major," said the colonel. "So we'll do our best to stick near cover as we move. I need you to cannibalize the surviving companies. Move everyone into a new combat team I'm setting up now. Should be on your screen."

Andres tapped through some screens slowly. Tech was not his strong point. "This it, sir... Uh... Strike Team Ranger."

"Affirmative, Sergeant Major. That'll be our designator going forward."

13

Three-Six Armored Cavalry (Fast Attack)
Twenty-Second Street and Zonda Road

What remained of the 931st Artillery wasn't much. Most of the guns had been disabled during the Savage drone strike. The Three-Six Cav, in convoy now with seven vehicles left from the original recon force, rolled up on what had been the 931st's established perimeter around a grand fountain at a massive intersection just outside the downtown financial district.

After the bad drop, the 931st's commander had ordered the unit to deploy its massive counter battery guns until the next bugout. The gun bunnies, Sergeant Greenhill's term for artillerymen, had deployed the automated guns and set up the command interface fire request network.

A few sentries were dispatched in teams to set up defensive heavy machine-gun positions guarding the access points into the main square where the massive guns were slowly unfolding skyward. When the drone swarm swept through the streets, it slaughtered the sentries in one pass. Seconds later the teams setting up the main guns were similarly dispatched, and then the drones, having identified the military equipment, set about to ramming themselves into the guns in order to disable the field piec-es. As they slammed their ceramic explosive-laden bodies into the fire control comps, they knocked out some of the big guns. Barrel strikes didn't bother the behemoths in the least, but the destroyed targeting computers effectively killed the weapons. Operationally speaking.

Once the remains of the cav troop showed up, Greenhill ordered a dismount and a check for survivors, though he didn't have high hopes. This once-ordinary intersection, typical of many such in all the colony worlds, was littered with dead bodies.

At the center of all the carnage was the fountain that commemorated the colony's founding. A small stone ship rose from the hands of various long-dead people who seemed to hold it upward toward the stars. If the city's wa-ter and power had been on, the fountaining jets of water would have looked like exhaust thrust.

Or something along those lines, thought Greenhill ab-sently as he stared at all the death and waste and tried to figure out where to begin. His job, as a cav scout, was to find the enemy so that the enemy could be destroyed. Not find his own dead people.

"Schoolhouse, this is Four-One," he said once he'd di-aled into the CIC intel comm channel. "We got total unit kill on the Three-Nine-One. Guns most likely ineffective."

Then from over near one of the big guns, one of the cav troopers shouted, "We got one!"

Apparently someone had survived.

14

Team Ranger
Crossing the Line of Departure

The colonel was forward with the lead elements of the new team, and Sergeant Major Andres was at the rear. The surviving infantrymen of the Twenty-Fifth had formed into two columns on opposite sides of the roadway they'd been assigned as their lane for the coming assault into the Savage-held portions of the city. New elements, platoons, fire teams, and special teams had been broken down and filled. Team Ranger was slightly under company strength, but it was heavily armed, carrying as much as the men could manage, loaded for bear.

Marks gave one order over the comm before they crossed the line of departure: to shoot, move, and communicate as a team. Kill everything in their way with extreme and maximum violence, and protect the massive Espanian Sentinel tanks they would pick up ten blocks forward.

The route through the business district, along the main body of Strike Force Warhammer's right flank, would take them into an industrialized neighborhood called the Hopps, where the Espanian armor had been dropped by a heavy lifter squadron. That armor wouldn't move until it had infantry support, so of course Ogilvie had sent the disrespectful Colonel Marks off to shepherd the armor into the game.

Fine, the colonel had thought. What he really wanted to do was turn the whole place into a glass parking lot, but in lieu of that, the Espanian armor could do a lot of damage if it was left in peace to operate. His infantry could provide that service.

"Sir," said Maydoon, the LT from Delta who'd held the forward position and was now acting as the colonel's executive officer. Marks had selected the kid because he was the most professional officer the colonel had met since taking charge of the unit—and because there was every chance Marks himself was going to get killed advancing against the colony ship. If so, well, this kid was a killer, and a capable leader, and maybe he'd get the job done instead.

Getting the job done was all the colonel cared about.

And that job was killing Savages, regardless of what the politicians said.

"Yes, Lieutenant?"

"I'm talking with the air boss team and we're low on priority for tasking."

The colonel gave him an enigmatic look.

Maydoon didn't miss a beat. "I just wanted to make that clear in case we get into something. We probably shouldn't expect artillery support."

"Good to know," said the colonel. "Because we *are* going to get into something. Trust me on that."

The next ten blocks were hot and silent.

They passed no dead civilians. A few wrecked pieces of drone. And crossed a lot of hot streets. The Savage

artillery had fallen occasionally, decimating whole buildings and laying waste to blocks. The late morning air was
warm, muggy, and incredibly still, like it was waiting for
something. Wallowing black smoke was still drifting out
and off to the west of the enormous mech, in the distant
foreground of the enemy hulk. Apart from that, the city
was a graveyard.

The colonel kept his eyes forward and moved along
the street just behind a two-man point team thirty meters
ahead of the main column. The heavily armed infantry to
his rear were spoiling for a fight, or complaining about
the heat. Or watching the shadows nervously. Everyone
burned off the fear of an approaching fight in their own
specific way. And whereas the colonel had been a hard
charger since taking command of the unit in the hours before the operation began, he let this slide and ignored their
jokes, chatter, and nervous silence. They would need to get
themselves ready for what was coming, and it was too late
to teach them anything else.

He called a halt after an hour.

Sergeant Major Andres sent out a comm for everyone
to get off the street and swap out their socks. It would be
a long day and a lot of walking. Many of them, according
to him, probably hadn't changed their socks since they left
Spilursa Naval Weapons Station on Omaron.

The colonel found himself with the primary assault
team. Riflemen overloaded with fraggers and flash-
bang bandoliers to pin down the enemy and give the
heavy-weapons teams time to set up and lock in some
support fire. All of them were sitting in the darkness of the

clothing store they'd designated for cover during the halt, leaning against the walls, except the platoon sergeant, who was watching from the shattered doorway.

It was silent, hot, and still among the clothes the store had offered in the days before the Savage invasion six weeks ago.

The colonel sat down and dutifully changed his socks. Leadership began at the top, and though he might be in charge, it was the sergeant major who really ran things. And so everyone needed to see him, the colonel, obeying the orders of the toppest of cats. Change your socks.

One of the assault team members muttered in the darkness, "Shoulda done the whole planet with an orbital strike, or one of them trigger-nukes. I'm way too short to buy it on this rock."

A few of the others laughed. It was always the guys whose enlistment was up soon that got worried the most. That was as old as time itself.

"Yeah, for a war criminal," said one of the other soldiers, "Tyrus Rechs sure does know how to do things up right."

"War criminal?" said another. "Who says? Spilursa ain't part of that little confederacy, and they got no power to go around decidin' for the rest of us how things got to be done proper. Hell, hand me a few dozen trigger-nukes and I'd do this hellhole myself right now and wouldn't bat an eye. Biggs is right. I'm too short to get killed today. I been savin' up for a scout ship. Was gonna get myself my own planet out along the edge."

"You can't even fly, Dozz. You'll end up in a sun some-where. Or cooked by the zhee. They all up and over those worlds out there along the edge."

The rest laughed at Dozz until the platoon sergeant told them to "Shut the damn hell up and get your gear tight."

"I'll learn," Dozz promised them in a whisper.

And then the halt was over, and they were on the march again. They had a date, and destiny didn't like to be kept waiting.

Neither did death.

A few tense and quiet blocks later, they linked up with the command team for the First Royal Espanian Armor. Captain Alvaruz de Macha was a tall, lanky man who used long strides to cover lots of ground. He wore armor and a helmet and carried the standard TS-85 blaster, subcom-pact variant for tankers, on a sling around his chest.

Colonel Marks was heartened by what he saw. The man didn't rely on his massive tank to protect him. He didn't take chances, and he moved quickly in a business-like manner. If any of them were to survive the next few hours, excellent skills and good habits might make the dif-ference. Or at least, that had been the colonel's experience in the dozen or more wars he'd fought in. He'd lost count of the individual battles a long time ago.

"We are five Sentinels," announced Captain de Macha in accented Standard, a language once known as English on old Earth. On Espania they spoke a mix of old Romance languages that had all eventually succumbed to a Spanish variant, but de Macha seemed to know his Standard well; it was the language of the galaxy. "Our weak point is our flanking armor and weapon arcs. I try to keep the men good with the co-ax machine gun on top of my beasts, but they often put too much... how do you say... faith... in the forward armor and the very mighty main gun. That is where we are *muy mejor*... the best."

"Good," said Marks. They had come inside the perimeter of the tanks, and now Team Ranger was breaking down to assist each tank with protection along the flanks and rear. "We'll keep a point team forward and to the right of each tank. Please tell your men not to fire unless my troops have a heads-up from your track commanders. Just have the TC identify and state 'engaging forward' over the general comm. That should get them down and covered. The rest will trail the tank and react to any fire or attacks from the flanks."

The commander flipped out his battle board, making it suddenly three fully integrated screens, and pointed. "Command wants us to follow this road right off the main body. That should put us up on Hilltop, where we can provide cover and overwatch once the main assault begins on the Objective."

The ancient Savage colony ship, the ship the philosophers who'd set up this mission to save New Vega from an apocalyptic solution had called the Nest, had been tagged here as Objective Black Widow.

15

Four streets farther south, they met their first refugees coming out of an industrial warehouse along the street. Under heavy guard, the refugee leader, a man who identified himself as Jhan Carstairs, a doctor with the University Hospital at New Vega, was allowed through to meet with Colonel Marks and Captain de Macha. One of the medics came forward to give him water and check him over. The rest of the men watched him and the other refugees suspiciously.

"It's been horrible," said the trembling man. "A living nightmare since the dreams began." His eyes were haunted and far away.

He was still under guard, as were the thirty-odd refugees huddled under the watchful barrel of the main gun of the lead Sentinel.

The colonel had heard Captain de Macha order his gunner to burn them with a Spitfire round if anyone made a false move. Reports of refugees exploding or attacking the strike force during the first engagements after the carrier drop had circulated enough that Ogilvie had issued a directive toward vigilance when handling refugees. Marks had been in the Tactical Operations Center and had seen how much duress the man had needed to be put under—protesting about the optics—for his troops to remain safe.

The deciding factor came when one of Ogilvie's staff officers assured him that needless casualties would play as badly in the media as dead refugees—and that higher casualty reports might result in subscribing members of the confederacy backing out if their troops unduly bore the brunt of such suicide assaults.

And that would be his, Supreme Coalition Commander Ogilvie's, fault.

So he'd reluctantly issued the directive.

"We knew something was up at the hospital the first night, over seven weeks ago," continued the haggard doctor as he gulped at the water in the canteen he'd been given. "Sure it was a full moon, always crazy, but the usual reports of bizarre behavior were off the charts. Within hours our predictive data algorithms identified that a vast majority of our cases involved law enforcement and government personnel. That didn't make any sense. We had a council member come in, hallucinating and in full tachycardia. She attacked two security guards and killed them both with her bare hands."

"Say again?" said Marks.

The doctor nodded in a tired, haunted manner. Like dwelling on the memory fatigued him. "Ninety-pound woman. Then she just stroked out. Wasn't right, and at first I suspected some kind of virus."

"But no longer?" asked de Macha.

"I'm pretty sure, now that I've had time to think about all this while we've been hiding, that they were using some kind of targeted nanovirus keyed for specific DNA. The Savages, I mean. And you know what that means..."

Neither the colonel nor Captain de Macha knew what that meant.

"Enlighten us," said Marks.

But the wild-eyed doctor seemed not to hear him and just continued moving his head up and down erratically as though confirming something he'd been so sure of all along. And still felt responsible for nonetheless.

His voice shook as he started backing up. "They were here for weeks, possibly months even, before the ship came in, and they were quiet as a mouse, sneaking around and up to no good. Quiet. As. A. Mouse. They hacked our DNA and Med Archives. We keep files and samples for every citizen. State-of-the-art processing and archive center down in the Old Colony. Somehow they got in there, hacked the data banks, pulled out physical samples, and had enough time to spin up targeted nanoviruses on our leading command and control systems. That first wave was here for, maybe... at least two weeks before everything began going to hell. We..."

He drank more water.

The colonel used that as an opportunity to change the subject and see what other intel the obviously fractured man might be able to provide.

"We've had reports of compromised citizens attacking the strike force. Being used as IEDs. What can you tell us about that?"

Captain de Macha didn't even blink when the colonel failed to use the proper Coalition term *rescue force*. Instead he added, "And how can we be sure your group isn't also compromised?"

The ragged doctor nodded emphatically and guzzled more water, sloshing it across his scraggly beard. "Red striations. Like a rash all over the neck. We identified that early on and the only cure was to quarantine your own group. Not quarantines for the sick; quarantines for the healthy—keep the good shut away from the bad. It was the only way you knew people weren't infected, so you could trust them."

"This illness is what causes... people esploding?" asked Captain de Macha.

"Yes. In the sense that it makes them willing to do it. The red striations are the result of some kind of neural control toxin. Something they were injected with before the surgery."

"Surgery?"

"Yes," said the doctor, moving from desperate survivor to clinician. Calmer now as he turned toward the business he understood. The interface of medicine and survival. "Infected survivors exhibiting the striations would attempt to infiltrate other survivor groups. The Savages at first were trying to get down into the bunkers along the subway and into Old Colony itself. More than a few episodes of self-detonation—not always explosive, mind you; there were reports of nerve gas and other chemical agents as well—but these patterns were nonetheless identified by the survivor network using the emergency survival protocols we've trained for our whole lives. And we developed a response."

"What was it?" asked Marks, eager for any insight into this particular band of Savages.

"Simply put, we cut ourselves off from each other. The most dangerous part, I suspect, right now, is that as the refugee groups are leaving their bunkers, coming out to be rescued by you, these lone bombers—that's what we've been calling them—will attempt to mix in and detonate within your ranks. Expect it."

De Macha whistled and swore.

The medic had given the doctor a low-dose sedative, and he was growing calmer by the second, even appraising, as though only just now fully appreciating the grand perspective of the hell he'd just lived through.

"I'll tell you this," he said, watching something off in the distance that no one else could see. Something only he saw because it only existed in his mind and memory. Marks had seen that look thousands of times before. "It speaks to the Savage ruthlessness that they'd devise such a cunning strategy. It was almost as if they knew you'd respond in force, and they wanted to be inserted among us, or even posing as a whole group of refugees, so that when the time came, when you showed up, as it were, they'd disable your ground forces by masquerading as the most desperate of us."

He frowned. "I am... or rather I was... a student of history. Old Earth history. I don't think I ever will be again. I couldn't possibly be after this nightmare from our past suddenly showed up on our doorstep and ruined everything we've built. But I was. And what the Savages are employing, the IED trick—it's timeless. It still turns up occasionally in our modern conflicts, but back on Earth, before the Big Uplift, before the Great Leap, it was very common in dealing with superior numbers and an over-whelming technological advantage held by the enemy force. Especially among the fundamentalist radical types. Ideologues."

"Nothing new under the sun," Marks said, rubbing his face. He hoped the doctor had something more useful than fourth-rate military history to chatter about.

The doctor nodded. "What this tells me about this par-ticular brand of Savages—and I know this is shockingly naive, you types are all briefed in their behavior mecha-nisms and patterns—but this tactic, this is like a window into their soul. Which is really a window into *our* souls, as it were. The Savages are who we were before the advent of the hyperdrive. Before the colonies and the new empires. We're getting a look back at ourselves, how we used to be-have, and it's absolutely barbaric. Turning other humans into bombs to blow up your enemy where he's weakest. Where he's giving aid and mercy to the desperate. Terror campaigns."

Marks didn't have the heart to tell the trembling aca-demic just how nasty war was out on the fringes, far away from formerly safe and civilized worlds like New Vega.

"When your men get wind of this," the doctor contin-ued, "the terror will spread just as it did then. And suppose this invasion is a sign of what's still to come? What do we know of the Savages? Really? Their numbers? Their abili-ties? Their coordination? Suppose we see more of this, and the panic grows. And the worlds we call home catch fire in a frenzy of terrorized angst, and all the other fractures are revealed. One bombing in some high-end restaurant could be all it takes to make an empire capitulate to the Savages. It's happened before. To us. This *was* us. *They* were once us. That's who were facing out here. Except now... they're post-human. And what, exactly, does that mean?"

No one said anything.

"Can you tell me?" asked the doctor.

But no one could.

So no one answered.

The doctor shook his head rapidly, as if clearing it of all the thinking he'd done during the six weeks of stark raving hell since the survivors had bunkered. "There's one other thing. Their strategy... capturing strays, pumping them full of neural control toxin, and then performing a bomb-install surgery... it hurts them too."

"How so?" asked the colonel. He always keyed in on ways to hurt the Savages.

"Why, they're cannibals now. Haven't you noticed? They're needlessly wasting calories just to terrorize us. Look around. This city had a population of ten million. Do you see any corpses in the streets?"

16

The Wild Man
Thirty-Second Floor, Cyrus Gardens Luxury Apartments
Hilltop District

He'd come to hunt.

Hunt Savages.

Six weeks after the infection, invasion, call it what you will, when all the planets of the not-even-yet-formed Confederacy, sometimes it called itself a Coalition, had put out the general warning to avoid New Vega at all costs, possible Savage outbreak in the stellar region, he'd arrived.

Why... he'd headed straight for it.

The only option for a lone traveler was to find an old scout ship from the past. There always was some soul foolish enough to buy one and think they could avoid all the traps of stellar navigation and light speed in order to find some fabled lost planet of gold, treasure, or tech. There always was such. The galaxy seemed to breed them by the dozens.

He wasn't that breed.

He wasn't a scout. Or an explorer.

He was a shooter.

Always had been.

He was a shooter even before he left his father's ranch on Stendahl's Bet. A shooter when he joined the militia. A shooter when he got sent to fight separatists on the southern continent—a nasty battlefront in a subarctic wasteland of ice plains, cruel mountains, and frozen seas.

All of it on a forgotten world. A lost world.

You can't find Stendahl's Bet on the maps anymore. The stellar charts. It's gone. Gone baby gone.

That was ten years ago.

Just gone like that.

Savages came one day, and they lost half the planet in a week. It had never been too populated to begin with. A colony world. A lot of ranching. Off-world beef exports had been the main source of business. But there had been a few big population centers. Hasting. Willoughby. Corazon.

Gone by the end of the week.

The militia had been deployed to protect the pop centers. And he went off to fight. Never mind the wife and baby. He went. Deployed first against the assault on Corazon along the eastern seaboard.

They lost big-time there. At Corazon. The Savages had put down a pretty significant presence. Like they were going to march across Stendahl's Bet reaping their booty no matter who stood in their way.

There would be a fight.

And that's all he'd ever asked for. For a fight. Not fair. Nor good. Those things were for movies.

But a fight. It's all he'd asked for.

I mean, it wasn't all he'd *ever* asked for. But it's what he'd asked for ever since Stendahl's Bet ceased to be a place. Just a fight. Within range. A good sight picture. And the chance to fight them. And kill them.

He'd asked for that ever since.

Ever since the wife and baby...

Those Savages. The ones who had tried for Stendahl's Bet... they hadn't been calorie hunters like these on New Vega he watched through his high-powered scope from the thirty-second floor of an apartment high-rise at the edge of Hilltop. Those Savages on Stendahl's Bet had been metal scavengers. Anything that was metal, they'd hauled it off in their salvage vessels. Back up to their big hulk to be taken off away and forever. That had been their booty. Yeah, they were makin' somethin' out there in the deep dark where hyperdrive ships from all the navies of the worlds wouldn't ever find them.

During the worst days of the battle for Willoughby, when the wild man helped the fading defenses trying to retake the city, they found there was no city to retake. Nothing but a skeleton of that oldest of boom towns from back during the frontier days.

Some said Willoughby was named for the navigator on the *Horizon*. Stendahl was the captain. They came to the planet hundreds of years ago.

Captain got to name the world, as the old traditions went.

So say the old-timers.

But who would really know now? Less than a hundred people survived the Savage attack on that world ten years ago. Survived the attack... and survived Tyrus Rechs's rain of fire that cleansed the Savages—and everyone else— from the planet.

He didn't hold that against the crazed sociopath Tyrus Rechs, the man all the worlds hated these days. He'd been there on Stendahl's Bet during those last days. There was nothing left. Nothing but the Savages in the end. Only a fool thought wife and baby... y'know... might have...

Only a fool.

He didn't hold it against the war criminal.

But sometimes he did.

Because maybe wife and baby might have made it. Maybe the Savages hadn't dealt with them in the way they'd dealt with everyone they found in Willoughby and Corazon and a dozen other one-horse ranching towns across the continent.

The Trail of Blood.

He'd stopped using their names. Now they were Wife and Baby.

It was easier that way. Easier to package. Easier to ruck. Easier to carry.

He didn't picture them much anymore.

Unless he had a Savage in his scope. The powerful and dialed-in scope that sat above the large-bore rifle he used. He didn't picture them then either. Or at least, he didn't see them.

But he felt them.

Her standing just behind him. Baby on her hip. And that smile he'd fallen in love with. The smile when he did things for her. Things she couldn't do. Things that made her proud he was her man.

He could feel them in those moments. Those first finger-pad-on-the-trigger moments. Those slow-breathing, falling, almost gone...

Pull.

BOOOOOOOM thundered the weapon.

Moments.

And way out there, right up close in his scope, another Savage had a massive hole torn open in its chest. With his special rifle he didn't need head shots. The big rifle could hit them anywhere and they were done. Hell, if he hit them in the head, and sometimes he did, the head would just vape.

But he preferred to nail them center mass in the upper portion of the chest. Because... for a moment they knew they were dying. They had at least a second, sometimes more, to know that they'd met the wrong survivor.

That they'd met the wild man.

And now they were dying because of him.

And if you believed the rumors, the theories, the whispers that some spoke about the Savages, no matter what tech tree they'd followed, all the old rumors said that these, in whatever form they'd become, these were as old as the hyperdrive itself. Older than that, if you understood your histories. From the way back.

Once humans.

No more.

And now they were dying because he'd put them down.

In those moments he could feel her and baby behind him. Smiling.

Sometimes he could almost hear her voice.

"Another one, babe."

That's what she'd say.

He lived for that moment when he could almost hear her saying that.

"Another one, babe."

After Stendahl got nuked into oblivion by Tyrus Rechs. Right down into zero viability for a hundred years or more, because that was really the only way to deal with the Savages—or so said those who believed in the renegade criminal known as Tyrus Rechs.

Only way to be sure.

He'd hunted Savages ever since.

He never would've left Stendahl. But he was wounded at Gap Springs. Badly. Face and chest all scarred from a fragmentary device that went off close and suddenly just as everything went to hell for the militia. Next thing he knew he was on board the *Mercy*. United Worlds hospital frigate. They were in jump. Stendahl had been dead for more than a week, the doctor told him.

And the worlds were baying for Tyrus Rechs's blood because there had to be another way to deal with the Savages other than just nuking planets into oblivion.

The planets called it a raid. Tyrus Rechs called it a foothold.

A prelude to a living, breathing world of Savages.

But who knows? Maybe they didn't desire those things anymore. Maybe they had moved beyond the wanting land, sky, and water. Beyond the basic ken of a human understanding of those basic things.

Maybe.

In the darkness of the galaxy, who knew what was possible?

And so, after leaving the refugee center on Sudlow, one of the Britannian colony worlds, the planet on which he'd been established as an official refugee, he'd gone hunting on his own. Gone looking. Got had for an old rundown scout vessel called the *Sweetwater Express.* Belonged to some old scout who'd been dead nigh on twenty years. His daughter was more eager to unload it than she let on. She was more than happy to sell it to the wild man.

By then, that's what folks had taken to calling him. Big, brawny, scars like tattoos. Big beard and coal-dark eyes that seemed to burn for nothing but revenge and something that could never come back. He never told them the story, but they guessed it all the same. Pain's like that. Like an open window in your heart, someone once said. Everybody can see in and see that you've been blown apart.

Revenge.

Revenge was enough.

"Do another one, babe."

Yeah. Sure thing, girl. Anything for you.

And so, whenever the Savages, or the rumors of a Savage infection, outbreak, invasion, came over the galactic transcomm, he fired up that old scout that shouldn't have even run and took off for parts unknown, flying on baling wire and prayers.

He'd shoot 'em for as long as he could.

But in the end, Tyrus Rechs, or someone else, one of his true believers from another planet, a colony too close to the infected world to take chances, would nuke the planet until it glowed and the atmosphere itself caught fire. And then it was time to go. They always lost. Never won.

But sometimes the Savages would up and leave on their own after they'd taken everything they'd come for in the first place. Lives. Water. Metal. Food. Tech. They'd be off once again into the Big Dark, before the exterminators showed, sailing between the stars in their massive sublight colony vessels that were the height of tech... back before the hyperdrive.

And now, after all that contact and scavenging and stealing, maybe they were the height of tech again.

Savages.

Hard to believe they'd ever been the best and brightest humanity had to offer. Once. Long ago. The dreamers, thinkers, builders.

Or maybe that was just what they'd said about themselves to justify it all. Men and women of destiny. Because destiny needs justification.

Six weeks ago he heard the rumor that the Savages had come in and hit a sector giant. New Vega. A big player in the fledgling galactic scheme.

New Vega.

He checked the flight directives and found that the world had an off-limits advisory tag.

Surest sign of Savages.

So he fired up the *Sweetwater Express* one last time, barely got her into orbit, barely coaxed her into jump, and practically flung himself at New Vega on a best-guess trajectory.

It wasn't a crash. Not even a crash landing. But the *Sweetwater Express* would never leap into the hyper ever again.

So be it.

This world was as good as any to die on.

And he could shoot Savages all day long here.

There were more than enough of them. Even now. Even after all these weeks of hunting them and watching them. Watching them come out like cowboys back on Stendhal to ride the herds of survivors back into the ship.

He'd taken the occasional shot.

Just one shot.

Always just one shot.

And then he'd watch. Dialed in close on the scope as the targeted Savage flung back its faceless helmet and died looking at the sky.

"Do another one, babe."

And now he was watching them. Big fight shaping up. This wasn't Tyrus Rechs. This was the Coalition of Worlds, or whatever they were calling themselves these days. Coming in fast to attack... and what?

Drive off the Savages?

Annihilate the Savages?

Study them?

Take what they learned for themselves?

That was all... That was all like a sin to the wild man. You couldn't reason with Savages. Couldn't annihilate them. Couldn't study them. Couldn't even understand what they knew.

Why...

Why?

Because they weren't human anymore.

And you wouldn't, in fact no decent person would, want to know what they knew. What they'd discovered out there in the Big Dark. Dark knowledge never meant to be known.

How do you know that?

He didn't hear that voice much anymore. He liked to hear hers instead.

Almost a laugh in her voice.

A lilt? Was that what they called it?

"I don't know," he whispered as he watched them through the scope. Watched them gathering for the big fight at the bottom of the hill. Three spears, three prongs. Three elements of the Coalition going straight into a hornets' nest of Savages.

They had no idea what they were walking into.

He could've warned them.

But he didn't have a comm.

Just the rifle. His personally loaded ammunition. And some gear to survive on, crawl away with, and shoot another day by.

"Do another one, babe."

"Yes, ma'am," he whispered.

The baby was on her hip, cooing. He was a proud daddy.

Thirty-second floor watching the Savages getting into place all along back streets and alleys. Coming up out of the subway they'd been so busy trying to crack into during all those quiet weeks when it seemed he had the city to himself.

What's down there? he wondered in some distant part of his mind.

Once the fighting started between both sides, he could probably sit up here for a few hours and counter-snipe the Savages attacking the Coalition forces. They'd have bigger concerns than him blowing off the occasional head of one their elites.

Big mothers.

Head shots handed out all around on those.

That was for sure.

He swam the scope across the city. There were so many to shoot. Both sides were walking right into each other.

And the fun was about to begin.

Good times.

"Do another one, babe."

Sure thing, darlin'.

Sure thing.

17

Team Ranger
Hilltop District

Forward elements of the main thrust under Ogilvie were already coming under direct fire at the bottom of the skyscraper-laden Hilltop District when Team Ranger made their first contact with the enemy. The Savages were entrenched along an improvised wall of destruction that blocked all entrance to the streets located deeper in the neighborhood.

Over the comm, the colonel could hear Ogilvie ordering his lead units to attack en masse and push through the resistance they were encountering within their designated avenue of approach.

"Push on, lads!"

He was issuing commands over the radio as though he expected them to be remembered for all time.

"Have at them, my boys."

"We're almost through!"

And…

"Give 'em hell!"

Meanwhile casualty reports and calls for medical evac over the battle boards monitoring the Coalition net were coming in fast. After half a block of heavy fighting, it was clear that there *was* no pushing on, pushing through, having at them, or any other such nonsense as dispensed by a field-grade officer not under direct fire.

Nonsense is still nonsense, even when spoken by generals.

What those *lads* were doing was dying.

There was no artillery support. The carrier hadn't finished rearming the tactical bombers for close-air runs against identified enemy positions. Some units were communicating. Some weren't. A few were missing altogether, and the cav, operating in the rear for some bizarre reason, was reassigned to check on those units and make sure the Savages hadn't flanked.

It definitely did *not* look like the Savages were conducting a simple planetary raid, nor did it look like they were scrambling to evacuate back into the stars now that they had been caught by the Coalition. If they were even going to push off for deep space at all, they weren't in much of a hurry to do so. In fact, to almost every commander involved in the operation—every commander except Supreme Coalition Commander Ogilvie—it looked like the Savages were interested in sticking around for a fight.

But even if the Savages managed to win today, even if the Coalition strike force went down in utter defeat, there was no way one single Savage hulk was going to stand up against all the human worlds combined. A defeat here would send almost every navy speeding here at max jump. And then there'd be no doubt that the Rechs Option would go into effect. The planet would burn along with the Savages who'd thought one colony ship, no matter how big it was and how much tech they possessed, could stand up to the entire weight of the Coalition and its several navies.

The numbers didn't support the survival of the Savages in that scenario.

Not ever.

Not even remotely.

To stay and fight—to dig in—had never been the Savage game. They had proved that time and again in their random menacing of the known worlds. Hit and run. Loot, take, steal, and then disappear out into the stellar dark for another years-long haul at just shy of light speed to the next planet. That was their method. They were safe out there in the dark.

Too many options. Too hard to track.

Worlds with hyperdrive-capable ships didn't go out that far into the empty space between worlds. Didn't need to. There was nothing out there. So it was a safe space for the Savages. If they could stay out there forever, they probably would; it would give them all time in the world to get up to their utopian madness and diabolical experiments.

But...

There were no resources out there in the dark between worlds. You needed stuff to build stuff. Materials.

Nothing but cold out there.

And a black darkness that swallowed everything and gave nothing back.

All the Savages had was that powerful scream of engines doing their best to push mass between the worlds at speeds so slow that, compared to hyperspace travel, forward progress seemed negligible to the point of immeasurable. Travel was measured in decades as opposed to days, and each massive colony ship became a world unto itself, pushing along untethered and untetherable. And unless they managed to get ahold of hyperdrive tech, they were pretty much stuck in place while the galaxy continued to grow around them.

Team Ranger, riding shotgun on the right flank of the main body, had come up against the Savages' improvised wall of debris. Colonel Marks was at the head of the column, standing in front of the lead Sentinel, designated as Alpha Zero One, when the point team spotted the wall of destruction that had been thrown up just a few streets away in the urban sprawl of Hilltop's western slope.

It looked as though someone had taken a massive bulldozer and simply scraped up the street while simultaneously demoing all the buildings on the near side. Thus creating a wide kill zone and then a wall from which the enemy could shoot at any approaching Coalition forces seeking to penetrate the district.

The colonel called a halt and ran forward to the point teams, dropping down with his pulse rifle as he got close and finally crawling up behind a pile of debris to put eyes on the obstruction.

"Looks like they don't want us to go on through, sir," remarked the sergeant in charge of the point team. They were lying just below the rim of a pile of ruined building materials. Around the colonel the stripped-down weapons team hugged concrete and waited for the shooting to start. The air had that pre-game feel, that sense that something was about to go down in short order.

In the distance behind them, they could hear the rumble of the powerful Sentinel tanks—the premier ground offensive weapon of the Espanian military. Four massive turbines, which howled like banshees when the throttles were opened up to full, now whispered in a silent, menacing, low-pitched scream that made everyone uneasy.

Tanks were dangerous to everyone on the ground. The infantry knew that well.

"Remember," Captain de Macha had announced to Team Ranger over the command net. "I have five weapons on each of my beasts. A 140-millimeter main gun. Heavy twin blaster. Automatic grenade launcher. And the right tread. And of course, the left tread. So please... stay out of our way, *amigos*. If we smell the enemy... well then, we will turn loose like wolves among the sheeps."

The message, despite the broken Standard, had been received and understood by all.

"They're trying to channel us into the meat grinder Ogilvie's sending everyone into," muttered the colonel beneath his 'nocs as he studied the high wall of debris on the far side of the open wasteland kill zone.

To the east, UW interceptors at twenty thousand feet shot down through the atmosphere and ran ineffective strafing runs against the streets the Coalition was sent to take. The bombers were being held back until enemy concentrations could be identified. Unearthly squeals of air-to-ground blaster fire tore through the canyons of the posh Hilltop District off to Team Ranger's left. The fighters came in low, dangerously low, streaking through the canyons of street and skyscraper to make their passes against the Savage defenses firing down the hilly streets into the oncoming Coalition forces.

Portable surface-to-air missiles from the Savages streaked upward in response, trying to catch the fleeing fighters, but to no avail. The interceptors turned this way and that, popping flares and dropping chaff clusters as they dodged their mindless pursuers.

The intensity and volume of blaster fire from that direction rose in a sudden storm of noise. Ogilvie had ordered another ineffective push.

Moments later waves of gunfire, heavy automatic mixed with impressive booms of single shot, replied to the Coalition advance. And replied again. And again. Until the waves of gunfire drowned out the diminishing returns of blaster fire. The attack was stalling, stalled, and probably in retreat. The dead would be left in the streets where they'd fallen.

Heavy booms spat out across the cityscape as armor moved in to cover the retreat.

It was ominous listening to the battle a few blocks over and facing a calm wall of destruction, frozen like some arctic wave of crushed pack ice waiting for Team Ranger to assault. And that counterpoint—the silence here, as opposed to the cry of death and destruction on every level a few blocks over—was not lost on the wordless recon squad crouching in the debris. Or the infantry covering behind the tanks to the rear, waiting for the order to move forward.

Ogilvie was back on the command comm. Ordering more units forward with more inane motivational babble.

Somebody had to do it, and he wasn't going forward himself. Commanders of his caliber didn't actually lead real people into real battles against storms of real gunfire.

Obviously.

"So what are we gonna do now, sir?" asked the recon sergeant lying next to the colonel in the dirt.

A long moment passed in which nothing was said and all were certain the new colonel had either not heard the question or was ignoring it entirely as he stared at the obstacle through his 'nocs.

"We're going through, Sergeant. Then we'll be where they don't want us to be. Which is where you really want to be when the shooting starts."

"Seems smart," remarked the sergeant, whose dry manner seemed to indicate it was all the same to him.

Then the men of the recon company began to shed their rucks and excess gear. They knew what was coming. And it wouldn't be pretty.

18

"You never know what they have until they shoot it at you," remarked Captain de Macha once the colonel had finished relaying his plan to breach the debris wall on the far side of the kill zone.

"Yeah," replied Marks. "I've found that to be true. More often than not."

De Macha smiled and moved off toward his tank commanders to inform them of the plan. The massive Sentinels were idling on a side street that opened up onto the main approach that would take the assault across the no man's land of cleared rubble and into the Savage defensive force. The infantry was staged and ready to go.

Ogilvie's main assault had bogged down to the east and was now concentrating on regrouping, staging for another attack, and getting the wounded back to the *Porter* for evac off-planet. Rotary-winged dropships of the United Worlds design, their four massive blade housings hanging above a central cargo fuselage with an armored pilot and weapons officer cockpit nosing out and down, came in from the north to collect the wounded and depart under Savage artillery fire. And through it all, one of those massive mechs, at least four stories high and held well back from the fighting, was reported to be lobbing shells almost indiscriminately across the battlefield from its twin pom-pom artillery pieces.

Three minutes from go time and Ogilvie finally green-lit the supporting assault, if only just to relieve pressure on the main body that was getting torn to pieces. And with that the mighty Espanian Sentinels, hexagonally segment-ed, four massive treads turning slowly, grinding rocks and debris to powder, eased out onto the road that would be-come the axis for Team Ranger's supporting assault.

The tanks fanned out into a rough wedge once they en-tered the kill zone, and the infantry crouched behind them.

The incoming fire started up almost instantly. Squad-designated marksmen and dedicated sniper teams re-turned fire from back in the rubble as soon as the Savage machine-gun teams opened up, and within seconds burn-ing tracer rounds and hot depleted-uranium slugs filled the air. The ricochets off the tanks sounded like trays of silverware being repeatedly dropped, over and over, again and again.

Just behind Alpha One, the lead tank, from which Captain de Macha commanded his "beasts," one of the as-sault team members who had swapped positions with the recon team remarked, "They're just straight up shooting at it!" Like he couldn't believe that the Savages had missed the obvious fact that neither blaster fire nor ancient chem-ical-based firearms were going to do anything to the for-ward armor of the infamous Sentinels.

The colonel was about to tell the man that the Savages were testing. That to the Savages, in his experience, every-thing was data. And that before they could do anything fully, they would test everything to find out what their options were.

There were advantages for the Savages in being cut off from the main of humanity out there in the dark for so long between worlds. No one facing them could guess how things had evolved. What their technology had become as it moved down the particular path they had chosen—and, in some cases, worshipped.

But the Savages didn't quite know what they would be up against either. So they had to do some testing as they returned to the main line of development, as it were. Like some accidental time-traveler checking the calendar in a room they'd suddenly appeared in.

But the colonel didn't get a chance to say all that.

"Engaging," announced Captain de Macha over the comm. Businesslike. Efficient. Just another day at the office and certainly not headed into a storm of bullets. And a second later the powerful Sentinel erupted with her 140-millimeter main gun on a target across the killing field.

"Damn!" shouted one of the infantrymen as a dust storm erupted, enveloping the men surrounding the massive tank. This was heard on the local comm net, as everyone had activated the noise-canceling effect systems in their comm-linked earplugs.

The colonel was watching the thermal targeting imaging feed from Sentinel Alpha One on his battle board while he followed behind the massive death-spitting monster. The Sentinel's round was smart-enabled, so there some course correction on its track-to-target over the four-second flight time before it founds its first target and exploded, throwing debris up and out into the kill zone. What appeared to be the ghostly heat signature of a Savage anti-armor team of three was suddenly obscured by smoke and explosive vapor expanding away from the hit.

"Got 'em," said de Macha with a touch of competitive pride.

A moment later, without any letup in the hail of incoming automatic gunfire coming from across the forward radial of the attack, a micro-missile lanced out from the Savage line, somewhere off along the rightmost flank, and smacked into the forward right tread of Alpha One.

Sparks and debris shot up into the air like a pyrotechnic display at a festival, and the tank came to a sudden halt.

"Technical difficulties..." said de Macha over the comm. Damage control alarms blared out over his feed. "ECM should have pushed that away. Give us a second. We'll feather the tread and continue on."

Meanwhile both of the forward-flanking Sentinels surged forward to cover their commander, racing out into the no man's land like mad bulls charging through a firestorm of dust and flying rounds zipping through the chaos of the charge. Their sudden burst of speed was so rapid that trailing infantry were almost left in the dust. Sergeants hectored the weapon-laden men to hustle forward if they didn't want to die of exposure to incoming fire.

One Sentinel engaged some distant target, roaring out with a massive boom heard even through the noise-cancelers installed in the helmets, then the other Sentinel followed suit. Two targets, sheltering inside buildings facing the kill zone the Savages had constructed, exploded.

Seconds later the faces of those two buildings slid down into the edge of the kill zone in a waterfall of construction materials and office furniture.

Then the ground jolted, hard, once, and both Sentinels went nose over into a crevice that had suddenly opened up in the middle of the field. The trailing infantry, now exposed, scattered for cover. Dozens were shot to pieces within seconds from zeroed Savage ground fire.

When the dust cleared, the colonel saw that the leading compartment of both Sentinels had gone down into an underground trench. The subterranean route of their local transit system. The rear section of each trapped Sentinel was attempting to reverse out, pulling hard and making some headway. But then the anti-armor fire from a few stories up inside the fronting buildings began to streak down onto the exposed tanks' topsides.

Three high-energy rounds punctured the dorsal armor of one of the Sentinels. The tank caught fire as its internal ammunition racks began to cook off in successive *whumps*. The nearby infantry scattered and began to take what little cover they could. Some even ran forward and tossed themselves into the open subway line despite the exploding tank.

Counter-sniper teams, operating from the buildings and streets the Coalition force had come from, opened up on these anti-armor teams, and Alpha One's electronic warfare operator was given the green light to scramble the battlefield. Meaning any directional or wireless weapons were about to become useless for the next two minutes as the tank emitted a powerful EMP pulse. The infantry turned off their comms and switched off the electronic scopes on their pulse rifles to protect against the effects.

There was nothing to indicate the pulse had gone off above the din of Savage gunfire ripping up the dirt and bouncing off the bent rebar and chunks of concrete.

As the colonel scanned the battlefield, he spotted the eruption of a massive muzzle flash from high up along a nearby tower. He was about to call in a report that there was a Savage sniper operating in the rear when he noted that whoever it was that was firing, they were firing into the Savages ahead of his position. Slow. Methodical. Smooth. Incredible shots of an almost titanic nature. And not blaster fire.

As far as the colonel knew, none of the militaries in the Coalition used old-school firearms.

Alpha One was still engaging Savage troops huddling in the rubble ahead when Captain de Macha came over the comm.

"Forward right tread is feathered. But we can't move ahead until we have something to cross the obstacle."

"Ideas!" shouted the colonel over another concussive *BOOOOM* from the main gun.

"Stand by," said de Macha.

A few seconds later the rearmost Sentinel came forward at a rush. A shovel-scoop unfolded itself from along the sides and rear of the armor, then it was plowing into the ruined debris and dirt, pushing forward a growing wave of material almost effortlessly. A medic dashed out under enemy fire and grabbed a wounded infantryman lying directly in the path of the oncoming behemoth and dragged the man out of the way. Infantry from across the field provided covering fire for the brave medic.

Despite having gathered what seemed an impossible amount of mass to move forward, the tank didn't even slow, leaving a steadily declining trench in its wake. When it reached the chasm, it pushed the debris down into the gap, filling it. Then it reversed slowly, raising its scoop, and launched itself forward over the filled-in gap with a burst of speed.

The colonel didn't think the gap was quite filled in enough, but the utility tank managed to grab the wall on the other side—deploying some kind of internal spike-climbing system embedded within its treads—and pull itself up and over.

"Well, I'll be..." said a soldier hunkered down next to the colonel as gunfire ricocheted off nearby piles of debris and exposed metal bars.

"Moving now," said de Macha over the comm.

Alpha One lurched toward the gap, meters ahead of the main body. It had fewer problems scaling up the ruined far side of the trench than did the dismounted infantry.

With just fifty meters to go until the crushed and ruined buildings that made up the Savage line of defense, the tanks flashed and thundered with their main guns, showering the debris wall with clouds of spinning micro-grenades. Gunners deployed from hatches and fired into the Savages shooting from positions inside the rubble. Pulse fire rang out in staccato bursts as the heavier weapons of Team Ranger contributed to the developing crescendo of chaos.

The colonel was on the run and moving forward, issuing orders for his team to assault into the debris. He grabbed the sergeant of the assault team and pointed to a gap in the ruins. "Send your men through that gap, right now! Send frags and flashbangs first for breach! Don't be stingy with them!"

Teams of men raced forward, found cover, and tossed in explosives and flashbangs before rising up with shouts and storming the positions. Other soldiers stacked around their targets' ingresses and waited for the bangs to go off. They swarmed inward right behind the booms, spraying blaster fire and praying that they were covering every possible angle.

And behind them lay all the dead who had not made it that far.

19

Three-Six Armored Cavalry (Fast Attack)
931st Artillery Perimeter

Sergeant Greenhill had been ordered by command to get the artillery up and providing fire support ASAP.

Problem was, everyone trained on the guns was dead.

Or so it had seemed at first. Until the lone survivor of a gun battery literally climbed out of an open breach to avoid being torn in half during the Savage anti-personnel drone strike.

Private Donal Makaffie was one sketchy dude as far as the no-nonsense Sergeant Greenhill was convinced. He'd seen the type before. Had been given the choice between prison and military service. You got the "Serve or Serve Time" from a lot from the enlisted UW types. And apparently Makaffie had been convicted of attempting to overthrow the government at some point in his pre-military days.

Nice.

It was some nothing rebellion of a couple of dozen junkies back on Earth. And Makaffie, with his degrees in chemical engineering, computer science, and speculative fiction with an emphasis on golden age pulp sci-fi, financed it by manufacturing and distributing drugs. Something Greenhill had never heard of.

"Call it H8, man!" Makaffie whined, giving everyone who didn't ask his life story. "It's my special blend. Lot of synthetics, which the galaxy is full of if you know where to look, that really get you there. Know what I mean? Make the world how it should be. How you want it to be. That's why I call it H8. 'Cause you hate the way things are."

Curts, the driver, scratched his head. The rest of the surviving cav troop was either setting up a perimeter, or trying to find something that would teach them how to operate the 931st's guns.

"If it makes everything how you want it to be," began a confused Curts, "then how come ya call it hate? That don't make no sense."

Makaffie cackled like a goat. Grabbing his skinny belly as he did. He was shirtless and only wore combat pants and boots. From around his sunken chest dangled a necklace of ancient keys. His wild eyes stared out through crooked military-issue glasses that had been broken and taped back together at the bridge. That was a rarity: glasses. There were only a small number of eye problems that still required them.

"Ha ha!" said the crazed private. "That's because those are the chemical identifiers. It's a play on that, man! But really, it makes you hate the world the way it is, and when you trip hard, you come out of it with a desire to make everything the way you saw it in the vision. It's all vision. *Everything's* vision. You gotta know that up front."

"All vision?" asked Curts, who'd literally been a farm boy for some big collective on a backwater colony world before he joined up with the Spilursan army. "What do you see in these... visions?"

"Doors, man. Doors to perception," said Makaffie. He spoke in a hushed whisper like he was sharing the greatest secret the galaxy at large had never heard. "And to see 'em... you got to have the keys." He grabbed his key necklace with one dirty hand and shook it frenetically. "And I got the keys, man."

Then the diminutive Makaffie devolved into wild, maniacal laughter.

"That's great, Private," said Sergeant Greenhill easily. Now was not the time to play drill sergeant hard charger. Which he'd sent the application in for as his next duty assignment. He knew this low-speed all-drag private could care less about the mission, or that arty was desperately needed forward. But he was the only one present who might have an idea how to operate the guns.

The guns that very much needed to be operated.

As if to punctuate the point, an incoming Savage round fired from deep in Hilltop smashed into a luxury condo tower down the block, sending waterfalls of glass outward and down onto the street. Alarms went off along the avenue. Alarms that must have been hardwired into some kind of emergency backup power within the building.

"I don't know if you've noticed current events.... uh, Private Makaffie..." began Greenhill.

"Call me Donal, Sarge," said the emaciated private with a smile. "We should be more informal if we're gonna do some synergy here."

"Uh... yeah... I don't know nothin' 'bout synergy, just a grunt who gets to ride around with the cav for this rotation and all, but if you hadn't noticed, we are currently engaged with the, uh... enemy, as it were. And the higher-ups back at command would very much like us to shoot these guns at the, uh... Savages who are currently shooting at our boys forward."

"Ha... Savvies..." Makaffie goat-laughed once again. "Ain't no such thing. We're all Savages out there beyond the known, Sarge. Reality's an illusion foisted on us by the Britiannia-UW military-technology complex. Mind if I smoke a joint, Sarge?"

Greenhill couldn't believe what he'd just heard. He felt himself rise up on the balls of his feet and suck in a deep breath in order to light this little dirt weasel up good and proper... and then thought better of it.

He chuckled nervously. Except it wasn't nervous. He was trying to hold in both disbelief and rage. And the thing that was making him do this was that every time he flicked his eyes away, like a good NCO constantly watching all his men, the perimeter, the skies and everything he was responsible for in order to get everyone back to base in one piece... he kept seeing the dead of the 931st lying on the street all about that battery.

And that reminded him that he *needed* the little goat-laughing dirt weasel standing in front of him. He would have preferred to need any other man from the 931st. Any other man.

But this one had an advantage over those other men.

He was alive.

For now.

The fact that Makaffie was almost forty, or so he appeared, a private, and seemed to lack any kind of discipline—or a strong connection to reality for that matter—did not imbue Sergeant Greenhill with the confidence he would have liked to feel regarding his current mission at this particular moment. The mission to get the guns up and firing.

"Well now," began Greenhill affably, "now might not be a good time to... use... get high. Hey—!" he added, as though suddenly experiencing a lightning bolt of an idea. This was all play-acting on his part. "Any chance you know how to fire these guns, Private?"

He added "Private" subtly, but with just enough emphasis to remind the dirt weasel he was still serving in the military.

"Do I?" goat-laughed the dirt-weasel private standing before the powerfully built high-speed low-drag sergeant with dried blood all over his combat fatigues and boots. "I know how to run these things better than they ever did. Yes, sir. I mean, Sarge. You work for a living and all, I get it. We can do shot out... and everything in fact. Just get me some coordinates and tell me what you wanna hit it with, and I can oblige with some glorious destruction. You see, I'm all about destruction, Sarge and all. It's when stuff's breakin' that you see the doors. And then we just drop a little H8... and you can slip through and disappear on over to the other side."

Greenhill stared at the private in bewilderment. But he caught the gist of what had been said. Mainly the part about operating the guns. He slowly nodded.

"We, uh... can provide the coordinates and ordnance request, Private. I'm sure that won't be a problem."

20

The Wild Man
Thirty-Second Floor, Cyrus Gardens Luxury Apartments
Hilltop District

He hadn't had a good sight picture on anything in the main assault going down on the streets below; some heavy-duty financial high-rises, corporate headquarters types all sleek and curving, had blocked much of the action down that way. But he could see into Hilltop pretty clearly. The Savages were throwing everything they had at defending the corridor they'd tried to channel the Coalition forces into.

A kill zone meat grinder. Entrenched positions all around.

From his vantage point, the Wild Man could see the tall artillery mech the Savages had deployed in a park near the top of Hilltop—up around all the grand government buildings and the original landing site of the old colony ship. The big machine was shooting artillery at random along the Coalition's flanks, just to make it clear that it was a bad idea to go any way but the way the Savages wanted their enemies to go. Savage ground troops were focusing on the one way the Coalition had up into Hilltop. The rest of their defenders were spread out along the flanks.

It wasn't until Team Ranger—of course he had no idea they were designated as Team Ranger—began its drive on the defended flanks that he decided to assist. From his vantage, he could put massive rounds into whatever key defenders he wanted on the Savage side. He'd already knocked out two machine-gun teams that had definite interlocking fields of fire set up and ready to go on the Coalition forces starting out across the no man's land covered by tanks.

First he hit the gunner, blowing a massive hole in the Savage's mechanical-part-laden chest cavity. He calculated badly and came in too low. Then he adjusted for drop, chambered a new round, centered the reticle once more. Took a breath and pulled the trigger again. Just barely.

The small cannon he called his rifle went off with a tremendous *BOOM,* despite the integral suppressor and landed the massive twenty-millimeter cartridge loaded with a sixteen-hundred-grain bullet right where he wanted it to land. The Savage weapons team had just sat down next to their ancient matte-black machine gun inside their fighting position when the round fired from the Wild Man's big bore rifle, moving at almost a thousand meters per second, hit their comrade dead center. The bullet moved right through the body and sent dirt fountaining a fraction of a second before the Savage fell backward onto the ruined ground.

Time enough to realize its end, he thought, as the massive rifle chambered another round.

"Do another one, babe."

Yes, ma'am.

He felt that smile. Her smile.

Then rinse and repeat on the other Savage weapons team on the far side of no man's land. Better shots that time. They realized it had ended, whatever *it* was for them, here. Because of him.

Now, as he watched the Coalition tanks and infantry move out into the cleared space before the rubble barrier, he had a sickly sweet feeling. Like he'd eaten too much candy or something. Or drank too much. Or stayed too long at a party.

Only he was behind his rifle. He'd had that feeling once long ago behind a rifle.

In the woods at dusk back on the world he came from. Stendahl's Bet. Trailing a viperfox that had been raiding their calves. Hearing his ma's dinner bell across the lonely hills and quiet groves. Knowing it was late and time to be home soon.

He looked away from the scope his eye had been centered on. Took a breath and checked the sky to see what world he was on.

It was New Vega. And it was almost noon.

Not dusk.

And there was no home to go to anymore.

His face touched the familiar spot on the rifle, centering his eye through the scope, and he thought about that sickly sweet late-for-supper feeling he felt in his stomach. And he knew why it was there.

Too many shots.

Snipers—real snipers—didn't take two shots in succession. Enemy could find you that way. The human mind could locate the likely firing position on just two shots. The first always surprised. Details and facts didn't calculate in the equation of finding the sniper. The second shot helped the mind to reveal the shooter's location.

Two shots told too much.

They'd come hunting soon.

He'd learned that from a special weapons and tactics sergeant during his advanced training back on Stendahl.

And that's what he'd done ever since. Tracked, hunted, and found the Savages, and no matter how many there ever were... he'd only ever taken just the one shot.

One was enough.

And now...

Do another one, babe.

Sitting here above a real live battle the likes of which the galaxy in its modern form might not have ever seen... he was like that kid in the candy store with the opportunity to eat too much of all the sweet things on display.

A shooter with a view to a kill, and ammo to burn.

He loaded his own special cartridges. He took care to weigh every charge and precisely seat every sixteen-hundred-grain metal pill.

They were too busy dying down there.

He could stay up here all day.

Do another one.

Babe.

He found one. An elite. Bigger than the rest.

Then he pulled the trigger on that bad boy.

And she smiled.

21

Team Ranger
Front Street

Captain de Macha pushed the massive Sentinel tank up over the defenses the Savages had constructed and smashed it right through the wall of an old building on the far side. It was an ancient structure from the New Vega frontier past that was being retrofitted, or gentrified, round about the time the Savages showed up.

Some kind of Savage engineer team—they were armed with what clearly looked like explosives—were setting up to bring the building down as the attackers pushed through.

De Macha's loader popped out from his secondary hatch next to the commander's, screamed the Espanian equivalent of "Surprise," and lit the Savage engineer team up with a brutal burst from the coaxial heavy pulse rifle.

Colonel Marks's infantry swarmed into the breach, covering behind the tank and the ruined walls, and shooting in every direction within the open floor plan of the old building. De Macha appeared in the track commander's hatch and signaled that they were moving forward.

"Watch that demo gear," ordered Sergeant Major Andres over the whine of the tank's howling engines.

Then, to the colonel over the command comm: "Best we get through this quick, sir."

The tank pushed through the massive building's main floor, encountered another wall, and punched through that one too, sending ancient mortar and brick flying in all directions, mindless that it might be a load-bearing wall and bring the entire structure down on them. The infantry followed close behind.

And that was when the Savages came at them from the flanks, swarming through access doors that led in from the outer lobbies of the building. A grenade rocked a forward assault squad covering behind de Macha's flank. No one saw it, and when it went off, the entire squad was ripped to shreds by its needle-sharp fragments.

The soldiers of the Twenty-Fifth started firing as Savages came from gaps in the walls, or from two corridors that opened up onto the space they were fighting in. What made their attack disconcerting, realized the colonel as he directed fire, was that unlike most people, the Savages moved and fired at the same time. And their targeting wasn't half bad despite their mobility.

"Let me through!" A medic sprinted up, wanting to get out to the team that had been rocked by the grenade.

The colonel held the kid back. "You wait until the assault teams put down the first wave!"

"We can't set up a collection point here," said Andres over the comm. "They'll just demo the building with us inside, sir."

"Affirmative on that," said the colonel. "Leave the dead and carry the wounded. Follow the tank through to the other side."

"Uh..." said Andres. "Sir, I don't like—"

"No other choice, Sergeant Major. I get that we're strung out. But this is the breakout in an enemy-held defensive line. It's the only way we free up the main assault. Once the Savages know we're in, they'll react and try to seal it, cutting us off. We push now while we have the opportunity."

De Macha's Alpha One bulldozed through another wall in the gutted building and entered a grand opulent lobby. Tall leaded windows provided a view onto the street— and an entry point for the anti-armor round that smashed through the glass, glanced off the tank, and went fishtailing up into an ancient red crystal chandelier.

The ornate piece crashed to the floor and the giant leaded windows came apart as the Savages filled the space from every quarter with as many rounds as they could.

"Buttoning up!" shouted de Macha over the comm.

"Good idea," replied the colonel. "What's your thermal imaging look like?"

There was a humming lull in the comm while the real world turned into a cacophony of stray rounds, smashed glass, and distant gunfire.

"Nothing," replied de Macha with frustration. "She's smashed. We're blind."

The colonel turned to his two assault team leaders. "Both of you take a side exit and set up an ambush. Maydoon, you make sure it happens!"

The LT serving as his XO nodded and moved with a "Yes, sir!"

Marks pulled out his battle board and dialed into the ad hoc Coalition fire support request screen. Using a real-time map of the city provided by a Hawkeye drone, he centered on his coordinates, tapped out three target reference points, and asked for high-energy incendiary rounds to be used.

The response came on-screen.

Fire mission online.

The colonel waited.

Shot out, came the message.

A round whistled in from above and smashed into the street. The colonel chanced a peek from the room they were covering in and saw the flash of bright gunfire coming from the building across the way. At just that moment another smoking anti-armor round smashed into a silver marble support column and exploded.

The colonel adjusted the shot location on the battle board and waited.

Shot out.

Again another massive round whistled in from above. This one hit the building across the street. Smoke and debris erupted from its portico, but the building seemed relatively unharmed.

The colonel touched the "fire for effect" request button.

Affirmative, came the reply.

"Uh, sir..." whispered the sergeant major from along the wall. "Any chance a full barrage is going to set off the explosives that were supposed to bring this structure down?"

The colonel made a gesture with his head indicating he had no idea. And that they had no other option.

Five seconds later artillery rounds started falling all over the building on the far side of the street. For a full minute rounds slammed into everything. Glass fell from shattered windows. Drywall and plaster shook loose and came down in great sections. Some opulent staircase from New Vega's frontier past groaned and collapsed in a dusty cascade.

Dead silence followed the thunder of the falling artillery barrage.

"Moving forward," said Captain de Macha over the comm. Not wasting a moment. Taking advantage of the enemies' disorientation.

Colonel Marks wasted no time either. He had few soldiers left; they needed to be swift and mobile. "Flanking teams hold. The rest follow the main element."

The Sentinel crushed the massive bronze entry doors and bounded out onto the street. Its main gun, and the coax on remote, rotated on hydraulic whines, looking for targets.

The colonel's ear picked up an ominously wrong clanking sound in one of its tracks. They'd pushed through, but the feeling that they could be overrun in an instant weighed on Marks.

There were no Savages on the street. The building across the street, along with several others nearby, had collapsed in a great pile of ruin. Dust still rose up into the sky.

Team Ranger took up defensive positions on the grand steps of the building they'd just exited, some covering behind ruined statues. The colonel again brought up the battle board and accessed drone recon, only to be greeted with a black screen.

It had been shot down.

Twenty minutes until replacement, said the flashing message on the board.

Inwardly the colonel sighed because he'd had this thought before, and it was a ridiculous thought to have now. Both because it was true, and because it was false... in a sense.

This was no way to fight a war.

But when had there ever been a way to fight a modern war? Everything always went wrong. The best plans fell apart within seconds. All that had ever served him was being able to adapt and react faster than the enemy. Because the situation changed moment by moment.

It always did.

That had meant life or death on many occasions.

And... things were always different with the Savages.

In the distance, several blocks up to the east, he could hear the ongoing firefight from Ogilvie's force. He checked on the casualty reporting.

That was down too.

DNS Attack in Progress flashed across the screen.

Well, thought the colonel grimly, *that makes sense.*

The Savages loved to play cyberwarfare games. So of course they'd fight hard in that battlespace too. Lie low like they didn't want to participate in that space, assess, and then when things were nice and messy... unleash a DNS attack.

Effectively the Coalition was now blind.

Marks climbed up on de Macha's tank as the captain opened it and struggled out into the daylight. His face was caked with soot and running with sweat.

"She's hurt pretty badly, my friend," he said. "But we still got Alpha Four and Five. They're coming up now."

"Roger that," said the colonel. "We hold here for now. I'm taking half my men and I'm going to flank the Savage positions working that crossfire on the main body. Once I link up with the commander, we'll move forward together and see if we can give the Savages something to think about besides Ogilvie's force."

"Got it," said de Macha, who was already dragging out some kind of toolkit. "We'll try to effect some repairs if the men you are leaving will cover us a little."

He smiled guiltily like this request was imposing too much on the new colonel.

"They'll cover you a lot, Captain," replied Marks as he climbed back down. "You saved our bacon today. Thank you."

"Well, you know how it is... brains in the head, as they say, save the blisters on the feet."

And, thought the colonel, *prevent body bags from being filled. Which is why you came along on this little adventure, isn't it?*

Marks pulled two squads, one heavy and one assault, to take with him against the Savage defenders obstructing Ogilvie.

A Savage artillery round randomly whistled in from overhead and landed a few buildings back. Its detonation echoed across the hauntingly empty streets of New Vega City as the colonel left Lieutenant Maydoon in charge of the team guarding the tanks.

"Cover him," he said, indicating the armor captain.

"Affirmative, sir," said the young lieutenant quietly. "His tank doesn't sound too good. We're going to collect the wounded and try to get a close-support evac off the top of the building. You good with that, sir?"

The colonel wasn't.

And he knew that was a shortcoming of his. Mission was everything. And only he knew how bad this was shaping up to be. Wounded? They'd all be dead if things didn't turn around fast.

He thought about the special package back in the crawler. He could order the crawler forward now. But the crew of the massive APC would basically be on their own; if they got jumped, his ace card was compromised. And the more this situation progressed, the more it looked like he was going to need to go to Plan B.

But he knew that soldiers *had* to take care of their wounded if they were expected to go on fighting. They had to have that assurance that someone was going to do the same when their time came. That their buddies would carry them off the field. They had to know that.

Otherwise they got hopeless and fatal. And that got dangerous for everyone.

"Make it happen," he told the young lieutenant. "And make sure the dustoff birds have some interceptor cover when they come. We don't know how much anti-air cap they've got around here."

"Can do, sir. Setting up the LZ for dustoff now."

And then the young officer was off and making things happen.

22

The series of artillery strikes, as observed from high up in the building from which he saw the assault unfold, were incredible. He watched the ghostly trails of the rounds as they arced out across the sky, then fell into the war-torn streets like dying angels.

He imagined all the Savages that were destroyed under the collapsing buildings and exploding munitions from the barrage. He imagined this, and it was good to him.

A battle, when you were in it, was confusing. Everything was chaos. Nothing known could be counted on as true because so much of it depended on deception. And you had to center yourself and find out who was shooting at you, so you could shoot back at them. Shooting was always the first priority. Whether you got to shoot first or last. And if you were lucky and found someone to shoot who didn't know you were about to shoot at them... well, that was all just bonus round. The best of all positions one could desire.

The sniper's way of life. Which was death for those out there in the scope.

Bonus round.

Another one, babe.

Since Stendahl, his life had all been bonus round.

Think about that, he told himself as he watched the city.

There were only two battles in progress he could observe along the bottom of Hilltop. Full-scale, pell-mell, shooting-at-each-other-with-everything-you-could-get-your-hands-on battles until one side was good and beat down. He'd seen a few other smaller skirmishes go down—sudden violent encounters that didn't last a minute before someone had been annihilated. Sometimes he'd even added a round or two, vaping a Savage's headspace like some divine act of retribution.

Which wasn't cheap for him. The rounds he carried were anything but.

It wasn't like he was carrying a blaster that relied on rechargeable energy packs. He was using old-school chemical-based propulsion rounds. And he made his own. Back on the *Sweetwater Express* he'd had a whole loading shop set up to while away the hours and days in hyperspace. In the silences between worlds his life was perfecting the loads and working the rifle. The ancient rifle, a family heirloom that had journeyed out to the frontier with them. Long ago.

To Stendahl.

A place that once existed.

A place where the Wild Man didn't.

People didn't begin to call him the Wild Man until after Stendahl. Living on the fringes of one backwater world after the next. Out where the grav-rail lines ended. Beyond the last prefab shacks at the end of town. Doing odd jobs and the occasional varmint-cleansing for some rancher or grower. Waiting. Just waiting for the Savages to pop up somewhere. Just like all varmints.

Every so often he'd do a little bounty hunting. Most of them little more than local-government-sanctioned hits when some particular person offended the locals enough for them to put together a pot to get the offense handled.

But that, all of that, had just been work. Odd jobs. And he'd felt less and less of her in those times of waiting. Like she wasn't even there in the abandoned shacks he'd made his own for a cold winter's season. Like she was out wandering the forest paths in the night and asking him when he was going to…

You know…

Do another one, babe.

But he *had* to wait. He had to wait for the Savages to show up somewhere. Following the rumors and hope the *Sweetwater Express* would hold together for just one more run. Hauling him and the big rifle and all the ammo he'd loaded himself out there.

So he could hope.

And sometimes pray, though he stopped believing a long time ago.

He would sometimes find himself on a quiet, mostly dead world where the Savages had never been. Or where they had come and gone, and that was why the world was dead now.

They were locusts.

But this, here, watching the day turn toward the hot afternoon and seeing a quiet battle lull as both sides figured out their next move... hauling away the wounded, moving around for advantage... this felt different. Different from those other worlds. Those other raids.

He ran his scope over the Savage colony ship out there in the distance. It was a thing so gargantuan and huge, so alien, that it might as well have been a painting, or some special effect in an entertainment about such things.

It didn't look like it was getting ready to pick up and move anytime soon. It looked like the Savages were here to stay.

That's what it looked like.

He looked down at the newly quiet streets, at the gaps in the wide-ranging battlefield. The right flank of the Coalition forces was breaking up. One force was moving off to the east to engage the Savages that had pinned down the main element.

He thought about that for a second.

Then he was up from his hide and grabbing his ruck and gear, all of it by some automatic programming from an unaccountable amount of one-shots and position shifts he'd been doing since Stendahl. That had always been his advantage over the technologically superior Savages threatening to wipe out humanity. Every time they showed up in some part of the expanding sphere of human presence within the galaxy, he'd gone there, hidden among them, and made one shot at a time. Shifted. And shot again.

Do another one, babe.

That's how you kept on going. Sure, you could shoot down a few of them. But then they'd know where to find you. Shoot one and move. Words to live by. Words he *had* lived by.

But now he'd spotted another building. Forward. Across the no man's land of ruin the Savages had created to keep the Coalition back. If he could get there, he could hit more Savages as this new element broke off to stab into the Savage side somewhere along the main battle down there in the streets.

He felt her smile as he heard his breathing. Hard and fast as he sprang into motion. He had to move fast, or he'd miss the show that was gonna happen over there beyond the ruin.

And that wasn't an option.

23

Team Ranger
Movement to Contact, Savage Flank at Triangle Square

Moving quickly with as much infantry he could spare, the colonel ordered his team into a patrol column. The platoon sergeant had assured him that Specialist Lucas Martin was the best point man they had. Martin was thirty meters ahead and taking them along a remarkably wide and clean alley that ran along one of the main streets heading east toward Ogilvie's main body.

Sudden storms of gunfire rang out at random intervals in the distance ahead. There may have been some return pulse rifle fire or the odd blaster. But it didn't sound like the general's thrust was all that motivated to break through.

"Probably probing, sir," said Andres in these moments as the column held up in the shadow of some ruined building or covered behind a slope of loose scree that was once an office tower or apartment complex.

Martin held up his left fist and crouched behind a dust-covered service vehicle that had probably been left in the alley weeks ago. He pointed toward his eyes with two gloved fingers, then stuck his index finger up.

"Eyes on one," whispered Andres over the comm.

Martin fed the image from his pulse rifle to the colonel's battle board. With the entire column hugging the wall of an ancient brick-and-mortar building that hadn't been swept away by New Vega's recent wealth boom and gentrification push, Marks watched the image of the Savage marine.

He was obviously on guard duty. Whether it was watching the flank, or forward as some kind of observation listening post, wasn't clear. The Savage was crouched in the basement stairwell of a building farther down the alley, well concealed. Martin could have easily walked right up on him and gotten the whole column killed. But the point man had lived up to his eagle-eyed rep and spotted the fantastically obscured Savage hiding just below street level.

Armor system just like they all wore. Faceless helmet. Some sort of cloak. Wicked matte-black assault rifle.

There really was no way to sneak up on the guy.

The colonel called the squad-designated marksman forward over the comm and showed him the image. The shooter, a small kid with nervous eyes, studied the Savage while slowly working over some gum in his mouth. Then he looked around and selected his spot.

With no fanfare he got down on his belly and began to inch out into the alley a little at a time. It wasn't how the colonel would have handled the target. He would have gone forward. But he wasn't a micromanager. If the kid was good, then he knew what worked best for him.

The marksman waved Martin back to the alley wall and away from the service vehicle. At that moment it became clear what the kid was going to do. He was going to shoot underneath the truck and take the sentry through that small window of space.

The colonel crouched along the wall. It was a difficult shot at best.

Marks took a moment to study the sniper's weapon. It wasn't the standard pulse rifle variant; it was a charged rail gun. The colonel had used those a long time ago and was always glad to see the back side of them. Great for direct-fire engagement and targeting; terrible in combat environs and susceptible to EMP-based warfare. There was a reason they'd called them Brittle Betties back in the day.

The kid fitted in an electrical charge pack. One shot per. Sighted, blew a bubble, and fired. The brief electrical discharge of the rail gun popped the bubble. But other than the muffled electrical *snap* of the weapon, there was no sound.

That was smart thinking by the kid, Marks told himself. *Dial down the velocity to stay below the sound barrier. To stay quiet.*

In the time it took the colonel's eyes to refocus on the target, the Savage's brains had painted the wall of the stairwell.

"Nice shooting, Private," the platoon sergeant whispered before turning to Colonel Marks. "Good to go, sir."

They were just a few streets away from the main axis of advance for General Ogilvie's team. They sent Martin and three others into a building after hacking the electronic lock at street level; the security system was running off an independent power source not connected the city grid.

Martin swept the building quickly, moving fast, and came back over the comm once it was clear.

"Top floor," he whispered quietly. "We got a view of what's going wrong, sir."

"We're coming in," announced the colonel.

"Copy that."

Two minutes later the platoon had eyes and muzzles watching every entrance to the building—some kind of plumbing supply warehouse. Marks and the point man made the roof, and a moment later the sergeant major joined them.

What they saw made plain why the main body was getting murdered every time they came up the street to attack the Savage forces holding there. It started with a wide, triangle-shaped intersection. The smashed and still burning ruins of APCs and a few tanks littered the intersection—as did the bodies of the infantrymen from the various worlds that formed the Coalition forces. On the Savage side, the south of the triangle, the Savages had been firing from sturdy-to-the-point-of-hardened buildings down into the open end of the triangle the Coalition forces were coming through. Furthermore, the buildings not occupied by the Savages had been demoed so that only skeletons remained, the floors and stairwells revealed. Any Coalition troops trying to get into an overwatch firing position would be sitting ducks for Savage counter-snipers.

The three of them—point man, colonel, and sergeant major—were seeing this whole scene at distance, from inside a stairwell that led up to the roof. Within the dark recess of the roof access, as the day began to fade into afternoon and a gray acrid misty smoke hung over the city, they could spot Savages in position, or moving around, waiting for the next assault from the Coalition.

After studying the situation, Marks led everyone back down into the dark of the uppermost floor. It was a musty-smelling business office.

"Get me Ogilvie," Marks told his comm tech.

"Patching you in, sir."

Marks waited until he heard a voice on the other side, one that didn't belong to the Supreme Commander. "Who's this? I need to talk to General Ogilvie."

"General Ogilvie is unavailable. This is his adjutant. What do you need, Colonel Marks?"

"You tell the general that my boys and I have pushed past the Savage lines and have eyes on what's chewing up his damned offensives!"

This seemed to stir the adjutant. "Stand by for the Supreme Commander."

The colonel ducked from the sound of a boom—close enough to make him react, but too far away to represent any immediate danger.

"What's this about, Marks?"

It was Ogilvie.

Colonel Marks quickly ran through the situation and highlighted the forces facing Ogilvie.

"I'm well aware of why we're being slaughtered, Colonel," said the clearly irritated Supreme Commander of the Coalition. "It's impossible to break their anchor at the south end of Triangle Square, as the locals call it. Ridiculous name, isn't it? This is New Vega's high-end premium shopping district, and that building the Savages are using for an anchor is the old bank. Built like a fortress, strong enough to resist pirate raids, and armor and artillery aren't doing much. But..." added the colonel, as though he were personally trudging up some impossible mountain to lead a surprise counterattack, "I have scout teams probing the back side of Hilltop, and we may well yet find another street to go up in a few hours' time. We've pinned them here; they won't be expecting us there when we decide to move."

If, thought the colonel, *a there exists.*

And knowing the Savages as well as anyone could know something that had shed its humanity, Colonel Marks didn't think they were going to miss a trick and leave some undefended route into their rear. It would either be trapped or full of surprises. Like being targeted and ranged for some artillery they had yet to reveal. That was their way. More soldiers would get killed learning something the hard way that the colonel could have told them in the first place.

But it was clear that Ogilvie and his lot weren't listeners.

The truth was, Marks ruminated silently to himself for not the first time within the last twelve hours, *they should've turned this place into a glass parking lot the second the Savages showed up.*

Couldn't reason with them.

You just had to destroy them. And to the colonel, that meant also destroying planet they'd infected.

Because with something like the Savages, something post-human and cunning and living in the dark, how else could you be sure you really got them all?

It was the only way.

The only way to be sure.

"Yes, sir," the colonel finally replied over comm—after first muting it long enough to take a deep breath.

This was not his normal mode of getting things done. But it was the only way to get things done right now. Now that they'd collectively tied their fates together in this— what was really looking like an insanely bad idea—*coalition of the willing*, as the politicians back home had all been saying in the weeks leading up to this.

The goal of the whole operation had been to save the valuable world of New Vega. No matter how many lives it cost. The ones making the decisions weren't the ones paying. The feast was ordered. The slaughter was now served.

"But, sir," continued the colonel, "as you've noted, that could take hours. And having moved as far in as my men have, I'm not confident there actually is another way into the Hilltop District. Taking out the forces at the Triangle is our best shot at getting to the... Nest. I have a plan, if you're willing to hear it out, sir."

24

The colonel laid out his plan, and to his credit, the supreme Coalition commander agreed with it.

Eventually.

Initially, the general's "strong and measured inclination," as he put it, was to wait and see if his scouts could find another way into the district. It seemed to Marks that the main allure of the "wait and see" plan seemed to be the possibility of General Ogilvie coming off as a tactical genius if the scouts got lucky and actually managed to find a route up into Hilltop.

Assuming everyone didn't get slaughtered trying to take that route.

But if it paid off, that's how legendary status was achieved. And of course this would become a political campaign talking point going forward. Win-win for everyone.

Except the dead.

"And besides, Colonel," said the general with alacrity and general optimistic goodwill from his position located much to the rear of the forward line, "we may catch a break and they could engines up and shove off altogether. That'll look like a vic for us at this point."

A vic, thought the colonel.

Victory. As if there ever was such a thing when two sides started shooting at each other. The victory would be for those who didn't have to die today. Who merely had to live with the horror of what they had witnessed for the rest of their lives.

That was the real victory.

"I hope so, sir," said the colonel, knowing no such outcome was even remotely possible. None of the Savage forces he'd observed, and that were still under observation from his team located right inside the enemy line, looked to be falling back to their ancient colony ship for emergency departure.

No. The Savages were not leaving. Not now, not any time soon. Which bothered the colonel on a level he didn't have the time to consider.

Yeah. Trigger-nuke dialed into max yield would've done the trick in a heartbeat. Still might.

"There is a question that bothers me, sir," continued the colonel. "If the Savages do pick up and go, they will most likely be departing with a significant portion of the population. We're seeing no civilians this side of the line. No bodies. No mass graves. No survivors. My guess is they've been taken into the… uh, Nest. Sir. If they go, if we are able to declare… a… victory…"

He couldn't bring himself to say *vic.* He was too fine a man for that.

The term was phony, like it was some benchmark on an officer evaluation report officers were forever writing about one another.

"Then we're going to face some hard questions about why we didn't do everything we could to rescue the civilian population when that was our primary mission here. Sir."

Your primary mission, General was the unspoken card the colonel had played like an old hand. Because it was all manipulation to the colonel. Playing the pieces, moving them around. Getting things done as he saw best.

There was a long pause on General Ogilvie's end.

The sense of dithering that came over the comm from the general, at the extreme rear watching the battle with as much data as could be safely gathered, to the colonel, forward in the thick of the fight, was palpable.

"I believe you are right, Colonel," began Ogilvie slowly. As though thinking his way through this new conundrum. "I'll order a fresh next attack in fifteen. You'll be in position by then?"

"We will, sir."

"Well then," said the general as though only now realizing that the man he was talking to was the one who was going to be doing the actual killing. The one at the tip of the spear. The one putting his life on the line. Which, when you really thought about it, as the general was doing in that moment of clarity, was the biggest gamble of all. The gamble to sign on the dotted line, raise your right hand, and bet your own life.

"Good luck, Colonel," said a somber Ogilvie. "To you... and your men."

25

Following Martin, the assault team once more formed up in a wide-intervaled column and made its way up through back streets alongside the posh shopping district the galaxy had called Triangle Square. It was still called that on the battle boards and TacAn maps. Except now it was a battlefield.

A few more Savage sentries had been silently disposed of, and within minutes the team was watching from inside the dark shadows of a high-end restaurant that had been dark since that day six weeks ago when the Savage ship first came out of the skies above the gleaming gem of a city.

Across the street stood the ancient First Bank of New Vega—a literal fortress. Or literally the remnant of one. Back before New Vega City was even a city, the early colonists had guarded their fragile wealth from the pirate cartels here, in this central fortification. In this blocky, triangular, twenty-story high building.

There were no windows below the fifth floor, and a well-defended entrance provided the only way in. One heavy machine-gun team was bunkered in front of the entrance at ground level, and two more had taken reinforced positions on the second floor in stone architectural balconies that, ornamental or not, seemed hardened to withstand attack.

All Savage forces were clearly oriented to engage anything the Coalition threw at them down the main street— Grand Avenue.

In five minutes, Ogilvie would order his armor and remaining infantry forward at slow speed, using maximum cover. From the west, Captain de Macha and his three tanks, with a platoon of infantry under the command of Lieutenant Maydoon, would attack into the Triangle and absorb the attention of the leading Savage elements located along the eastern side, bunkered in glitzy stores and fashionable high-rises that formed multi-tiered garden grottos. With the eastern side of the Savage defenses engaged and the southern end of the triangle attacking the Coalition forces coming from the north along Grand, the colonel's team would then assault the main entrance of the bank from an angle that was roughly behind the heavy machine-gun team stationed at the entrance. After breaching the door, they'd engage and clear the Savage defenses located within.

It was hoped that the Savages would react defensively once the bank, the anchor of their defenses, came under assault. If they were forced to refocus on the threat from within, or even tried to retake the building from without, the Savage units would stop engaging Ogilvie's troops, allowing them to take Triangle Square.

Or at least that was the plan.

Sergeant Major Andres was sweating when he checked his watch. It was hot. Outside, the last of the day's zenith of heat was fading, but not so within the quiet dark of the abandoned restaurant.

He checked his watch.

Two minutes.

"Everybody up," Andres said. He may have been scared to death, but there wasn't an ounce of fear in his voice.

"C'mon, pretty boys. Nap time is over. Time to earn your pay and kill some Savvies. After this, fortune and glory. And maybe your mommas can buy a new forge printer with the life insurance they're gonna get if you don't come home."

No one laughed. They'd seen enough of their comrades die to feel like their luck was out. That to keep fighting was to tempt fate just one time too many. The reality of their pending deaths weighed in such a way that no amount of levity could lift it at that moment.

Weapons had been checked and loaded. Triggers were live. Gear was shucked or tightened. But there was no laughter. The work was quiet and businesslike.

At one minute everyone was staged in two-man teams to exit the building. They'd move forward covering angles and engaging.

Objective one was to neutralize the ground-floor machine-gun nest at the entrance to the building.

In the distance, Coalition armor, probably Sentinels or Wolverines, opened up at range. The powerful *booms* of their guns could be heard echoing throughout the canyons of the city, shattering windows, shaking tables and forgotten dinnerware.

A few shots smacked into the bank several stories up and did little more than send forth sprays of concrete.

The Savages' heavy machine-gun teams immediately answered from across the square. They were sending armor-piercing rounds at the tanks, APCs, and the infantry on foot.

"At least that got their attention, sir," whispered the sergeant major over comm at thirty seconds to "Go."

The colonel nodded once but said nothing.

His gaze was out the door and on the machine-gun nest down the street. It was barking on continuous automatic fire, and even from here, forty meters across and down the street, bright brass flew out and away from over the sandbags. The Savages' guns were gas-fed twin-barreled murder machines. To get caught in their deadly cone was to die badly in several places all at once.

There was nothing from the colonel in the seconds before they moved. No words. No assurances. No hope. Everyone knew their job. To look at him was to know that he was going to do his job. And yours too if you died trying.

No one failed to notice the contrast of the quiet inside the darkened dining establishment, as measured against the maelstrom of death unfolding in industrial-sized doses out there on the street. These things were present in the minds of men about to run from one to the other.

Except maybe the colonel. He seemed not to care about the weight of the moment. His eyes were cold and murderous.

Go!" shouted the sergeant major, and then they were breaking out from the restaurant. Running and not shooting. Not until the last possible second.

To their right, from some distant building, a lone Savage sentry got on the ball quick and opened with a sudden staccato full burst, spraying the line of men running to engage the pit.

Three went down in the street, including the medic.

The rest kept running, moving as fast as they could to get across open ground.

The colonel was fastest. Flat-out sprinting, his rifle bouncing in his hands with each stride—anything but at the ready. He was determined only to close the distance as quickly as possible. Other teams moved more slowly, following sights in, ready to engage targets. Still others were hustling to set up fire on possible enemy response avenues.

Someone decided it would be good to fire at the sentry before he could shoot more men down in the street. That one hollow bark of the pulse rifle, ethereal and sudden—an alien sound amid the din of heavy machine-gun fire—alerted one of the ammo loaders in the Savage machine-gun pit they were about to storm. One of the faceless Savages, features covered by the dull gray surface of his helmet, pulled an old-school sidearm—a big old massive hand cannon—and fired at the colonel. The rushed shot went wide and smacked into another soldier.

The colonel was already firing as his rifle came up. It was wild until he walked it to its mark and knocked down the Savage with the pistol. Without slowing he slammed his shoulder into the sandbag barrier that formed the sides of the pit. He could hear the team of Savages inside reacting. It was alien almost, high-speed electronic chatter that sounded vaguely familiar.

"Frag ready!" he shouted at a trooper who'd come in behind him. Then he stood suddenly and sprayed pulse rifle fire over the barrier on full automatic. Not even looking. Just holding the weapon over his head and pointing it down on the other side.

He ducked back down and screamed "Now!" at the man next to him. The soldier had already cooked the frag like a pro. He popped up, dropped it onto the other side of the barrier, and dove onto his stomach. A moment later the explosive rocked the pit, killing the Savages on the other side.

"Move! Move! Move!" shouted the sergeant major to the rest of the troops.

Time for objective two: breach the old bank.

A soldier who hopped the barrier slipped in Savage brains that had been blown across the pit. The twin-barreled heavy machine-gun was a smoking ruin. And above, on the two armored and reinforced balconies, the other Savage machine-gun teams were still engaging Coalition forces down the street. Apparently unaware of the breach taking place closer at hand at that very moment.

The colonel was distantly happy that they had a little surprise still going for them. However the Savages communicated, they hadn't realized the anchor point of their defenses was under direct assault.

It was time to exploit that to the fullest.

Infantry stacked on either side of the ancient security door. The thing was a massive chunk of reinforced steel that had once guarded the fortress from pirates with blowtorches, explosives, and firearms.

"Do it now, sir!" shouted the sergeant major once everyone was staged to follow on.

One of the infantrymen rushed forward with a large two-handed canister. He studied the massive lock for only a brief hesitant second before rearing back with the single-usage lock-breaker canister and swinging it with all his might, activating the rail-driven depleted-uranium ball within. The massive slug shot forward at incredible speed and destroyed the locking mechanism—and much of the door—using relativistic force.

The infantryman dropped back away from the door, tossed the spent canister, and pulled his primary while one of his fellow soldiers shouted, "Doorkicker for the win!"

Someone tossed in flashbangs. Then grenades. And then they went in shooting at everything that moved.

What they found on the other side shocked them.

A Savage reaction force of about twenty in dire black armor had been tasked with holding the security lobby. The flashbangs had disoriented them; they stumbled about placing big armored gauntlets on walls or surfaces to stabilize themselves.

But the frags had done... almost nothing.

Explosives that turned men to red goop and missing body parts. That generated the mechanically equivalent outcome when it came to light-skinned machines, mechs sometimes, and even the heavy troops of some worlds that skinned in similar armor to the Savages. That had killed all of the Savages in the machine-gun nest.

But those same explosives had done far less damage to *these* Savages. A few had smoking limbs that had once finished in a hand, or rather a gauntlet. These waved their stumps about. Another Savage had been cut completely in half, no doubt due to an unfortunate proximity to one explosion. And a big one, an elite as they'd been tagged by CIC battlefield intel, wobbled around with both massive gauntlets gripping its helmet. The rest of them bore only smoking fragments in their armor as they tried to regain their feet.

Then again, none of them looked immediately capable of firing back. A few struggled for their weapons, but with little success.

The Spilursan infantry, and even the colonel who'd followed the first of them in, after swapping out a new charge pack for his rifle, fired almost point blank into the frozen and surprised Savage quick reaction force. And every one of those soldiers noticed something as they burned through full charge packs, slaughtering their stunned enemies.

There was no blood in the massacre beyond the ends of their stuttering barrels.

Within seconds the Savages were dead. Or rather, lying motionless in their armor. No longer struggling to reach their weapons. The biggest, the elite, was the last to go down. It had gone to its knees—after taking several hits—yet stayed upright, almost defiantly, its massive giant gauntlets still clutching at its fractured and smoking helmet where the flashbangs had injured it. Him. Or whatever it had once been.

Sergeant Major Andres, breathing heavily, sweat streaming down his chocolate skin, stepped over, pulled his sidearm and put two pulse shots into the big giant's head. It crashed to the floor of the old bank's security review entrance.

Silence took over for a moment, though there was a full-scale battle going on just down the street.

Smoke and burnt ozone lingered in the air.

"Go three," Andres said, croaking out the words.

The infantrymen moved on to objective three with businesslike professionalism. Now it was time to wipe everyone out inside the building in teams. Get the Savages to react to the threat close at hand—and fast, so that Ogilvie's forces could finally take the square.

Colonel Marks could hear Captain de Macha's Sentinels rumbling into the battle. According to the plan, the massive tanks were coming down Third Street and firing high-powered anti-personnel rounds at close range into the Savage defense on the eastern side of the square.

The teams moved quietly on toward their assigned floors. If Savage comm was down—that was the only explanation Colonel Marks had for how little resistance they had faced in taking the building—then a little more surprise might help. Not only with the mission, but with surviving long enough to link up with de Macha's tanks.

The colonel and Martin moved to take the roof and try to put down the indirect fire coming from there. Andres stayed to hold the entrance with a small team in case the Savages tried to retake the building from the ground floor.

"You get overrun, Sergeant Major," said Marks as he stepped into the stairwell, "let us know."

Meaning if you're about to die, tell us.

"Ain't gonna happen, sir. Always wanted to own a bank. Now I do. Ain't gonna let it go just like that. My momma woulda thought she raised a fool or somethin'."

The colonel smiled at this. Which wasn't a thing he was given to.

"Hey, Colonel," said Specialist Martin, standing above the body of the big elite that had been the last to go down. "Come back and look at this before we move, sir."

The colonel stepped over. The giant had been hit by at least thirty pulses. The beautiful black armor, which up close seemed to have textures like circuitry whorls and even braille-like dots along its surface that hadn't been observable from a distance, was ruined in several places. As with the other defenders, there was no blood running out onto the ancient golden tile of the bank. There was no burnt flesh or shattered bone. No intestines running out onto the ground like the colonel had seen in every other conflict with the Savages so far.

No gore.

Nothing of the awful horror that bodies look like when they've been ruined by weapons. Fascinating and terrible in the same moment. When you're struggling to reconcile that the macabre corpse before you is a life. A life with experiences similar to those of the one who took it.

There was none of that.

Except inside the helmet of the dead Savage giant. Within its fractured fastness were the remains of a human brain.

The colonel stared at it, and for a moment it seemed to waver before his eyes. But that was in his mind. His eyes saw nothing more than the gray goo and spatter.

But the waver...

The waver had been his perception and reality meeting. His own mind not wanting to agree with the data it encountered.

The Savages were post-human. There was never any doubt about that.

But once, long ago...

They'd been just like him.

With a brain just like his. Just like all of theirs.

Surrounded by a body and humanity in all its messiness and beauty.

The difference was, these Savages had kept the brain and lost the body in their long night march toward perfection.

The brain was the only thing left of what they once were.

26

A wild firefight inside the bank lasted for the better part of the next hour. At first the Savages weren't dialed in to the fact that their line was under attack from so close. The heavy anti-armor fire coming from the bank-slash-fortress was still focused on the surging main body of the Coalition coming up Grand Avenue into Triangle Square.

Captain de Macha lost one tank in the charge down Third Street, but he kept most of the infantry safe. Firing from across Triangle Square into the Savage-defended high-rises produced devastating effects on the structures the enemy was fighting from. But the Savages never let up, even with rubble exploding all around them. They refused to be dislodged by effective crossfire. Ogilvie's main force of mixed mechanized infantry and armor support, struggling up into the square, could not link up with de Macha's. No matter what they did, there was no pressing across the main square without taking heavy casualties. Triangle Square was a light show of tracer rounds, pulse fire, and the occasional sidewinding blur and following smoke trail of an anti-armor rocket.

The assault bogged down as Ogilvie held up for five minutes and called for additional tac air support before attempting the next push. During this pause he departed the

TOC in the rear and moved forward in an APC—armored personnel command car—to better direct the battle from closer to the units supporting the heavy fighting.

The colonel was listening to all of this over the comm with only half an ear. Following Martin, his team was moving up the stairwell toward the roof. But by now the Savages were aware of their incursion.

"Better hurry up, Colonel!" Sergeant Major Andres shouted into the comm, the concussive sound of pulse rifles filling the background. "Savages are massing across the street to retake the bank from the ground entrance."

"Roger."

At every landing of the stairwell, the colonel could see for himself the Savage response.

A wide central well bored upward through the first eight floors of the bank, ringed by broad hallways with beautifully tiled floors and sculpted brass railings. Those opulent corridors were now lines of attack for Savage teams advancing to stop the assault on the stairwell at one corner of the well.

The resistance was fiercest on level four. The entire team was stopped cold, engaged in a vicious firefight against a host of Savages. Not unwinnable, but certainly not something Marks and his men could speed through.

"Sir!" a sergeant shouted to Marks. "You and Martin should move up—get to the roof. My team can hold the counterattack!"

Marks nodded after assessing the situation for himself one last time. Pulse rifle charge packs were quickly littering the impromptu fighting position. Short controlled bursts dropped Savage marines or sent them covering in office sprawls. Firing, targeting, and firing again seemed to be the only way to get a knockdown on the heavily armored Savages.

The Spilursan infantry were adapting to the situation.

"All right, let's go," Marks said to his point man.

Martin led the way up into the next floors, following the barrel of his brutal assault pulse rifle into the shadowy dark above. Two more flights up, a lone Savage marine came charging down toward them. Martin fired on full auto, drawing a line of pulse impacts across the wall, and then the Savage shapeshifted from a man into that cartwheeling human-like spider and was suddenly flying toward Martin's head.

Marks joined in the firing.

The Savage went limp, dead in midair, trailing ruined ceramic plate armor and bleeding hydraulic fluid trails. It smashed into the wall and fell to the landing with a thump.

The colonel wasn't taking chances. He stepped forward and put two pulses in its ruined helmet for good measure. The blue flash of the weapon turned his face suddenly stark as Martin watched and waited to make sure they were ready to go on.

Like the colonel, Martin wasn't a talker. The merest of glances from either seemed to serve as an agreement, a plan, or a direction. They were a fighting team now. Rank faded away.

The sprint up the stairs lasted all of two levels before the Savages decided to blow the stairwell from above. The unexpected blast was like the loudest dry stick that ever snapped, rising above the cacophonic chatter of assault and pulse rifle fire, reverberating through the gloomy shaft of this ancient fortress of a building. The war outside in the square to the north was completely drowned out.

Marks felt the stairwell beginning to buckle beneath his feet. He grabbed Martin by the LCE and dragged him out onto the level's balconied hallway bordering the main well. A moment later the entire stair collapsed onto the lower levels, a landslide that sent dust and debris flooding out in a cloud—likely right on top of the boys they'd left behind on the fourth floor, unless they'd been able to push their way past the Savage defenders.

Just down the balconied corridor the colonel had escaped to, a Savage machine-gun team, firing from a leaded cathedral window that was now filled with smashed shards, looked over in surprise at the two invaders who'd appeared on their flank.

Marks was already rolling over onto his belly. He dumped a full charge pack into the Savage loader, who was in the midst of feeding a belt of massive rounds into the wicked-looking light machine gun. Brass links lay scattered across the floor.

The first burst caught the Savage full-on dead center.

The thing merely sat down hard on its butt, a dozen smoking holes in its chest plate. Undaunted, it pulled its sidearm and began to fire back.

The colonel had fired his pulse rifle dry.

But Martin hadn't fired at all.

He didn't kill the Savage, but his spray of pulse rifle fire did manage to blow off the arm attached to the hand holding the thing's weapon. The sidearm went skittering off along the floor as arm and body parted ways.

As if in slow motion, the Savage merely looked at the missing limb and moved to pick up the weapon with the other hand.

The Savage gunner was dragging the powerful automatic weapon, likely loaded with armor-piercing rounds, from off the ledge of the massive window that looked down into the war-torn square. He hefted it around to unload on the two infantrymen.

The colonel was slapping in a new charge pack when the interceptor Ogilvie had called in for an airstrike overshot the laser-designated target in the square below and unloaded a massive volume of pulse fire on the upper floors of the bank.

Both Martin and the colonel watched in amazement and relief as the two Savages were suddenly torn to shreds by the air-to-ground fire that swarmed in through the smashed window at the end of the corridor. It was lucky, but both men were happy to take it.

"C'mon," muttered the colonel in the yawning silence that followed. "There's another set of stairs on the other side of this floor. Hopefully Savages didn't blow them, too."

Then they were up and moving, racing across the slaughtered remains of the two Savages, the ruined heavy gun, and the piles of skittering empty brass casings as the fire from the strafing run licked up in small pockets of flame, burning out on the floor.

27

"Savages! Incoming!"

There were maybe fifteen Savages marines, moving fast and covered by light machine-gun fire from the buildings along the eastern edge of the square. The first force seeking to retake the bank. It was clear they intended to rush the entrance.

Specialist Makneil, Private Hurr, and Sergeant Major Andres alternated fire from the bank's smashed security entrance. The running, cartwheeling Savages died halfway to their objective.

"Colonel Marks," Andres attempted over the comm, "how copy?"

In the fortress-like confines of the bank, the comm was going in and out. The sergeant major could reach some of the squads clearing the building, but he'd lost contact with Colonel Marks altogether. It was the senior NCO's conclusion that either the colonel had been killed or that something more than the building itself was interfering with comms. Maybe the Savages were using some kind of sophisticated directional jamming equipment to isolate the defenders at the main entrance. He suspected the latter. Or maybe just hoped. Colonel Marks didn't seem like he was gonna die all that easy, but in war, strange things happened. Amateurs got lucky, and incoming fire didn't discriminate.

"They comin' at us again, boys," Andres yelled after dumping a charge on full auto to keep a Savage's head down out there. "I get killed, you hold this position with your lives. Is that understood? We can't have 'em cutting off the rest of our boys from escape if they need to pull out. Got me?"

Both soldiers, one checking the sights on his rifle, murmured their understanding of the standing order they'd just been given.

About a minute later a high-powered round, fired from some Savage sniper weapon system out along the eastern side of the square, probably from back in the recessed dark of the one the artillery-smashed buildings, took off Private Hurr's head. Or rather it blew the back half off, leaving a red spray of mist hanging in the dry and smoky air. Painting the rear wall of the security entrance in gray matter.

"Oh, shit!" Makneil shouted.

The sergeant major, who was crouching beneath Hurr while the kid scanned the street for the next assault, caught the boy's body and lowered him to the floor. He knew the private was dead already. Time in grade and various hot spots had taught him thus.

"Stay back and watch," Andres told Specialist Makneil as he dragged Hurr's body over toward the other side of the room where it would be out of the way for the rest of the fight. Where some recovery team would come and find him once the battle was done and all the Savages were dead. He took the kid's weapon, charge packs, and remaining explosives. The rest of his platoon would need those. He quickly folded the young man's arms across his chest.

"You just rest now," Andres heard himself say from some distant part of his mind. His voice a wheezy gasp in the hot afternoon of this unending day. The other part of his mind, the present situation part, had been working the NCO's constant problem of supply and redistribution to care for those who remained. To get as many as he could home.

He stopped when he heard himself.

And then he decided that was okay. As long as he kept moving.

"That's all right," he whispered to himself, leaving the body and rejoining Makneil. "It's okay if you tell 'em it's over now."

That too is an NCO's job.

Then he was back to the present and all its demands of attention, return fire, and constant supply.

Another Savage assault pushed from a building closer at hand. Near the restaurant Team Ranger had initially assaulted from. Firing as they moved. A heavy gunner at their center unloaded a brutal hail of gunfire at the entrance while two teams spread out and rushed forward from the gunner's flanks.

"'Nades, young specialist," hissed the sergeant major with his hands out. "Sense of urgency would be good right about now, in fact."

Makneil pulled a frag from off his vest and handed it to the sergeant major, who fluidly armed it and rolled it into the pit the Savages were racing for. Then his hands were out for another. Makneil held it out, and the sergeant major took it and waved the specialist back against the wall.

The serjeant major waited, kneeling, one hand holding the fragger, the other with his fingers out and ready to arm it.

The first explosive detonated and probably killed some of the Savages as they swarmed the empty weapons pit. But their heavy gunner was still shooting, still moving forward slowly, raking the door with as much fire as he could place there despite the jumping weapon. He was smart. He was firing for suppression, keeping the defenders back from the entrance so the Savages could get close enough to put their own grenades in play.

An explosion in a tight confined space like the security lobby would be more than enough to do the job.

Andres bided his time. "Keep comin', you mother."

At the last second the sergeant major tossed the grenade out the door and onto the front steps, hoping the Savages were getting close now. Hoping that after the first grenade the Savages would suddenly surge forward, seeking to seize the momentum. Recognizing that the window for another grenade was just bare enough for them to breach and spray the lobby. To get their kills and meet their objective.

That's what Sergeant Major Andres wanted some lost human part of the Savages might still be thinking. Grabbing for moments of desperate survival and not weighing the odds. Surrendering to time and chance. As though there were cosmic do-overs for the losers.

The sergeant brought up his rifle and fired on the doorway without waiting for a target to appear. His pulses were already hurtling toward the doorway as the first Savage filled the smashed frame of the entrance in its hulking faceless armor. Andres's pulse fire tore the thing's head from its torso.

A split second later the frag exploded violently and a little too close for comfort.

"Ah! Dammit!" Andres shouted.

"You hit, Sergeant Major?" Makneil yelled above the din of his own rifle firing.

Andres felt a sharp pain in his chest and for a chaotic moment thought he might be having a heart attack. But when he pulled away a probing hand and saw it bloodied, he knew a fragment had struck his left pectoral muscle. He could feel it now, sticking out of muscle and skin. He grunted in agitation each time it brushed against his clothing and armor.

"I'm all right," he yelled back, sitting with his back facing the wall, watching the entrance. "More're comin'!"

A Savage stumbled through, missing both its arms, half its helmet sheared away, its brain smoking from within the ruin of its head.

SGM Andres would remember that. Could never forget it.

The thing's brain, buried inside that faceless helmet, was on fire as it stumbled through the doorway.

Makneil opened up and dropped it with a brutal burst from his pulse rifle.

And they waited for more. And waited. But none came.

For now.

The plan had involved the colonel and fire teams reaching defensive positions quickly. The three—now two—soldiers at the entrance couldn't keep the Savages at bay all by themselves. That wave had only been barely fought off.

"Let me help you, Sergeant Major," said the specialist. "Hold on while I clear the door."

Makneil stepped almost gingerly through the debris, hugged wall near the entrance, and checked the opposite side of the street from an angle just below line of sight and along the bottom of the entrance. Then he ducked and crossed to the other side of the frame quickly. He stood, carefully, and checked the street once more.

The sergeant major distantly remembered that was not far from where Hurr had been killed.

Poor kid.

But Makneil's head didn't explode.

A second later he was back to the sergeant major and assessing the wound.

"Ain't bad, Sergeant Major. I can treat this." He pulled out his basic medical kit. "You just watch the entrance. Anything shows up, tell me to get out of the way and end it. Okay, Sergeant Major?"

Andres felt cold and sweaty, but he managed to nod.

He'd never been hit.

Nineteen years in, and he'd never been hit.

Don't that beat everything.

Makneil worked fast getting a clot-shot in near the wound and stopping the bleeding. Then he pulled the shrapnel and hit the ragged tear in the sergeant major's skin with superplastic from a one-shot injector every soldier carried. Finally he slapped a self-adhesive pressure dressing across it. The smart bandage ran through its diagnostic and turned green, indicating a good seal.

"You want some Chill, Sergeant Major?"

Yeah... thought Andres distantly. *That'd be real good. 'Cause this is gonna hurt like... well... like a....*

He stopped.

He knew he was getting foggy. Maybe a little shock. Checkin' out and getting evacked might be nice. But not now. He had troops who needed him. It wasn't time to go home yet.

"Ain't got time for that, Specialist. Good to go. Help me get up."

The sergeant major used the butt of his pulse rifle to help get to his feet. His left arm didn't want to work, and he was afraid of tearing the bandage. That was something he didn't have time for either.

Then comms went live, confirming Andres's suspicion that it was the Savages outside the entrance that had jammed it. But before the sergeant major could check in on his men—and the colonel—the Coalition air boss, call sign Wizard Actual, gave a priority address across all channels.

"Targeted airstrike inbound. Heads down on the ground."

A moment later the roar of inbound strike fighters off the *Indomitable* came in, weapons hot. They filled the street with as much pulse fire as they could lay down along their pass. It sounded like they were coming down the middle of Grand Avenue, shooting at everything as they blazed by before streaking off, roaring into the late afternoon smoke and haze.

"It's good to be infantry," said the sergeant major as he and Makneil fell back to their next position—an inner office designed as a final bunker before access to the bank was granted. Covering behind concrete slabs that had been installed as barriers against the long-lost days when pirate merchant princes had blasted off with an entire planet's worth of cash and gems in their old pirate junks.

The Golden Age of Intergalactic Piracy, someone had once called it.

"Infantry seems like a pretty lousy place to be this afternoon if you ask me, Sergeant Major."

"Nah," said the old NCO with a wry smile. "My ex digs scars."

On the other side of this, he wanted to look her up. Maybe say he was sorry. Maybe get another chance.

Or just show her his new scar and see where things went.

28

The Wild Man
Hilltop District

The streets were empty and desolate. At least between the major battles and the smaller flanking skirmishes of both opposing sides, Savage and Coalition. Everything the Wild Man looked at appeared haunted, abandoned. Weeks earlier this had been a thriving metropolis of close to ten million.

Now it was lonely and forsaken.

It reminded him of Stendahl.

After the big battles the local militia had lost against the Savages that had come out of the skies one rainy night.

In the weeks after the street fighting, back on Stendahl, the world that didn't exist on the stellar shipping lanes anymore, the Savage haulers and heavy cargo lifters came in, carried off their stolen booty—looted wealth, plundered food, and loaded newfound slaves. The world became emptier and emptier by the day.

The Savages set up massive detention camps beyond the limits of the burning cities, remarkable in their sudden appearance and horrifying in their purpose. What few remaining forces of Stendahl's government-in-exile tried to retake those locations through guerilla raids, often joined by bands of local militia made up of crazed family members or grief-stricken survivors willing to do anything on the chance that just maybe, possibly, their relatives might be in the next camp. Might still be alive.

Storming the wire at night had been standard operating procedure in those last moments. Doomsday klaxons and bone-white searchlights from the big ships winding up as the Savage marines reacted to the incursion. Their reaction... was to leave. To herd the desperate and captured aboard as the militia came through the wire in force. Then those heavy lifters and cargo ships, under fire and full of newfound slaves, climbed up into the night and disappeared forever. Taking lost family members with them.

He always told himself they'd been killed.

That they hadn't been taken.

That they'd been murdered by the Savages.

But here, in the silent quarters of ruined New Vega, where he'd come to fight the Savages once again, he wondered. Was that really true? Had they died in the fire that swept their township? Or had they, too, been taken up in the big lifters, burning for rendezvous with the Savage hulk? Hauling out of orbit and making for the dark between stars.

Lost forever now. Lost.

He wondered about wife and baby.

It's got to be that way, he thought as he ran along the empty street and under a shadowy arcade that must once have been filled with shoppers and tourists coming to the gem of this sector to see the latest shows and attractions, spending their vacations and accumulated wealth on a day they were supposed to remember for all the rest. Behind windows, smashed and un-smashed, lay all the luxury goods anyone could ever want.

The Wild Man stopped suddenly and listened to the yawning silence that hung across this section of the city.

In the distance more Savage artillery left the gun tubes. A moment later it fell somewhere to the rear, on what must be the Coalition lines, because there was no one else. Except him.

Tall buildings rose up from wide sprawling blocks of commerce and prestige in the streets ahead. Grand palaces of business towered over opulent hotels and once-optimistic design and advertising firms. Farther down the street one of these proud buildings had collapsed into the street, forming a great frozen wave of debris and wild beams.

Coalition interceptors streaked through the sky overhead. Tearing the air to atoms as they ripped across the heights of the tall towers.

They'll come in soon to hit their targets, he told himself. *They're just takin' a high-altitude peek before they make their attack runs.*

He'd seen it all before.

Seen it on Stendahl, the home that no longer existed. Seen it in other battles on other worlds where the Savages had come to loot and plunder. Seen it on archival footage of past Savage attacks, going back to what seemed like the dawn of intergalactic space flight. Only it was closer back then. Those short jumps.

Yes, he'd seen it all. Had seen *them*. The very real boogeymen who came out of the dark... and carried away...

Wife and Baby?

He was moving again. He didn't want to stay in the shadows of the silent arcade any longer. He needed to do another. Needed to feel her smile once again at what he could do.

Hear her.

Do another one, babe.

He needed to hear that.

His massive rifle was held at port arms as he stuck close to the sides of the tall silent brooding buildings, making his way toward the fringes of the big conflict shaping up at a triangle of open space. From atop his lofty perch, raining down single-shot death on the Savages that had the misfortune to enter the world of the scope mounted on the big rifle, he'd spotted that big empty triangle within the packed urban sprawl. An open grand plaza kind of space that Stendahl had never had the chance to getting around to developing. That lost colony world had been too new in the grand scheme of things. Everything had been utilitarian.

Stendahl had been a hard world.

But that triangle, grand as it was, was where the big fight was going to go down between the Savages and the Coalition. Both sides, whether they knew it or not, were committing everything to that small space. You just had to have a bird's-eye view to see it and to know what was coming from both sides. Like two storm fronts on the local weather radar when it was time to go out and round up the cattle to come in. You could see it all shaping up, and it put a nervous fear in your gut that was kind of electric and exciting at the same time.

He wondered why the Coalition, with their fighters and orbiting ships, didn't see it. But maybe they did. Maybe they wanted to have it out right there. Fighting on battlegrounds of their own choosing.

As he'd picked up the spent brass from around his last hide, he'd also seen the Big Walker, the mech the Savages had deployed at the top of the hill, moving down along the streets, firing smoky barrages of rockets and rounds over the tops of the tallest buildings to land in the Coalition rear. After losing a few fighters, the Coalition had given up trying to take it down. They just took what the beast had to dish out, trusting in attrition to win the day. Two other walkers had also deployed from the belly of the massive Savage hulk, and he was willing to bet that old ship was full of surprises like a carnie show come in to fleece the local rubes on a death-rattle freighter that didn't look so much like a spaceship as it did a junkyard in loose agreement with itself.

In the middle of a side street he found a dead UW soldier. Matte-gray body armor. PDB Type 76 blaster rifle. He'd only been dead a few hours. Probably came in with the first wave to breach the no man's land and either got separated or picked off by a drone. Probably the latter, judging by the look of the man's torn-open abdomen.

Despite the fresh gore turning putrid in the late afternoon heat, the Wild Man stripped the body of what gear he could find. Mainly rations. Someone had taken the charge packs for the rifle and whatever explosives the man had carried. But he did find the comm that attached the dead soldier's helmet, and he quickly stripped that out too.

He could hear unit chatter, tinny and small, still being exchanged.

Might be good to know what's going on, he thought to himself as he finished up.

He looked around watchfully, guilty almost, then left the dead man in the street and headed off once more toward the battle.

A few streets over, after the interceptors had streaked in and shot up the area, as he heard distant tanks rumbling forward, spraying death across their front arcs in tremendous booms, he found a suitable building. One that might provide a glimpse into the Savage lines. He smashed the glass at the front door and let himself in with little fanfare.

The lobby was dark and quiet. Cool and paneled in rich dark wood. The carpet was plush, and there were big overstuffed leather chairs that would either rot with time or perish in a nuclear fireball if Tyrus Rechs ever showed up and solved problems the way he tended to.

And maybe, he thought, as he began to climb up through the dark stairwells of the building, maybe that wasn't such a bad idea.

29

The TOC was jumping. Savage artillery pieces operating from Hilltop had struck the power generator vehicle, wiping out power. The truck was close enough to the TOC that everyone inside was buzzing with the adrenaline from the near-miss. Supreme Coalition Commander Ogilvie was listening to his staff officers and shifting position in the mobile TOC that was supposed to follow the second echelon forces forward.

"Sir," a staff officer said, his voice tense and his eyes fighting fear. "We need to shift back to the rear. We're too close to the lines."

Several more of his staff nodded in support, to the point that Ogilvie sensed an outright rebellion against his command if he didn't move back. These staff officers weren't interested in getting killed the way the infantry, armor, engineers, and special forces were currently getting killed trying to take Hilltop.

But the plan—Ogilvie's plan—called for him to follow the second echelon forward. And the Supreme Commander continued to feel, quite strongly in fact, that the optics of saying something devil-may-care and "fighting on" from closer to the fighting would play well come some future election.

So at the moment, he was undecided.

About everything.

Despite the moment-by-moment wholesale slaughter going down on the streets of New Vega, as far as he was concerned this was all still movement-to-contact. The *real* battle had yet to begin. But this preparation, this throat-clearing, as he had come to think of it, was not going well. No less than thirty-seven different operations were underway within the Coalition umbrella. And all of them were going badly.

The 247th Sappers out of Epsovulc had disappeared trying to enter the bunker system beneath the old colonial district of Hilltop.

The Spilursan marines from off the *Indomitable* had missed their LOA and walked into a brutal crossfire halfway up Assault Axis Grand. Their surviving officer, a mere captain of all people, was reporting seventy percent casualties. Ogilvie scowled at the thought. That captain had clearly done something horribly wrong.

The Ninth UW Infantry (Mechanized) had failed to take Triangle Square in the initial push. As had the Second Armor and the Rigelian Mech Lancers. All three of his heaviest assets were now stalled along the Grand Avenue assault corridor.

A special operations unit assigned to knock out the indirect fire atop the anchor in the Savage line had been shot down. Their helicopter took a direct hit and spiraled in somewhere down along Fourth and Commerce. Drone recon confirmed total unit kill.

The list of tragedies, which the general thought of as failures, failures that would be personally attributed to him in the history books, was growing rapidly.

This was not good for his career prospects.

But he coldly appraised his future ambitions, and found they were still intact. The more devastating the battle, the more glory there was to be had when it came time for victory. A not distant part of his mind calculated that a win, in the end, would look even better not despite of, but *because* of all the casualties.

I know, he hectored himself, *I'm a true monster. But it's not all war. Sometimes it's politics. And I didn't make the rules. They were that way before I ever showed up.*

So just play the game, Oggie.

Play the game.

Ogilvie held up a hand to the officer who'd pleaded for them to fall back. But before he could speak, an S-3 running overall combat operations for Warhammer entered the circle of huddled officers.

"Sir," said the S-3, "I need to advise you that we have an open option right now if we're going to knock out the Nest without resorting to nukes."

The general raised a droll eye. A look that he hoped said, *Oh come now, it's not that bad... yet.*

But the sober look on his heavy-browed staff officer's face said that it was indeed that bad.

Oh, bother. Staff officers are always so dire. That's ever their way. The problem with them, the general thought as the man began to lay out the seriousness of the current situation, *is that they don't have vision. They don't see the grand picture—where all this is leading. And if you don't have vision, well then, you don't have optimism, and so the rest is moot.*

After all, he reminded himself as the staff officer went on and on about casualty counts on forward units, *how do you think I got to where I'm at?*

"We can use the bombers to clear the square—*if...*" said the staff officer with a measured seriousness that communicated that he knew *exactly* what was in play: lives and careers. "If we pull back our forces now. The Savages might wise up, but our Titan bombers, sir, are carrying Alpha Strike armaments at present. They'll crater that whole section of the city in one pass. On the other side of that we can bring Strike Force Wrath into play and destroy the Nest on the ground before she bugs out."

Ogilvie bit his lip and studied the computer-rendered displays of the option he was being presented with.

"Titans, you say...." He said this just for something to say while he bought himself time to think about how this might affect his career. He wasn't thinking about the legendary UW bombers at all. He was trying to see how authorizing strategic bombing runs within the city limits of New Vega played out politically.

And what he saw was himself in front of a committee trying to explain high civilian casualties. And that was the start of a slippery slope to war criminal status. The next Tyrus Rechs.

"Do we have another option?" he murmured, almost to himself.

No one said anything.

"Option two?" he barked. Knowing what it would be.

The staff officer put the battle board down. He took a deep breath.

"Sir," he said stiffly. "We pull back and evac the planet. Then we release the nukes Wrath is carrying."

"Absolutely not!" screamed the general theatrically. "I was sent here to *save* the planet. Not annihilate it like that bloody Tyrus Rechs! What do you want, for all of us to end up war criminals? And what... millions dead if the survivor counts are right! We're at nearly fifty percent casualties ourselves. What then—we head back home and say, 'Sorry, we killed half the force and ended up using the nukes anyway'? Not on my watch! The next one of you that even mentions that option, be aware that I will press field charges and we'll have you shot for battlefield treason if the fleet JAG can swing it. Or..." He glared around evilly. "I'll do it myself and face the consequences on the other side of all this."

He was aware that some spittle was hanging from his lip. He licked it quickly and felt, or rather knew, his face was florid.

The staff officers swallowed hard and looked away, unable to make eye contact with the general.

Good, he thought. *Let them be more afraid of me than of the Savages.*

"Get me Admiral Sulla on the comm."

Staff hustled to make this happen immediately.

Astonishingly, the S-3 stepped forward. Alone. Not one other staff officer at his side. Ogilvie's mouth opened for a verbal scourging that would be remembered long after he was gone, when the men in this room—his protégés—were in the twilight of their own careers. But the S-3 spoke first.

"Sir, respectfully, I must ask what you intend so that I can send alerts for change of mission to the units forward."

The general straightened his battle dress uniform, folded his hands over his knee, and fixed the officer with a grave look. Then he smiled pleasantly. Once and quickly.

"Why, dear boy, I intend to use Wrath and the bombers in tandem. We'll pin the Savage forces forward and... crater them... as you so eloquently put it. Then Wrath will hit the Nest at the same time. Within the hour we'll have solved this mess, and by dark we'll be in sweep-up mode. Problem solved. Without nukes."

The S-3's face brightened. "Excellent, sir. Shall I send the orders for our forces to fall back?"

"Oh, no. We mustn't do that."

"Sir?"

"Broadcasting a change-of-mission warning ordering the forward units back is the height of folly if the Savages have broken in on our traffic, which is highly likely given the rate of mission failures in ongoing operations. They cannot find out about the Titan Alpha Strike or they'll scurry back down into their holes. Sweep-up would be hell, costing far more casualties in the long run."

The S-3 stared at his commanding officer in horror. But he said nothing for several tense moments. And right-ly so: this was no war to lose a career over. "To be clear, sir, we will be unleashing the strike Danger Close to forward elements?"

Danger Close. That was an understatement.

Ogilvie nodded tersely. "It's for the best."

30

Admiral Sulla regretted the time away from the CIC, though it had been necessary. He'd needed to attend the briefing with Ogilvie's commanders on the ground, and felt it was equally important to visually inspect the task force with a fly-by in the assault frigate *Carruthers*. But even these short engagements, followed by a flight off the planet and then a quick micro-jump out to the task force, had taken time he didn't have. Time in which the entire operation seemed to be going to hell planetside.

And now, as he walked into the combat information center at the heart of the massive United Worlds carrier, he received an alert that General Ogilvie wanted comm immediately.

The first officer of the *Defiant* couldn't control the roll of his eyeballs at this latest demand from their prima donna supreme commander. Sulla gave the man a look that reaffirmed his position that rank was to be respected, if not always the person on whom the rank was pinned.

The chastised officer nodded and patched the comm through to the digital sand table currently showing the developing battle on Vega.

On the board below Admiral Sulla's gaze were a lot of red enemy assets surrounding Coalition blue. The picture did not look good at all. Real-time updates from the *Explorer*, a scout-class United Worlds corvette holding at sub-orbit over the battlefield, showed an operation turning from dire to grim.

Sulla studied the continental map. The thing that bothered him the most was that they were having a hard time locking down a location on those Savage interceptors that had jumped the initial insertion fleet. Attacking from orbit into atmo, no less—which was a tech not currently available to the Coalition fighter craft and specifically the premier military United Worlds fleet. The most ancient of all the starfaring navies. And still the most powerful.

Atmospheric fighters and bombers had to be taken in by carrier, just as the *Indom* had done during the combat jump. She was now on station and out to sea at a kilometer above sea level, running flight ops against the Savages protecting the Nest.

And yet there had been no sign of those Savage interceptors since...

"Sulla!" shouted Ogilvie good-naturedly over the comm. As though they were merely old friends catching up, and not commanders waging a losing battle about to go seriously sideways. The noise of the operations APCC sounded in the background.

"Supreme Commander Ogilvie."

"Good, good. Well… we're having a hard time of cracking this nut. Heavy casualties."

"So I see…" murmured Sulla, turning away from his command staff hovering around the digital sand table.

He'd had higher hopes for this operation than the way this was going down. Many in the galaxy were ignoring the Coalition and planetary forces' successes in driving Savage hulks away. There was fear at play. And that fear was leading the galaxy to think that perhaps Tyrus Rechs and his ruined world tactics were the right way to deal with the Savage menace. A convincing victory on a planet as infected as Vega would have gone a long way toward putting an end to that reckless and unsustainable strategy.

But something had gone horribly wrong here.

These Savages weren't shoving off like they were supposed to. Like they always did after their raids. Loot as much of the planet as they could before the Coalition, or whatever body, could get a force together to stop them, and then head off once more into the interstellar dark in their nightmare hulks, taking their prisoners with them.

Slaves.

And perhaps worse.

Loved ones simply disappeared forever. The Savage ships, massive things, were often never heard from again. Maybe they found a home. Maybe they were destroyed by a stellar anomaly. Or maybe their ancient ships finally came apart at the seams.

Who really knew?

Sulla knew.

He'd been on one for fifteen years.

Few people still living knew that. Just a handful. Including the two other slaves who'd survived.

"So, what I'm thinking is that I see an opportunity here, Admiral," said Ogilvie, his eyes glinting.

"And what would that be?" asked Admiral Sulla, committing to nothing. Part of the deal he'd struck with the power brokers of the loosely confederated worlds was letting this idiot run things. The logical choice would have been someone else. A specific someone else. But that came with problems Sulla would have been unable to navigate.

And Sulla ever worked behind the scenes to make things happen as a combined effort. Because it had to be that way.

"I admit... it may," said General Ogilvie after clearing his throat, "look bad from *Explorer*'s sensor feed. But examined in another light, there's a moment of opportunity here for us to seize the reins."

"Let's hear it then, General," said the admiral a bit testily.

"I'm sending in the bombers," announced Ogilvie. "Full Alpha. Coordinated. All the bells and whistles. Savages are committed to our line. No civvies on the streets. Intelligence believes the survivors are bunkered, or... well, I'll be blunt here—that they're already inside the Nest. With civvies are out of the way for all intents and purposes, we realize the Alpha Strike, and then bring in Wrath to hit the Nest now. Immediately. Go with Beta Two targeting solution. Cripple the Nest's engines and establish a cordon denying liftoff."

There was a long pause. Static in the comm across the great distance of a solar system. Which itself was nothing more than an island in the dark sea of the galaxy.

The hypercomm was still years from being a reality. The leading, bleeding edge of intergalactic communication tech was tachycomm. Boosted quantum. Which meant it could *feel* like real-time at this solar distance... but it wasn't. There was lag. And across the void between the stars, it was like sending an ancient Pony Express rider.

It was during that pause that Admiral Sulla considered the general's proposal. That the general would pull his troops back before that strike was a given, meaning Sulla would have to determine what the true timetable of "immediately" truly was.

"That seems a reasonable plan, I agree. When will your troops commence withdrawal? "

This pause seemed longer than the last. Perhaps the distance between them. The mechanics of quantum.

Or...

"Troop withdrawals are already underway. I need you to jump in... just under forty-seven minutes. Can you do it?"

The admiral looked at the CIC clock. Then the sand table. The represented death still proceeding at an industrialized pace.

And still he said nothing.

The plan had been to wait until the Savages lifted off before engaging the hulk with a naval task force. Task Force Wrath. Wait until the Savages had removed themselves from the planet. Less chance of contamination and infection. Less chance of the Savages releasing whatever voodoo they might have cooked up in the dark.

This route, by contrast, would destroy much of that jewel of a city. Though the planet would at least be spared. All in all, it was something halfway toward the Tyrus Rechs solution.

Which would make some people happy.

What was being suggested by the desperate general, planetside and on the ground, wasn't the plan. But plans went out the door the moment the shooting started. Always had. Always would. And in the end, it would still end up proving Sulla's point. Rechs's strategy of using trigger-nukes to destabilize and ruin entire planets at the atmospheric level was not necessary. It needed to stop. And Sulla hoped what was about to happen would convince the bullheaded Rechs of just that.

"Agreed," he said. "Starting the jump clock for forty-six minutes to atmospheric insertion with Wrath. Stand by."

31

The comms still hadn't come back online as Martin and Colonel Marks started assaulting the Savages embedded on the roof of the old bank. Firing short controlled bursts after knocking out two positions with tossed frags, the colonel and the point man, taking sectors, advanced across the wide smooth rooftop above the battle. They reached the edge of the roof and began shooting down the Savage indirect fire teams absorbed with annihilating the Coalition forces on the streets below.

The work was short and merciless. In the course of the assault, one Savage indirect fire team, operating what looked to be some kind of micro-mech-based mortar system, detonated one of their own rounds, taking out an emplacement next to theirs. Hastening the destruction of the Savage counterassault force massed outside of the bank.

Within a minute the work was over, and Martin and Marks fell back to the building's edge near the roof access and knelt next to the short wall that separated them from the twenty-story drop below.

The colonel attempted to reach Ogilvie's CIC. "This is Ranger Actual to Doghouse. Objective Anchor has been neutralized. How copy?"

There was no reply from CIC call sign Doghouse.

"Can't get through to doghouse," Marks said to Martin.

The point man nodded.

The colonel tapped for the sergeant major. Still no reply. Andres had either been killed, or was having comm problems also.

He tried again, hoping that sheer persistence would succeed.

Amazingly, he got a connection. Automatic pulse fire reverberated in the background of his senior NCO's feed as it skipped in and out.

"... engaged, sir. But we'll hold," came the reply after identification exchange.

The colonel decided his top NCO was too busy to try to connect with Doghouse from his end. But at least he was still alive.

"Copy that," replied the colonel and broke comm.

"Sir! Titans!" shouted Martin, pointing to incoming Titan bombers sweeping in off the ocean at bomb-run altitude.

Titans were massive eight-engine bat-winged UW craft that could be dropped from the underside of a carrier. Marks watched as they closed in on New Vega in perfect formation. Ahead of them a swarm of twin-tailed interceptors, engines on max burn, swarmed across the city, streaking in from far to near at thunderclap speed.

Ogilvie had gone strategic.

"Get back inside!" Marks shouted.

It was their only hope now.

They were running for the rooftop access door when all hell broke loose across the city below as a wave of destruction swept toward them.

32

The wounded Sergeant Major Andres had no inkling at two minutes out that a flight of Titans, eight in all, were about to drop fifty-six thousand pounds of explosives on the eastern side of Triangle Square and up along the Hilltop District onto the very Nest itself. Most of the bombs in the mix would be high-impact confined-radius dumb bombs with a sensor-directed munitions package. But the real kickers were the four deep-impact explosive giant bombs, called GeeBees by the UW navy. These would crater bunkers that had been buried deep. And all four were to be used against Triangle Square.

Yet even had the senior NCO known of the impending airstrike, it still would not have been the most lethal problem confronting his defense of the main entrance to the First Bank of New Vega. He and the agile Specialist Makneil had fought off two waves of Savage attacks against the entrance to the bank fortress, burning through charge pack ammo and firing on full auto, but already another attack was coming in fast from the Savage lines, and this one was... different.

It hardly mattered that UW armor and infantry could be seen rolling into the far end of the square. The final push was on. Even with help in sight, the horrible end seemed near at hand.

That end took the form of a massive armored Savage marine—either an enormous human in gargantuan armor or a nine-foot-tall mech. He lumbered across the square, backed by smaller armored Savage marines in support, and carried what looked like a flamethrower. Except it wasn't flame it was dispensing, but hot jets of molten metal that spewed forward in unexpected bursts that were almost mesmerizing.

A burst of the liquid metal caught Makneil in the doorway, covering him in what looked like molten burning brass. He probably screamed, or tried to, but the heat and molted slag denied him that final act, mercifully cooking him to nothing within half a second.

The sergeant major swore in shock and anger as he backed away, swapping in his last charge pack.

The Savage giant was ten meters from the entrance when he let go with the molten sprayer again. This time he sent his hot jet of liquid metal right through the doorway and into the smashed and shattered security lobby. Any portion of the walls and floor that was touched ignited instantly, and the glowing orange-red slag oozed down the heavy cement barricades.

The heat was almost unbearable, and the position was immediately no longer defensible.

Andres heard the trundling servo-assisted gait of the giant coming up the steps to the bank, crushing the ancient marble as it moved. Hinges and joints whining with hydraulic sighs.

At that moment he got a flash priority communication override from Combat Information Center Doghouse to every asset on the battlefield.

"FLASH. FLASH. FLASH."

It was the AI override message. Then a voice. "GeeBee airstrike inbound. Shelter in place. Seek cover immediately if you are in the open."

No one would know it, because the strike would kill the S-3 and everyone in the TOC, but the staff officer had disregarded orders and was at least attempting to warn everyone on the battlefield of the impending massive airstrike with a short terse verbal message that might save some.

A moment later the bombs began to fall, well behind the forwardmost line of engagement.

33

"Latest update from the *Explorer* matches our jump calc, Admiral. Bombers inbound for Alpha Strike."

Sulla studied the readiness display from his task force.

The *Omari* was their lead combat ship—a Spilursan battle cruiser that had seen action at Tellae and the Battle of Shirawa. The capital ship was supported by two UW destroyer escorts, the largest ship the failing government could afford after production of her iconic super-carriers. But both the *Isolde* and *Galahad* had top-rated crews who'd faced pirate actions countless times. Combined with the support of the Espanian missile frigate *Campeche*, that was more than enough to knock out a lone Savage hulk—provided they caught her in atmosphere. Or at least it had been before.

Normally fat and slow, the old lighthuggers the Savages used, when caught before ramping up to their incredible sub-light speeds, were easy pickings for even just an assault frigate so long as it was carrying the proper ordnance and the Savages being pursued hadn't developed a means of staving them off with interceptors or other tricks.

Following the *Omari, Isolde, Galahad,* and *Campeche* would be Sulla's own flagship, the carrier *Defiant,* and her tiny escort group composed of the secondary assault frigate group and the defensive escorts *Bauer* and *Joan D'Arc.*

All of this was simply overkill for a single Savage lighthugging hulk.

But this entire operation was supposed to be an exhibition. An example to show that even a planet as infected as New Vega could be saved—instead of annihilated and made unusable—by the growing confederation of post-Earth galactic worlds.

So far, the army was getting beat bad. But the navy could come in and end this. Which was what was about to happen on the other side of the micro-jump.

But there was another objective—a secret mission that few knew about. Annihilating the Savages to the point of nonexistence was always the public goal. The declared goal. But there were bonuses obtained from within the flotsam of the wreckage of a burning Savage hulk. Out there in the dark, the Savages, once the best and brightest of Earth, had perfected technologies over the span of their long hauls. Oftentimes producing results that strayed so far from the galactic evolution of technology that they were effectively wonders.

Sulla had witnessed that much firsthand.

Fantastic results. The stuff of miracles.

The fabled longevity some of the Savages were rumored to have, for instance, Sulla knew to be real. That particular technological breakthrough had escaped the Savages' human descendants. As had other equally wonderful techs acquired within the occasional ruin of Savage madness, or through interrogations on worlds the stellar charts had conveniently edited out of existence.

UW's star might be fading, but the navy and military-industrial complex that had ruled what was considered the core of the galaxy these last two hundred years was not without teeth.

And if all went well...

... if *today* went well...

Then maybe something new was on the horizon.

A republic of stellar nations reaching all the way to the edge of the galaxy.

"Stand by for payload. Bombers almost to target."

Sulla unclenched his fists.

Almost there, he told himself.

Almost.

The Savages were a cause the various galactic nations could unite behind. Destroying them decisively would bind the worlds together.

Today could be the beginning of a better thing the galaxy had never known. A galactic republic that would bring peace and prosperity to all.

A combined force, a true coalition of nations, coming together to defeat a Savage hulk that had managed to ruin a premier world... and then that world coming back online in the next few years as every nation lent a hand to rebuild... *that* would be the argument to band together. That would be the example. The lesson.

Working together to achieve great things.

They would show all that not only could it be done, but that it was vital to do so. Today, they would make that argument.

Yes... thought Sulla.

They will see.

34

Dropped from the *Indomitable*, the massive B-500 Titans came in low across the ocean, out in the waters beyond New Vega City's eastern and southern shores, then started their climb to pick up altitude as they crossed over the cliffs that lined the coastline to the east of the city. The 538th Interceptor Squadron, Phantoms, streaked ahead to clear the target of A-A fire and ground fire, ready to engage any interceptors the Savages may have been mysteriously holding back from the battle.

The initial pass by the Phantoms yielded little to no A-A fire, as all units were engaged in fierce ground fighting in and around the target. But within twenty seconds the interceptor leader, call sign Spitball, picked up multiple bogies inbound from twenty thousand. He ordered the Phantoms to break and engage now that the bombers were nearing the strike zone.

Meanwhile the Titan leader had greenlights on all bomb systems and was tracking good on the drop. Ordnance was armed and they were standing by for weapon release.

"Sir," Titan Leader's bombardier said, "I'm getting several warnings: friendly targets in the zone."

Titan Leader frowned. His bombardier was tasked with overseeing the elementary targeting software. "Maybe too many different ID tags from all those Coalition forces?"

"Maybe, sir. But we're supposed to have them all linked into the system."

That system was a smart-release ordnance safety meant to protect targets identified as friendly. Military organizations often worked to maximize damage and minimize friendly fire by allowing targeting software to update in real-time who was friendly and who wasn't.

"Hadn't we better call it in?" asked the bombardier, surely aware of how this might scrub the run.

"Yeah," Titan Leader said, switching to his wing comm to call off the attack.

"Wait! It's cleared up! I've got clear locks."

Titan Leader let out a heavy sigh. He switched to the wing comm. "Watch for targeting anomalies but be ready. Those Savage interceptors are giving our Phantoms a tough time."

Ahead, fighting over the massive Savage hulk—the Nest—were scores of fighters locked in winner-take-all dogfights. If any of those Savage ships were able to break off and get to the Titans... Titan Leader didn't want to think about what that might do to the formation.

The bombardier sat watching his displays, waiting for his window to go green.

"Titan Eight, bombs out!" came the call over the wing comm.

The bombardier turned to look at Titan Leader in the cockpit. The pilot, along with his co-pilot, met the man's gaze, concern on all three faces.

It was too soon. They couldn't be over target yet.

But before any of them had a chance to question it, another voice came over comm: "Titan Six, bombs out!"

"Titan Seven, bombs out!"

And so it went until the bombardier's display went green. "Firing solution acquired, Titan Leader."

"Drop 'em," replied the pilot.

Because the Savages were bearing down hard, breaking away from the Phantoms and screaming toward the formation. And this bombing run... was everything.

"Titan Leader, bombs out!"

***

Titan Eight, the last Titan in the strike, had been the first to release her ordnance, dropping her explosives well behind enemy lines. Or so the ship's bombardier believed; so the ship's sensors had told him.

In reality, the release devasted the rear echelon of Coalition forces. The Coalition's mobile TOC was vaporized, as were several supply units, along with a field-action surgical team operating close to the lines in support of combat operations.

Had Titan Eight's bombardier been trained in the subtleties of electronic warfare, he might have noticed that the smart-release ordnance safety had suddenly reconciled by throwing friendlies much farther back than they had previously been on the grid. And had he noticed this, he would undoubtedly have questioned such a potentially disastrous shift of assets on the map.

But he didn't notice. Didn't question.

It didn't even occur to him—or to anyone in the strike—that the Savages had reacted to the incoming threat by changing the playing board. Effectively, they had painted friendly forces as hostiles.

With devastating success.

Titan Six followed in short order, dropping seven thousand pounds of ordnance on the main element of Coalition forces coming up Grand to attack the eastern edge of Triangle Square. Infantry caught in the open or sheltering behind the big Sentinels and Wolverines fighting their way through heavy anti-armor fire were blown to pieces as the first of the ground-penetrating weapons slammed into the street, sending explosive blasts rippling through the lines.

More ordnance airstrikes detonated roughly five stories above the surface. Buildings were literally blown in half and collapsed onto other neighbors or into the streets. Teams of both Coalition and Savage operators fighting for these high vantage points were instantly killed by storm fronts of flying debris.

Someone running the data from *Indomitable*, looking past the horror of what was transpiring, estimated the main body of the Coalition assault suffered at least ninety percent casualties within the span of ten seconds. Tanks were flattened or blown off like children's playthings. Blast waves of glass and molten steel spread out into other streets, killing flanking units and causing casualties as high as fifty percent in tertiary assault support units.

Those aboard Titan Six would, perhaps mercifully, never know what they had wrought. Moments after dropping its load, Titan Six was riddled by Savage interceptor fire and crashed west of Hilltop, going up in a swirl of flames and belching black smoke that promised there were no survivors.

In almost the same moment, Titan Seven released both of its GeeBees, the immense bunker-busting weapons. GeeBee One scored a direct hit after boost, penetrated deep into the subterranean levels used by the New Vega Transit Authority, and went off like the biggest firecracker short of an actual nuclear weapon. GeeBee Two cratered Triangle Square, killing much of the infantry fighting in the surrounding buildings as well as supporting armor.

It was worse than anyone could have possibly imagined.

At least the Savages, despite their victory over the Titan targeting systems, were not free of casualties. Most of their forces operating forward of the Nest were wiped out along with their Coalition adversaries.

Still, it was better for them than it could have been. By far.

The Titan strike leader was the only ship that actually dropped on target, deploying a long line of bombs up to the Savage colony ship set down on the eastern side of the Hilltop District. Yet the damage, while terrific, did little more than ruin streets and devastate buildings of little tactical value. It wasn't expected to do so. There drop was a calculated precursor meant to clear the way of any hidden, last-resort A-A emplacements that might be waiting to take down Titan Five as it roared to drop the two remaining GeeBees on the Savage Hulk itself.

Titan Five was in the sights of another Savage interceptor that had managed to break through the line of defenders from the 538th Fighter Wing. The Savage fighter scored several hits on the Titan, but the big bomber managed to release one GeeBee anyway, dropping it short, just west of the Nest and close to Hilltop. The blast collapsed an entire city block that was most likely unoccupied by Savage forces. The second GeeBee refused to release and went down with Titan Five when she crash-landed in the government district, detonating with the ship and leveling buildings from the thunderous surface explosion.

And then it was all over. The surviving Titans raced to return to mother while the Phantoms provided cover, too focused on staying alive and shooting down their opponents to notice the stunned silence coming from the command comm.

Strike Force Warhammer had been reduced to combat ineffectiveness within the span of less than a minute.

35

"Sound off now!" shouted the sergeant major over the comm in the aftermath of the series of tremendous explosions that had rocked the bank—and the entire city.

Some of the men of the Twenty-Fifth Spilursan Light were answering. Many were not.

The colonel rolled over onto his side in the dust-filled stairwell. He and the kid, as he thought of Martin, had made it back inside just before the bombs began to drop.

That had been an awesome sight.

Seeing those eight bat-winged bombers, among United Worlds's most iconic war machines, sweeping in over the city at low altitude. And then beginning to drop.

Awesome... and terrible. A holdover from the old shock-and-awe glory days.

The colonel felt hard concrete steps underneath him, but he could see nothing. Just dark.

He felt for his battle board and activated the beam. Suddenly the stairwell was bathed in harsh white light. Dust swirling this way and that. Each mote a world. Surrounded by all the worlds the galaxy had to offer.

Distantly he heard alarm bells ringing. He wondered if that was just his ears. If his eardrums had been ruptured by the massive concussion effects and barometric drops that accompanied the fabled Alpha Strike the Titans had devastated other cities and worlds with.

He got to his knees and tried to stand.

The stairs above the one he was lying on had been damaged, but had not collapsed fully. Cracks showed ominously in the pristine white concrete. They had almost been crushed.

But he could stand. He had balance. He wasn't dizzy. His eardrums hadn't ruptured.

"Specialist Martin!" croaked the colonel as he waved his arms through the sea of floating dust.

Nothing.

"Martin!" barked the colonel hoarsely. His voice cracking as dust swam and swam with seemingly no place to go but around him while those distant alarm bells kept ringing as though someone would respond shortly and come to help. But he knew that would never happen.

He swept his hand from side to side to clear away more dust.

He saw the blood, mixing and congealing with the silty dust that powdered everything like an alabaster covering.

And he saw the source of the blood lying halfway down the stairs.

Moving cautiously, unsure how stable everything really was, he reached the kid. Martin wasn't dead, but he'd taken a pretty good knock to the head. Maybe a concussion. Maybe a fracture.

The colonel sat down and thought about where he was. What the situation was. The ringing kept on, unabated.

The sergeant major sounded on the comm again.

"Sound off if you're there."

Then...

"Here, Sarge. Bryans."

"Copy. Tark here. Got Sutton and Willis. Willis is hurt bad. Think his back is broke."

"Norris here. Can't find the rest of my team. Sixteenth floor."

A few others. But nowhere near the entire team. Not at all.

Martin groaned.

If he threw up, it was a concussion. If he couldn't see straight, it was a fracture. Maybe.

The colonel thought he'd see how good the kid did before he made an issue out of it.

Then he tapped his comm.

"Marks here. Twentieth. Sergeant Major, can you raise comm with Doghouse?"

Silence. Not just over comm. But everywhere out over the city. Except for those alarm bells that were still ringing in the distance. And those were always there—had always been there, in all the other wars and disasters he'd been through. Alarms crying out like they'd gone mad at the injustice of all the destruction that had suddenly come without warning.

But only after the fact.

Funny, you never heard them when it was rap and slap, run and gun. Only after, when you could see the dead bodies in the street. When the fighting was either over or on hold, as both sides caught their breath and prepared to come at each other once again.

"Uh... that's a negative, sir," replied Andres. "No contact with higher elements at this time. Not even the ships on the net. Thinking—hoping—maybe we just have squad comms. But from what I can see of the street, sir... uh, we might be the only ones left."

Someone had messed up. That was for sure.

And the colonel had a pretty good idea who.

36

The Wild Man
Near Triangle Square

He'd been firing into the Savage lines along the complexes that lined the opposite side of the Triangle. Target-rich environment over there.

To say the least.

The fighting had wound up into a full-tilt, no-holds-barred battle royale for all the marbles in the moments before the Titans arrived overhead.

He'd taken up a position on the eighteenth floor of an office building that seemed to be the kind of place he and his wife had watched in one of the entertainments. A show about beautiful and successful people, lawyers, who worked in just such an office. They were always slapping each other and then kissing. A lot of crying too.

They'd watched those. She'd liked them. It was like peeking into a different world. Not the little stead they kept on the edges of Stendahl.

"Do you think that's what the big cities on the top worlds are like?" she would ask him sometimes.

This office he was shooting from was that kind of place. The kind of place they, those people in the entertainments, would have worked in. Slapped in. Kissed in. Cried in.

Lived in.

That was what the entertainments made you think life was. Slapping, kissing, and crying.

In hindsight, he'd thought as he made his way with his big rifle up through the silent levels of the lifeless place, *they might not have been so wrong. Maybe that was what life was supposed to be. Instead of killing each other.*

Maybe.

The Wild Man landed the scope on a Savage hunkered in the ruin of a luxury tower across the way. The thing had some type of advanced tricky binoculars. A spotter of some sort.

Sure. Maybe life was something else. But not here.

Not today.

He blew the Savage's head off. Thinning the population.

They'd stopped being human a long time ago. They were nothing but animals now. Pure and simple. Predators come in to prey on the herds.

He found another, because that's what she wanted.

"You smilin', babe?" he asked the quietly carpeted luxurious office he was firing from. A place they'd probably done all those kissing, crying, slapping things in. People who were now either dead, or...

He was shooting from well back near the wall, against the central elevator core. Almost in the hall. Just picking targets out between the desks and narrow spaces that opened up onto the Savage lines below and across the Triangle. One after the other.

BOOM.

BOOM.

BOOM.

Like some song perpetually on the edge of beginning the backbeat. The rhythm. The chorus line. The chord change. All that stuff that would never be.

BOOM.

He didn't even hear the bombers come streaking in over the skyline. Vapor contrails rolling out aft of their howling engines.

He did see one of the United Worlds interceptors streak down the broad main street where everyone was fighting. Twin engines burning like a screaming banshee. Howling like one too.

That moment filled him with something.

Like...

Like he wasn't alone, fighting these Savages all by himself. Which was what he'd been since Stendahl. Alone. Fighting. Killing them one at a time from range.

But now, here, with UW and whoever else throwing in on this, swarming the Savages together... he wasn't alone. Even if they didn't know he was here helping them.

He was helping them.

And they were helping him to kill all the Savages.

All of them.

And then what, babe? What're you gonna do once they're all gone?

"I don't know," he whispered as he sought another target.

Go there... he thought. *Where you are.*

He heard the incoming Titan bombers. But he'd never witnessed the fabled machines in action. So he had no idea that the hurricane of engines rolling in from the south was about to devastate the city.

He found another Savage.

Took a breath.

Began to let go...

Boom.

This one had time to die.

It knew it. It sat down. Massive hole in its gut. And it looked up at the sky with its faceless helmet as the whistling sky-screams from the east, far down Grand Avenue in the low quarters of New Vega City, began to drop.

No boom here.

But colossal, titanic, *whumps* that successively hammered the world instead.

It was a badly timed chorus of monster *whumps*.

And then the secondary explosions.

They rocked the building he was in, and it felt, as he lifted his chin away from the stock of the massive rifle, that some great beast of justice, some monster as old as the galaxy itself, had had enough of humanity's galactic insanity, and had finally come to dispense a verdict.

Like it was walking across the planet toward all the killing at Ground Zero. Intent on killing everything once and for all.

The Wild Man always used ear protection. His rifle was like a small cannon. The ear protection always helped him. Helped him to hear her in those moments after...

Do another one, babe.

So when the first GeeBee powered up to boost and drove itself down into the side of Hilltop District and then exploded skyward throwing the barometric pressure all out of whack along with several blocks of buildings in every direction... well, he didn't go deaf.

The glass in the office window concussed inward as the building literally bent like a dandelion stalk in a strong wind. And he began to slide down the polished floor he'd been firing from.

Everything groaned. The superstructure of the building. The walls. Even the air, if that was possible. And for one brief unreal stomach-turning giddy second in which death seemed inevitable...

We're here, babe. Come along now.

He was looking at the last of the afternoon sky out the same window that had moments before been staring into the Savage lines across the broad street. The building had swayed that far back.

He saw interceptors tearing off and away.

Titans on fire and going down.

One hit along her portside wing and going in.

A daisy chain of explosions rising out toward that massive, almost alien colony ship, hugging the side of the hill south of the battle.

Other buildings simply snapped and fell in on themselves or were blown to disintegrating bits in seconds. Hurtling out across the district. Orange blossoms of fire engulfed the street below and rose up to clutch at the sides of the surviving skyscrapers.

And then the Wild Man's office building began to swing back the other way and he was sure, as he slid across the marble, clutching his rifle, and only the rifle, as he rolled end over end for the smashed window he was headed for, that the whole kissing-crying-slapping building would go over as he went down and out of it. Falling on top of him as he went.

He was sure of that in that seeming last of all moments.

Fine, he swore at the galaxy.

At the Savages.

I hope I crush them all.

That was his thought as it felt like the building was about to go over on its side.

But it didn't.

It leaned. Wickedly so. Like it *should* go over. Like that was inevitable and there could be no other possible outcome. But it didn't. Glass shattered and popped loose from gigantic captains-of-industry-sized panes. Furniture slid and whole office partitions collapsed.

But it didn't go over.

And he didn't slide out of it.

Not quite.

He got to his knees in the aftermath.

Things smashed all around him, filling the floors above and below with the sounds of things falling and slamming into one another. He heard the central core columns groaning like the spars of ancient ships. As though the very fibers that kept the building upright at even this crazy angle were ready to let go and slowly bend and break one by one.

Below there were explosions, but small ones. Black smoke filled the windows an instant later. Puffing and breathing like the belly of some great beast from the forgotten nether of the galaxy. Like something from a fairy tale meant to terrify wicked children. Something that came to take away the innocent forever. Something heroes fought and died for. Were summoned, sent for, and called to the stage for this moment and time.

There had always been a good-looking hero in the entertainments she watched. Someone not him.

"Aagh!" he groaned as he got to his feet. "I'm no hero."

He pulled himself along the wall into the inner parts of the building.

"And I'm not dead yet, babe," he whispered hoarsely, if only to remind himself of what was true and known.

He pulled his canteen and drank as he leaned against a leaning wall, unable to remember when he had last done so. He spared a glance out the window, now facing ominously downward. Twilight was coming. The day was done, and whatever had happened out there had ruined everyone's plans.

"Not dead yet," he rasped again.

No, babe. Not yet. But we're waiting... when it's time.

Do another one.

***

When he reached the streets below, he saw the dead. Or what remained of them. He saw tanks, full-sized Sentinels that had been tossed onto their sides like children's discarded toys. Ash rained down from above like gently falling snow. Alarms rang out from every shattered building. As though screaming at the injustice of all that had happened.

Savage corpses were mixed in with the UW dead and all the dead of all the other military units. Many of them had been burned alive or blasted into fragments that could never possibly be reassembled.

He saw one Savage, missing its lower half, crawling through the falling ash snow. Leaving a trail in the bare scrim starting to gather on the blackened street. It was crawling back toward the mother ship that had brought it here.

It's going home, he thought.

He'd unloaded the big rifle for the treacherous trek down the building's twisted and bent stairwell. He'd slung it to crawl, hand over hand, along collapsed stairs that had become nothing but traitorous handholds, some of the shards of glass that had raked his body when the windows blew inward still lodged where they had struck. The blood had run down his arms and dripped into his eyes.

The Savage crawling away from him now wasn't bleeding.

Not like us.

But it *was* trailing some sort of... slick mechanical-smelling fluid.

He unslung his rifle and pulled a massive round off his vest. He thumbed it into the breech as he walked toward the wounded Savage. His boots raised clouds of new ash. Crushed broken glass as he slowly closed the distance.

Not like us.

Not at all.

Do another one, babe.

He turned.

She was standing there with baby on her hip. Wearing that red Saturday-night dress. An apron. Her red hair and blue eyes always on the edge of bitter contempt and smoky lust.

"I can't tell if you hate me, or like me," he'd once said to her early on.

She'd laughed and told him there was a fine line between the two.

The ash was raining down on them. But passing through like they weren't even there.

And right at that moment he just wanted to eat the barrel of his own weapon and go to where they were.

But she wasn't smiling.

She only smiled when he did another one.

She was waiting.

And that smile... that smile had been everything to him. He'd move mountains for that smile.

He turned back to the crawling half-Savage.

The sky ripped in two as a group of starships came screaming in above the colony ship. Fast and hot, the clouds and smoke suddenly folding around them and their wakes, then flinging themselves out and away into nothing at the tremendous weight of ionic thrust.

Stunned by this sudden return to reality, the Wild Man stared skyward with his mouth open.

A fleet.

A fleet is what he would have called it.

Come to save New Vega. Come to smite the Savage ship.

All the ships high above him in the last of that fiery day bore down on the beached whale of a Savage hulk that was easily more massive than them all. Put together even. All of them.

Missile trails, smoking and sidewinding, were already racing down to hit the stranded monster ship that had come to ruin this world.

But that was their business.

Do another one, babe.

This was his.

He raised the rifle and targeted the crawling Savage that had been torn in half and had gone on living despite that. Dragging itself home like every wounded animal ever had since time began. Trailing little bits of machine and armor and oil. Little bits of itself.

Like no living thing.

The shot rang out across the empty ruined city. Its sound echoed and bounced from one wall to the next. As though looking for one other last living survivor to believe it. And then it faded out into nothing, because it had found no one.

The Savage's head had disappeared in a black spray of ruined armor and misty brain.

Like no living thing that was ever human.

He turned back to see her...

To show her what he'd done for her.

To see the smile.

He didn't see it. She was gone. There was only that ash falling as the massive battle began in the skies above.

Yet despite the end of that world, of everything...

He *felt* her smiling.

And to him... that was everything.

The End of the Way Things Were

Carrier *Defiant*
Task Force Wrath

Admiral Sulla was most concerned with fleet formation and positioning when they emerged from jump in the atmosphere over New Vega City. Quantum boost signal coupling had negated the early catastrophic errors that had plagued fleet ops of this type, but Sulla had been flying long enough to maintain a healthy fear of the horrors of formation jumping.

And they wouldn't have done it at all were it not a micro-jump. Only at short distances were these kinds of precise insertions possible. Small errors in calculation didn't expand into the major critical failures that could occur over incredible distances. In those instances, even the most remotely placed fractions of decimals could magnify to the point where ships could annihilate each other on a bad reentry.

The younger crew all about him, busy with their tasks inside the dark CIC, rushing from comms, to weapons, to power management and deflectors while he studied the digital sand table, seemed businesslike and heedless of what happened when two ships shifted back to real space and tried to occupy even the smallest bit of space-time in the same instant. Or tried to occupy some other object that was currently where they wanted to be. Like a sun, or a planet, or even a small asteroid that could be pushed out of the way by the effects of the hyper-destabilization bow wave.

A ship could instantly become nothing but a debris cloud expanding across the cosmic background in such a horribly miscalculated moment.

And the odds increased when two massive ships like the battle cruiser *Omari* and the carrier *Defiant*, along with their escort ships, hurtled through the void of hyperspace, whatever it really was because no one really knew, together. In battle formation. Ready to engage the enemy at broadsides.

Marines were ready. Gunners standing by. Pilots in the briefing rooms were receiving the forward scout *Explorer*'s data and receiving their strike targets on the objective. Every crewmember had moved to battle-station readiness.

Overwhelming, highly qualified forces were closing in on a single Savage hulk that had refused to take off.

Maybe she couldn't?

Who knew?

But why, wondered the admiral as he studied the static display—no new incoming data came in while in jump—did he have a bad feeling about all of this?

In the last instant before the entire task force tumbled from hyperspace, an atmo insert no less, the CIC suddenly grew quiet. Even the constant electronic murmur of traffic between the ships and throughout the ship's departments dropped off. And all that could be heard was the monotone voice of the fleet jump coordinator calling out the seconds until jump exit.

"Three..."

"Two..."

"One..."

"Exit."

The series of screens along the forward section of the darkened combat information center showed the view from the bridge. Admiral Sulla, like most deck officers, gave these an almost cursory, and really involuntary examination. Their eyes and ears were the data being assembled all at once across the CIC. They would be far more aware of what was going on by looking at these readouts, displays, and holographic projections, than by merely observing the forward bridge display screens.

But their eyes were involuntarily drawn back, helplessly, to the forward view.

To the apocalyptic amount of destruction in front of them.

A stunned silence enveloped the bridge.

The city was ruined.

The admiral barked out, "Targeting!" to refocus his dumbfounded staff and crew. To tear them away from what could not be unseen.

A ruined city. Impact craters, seemingly haphazard, carved out of entire city blocks. Oily smoke boiling up against a red sky. Shattered towers, collapsed buildings, entire sections of the once-brilliant city on fire.

"Update from the *Explorer*," called out the TacAn officer. Her job was to update the situation from what was known pre-jump, to what had transpired mid-jump, to what was now the state-of-play post-jump. "Negative contact with Doghouse. Negative update on ground operations from Warhammer Actual. No contact there either, Admiral. Titan Leader is under attack and broadcasting 'Badstrike' on the raid. Multiple friendly casualties confirming... *Explorer* confirms no damage to the Nest..."

Stunned silence followed. They had been in hyperspace for less than a minute. How could such disaster have fallen on the Coalition in such a brief time?

"Looks bad, Admiral," she finished. An apt summary. "But we have target lock on Objective Nest and are closing to firing range with turrets. SSM solutions are good."

And now was the moment of decision for the most veteran of UW's naval officers. Go with close-range fire for the capture, identifying and targeting critical defensive systems to disable that technological relic and ancient wonder, or destroy it and save as many assets as possible on the ground in the aftermath.

One scan of the real-time updates coming in from every asset's transponders, down to the infantry group level, told the admiral that the entire mission was a catastrophic loss.

"Confirm SSM use now. All ships engage at will."

An electric buzz shot through the CIC, and the crew bent to the firing orders.

This was, short of nuclear release, the most extreme option at his disposal. Ship-to-ship missiles rated at starship levels of hull penetration and destruction, being used in fleet fire support, would do massive damage to the city.

"Instruct all units to withdraw to the stadium and stand by for evacuation."

The sensor OIC was at his side.

"Admiral, *Explorer* is detecting an inbound hyperspace disruption."

The admiral's blood froze. Because this was unexpected, and there weren't any friendlies Sulla could think of who would come unannounced into a Savage war zone. But an enemy...

They had theorized over the years that something like that could happen. Theoretically... it might. Many had said no. Made solid arguments why it never would. But on a day when so many things were going wrong... then why not today?

Why not now?

"Scramble the interceptors," Sulla said. "Load the bombers with SSMs. We'll take no chances."

The CIC shot-caller who was standing nearby to receive any such orders opened his mouth in disbelief. The bombers had been loaded with anti-personnel and bunker-buster munitions to mop up identified Savage holdouts and hot spots on the ground. SSMs weren't used for those operations.

"Sir, it'll take twenty minutes to swap the ordnance out," he protested.

"Do it faster then," said the admiral through clenched teeth. "We may not have even that much time."

The Beginning of the Way Things Would Be

Coalition Fleet
The Skies Above New Vega

The history books would often get the Battle of New Vega wrong. The entertainments were even worse. For more than the next thousand years they would get it so wrong, and in so many ways, that no one at the battle could even have recognized that these epic narratives were meant to represent the actual event.

It was not fought in the middle of the day with super-heroes leaping between ships. There was no lovestruck couple, a junior weapons officer and an insubordinate female marine, riding the destruction down into the ruin of the Savage Nest planetside, sacrificing themselves to save the day.

That was just something invented by storytellers to sell downloads.

It was fought at dusk, and the sky looked like it was filled with strange behemoths from other worlds floating toward one another and hurling lightning bolts and smoking arrows across the sky as they closed the distance.

In that... it was mythic.

Epic even.

But the directors of the entertainments had wanted it to look prettier and be more visible. They changed the facts in order to earn more credits. And long afterward, when the truth had already all but been done to death in the dark ages of war to come, the stories were changed again, this time to fit the times and highlight issues to support the agendas of the now in those far-flung future viewings. Disregarding the truth of the then. Of that day.

What the Wild Man witnessed from the ruined and burning streets of New Vega, and what Sergeant Greenhill saw from the unfathomable destruction in the rear echelons, and what the colonel and his strike force and any other survivors saw unfolding in the twilight darkness above them, was beyond description.

Everything that would come, no matter the budget and despite the special effects, would pale in comparison. What happened that day... was terrible.

It began with the arrival of Task Force Wrath at twilight as the city burned like some tormenting plane in the lower hells. One Spilursan battle cruiser, the *Omari*, and two defensive escorts, the *Isolde* and *Galahad*, supported by the Espanian missile frigate *Campeche*, led the Coalition fleet's charge. To the rear and off the starboard side of that attack formation came the premier United Worlds super-carrier *Defiant*, supported by *Bauer* and *Joan d'Arc* along with three assault frigates, *Moreau*, *Sterns*, and *Chang*.

The captain of the *Omari* had first-strike authority and fired a full spread of SSMs, six in all, as the distance closed to less than ten thousand meters between the advance guard of the Coalition and the Savage hulk. Less than a minute later, both *Galahad* and *Isolde* released torpedoes and fired four SSMs a piece.

Suddenly the Savage Nest, an ancient colony ship built hundreds of years earlier in low Earth orbit and launched in the last days of the Big Uplift when elite colonists fled dying Earth for the promise of some found utopia out there in the stellar dark, erupted on the ECM spectrum with a powerful directional cone of jamming noise and electronic interference that activated failsafe codes within all of the incoming missiles that formed the Coalition first-strike response.

That lone pulse, powerful and immense, defeated the first wave.

But sensors detected a massive surge within the colony Nest's powerful reactors, and it was an *Omari* TacAn officer's analysis that perhaps this was some type of one-shot weapon.

SSM reloads were underway at two minutes out on the three lead ships when the *Campeche* was released by the *Omari*'s commander to engage with a full broadside spread from all missile batteries. The Espanian missile frigate wasn't carrying full payload SSMs, but rather the evasive and highly agile STORMs—systems-targeting om-ni-reflex missiles. These were AI controlled and capable of free-fire target acquisition on the fly.

The Espanian captain unlimbered all batteries and launched as the ship lumbered into a hard turn to port, breaking off from the main assault at an altitude of four thousand meters above the ruined city. The ship heeled over as missiles erupted away from all batteries along her port side, their smoking trails dancing and weaving toward their target: the Savage Nest.

The ancient white-hulled hulk once must have looked daring and impressive to those who prepared to leave Earth within it. But even before the missile strike from the *Campeche* ravaged the outer hull, the long years in space had clearly taken their toll. The hulk was covered in cosmic dirt and maintenance grime and ravaged by battle damage from other conflicts that had taken place somewhere along its distant travels. Strange mechanical blisters of unknown origin dotted its skin.

The STORMs found and acquired targets identified as weapons systems, drive propulsion systems, or comm engineering structures.

To the rear, as the forward three ships closed in, engaging in coordinated volley turret fire, the carrier *Defiant* switched to flight operations and deployed interceptors rapidly. Initial plans for the strike stated that atmospheric flight operations would begin once the Savage ground threat had been identified and neutralized. When targets could be selected during mop-up operations.

Some return battery fire, actual old-school twenty-millimeter chain-guns reeling off spent casings from the Savage hulk, engaged at max range. The weapons had little effect against the closing *Omari* and her powerful deflector screen and forward armor. Meanwhile the Spilursan battle cruiser was firing at will with her thirty-six heavy pulse batteries.

The ancient hull of the massive Savage ship was being torn to pieces as ship-to-ship fire ripped plating to shreds and destroyed critical topside systems along the dorsal sections.

It looked as though victory was at hand. And perhaps it would have been had the thing—the theory—that all others wrote off as an impossibility, hadn't come to be.

Admiral Sulla overrode all comms to issue high-priority flash traffic from the combat information center of *Defiant*. "Warning to all Coalition vessels and forces: expect more Savage vessels this sector. Hyperspace destabilization detection alarm has been activated."

Collectively, this was the first time such a phrase had been uttered within the consciousness of either the military or the galactic culture as it was known. The Savages did *not* work together. They were highly tribalized as a result of their closed, floating utopias. The differing lighthuggers had been rivals on Earth, seeking to remove themselves from one another in the expansiveness of interstellar travel in order to pursue their individualistic ideals of perfect. The galactic consensus was that Savages were just as opposed to one another as they were to any civilized colony they encountered.

A ripple of shock raced through fleet comm as commanders asked for clarification and crews struggled with the reality that the one-sided fight they'd been more than willing to participate in for glory and easy combat decorations might be turning into something far more difficult.

The contingent of Rossonian Crusaders, a heavy mechanized infantry unit from Ross-241 accompanied by their diplomat as part of their agreement to submit to the Coalition leadership, threatened mutiny, immediately demanding that the captain of the *Joan d'Arc* terminate the engagement and withdraw safely from the battle.

A similar scene played out on other Coalition ships as the fighting unfolded over the next few minutes.

Two pivotal events happened within the next thirty seconds.

The first would stun galactic culture, sending shock waves through the dozen capital worlds and the smaller colonies that had begun to flourish during the early golden age of hyperspace. Four massive Savage ships fell out of hyperspace at a range of just over ten thousand meters from the nearest Coalition war ship.

The second was that the Savage Nest fired a swarm of drones at the Espanian missile frigate *Campeche*. Thousands of ceramic-forged drones, similar to the ones used in the anti-personnel strike that had taken place earlier, shot forth at rail-gun speeds.

A moving cone of destruction erupted down the hull of the medium-sized capital ship—as though it were a tractor suddenly consumed by a swarm of locusts on a sunny country day. The powerful drones slammed into the forward sensors, upper bridge, lower command, and intel targeting, then proceeded aft through the crew quarters all along the ship.

Critical hull failure occurred when the successive drone blasts penetrated inward and hit missile stores, activating a cascade of explosions among the STORM warheads that were ready-racked for loading. The magazine explosion tore the vessel apart.

Only the compartment block containing engineering decks survived instant destruction; it managed an immediate emergency separation operation and fired the disconnection bolts to separate from the ship. But with the vessel at four thousand meters, deep in the planet's gravity well, there was little room for recovery or escape. The engineering section came down in the wealthy seaside district of Porto Suello along the coastal southern side of the Hilltop District.

There were no survivors.

For the first time in recorded history, the Savages had joined forces for a common cause. The next fifteen hundred years of galactic history would be defined by this moment.

The Savage Wars had begun.

37

Watching the battle on the forward display and letting the fighter intercept officers deal with this newly arrived Savage threat was all Admiral Sulla could do at the moment. The *Campeche* had suddenly flared and then gone up like a bomb off the *Defiant*'s starboard bow.

The crew of the carrier, men and women who'd seen countless pirates destroyed and had participated at long range in the Battle of Tellae, gasped as pieces of the missile frigate went in every direction. Smoke trails erupted from the fiery blossom, rising into the atmosphere hundreds of meters before falling down to land in the vast urban sprawl of a dead city, several boroughs of which were already on fire.

A senior deck officer began to cry, her sobs poignant reminders in the sudden silence that enveloped the stunned CIC that the game had just changed, and that it would be an all-in game. There would be losers, and perhaps... winners. Someday.

Sulla tore himself away from the image of destruction.

"Redirect all sensors! We need data on those four new contacts now!"

Suddenly the CIC was alive once more with chatter and motion as trained professional officers forced themselves into action. It was time to start fighting this battle if there was to be a chance anyone might survive.

Out there, off the starboard bow, the burning wreckage of the main spine of the *Campeche* fell like a burning Hollow Eve skeleton toward the city below. Not far off, the engineering section, which had disconnected at an extremely low altitude, plummeted along its own dangerous vector.

"They're not going to make it!" someone who was still watching called out.

But Sulla had no time for that. None of them were going to make it if things kept going the way they were headed. Already a distress signal was coming in from the scout vessel *Explorer* in low orbit, indicating that she, too, was under attack.

38

Three-Six Armored Cavalry (Fast Attack)
931st Artillery Perimeter

There wasn't much left of the detachment of motorized cavalry that had been sent out at just after dawn to recon the area surrounding Objective Rio, and which had instead become a loose collection of ad hoc gun bunnies attempting to execute fire missions under the direction of the wild-eyed drug manufacturer and distributor Private Makaffie.

The badly executed Titan bomb run had dropped ordnance all over the Coalition rear and on some forward operating units, producing geysers of flame leading all the way up the hill. The ground shook violently for several seconds after the strike. Trembling before fading at last into a dull, low-grade resonance. But none of that interrupted the detachment's work of acquire, load, and fire. Rinse and repeat.

What did stop the fire missions was the sudden lack of requests coming in. They just blinked out on the fire control computer that had been set up at the center of the gun battery.

"Makaffie," Sergeant Greenhill said, tapping his comm as he approached the guns. "Why aren't we being sent new targets? What's going on?"

"TOC control might be down," said the shirtless Makaffie as they clustered around it, dirty and sweating. "Or forward observers took a hit and all missions are off-line until solution integrity can be reconfirmed. Dunno?"

"Maybe they're all dead," said Curts, staring at the plumes of smoke and flames rising before them as buildings pitched and fell and Savage interceptors downed Titan bombers and Phantoms in deadly aerial fighting. "It looks bad, man."

"No," said Greenhill, shaking his head. "That can't happen."

But then Task Force Wrath jumped into the skies above New Vega City. A big war ship and her two escorts followed by a massive United Worlds carrier and her group.

"Don't matter now!" someone shouted in that tense moment that hung between triumph and whatever the state of the actual battle was. From back here, it didn't look like things were going too well at all. But the fleet above would change all that. "They show up and the war's over!"

Which seemed right. A done deal as it were. An entire task force against one Savage hulk still on the ground. No contest.

All the men standing around the battery stood back to watch the lead battle cruiser engage Objective Nest. There was shouting and whoops as the powerful ship-buster SSMs streaked out from the lead war ship, aiming down and forward, racing in toward their defenseless target on the ground a few kilometers to the south.

That was how it seemed. At that moment.

When the SSMs exploded before reaching their target, a few of the men groaned like naughty children whose fun had been suddenly ruined. But an ominous silence fell across the battery as they watched to see what would happen next.

"They gonna target the Nest and start firing," Greenhill mumbled to himself, almost willing it to be so. But who knew if friendly troops were that far forward? Battlefield intel had been silent for the last hour. Drones were down. They'd just been firing blind missions, trusting the coordinates and targets they'd been given.

"Oh!"

It was Curts who first shouted when the three massive Savage hulks showed up in atmosphere. When the survivors of the Three-Six Armored Cav stood witness to history.

The first ship looked like a massive low mountain ringed by a wide outer plane, an upside-down city hanging underneath the mountain's gentle slope. All of it matte-gray steel. That was an incredible sight.

The ship on its heels was a kilometers-long tube with a central disc. A massive blister forward of the spine looked to be some kind of command and control structure. At the rear, a wide block of ancient engines thrust the long ship through the atmosphere.

The third ship, almond-shaped on its top half, was constructed of the same white hyper-mold ceramic as the Nest. Its bottom hemisphere was shelved in decks and small cities all along its massive length.

Every one of these ships was a leviathan compared to the tiny Coalition task force that seemed to have been dwarfed right out of existence.

The massive Savage hulks moved at an incredibly high rate of speed. *That's what they gotta do to avoid smashing into the planet*, thought Greenhill, who'd always found starships fascinating things. Due to their goliath-like size, it seemed as though they were pushing slowly through the atmosphere, forging ahead in one pass over the battlefield. But in reality, they were moving very, very fast.

It was the grounded hulk that fired first. The Nest. A drone swarm erupted from its hull, like a hundred thousand ravens had suddenly taken flight. They raked the side of the *Campeche*, and the Espanian frigate exploded from stem to stern.

Greenhill felt as though he should give orders. Get the men into the vehicles and... do something. But they all just stood there, rooted in fear and wonder, unable to take their eyes away from the awful spectacle playing out in the skies.

The big half-almond-shaped hulk opened up with a weapon system that was nothing like a pulse or blaster. Massive rail guns spewed forth shadowy projectiles. The ghostly images of super-kinetic shots rocketed forth from the bow as the ship closed in on an intercept for the lead Coalition group. Four shots in all.

One missed.

The rest broke the Spilursan battle cruiser *Omari* in half.

"We in trouble," Sergeant Greenhill said.

39

In the moments before the *Omari* was fatally holed in several critical decks, exploding at an altitude of three thousand meters over the western edge of Hilltop, Admiral Sulla had high hopes for the *Defiant's* interceptor squadron now making runs against the new Savage hulks.

The pilots were calling in direct hits on the underbellies of the giant vessels, and one explosion—which appeared to critically affect the long slender ship with the massive disc at its center—indicated that despite their size, these beasts could still be hurt with conventional weapons.

Which was a thing that was known, but somehow also in doubt. As though the arrival of the new hulks had swept away everything once held as fact when it came to the Savages.

Previous engagements had shown that SSMs were sufficient to take down a Savage lighthugger. And even though Objective Nest had been able to jam the first strike from *Omari* and her escorts with a powerful electromagnetic pulse, that didn't necessarily mean they could pull that trick all day long.

The bombers on the lower hangar deck, seated in the belly of the carrier, were being reloaded with more SSMs as fast as possible. The armaments section chief was saying eight minutes until combat drop.

They would make short work of this little trick the Savages were attempting to pull.

Except... Admiral Sulla reasoned as he studied the tactical display... *this is a trap.*

Doctrine indicated Savages didn't work together. Didn't even communicate with one another. Perhaps couldn't. They were as alien to one another as they were to their distant hyperdrive relatives. But doctrines changed.

And this was no lucky-timed jump. No. The Savages had *purposefully* dropped a ship on New Vega, waited patiently for a Coalition strike that had taken six weeks to get here, and then jumped in with four additional Savage hulks that seemed to be working together.

There was nothing accidental, or lucky, about any of this.

"Target Three Zulu firing... something... sir."

Three Zulu was the identifier that had been assigned to the half-almond-shaped Savage hulk currently bearing down on the carrier.

"What is it?" barked Sulla.

A second later everyone in the CIC had a pretty good idea of exactly what the Savages had developed out there in the long dark between suns and worlds.

"Most definitely a rail gun system, Admiral. Massive proportions," stated the matter-of-fact TacAn officer in the tense darkness of the CIC.

Three shots slammed into the battle-hardened *Omari* and broke her in half. She erupted in such sudden fury that it seemed impossible to imagine survivors. Her burning remains plowed into a distant section of New Vega City.

Two ships in two minutes, thought Sulla.

And so far each Savage ship had shown itself to have some kind of massive end-game offensive weapon capable of knocking out an entire ship in one strike. But different designs, each based on that Savage tribe's brand of long-researched tech. Suggesting that this wasn't some particularly large Savage colony that had lifted off together to face the galaxy in unison.

"Interceptors concentrating fire on Two Zulu."

Two Zulu was the long-spined ship with the central disc.

"Stand by to jump now! Emergency escape protocols in effect on my order. Broadcast to fleet!" Sulla shouted so that there was no mistake about the order, or its urgency.

"Powering up jump batteries..." someone called out. No one dissented. No one questioned the decision.

"Rally calc locked in. Go for jump."

"Recall squadrons?"

"Negative recall," shouted Sulla over the chaotic din developing across the command deck. "Tell them to make for the forward airfield established prior to combat operations. Or link up with *Indomitable*."

He knew some would call him a coward. But they could do that *after* he'd saved the carrier. No carrier meant no fighters.

If the Savages had to keep moving through the atmosphere to maintain altitude, then they couldn't hold the field for long. Or at least, so Sulla gambled. They'd have to orbit in hard atmo or climb out beyond the Lagrange to avoid the gravity well. Either way they weren't sticking around over New Vega City unless they were intent on crash-landing. Which meant that by simply jumping away with what remained of the task force, Sulla could return within a few hours in order to effect rescue operations. But sticking around—that would just get his ships destroyed by whatever other superweapons the Savages were keeping back for just the right moment.

As of right now, it was clear they couldn't stand up to the Savages' firepower.

The reserve jump batteries released their energy and powered up the massive hyperdrive that would hurl *Defiant* from the battle. Ahead and all around, escort ships were violating protocol and leaping away before the carrier. All heading toward the emergency rally point. All desperate to save themselves now that the order to retreat had been given.

Tyrus Rechs had been right.

The planet would need to be nuked straight into the Stone Age.

It was the only way to be sure.

40

A massive piece of one of the destroyed starships, burning and coming apart as it fell toward the city of New Vega, barely missed smashing into the First Bank the soldiers of the Spilursan Light had been defending. The near-miss rattled the building and sent the Team Ranger survivors behind cover as new waves and dust and debris flew down the streets and through shattered windows.

As far as Colonel Marks knew, they were the most forward unit that day. A day now turning to night.

He watched from the massive gap where a section of the bank had been blown in. The entire building looked like a giant block of swiss cheese now, but in testament to those early colonists who'd built it to defend their hoarded new wealth, it had held up.

Out there, he could see one of the massive stories-deep craters that had formed after the GeeBee strike erupted through the city streets and down into the transit and maintenance tunnels. What remained of Grand Avenue was littered with dead Savages and dead Coalition troops from any number of worlds.

And in an odd counterpoint to it all, the city lights had come on where they had not been destroyed. Like some weird irony playing itself out now that the city had been turned into a deserted graveyard. As if declaring the war over and a return to business as usual.

The bloody play was finished and the house lights had come on.

Sergeant Major Andres put a hand to his ear, listening to a flash comm transmission. "It's the *Porter*," he said, relaying the message in real time for those who'd lost their comm abilities in the maelstrom they'd just survived. "Sayin' all Coalition survivors gotta fall back and evacuate. Assault frigate liftin' off with whoever shows up. Got a little less than two hours."

The colonel grunted.

"That's thirty clicks, sir," said the sergeant major. "We won't make that no-how."

They had three wounded. And eight men who could carry.

That was all that was left of the Spilursan Light he'd cobbled together into Team Ranger.

Marks shook his head, thinking. "Try to contact the LT at Delta and tell him to move the crawlers forward to the northern edge of Hilltop. We'll try to link up."

"If they're still there."

Marks nodded. "If they're still there. We might miss the *Porter*, but they'll send in other ships to pull us out."

"Hmmm..." said the sergeant major, like he didn't totally believe that what was supposed to happen would actually happen, but would accept his orders nonetheless.

"Everybody else," Marks said, pivoting to make eye contact with his battered and bloody surviving soldiers, "get out the carry slings and divvy up the wounded. Martin, can you still take point? We'll move back through our lines following streets we knew we were in control off before all the intel went down. We'll probably meet more survivors."

Specialist Martin, sitting on his helmet with a bandage wrapped around his skull, stood, wobbling slightly. "Good to go, sir."

Everyone was injured in some way.

But the seriously injured stood out. Immobile. Unconscious. One battlefield amputation. It wasn't the enemy, but the explosive-propelled debris from the errant bombing strike that had done most of the damage.

Marks was surveying the abandoned streets when Sergeant Major Andres joined him at his side. "Got Delta on comm, sir. They was a little beat up, but said they'd move on position."

"Good."

Andres looked out onto the night. "Weird about them streetlights, huh, sir?" He seemed to be just looking for something to say in the eerie silence that had fallen over a battlefield that only an hour ago had been turned up past eleven.

The lights shone down, sometimes at odd angles from those lamp posts that had been bent and twisted from the ravaging fight. Each one bringing into focus some grisly scene of death beneath its light. Ruined tanks, burnt or mangled men, and dead Savages everywhere. Sporadic fires burned like bright flares in the night, and the smoke from the fires had made the orange streetlights misty in the early evening twilight. Like something out of an ancient novel about the end of the world.

"Modern city, modern tech," replied the colonel.

New Vega didn't need a soul alive to keep working. If all the Savages and Coalition forces up and left the planet forever, the city would keep up its automated rhythm, indifferent as to whether it would ever again be appreciated. Predestined to perform its task until it could no longer.

That was not unlike how Marks felt about himself. Keep fighting. Keep moving. Until you can't do it any longer.

Ten minutes later they had the wounded in carry slings and were making their way to the rear. They used the ruined street as long as they could, then detoured through a building that miraculously remained untouched by all the chaos—as though it had been away during the fighting and had only just now returned to ease back into its foundations. But inside, that illusion that some part of this city had escaped the terror of the day vanished. The team found a dead Britannian commando in the expensive lobby, shot through, bled out, and huddled into himself.

"Died a while ago," said Martin after checking the body.

And then they moved on through the building and out onto a loading dock in a narrow alley.

"Let's hold up here," Colonel Marks ordered. "Martin, let's take a look up this alley."

The colonel and Martin reconned the alley and found a way back toward what had been Coalition-held streets. The hulking ruins of burned-out tanks, holed and gutted by Savage anti-armor weaponry, stood like smoking ghosts.

"Probably hit during the battle," whispered Martin as they scanned the dark spaces near and far. "Then the GeeBees blew out the fires. They do that. Saw it a lot on Huando."

The colonel said nothing and led them back to the group waiting on the loading dock.

Those had most likely been de Macha's tanks, and somewhere within the remains his blackened and charred body was probably lying on the deck of one of those heat-twisted behemoths.

De Macha had been a good officer.

A good soldier.

A few streets farther on, as they came down off the district called Hilltop, they linked up with more units moving to the rear. Streaming soldiers, sometimes in one and twos, sometimes in whole groups that seemed like they could have been cohesive units until you looked close and saw all the different gear and fatigues, were shuffling through the rubble and ruin, avoiding the dead and sometimes stumbling onto body parts and trying to force themselves to forget what they'd stepped on as they made their way to safety.

The colonel thought about what he'd seen. And what it meant. He'd watched much of the sky battle go down from almost directly below it. And though he hadn't been as stunned as everyone else when the four Savage hulks showed up, he'd been surprised. A little. But in a different way. Something other than what everyone else experienced. Finally seeing the proof of the thing he'd suspected all along.

"Had to happen," he muttered to himself as they crossed through a ruined parking lot, the march thrusting him further into self-reflection. Artillery fire had struck the building that watched over the lot, and it had collapsed in on itself.

"What's that, sir?" asked the sergeant major. "What had to happen?"

In their short relationship as commander and senior NCO, the colonel had not been given to long conversations, loose talk, idle chatter, or much communication beyond the business at hand. But now, lost in thought, stunned like the rest, Marks spoke about what was on his mind.

"Savages," he began tersely after a long sigh. "Some have suspected for a long time that they might actually be working together. Today... proves it."

The sergeant major remained quiet as they moved through the smashed parking lot and onto the street. The amputation casualty was dying behind them; he wouldn't make it to the evac point. But they were carrying him anyway. When it was time for him to die, he'd die with them. Not alone and left behind.

The dying man groaned and kept asking nonsensical questions. Conversation seemed to be the only way to get the poor bastard's plight out of your mind. Nobody wanted to hear that background noise in the eerie and vacant night.

"What about Delta Viridian Five, sir?" asked Andres.

The colonel knew exactly what the NCO was referring to. Everyone who'd ever made an effort to study the Savages knew about the Delta Viridian incident. Way back in the early days, when the Savages first started to show themselves in small, isolated incidents, a scout vessel came upon two Savage hulks fighting in an uninhabited system over a colonizable world. The two ships destroyed each other with what the scout vessel's captain described as "doomsday weapons."

Survey and reclamation teams went out to that lonely system and, aided by the scout vessel's visual logs, determined that there had been points in the battle where the two distinctly different Savage cultures could have saved themselves and fled. Instead they had chosen mutual annihilation through their voodoo superweapons. True believers in their own superiority, all the way to the end.

It was because of this incident, and a few others like it, that general theory held that the Savages didn't like each other. Hated each other. As much as they hated post-Earth humanity. Maybe even more so. And that theory grew in strength every time a lone Savage hulk attempted to take on a colonized world. Always alone. No strength in numbers. Relatively easy pickings for an assembled fleet to take care of.

Except today had made all that conjecture a lie and those past victories moments of grace. A pleasant lie for those who'd wanted to package the Savages neatly into an idea they found comfortable and reassuring. That the Savages were always their own enemies too.

But it was a lie. At least on New Vega.

"I guess things have changed," said the colonel. "There are so many reasons why this doesn't make sense, and one reason why it does. And now that it's happened, the best thing you can do, Sergeant Major, the best thing we can all do, is wrap our heads around it and realize that this is what it is. The Savages are allying. Forming into something cohesive."

They walked in silence for a while. The moanings of the amputee were more erratic.

The soldiers to the rear set the dying man down. He was going now. He kept telling them he needed to catch his breath between papery gasps.

The colonel and the sergeant major stepped away. Out in front, Martin watched the dark shadows of other units and stragglers making their way down into the lowlands of New Vega City. Off in the distance they could see the stadium they were all headed to. The place where it had all begun.

The *Porter* was there.

"They can't communicate," the colonel whispered to Andres as the dying kid fought to breathe. Marks didn't see it as his job to comfort the soldier on the way out. Let his buddies do that. Let him be surrounded by those who loved him. "Comm between known worlds and fixed points is one thing. We've established that with years of contact and vessel data confirmation. But the Savages are out there, in the vast distances between worlds we never go to. We've bypassed all that with the hyperdrive, but it's where they live—and the volume of that space is so massive it would be almost impossible for two ships to find each other and talk to one another. That's one problem that's always kept them apart."

Sergeant Major Andres nodded, following along.

"The second thing is their culture. Each tribe believes that only it knows the right way forward into the future. The Savage, by the very nature of his society, is convinced with absolute certainty that he is right, and everyone else is wrong. The utopia he thinks will save them all... that's the only way. Everyone else is a heretic. Everyone else has to die."

"Yeah, well," Andres said, working some saliva in his mouth and spitting. "That don' seem too different from most folks, you ask me."

"Put it this way..." continued the colonel after a pause. "Certainty. That's a Savage. Raised in a closed single-belief culture that aspires to a sort of godhood. That's any given Savage vessel. They pulled up and left Earth during her worst days. Creating cultures in their generation ships that aspired to make right what humanity on Earth had gotten so wrong. Sounds good, right? Every time any world gets into a political debate with itself, both sides start seeing the merits of the Savages... you follow. One voice. Unity of purpose. Everyone who doesn't think like you is mentally ill. Death to the heretics.

"And then... mass mental illness sets in. All the pitfalls that come with an inbred system of thinking like that—a listener that can only hear its own voice. They go mad out there in the void, and they begin to believe all the lies they've told themselves. Just to keep going. Cult-like leaders don't help much. And the Savages are rife with them."

"Sounds like crazy stuff," mumbled the sergeant major. "Way above my pay grade, sir."

The colonel continued like he didn't even hear the senior NCO's comment. As though the sergeant major were privy to the wheels that turned all the time inside the normally stoic officer. Conversations he'd had ten thousand times with himself.

"And so any two Savage tribes are not the same—not in any way, shape, or form. They are vastly different. And each is convinced that the other is societal poison. Mentally ill. Must be aborted. And the hierarchy, because there's always one within those ships, they'll do anything to convince their subjects to keep moving through the darkness because that's the only thing that keeps them in power. They breed paranoia, suspicion, and fear like some people breed cattle. They're like modern-day pharaohs. But more than. Much more than absolute rulers, if there can be such a thing. Power. Total power like you've never thought possible.

"Those hulks we saw today, each one worships some god, or gods, at its core. And *they* are the gods. Those cult leaders. Whole societies dedicated to one man, or woman, who's shed their humanity to rule over the others. All of whom aspire to be that god they worship. And the whole culture lives for that person.

"So when two Savage cultures meet... it's like two relatives who can't stand each other, trying to have a civil dinner with nothing but spite and contempt for one another. Before today, any scientist who's made a career of studying their history, the fragments, the relics of their cultures whenever and wherever we could find them, would have told you it's absolutely impossible for them to work to-gether. And yet today... they did just that."

"It's gonna be all right, buddy," said one of the soldiers in the distance, comforting his dying friend.

"Why, Colonel?" asked the sergeant major.

The dying man finally gasped, eyes wide open, and was gone.

Marks whispered, not wanting his voice to rise up above the still that had formed in the wake of the soldier's passing. "The one reason why, as opposed to all the rea-sons why not, is that if they don't... they've realized they won't survive. We pick them off. We show up like we did today and put them down..."

"... or Ol' Tyrus Rechs gets 'em," Andres finished. "An' after today I'm not so sure he ain't right about that, if he actually does exist beyond the little Hollow Eve masks kids wear. Lotta dead wish it'd gone that way today instead've the way it did, sir. That's for sure."

"Yeah," said the colonel. "But it's gone beyond that now. They're working together. This changes everything."

He said nothing more, and the usual silence fell be-tween them.

The sergeant major made ready to go. To get the men moving again. They'd tag their man and leave him. A big clean-up would come. But today they needed to survive. That and nothing more. And the less they had to carry, the better their chances were.

As the march began once more, the sergeant major fell in step beside the colonel and picked up the thread. "How do you know all that, sir? If you don't mind my asking."

Colonel Marks fixed him with a glare that he might not have known was on his face. He said nothing for a long minute. Then:

"I was a slave on a Savage ship for fifteen years. A long time ago."

And then he turned and went off through the twilight dark to the point man ahead. There was only an hour until the *Porter* lifted off. And they had a long way to go.

41

In the stunned silence of the aftermath that followed the battle between the Savage hulks and the surviving Coalition vessels that had fled off into who knows where, the remnants of the Three-Six Cav returned to their MTAVs for packaged food and drink.

Sergeant Greenhill tried the comm. Tried in vain to raise Doghouse.

Nothing.

Tried to get any other still-operating unit.

Nothing.

Maybe some EMP device had been deployed on the field and electronics had been temporarily knocked out. Most systems were wired to survive such attacks, but they took time to reboot.

He let the comm mic in the MTAV dangle as he watched the night come on. And he finally became aware, or maybe just accepted, that he was now in charge. All throughout the day, after the death of Colonel Dippel and the company CO, he had assumed that some staff officer would show up to take charge and tell them where to go, who to kill next.

But no one had.

Sergeant Greenhill weighed his options. They could link up with some unit, find another officer, and let that cat decide what to do next. Where to go. Who to kill. Or they could head back to the known at the stadium. Link up with the TOC at the *Porter*. Though he was pretty sure, as full dark began to settle across a city that was both glittering and ruined—and oh yeah, on fire too—that the TOC had jumped forward when the battle began. And that a lot of artillery had fallen all over the rear when the Titans made their strike.

So there was that. The possibility that the TOC, the overseer of the whole operation, had been hit and wiped out. Which was seeming more likely by the second.

The first survivors from the battle, carrying wounded in slings or helping the walking wounded to hobble along, came trickling through the silent battery of arranged guns in the circular roundabout. No one challenged them. And Greenhill should have thought about that. Getting sentries set up. Who knew if the Savages didn't have some kind of guerilla warfare plan to mix in and disable?

He'd seen that on Kimshana.

An officer covered in dried blood came up to the troopers gathered around the staged MTAVs. He was looking for whoever was in charge.

That was Greenhill.

Greenhill recognized the Britannian sapper by the iconic dust-brown beret they always wore, even in combat.

"Leftenant Higgs-Patel... Royal Engineers," he announced when the cav troopers had directed the questing officer over to their sergeant.

"Sergeant Greenhill, Alpha Three-Six. What can I do for you, sir?"

"Ah… excellent, Sergeant. After the strike, we received traffic to fall back to the *Porter* for evac. But our communications net has since gone down. I just want to clarify that those are still the standing orders from Supreme Commander Ogilvie. Would you happen to know if they are still in effect at this present moment, or are we to return to the offensive?"

Greenhill shrugged. "No, sir. We didn't even get the fallback message. Far as I know, after the drop the entire Coalition comm went down."

The Britannian officer sighed rather theatrically.

"Well, I suspect we should just return to the *Porter* and apologize if we somehow heard wrong. My men are out of charge packs altogether. Fighting was rather fierce up there along the rail tunnels. Thirty-five dead, fifteen wounded. Bit of pickle we found ourselves in, what?"

"Load your wounded, sir, and we'll take them back," Greenhill offered.

"Ah, smashing. Rather solid of you, thank you so much. Hope we're not a bother and all. My sergeant was killed. Head blown clean off by a sniper, I suspect, and… to be honest… I know a lot about mines and explosives, but really not much about getting things done. That was her job. And… well… as I said… she's gone now. So thank you very much indeed for seeing us out of this mess."

Greenhill could see by his red tactical light that the Britannian officer, despite the cheery tone in his voice, was about to lose his marbles. His left eye was twitching fiercely. And most likely the dried blood all over his uniform was that sergeant's. Or perhaps from his thirty-five wounded. Or fifteen dead.

"Have some water, sir," Greenhill offered. He handed over his canteen. Maybe the twitching was just dehydration. It had been a long day; shipboard time on the *Porter* had been two thirty in the a.m. when they had first call. And most had slept badly anyway in the tense hours before.

The *Porter*, possibly five kilometers away, howled to life and lifted off from the nightmare landscape of ruined shadows sticking up into the night sky like fingers from a grave, or dead trees in a cemetery after midnight. The central grid power had gone out over in the suburban sections of the city. Mass swaths of darkness made the area look like an old and long-abandoned graveyard.

"Where they goin'?" someone asked as the assault frigate climbed into the night sky. Others shouted at it.

No one knew.

How could they?

How could Sergeant Greenhill, or any of them, know that at the time of the Titan bombing run, Ogilvie had been shifting toward the front in his personal armored vehicle? His APC, strengthened and hardened enough to stand up to even tactical nuclear weapons, though not a direct hit? Ogilvie had wanted his staff photog to capture some battlefield shots of the commander at the front. You know... field glass to face and scanning the distance. Maybe a dead soldier in the road. The price of war and all. Ogilvie and his inner circle had been on the move from the TOC to the rearmost engaged units when the Titans showed up and annihilated the rear. And everything else that had the misfortune of being on the receiving end of those payloads.

Sergeant Greenhill could have had no idea that upon witnessing the destruction from inside the halted armored command car, and then seeing the Savage vessels show up moments later, Ogilvie had determined that all was lost, and ordered the AACV back to the *Porter* and gears up for emergency departure.

The captain had protested abandoning surviving units. There was more than enough room to take two full battalions.

The supreme commander had threatened to relieve him if the departure order wasn't executed immediately.

Now as the *Porter* climbed into the night sky above the fires raging out of control throughout much of the ruined city of New Vega, the general sat pensively staring out the aft passenger deck porthole on the command quarters deck, fully aware that his photographer was shooting him.

He affected a brooding, reluctant-to-retreat-in-the-face-of-overwhelming-force moodiness. As though he were still studying the battlefield. As though he were that kind of commander. As though his officers had insisted he retreat. Had insisted that the loss of their general, now that the tides had turned, would be devastating to the Coalition. Never mind all the ruined units they were leaving behind.

Men, women, and equipment could be replaced.

But not genius. Especially the tactical kind.

At sub-orbital altitude, Admiral Sulla sent transmission location idents for the *Porter* to rendezvous in order to assist with the emergency evac operations to get all the surviving task force personnel off the surface. Supreme Commander Ogilvie's most trusted staff officers denied the *Porter*'s comm officer permission to reply. Security risk. This was a desperate escape.

And so the *Porter* leapt away into hyperspace leaving the ruins of the battle behind and the Savages firmly in control of New Vega.

Heading back to the galactic core to warn of the Savage invasion—that was the mission reorientation the staff officers decided on. That was the most important task now, the general had "reluctantly" reasoned in concurrence with their arguments. That, and not allowing a senior military commander to fall into Savage hands.

And back on New Vega, the wounded continued to die as their surviving brethren stared into the night sky, wondering if any ships had survived. And if the Savages were coming for them, even now as the day finally disappeared into full night.

42

Team Ranger
Thirty-Fourth and Fulgham

She came out of the rubble when they left the last of the smashed downtown district. The colonel saw her making for their ragged column. The soldiers of the Twenty-Fifth saw her because she was tall and feminine and the opposite of everything they'd just been through. She was life after a feast of death.

Maybe to some she looked like just another refugee joining the long column heading back to the rear in silence. A soldier from one of the units females served in. A pilot maybe. Intel perhaps. A survivor caught forward when everything went to hell it what, in hindsight, now seemed an instant.

But to most she was a reminder why it was good to be among the living, and not the dead.

The roar of the day's battle seemed a foreign thing now in the eerie silence disturbed only by the sound of boots working their way over the rubble of a ruined world. Thumping on pavement or grinding broken glass and gravel under heel. There were so many retreating soldiers dejectedly making their way rearward now that their boots formed a discordant chorus.

There were no words in the columns making their way back through the industrial streets in which they'd first encountered the Savages. Those firefights were now old friends that would never be forgotten. The dead who'd been killed early in the day waited there still like memories that could not fade no matter how many times they were recalled. The corpses of dead Savages also waited, like the remains of strange creatures found on foreign shores.

As though all of what had just happened, had happened at some other time, to someone else not the survivors retreating back to the empty stadium.

The *Porter* had departed hours before, and so far no other ship had come in to take up position at Objective Rio, the original insertion LZ. A few crawlers, including the one assigned to Headquarters Company, Twenty-Fifth Spilursan, had moved forward through the streets to link up with their particular elements. The colonel was supervising the loading of walking wounded into the Headquarters Crawler when he spotted the woman.

She was blonde, her hair cut short, and wore green military overalls. A worn ruck was slung over one shoulder, and despite having been through it all, despite the dirt and grime and smoke that streaked her sculpted features, she looked determined. Maybe only because she was tall and beautiful and drew attention. Everyone else, even the colonel's own troops, bore the look of abject defeat.

The wounded moaned as they were loaded aboard the vehicles, and what meds were available were used to comfort them as best they could.

The colonel nodded at the woman.

"Think she could be one of those… human IEDs?" murmured the sergeant major beside him.

The sergeant major had been giving the colonel a casualty count update as more and more of the unit linked up or was found. Captain de Macha, to the colonel's surprise, had survived the battle, though his tanks had all been lost. He owed his survival to Lieutenant Maydoon, who himself was killed in action rescuing the tanks from an overwhelming Savage flank attack, leaving behind a wife and child back on Spilursa. That last detail had been included in the report at the insistence of Captain de Macha.

"I don't think so," said the colonel, eyeing the woman. He felt overwhelmingly fatigued. Like it was time to let down for now, or so the argument his body was making indicated. They'd been going at it since many long hours before the dawn insertion. It had already been a long day, and there was no end in sight.

He didn't mind that though, and he shrugged off the urge to let down with the ease of much practice. He'd had plenty of these kinds of days in his time. And there was still much to be done to get these troops off the planet—and to finish his mission.

"Well, I guess she looks like one of us. Ya want me to see what her story is, sir?"

The colonel shook his head. "Negative. Get these wounded aboard and head back toward Objective Rio. I'll see what she needs."

The colonel left the sergeant major and crossed the distance to the newcomer.

"What unit you with?" he asked as he approached.

She was sitting on a rock. One of the soldiers had given her some rations. She was eating them as though she hadn't eaten in days.

Marks held out his canteen, and she took it and drank gustily.

"What unit are you?" she asked between bites, not bothering to look at the colonel.

"Twenty-Fifth from Spilursa."

She swallowed hard. As though her throat wasn't used to so much food. Then she burped a little and gulped at some more water.

"I'm from here, Colonel," she said as she took another bite. "New Vega City. Just wondering if you were one of ours."

The colonel said nothing and sat down on a piece of fractured concrete opposite her.

"You're not from here," he said plainly as he pulled out one of his ration bars. "That doesn't bother me, but let's not start off with lies. And besides..." He waved his hand haphazardly as he tore at the seal of the bar. "Does whatever you're covering up really matter anymore? It's all gone."

She stopped chewing.

"How do you know I'm not from here?"

"You called me Colonel, so you recognize rank. You sit like you went to Annapolis-Houston despite the clear indications that you're starving to death. Or at least I think they used to call it Annapolis-Houston. They used to. A long time ago," he finished awkwardly.

She took another bite and chewed slowly, watching him. "A long time ago. Yeah. They called it that, sir."

"Oh." The colonel took a bite of his own ration bar. Waiting for her to go on.

"Captain Ivy Davis, commander of the frigate *Raven*."

The colonel smiled like none of that meant anything to him. "*Raven* wasn't attached to the strike force. Were you here when the Savage invasion began?"

She smiled and didn't mean it in the least. The gesture never reached her striking green eyes.

"So is that a yes, or classified UW voodoo and you can't tell me because you're pretty sure I don't have the clearance?"

"Classified," she replied bluntly.

"Figured as much. Well, Spilursa and Earth are on friendly terms last time I checked, so you can fall in with us and we'll try to get you back to your people."

She thought about that.

"Fine," she said after a moment, watching him as she took another bite of her rations. Then she added, "Thank you. I appreciate that. I really do. It's just been..."

And then she stopped.

Colonel Marks stood and dusted off his hands on his fatigues. He picked up his pulse rifle and checked it. He'd consumed his whole protein bar in just a few bites. Like every military man, he ate faster than most cared to notice.

He started to go, then turned back to her. "A hard five weeks, give or take?"

She said nothing, but the look of guilt in her eyes told him everything he needed to know.

Then he was gone, back to his troops and following the crawler to the rear. Back to the stadium.

Maybe there'd be another ship to pull the survivors off this rock.

Maybe.

43

The *Chang* had come in toward midnight. Contact with Task Force Wrath had been reestablished beforehand and comm with the *Defiant*'s CIC indicated Admiral Sulla himself was going to attempt to bring the *Chang* in during an orbital window when the Savage hulks weren't over the area of operation. The scout ship *Explorer* had been lost in the first assault by the hulks, but some satellite and drone recon was still active and available.

The hours before the *Chang* arrived were tense. Every hour, almost on the hour, one of the massive, almost otherworldly Savage hulks would cross the sky above like some high-altitude wraith drifting ghostlike through the night. The strange and ominous howl of its engines drifting down from the tens of thousands of meters it was running at washed across the graveyard city.

"They can't maintain any kind of altitude," one of the commanders said during an ad hoc organization of forces still on the ground. He then went on to tell everyone about the suspicions that repulsor tech was one of the few things the Savages hadn't perfected in their long crossings.

"They've got to keep circling the planet in low orbit, so they've broken formation to keep a presence over us at least once every hour," he explained.

And that did seem to be the case. It was a different ship every hour, always one of the three smaller vessels. The biggest did not appear even once.

"Those things were never meant for orbital insertion," said the supply captain, who seemed to know a lot about Savages. "They're almost forty kilometers long! They'd collapse of their own weight if they actually surrendered to gravity and set down. Probably."

Colonel Marks knew the truth of that.

He'd lived fifteen years on one of those ships and had barely explored it. From what he could remember, anyway. That was a long time ago.

Other surviving officers still fit for duty had gathered at the Twenty-Fifth Light's Headquarters Crawler to figure out who was in charge and what was going to happen next. There was only one other colonel left: a staff officer who'd been badly wounded and was expected to die. That put Colonel Marks in charge for the time being.

Contact was finally reestablished with Strike Force Wraith, and it was decided by Admiral Sulla that the *Chang*, under-crewed, would come in and try to pull what remained of the task force off the planet in one go. Then what was left of the fleet would jump for home, and they'd let the higher-ups sort out this mess and next steps.

For the next hour the wounded and the details assigned to get them aboard the *Chang* as fast as possible were sussed out. A lot of equipment was being left behind and sensitive systems were being demoed as evac preparations got underway.

The *Chang*, a boxy assault frigate with a central bridge built right into the superstructure, came down through the atmosphere and drifting smoke fast. Diving through the skies after a calculated pass by one of the Savage ships. And just as quickly, appearing from out of the night sky all around the city, friendly United Worlds interceptors still operating off the carrier *Indomitable* hidden somewhere out to sea took up positions to escort the assault frigate to the LZ.

Everyone held their breath, watching the landing lights of the big ship come on at the last second and wondering if the Savage Nest was going to shotgun a broadside of drones into the *Chang* as she made her approach.

Which would most likely seal the fate of the survivors, stranding them on the planet for what little time remained to them.

But that didn't happen, and soon the *Chang* was dropping her four cyclopean ground struts and coming in to hover over the shell-riddled stadium that had once occupied pride of place between the industrial districts and the suburban living areas of northern New Vega City.

Once the big ship was down, medical teams poured forth as though coming out under fire. Soldiers and wounded were quickly moved forward and onto the loading deck as crew chiefs swarmed the ship checking for structural damage and getting ready for a rapid departure.

What those on the ground didn't know, didn't expect, hadn't been told, was that the admiral himself was aboard the *Chang*. And Admiral Sulla stepped off the frigate and paid a visit to Colonel Marks just as the colonel was shucking out of his bloodstained fatigues near two cargo containers he'd had loaded aboard the crawler before the operation had begun.

One was large.

The other was about the size of a man.

The sergeant major and a few of the men, including the woman, watched the colonel from nearby and just figured he was an officer doing that officer thing where they always looked ready to lead. Swapping out the ruined and bloody uniform for a clean one. As though combat operations were likely to resume at any moment and he was expected to be ready.

The engines of the *Chang* were kept live and howling in case one of the Savage ships appeared overhead and started firing.

The admiral swept into the area behind the crawler, his naval trench wrapped about him like a tightly pulled shroud. His security team took up overwatch positions along a rough perimeter of which he was the center.

"Need you aboard now, Colonel," Sulla said.

The colonel shook his head and returned to the case he was busy opening. The one about the size of a man.

"Negative. Job's not done. We did it your way. Now I'll do it mine."

The admiral opened his mouth like he was about to say something, thought better of it, then unconsciously glanced toward his security team.

"Don't, Casper," said the colonel, sensing what the admiral was considering.

No one, not even the security team, had ever heard Admiral Corrin Sulla called by the name *Casper*.

"There's no other way today," said the admiral through gritted teeth as he looked around. Clearly, he was not happy about something. "Not even *your* way. They're on full alert, or whatever passes for full alert for them. You know that... Colonel. They'll know you're coming. Get on the ship and we'll figure out an alternative."

The sergeant major and the woman, along with a few soldiers, had come closer to listen in on the showdown between the two officers. The cav company who'd been assigned as a rear guard was busy hustling the last of the survivors aboard.

"Disagree," the colonel said. He nodded toward the *Chang*. Engines hovering. Everything about her said they were ready to get up into the night sky and through the wispy stratus and off this rock forever. Never coming back again.

"How so?" asked the admiral, without indicating in the least that he actually wanted to hear an answer.

"Once you lift off, they'll think they've won," said the colonel. "I might catch a few with this."

He opened the big cargo container.

"Uh..." said the sergeant major as soldiers began to swear and back away from the large case. "Is that what I think it is, sir?"

The colonel ignored him.

Everyone had seen what an old-school trigger-nuke device looked like. Every time Tyrus Rechs, war criminal or hero, depending on whom you asked, used one, the news networks filled their show segments with information about the highly illegal weapons. Banned weapons. Weapons of mass destruction, in the purest sense of the words.

Doomsday weapons.

"Now wait a minute..." began Andres slowly, putting two and two together. "That's... *your* way? Sir, are you telling me, sir," he said, getting excited. "Are you telling me that you're... that you're *him*? In the flesh? All along, sir! Are you telling me that?"

No one said anything.

Then the admiral muttered a curse.

"Soldiers," he said, making a bitter face. "Meet Tyrus Rechs."

PART TWO

44

The admiral cleared everyone away from Rechs as he began to skin into his armor. But they didn't go *too* far away, and in fact still more gathered to watch as word that Tyrus Rechs, *the* Tyrus Rechs, was on site and getting ready to go his own name on the Savages. The name of the infamous war criminal had become synonymous with excessive destruction in the collective zeitgeist of pop culture and on the never-ending bleat of news streams.

Some who'd been ready to evacuate, even wounded, had suddenly asked to disembark the *Chang* in order to help any way they could. Casts were cut, painkillers popped, and sedatives used in high doses to restrain those hovering between critical and last rites. Others from a variety of militaries merely grabbed a ruck and whatever rifle they could get their hands on, tightened their bandages, took two tabs of Chill, and left the ship despite being threatened with every possible military punishment.

But now Rechs and Sulla were talking alone. Or rather Sulla was hectoring the infamous legend. Practically shouting in Rechs's face. Which was not something most citizens in the galaxy could dare to do and go on living. But the admiral and Tyrus Rechs had a history no one knew about.

"You brought one of those damn trigger-nukes along?" Sulla shouted. "Tyrus! We were supposed to try it this way in good faith."

"I did," said Rechs as he shrugged into the old armor he'd taken off a Savage ship years and years before. High-tech stuff the best R&D in the galaxy had never quite been able to match. It stood up to blaster fire most of the time and shrugged off projectiles with ease. Jump-jet capable. A defensive shield that could power up and deflect damage for short periods, rated up to a direct hit from a nuclear weapon. Physics was another story, though. Physics didn't care how rated your armor was. It would pulp you all the same.

And then there was the helmet. One of the most advanced tactical HUDs humankind had ever produced. Although it wasn't necessarily totally human in the original sense of the word. More shadowy science of a particular group of *post*-humankind that had gone off and touched the data void known as the Quantum Palace. A place listed on most stellar charts as the last known position of a number of disappeared ships.

And that bunch were long dead. Thanks to Sulla and Rechs and a detachment of Martian light infantry. All that was a long time ago.

"And now you're going to... what?" asked Sulla incredulously as Rechs pulled his helmet from the shipping clamshell it had been stowed in, hidden within the crawler. Alongside the banned weapon of mass destruction called a trigger-nuke. "Waltz into the Nest and set it off? Ruin another planet? Y'know, we're running out of those. There are only so many conditionally habitable ones left. Zero viability for the combined galactic population is actually a thing again, Rechs. All that for just one ship?"

"Well," began Rechs. "I'm hoping for one of the other ships too. Coming in to assist once they recognize the threat. That'd be somethin', wouldn't it, Cas? Two-for-one special."

Rechs had tried a smile. But he was not a man to whom humor came naturally. That he was trying this unfamiliar tack spoke of how much he respected the admiral, and what their long history meant.

Sulla saw this and looked off, his face storm-cloud dark.

Rechs pulled the old hand cannon that he'd kept at his side for ages. A massive sidearm that fired fifty-caliber slugs on full auto, stabilized and auto-fed by the armor's impressive internal systems. He checked the initial load and holstered it on his plated thigh.

"Listen…" said Rechs, coming to stand in front of his old friend who wouldn't see him. "I get that you're pissed, Cas. But maybe it's not at me. Maybe it's about the fact that you had a good plan, and it was poorly executed through no fault of your own. Where's Ogilvie?"

Sulla said nothing for a moment because his oldest friend had just scored a direct hit and made his point in a bare minimum of words: *Where's Ogilvie.*

Typical, he hissed inwardly. So he just continued to stare off at the dark and ruined city and the fires burning out of control.

Then he finally spoke.

"Supreme Commander Ogilvie departed aboard the *Porter* with almost no evacuees… and bolted for the core. Declared it was of supreme importance that he personally advise the UW of this development in the Savage situation, then promptly turned evacuation operations over to the navy. Me, to be specific."

Rechs made a sound through his teeth, something along the lines of "Figures." The pure mutual disgust for Ogilvie dialed the mood down between the two men.

"They're up to something here, Cas. Something big," said Rechs. "We both get that. You and I have talked about this particular scenario before. We always wondered if someday they'd finally start working together. Well…" He nodded toward the sky. "It looks like that day is today. Whether anyone likes it or not… the game just changed." He let that hang in the air between them for a moment. "We have to annihilate them once and for all, Cas. If humanity, and every other race we've encountered out here, is going to have any chance… we *have* to do it. Plain and simple. And that starts today. Right now."

Sulla dropped his head. Rechs knew that meant his oldest friend was thinking. Or rather coming to a conclusion he hadn't wanted to be true, but was finally willing to accept in light of current events. Rechs had seen it before. They'd been through hell and back and all the hot spots in between, before, and after. They'd known each other longer than any of those watching ever would have imagined.

"So," continued Tyrus Rechs as he pulled on his gauntlets. One containing an interface that ran comm and other armor functions. The other fitted with a small yet powerful grappling dart. "Gears up on the *Chang* and get everyone out of here. I can finish this now. And if I don't, then get back to the worlds and tell them, whether they like it or not, it's time to form a galactic-wide government that can field a single military force to finally deal with the Savages."

"Just like that," Sulla said, despite the fact that Rechs was telling him to do exactly what he'd been wanting to do for ages.

"Yeah."

"These things... they're complicated. Lots of moving parts. Concessions, threats, coaxing. I'm not sure—"

"You can make it happen."

Rechs threw one gauntleted arm out across the destruction in the dark that surrounded the evacuation point. "Today wasn't one hundred percent Ogilvie's fault. Too many independently developed weapons systems and tactics trying to work together... they were ripe for interference. A disaster like this was bound to happen."

Sulla nodded. "The man should never have been in charge in the first place. It was a symptom of the Coalition's mutual distrust. Their fear of a strong leader arising from any one faction."

Rechs shrugged. "We'll learn from it and make a fighting force that's cohesive. And Casper... we'll make it the best the galaxy has ever seen."

"That's your job, Tyrus. I just fly starships."

"Like hell."

Sulla let out a sigh bordering on annoyance. "None of it is going to happen if you blow yourself to nothing just to take down a couple of hulks. Unless you've got your own freighter stashed somewhere nearby..."

Rechs turned to look at the city. One of the massive Savage ships was crossing the night sky overhead. Smaller ships were dropping away, flaring jets of blue flame as they set down along the ruins of Hilltop.

He turned back to Sulla.

"I've got to set this thing off. And I've got to get it inside that big hulk to do it. I'm optimistic, but I'm not unrealistic. We can det this thing right here and maybe hurt them. But det it inside, and I'm sure to destroy at least one of their ships before it lifts off. And in the end, that's how I've done it every time before, more or less. Get the one you're shooting at. Worry about the next later, or let that be someone else's problem. Slow is smooth, smooth is fast."

Sulla laughed scornfully. "Someone else's problem. Sure, Tyrus. Except it's the galaxy's problem now." And then he nodded once, seeming to reach some kind of decision. "All right. I'm not going to talk you out of it and I'm not going to fight you over it. I'll get the wounded and the survivors out, and then I'll be back before sundown tomorrow to pull you out. Dark, we lift off. Be here. And don't let me find a big smoking crater, Tyrus. I mean it. Game's changed. That's true. But that only means we need you now more than ever. We need you to form that cohesive force. I'll do the rest."

Tyrus nodded slowly, appraising his oldest friend. "So you're in."

"No. I'm not in. Not unless you promise to come back alive. It's either that or..."

"Or what?" asked Tyrus.

"Or..." said Sulla, deadly serious, "I'm going in there with you to set off this trigger-nuke, and I'll let everyone else figure out how to get off this planet and how to save every other world. Because if you're not making it back to the LZ alive, neither am I."

"That's stupid."

"No, Tyrus. You don't comprehend just how important your being there on the other side of this is to making the galaxy what it ought to be. What we both know it's capable of becoming."

Rechs held his friend's gaze for a long moment, trying to figure out how serious he was.

Then he nodded.

"Deal. I'll be here when you get back."

In the small crowd watching them, no one said a word. A few had snapped pictures on their personal devices. If just to get a shot of the legendary hero, war criminal, and all the other titles Tyrus Rechs had acquired in his almost mythic trek across the galactic frontier. How much was rumor, how much was true... no one really knew. No one ever would. Some of those stories were so old—even going back to the days when the first worlds began to hold forth as going concerns out in the stellar dark beyond distant Earth—that there was no one left to confirm or deny.

Except Tyrus Rechs himself.

And Casper.

"I'm going with you, Rechs."

Both men turned to see the female UW naval officer, Captain Ivy Davis, standing close by.

Rechs shook his head. It was better if he just did this alone.

But that didn't stop her. "I have a mission to complete, Admiral. Going in with... Tyrus Rechs... is my best chance. And I can probably be of some help."

"What's your mission?" asked the admiral.

"Classified. Can't say."

"I think we're beyond that now, Captain Davis," said Sulla. "I have a pretty good idea what department you're assigned to, and I have a fairly good idea of who sent you here, and why, even if the specifics elude me for the moment."

She thought about that for a second. Then she spoke.

"UW knew New Vega was developing an advanced communication system that could use hyperspace to establish direct comm." She stepped closer to the two men. "While my original mission of getting it for United Worlds might seem... petty... in light of current events, the truth is, it's probably even more important now. Strategically speaking."

"How so?" asked the admiral.

"Sir, if the Savvies are working together, then they're communicating. Probably at the same speed we currently use. Unless they've made some wild intuitive leap we haven't yet, and from what I know... that could be possible. Either way, the hypercomm is of significant value in future operations against them. If they haven't developed advanced communication over interstellar distances, and we do, that gives us a huge advantage. Whereas if they have, or get, access to that tech, and we *don't* have it, then their ability to communicate in real-time over vast intergalactic distances, while we're limited to current capabilities, gives *them* the distinct advantage. Wouldn't you say, sir?"

"I would," said Admiral Sulla soberly.

"So, my mission is this. I either go back in there and get it, or I destroy it so that they *don't* get it. But I have to make sure either way. I have to know. Because we, every planet in the Coalition, if that actually becomes a thing, need to know the situation. If the Savages can comm faster than us... well, we will adapt and overcome. But only if we know."

Captain Davis cleared her throat. Shook her head once like she knew she was giving up too much. Classified stuff that would have gotten her a stiff treason sentence, probably landing her on the cleanup crews in the nuclear wastes of some old war-torn UW planets. Which was basically a death sentence.

But somehow, Savage hulks fighting together like a fleet, the ruins of New Vega, and the destruction of the mighty and much-touted Coalition strike force, seemed more important than her doing time in a paper-thin hazmat suit in some jungle cesspool crawling with mutated poisonous snakes, bloated disease-carrying flies, and background radiation that would cook her insides slowly over the course of twenty years. If she lasted that long. Which few did.

She sighed and showed the rest of her hand.

"When U-Dub intel got the word that New Vega was under attack, they sent the *Raven* in with a team of marines. The original colony ship of the first planetary settlers, buried beneath Hilltop, has become New Vega's research base... a kind of house of secrets. Most likely members of the government are down in there right now waiting for you guys to pull them out. But they weren't our mission. Our mission was to break in and snatch the device regardless of the outcome of the Coalition effort."

"Before the Savages... or, say, any other government... got their hands on it?" asked Rechs sharply. "UW wanted it all for themselves."

She didn't answer. Didn't need to.

Rechs shook his head. "Good old U-Dub. Some things never change, do they, Sulla?"

The tension between the three was thick enough to cut.

"The situation makes that comm device valuable to everyone now," said Captain Davis. "I get that. But... all the more reason to complete the mission. And I'm your best chance of doing that."

She folded her arms and stood back. Daring them to challenge her.

"Best chance?" asked Rechs, like a poker player calling in order to see some cards.

She didn't blink. "Yes. Best chance. Because I know the way. The entire place is like an underground fortress, or labyrinth, and for the last five weeks, until you showed up, I've been surviving down in the underground bunkers and tunnels below the city and avoiding the Savages who were trying to get in. Which means I'm *also* your best chance to get your weapon"—she nodded at the trigger-nuke—"into the Savage ship alongside Hilltop. You help me get the comm device, and I'll take you through the maze and right to the Savage doorstep."

Tyrus Rechs said nothing for a moment. Everyone watching was sure he was going to tell the tall female United Worlds captain that there was no deal. That he'd do it his way, which meant any way he had to. Even the hard way if necessary.

But instead...

"Grab some gear," he said. "We leave in thirty."

She turned on her boots and went to scavenge from the discarded gear piles that had been left behind to make room for more evacuees.

"Sir," said Sergeant Major Andres, stepping forward. "If it's all the same... I'd like to go along with you too. You *are* still my commanding officer."

"Yeah," said Specialist Martin softly from the shadows near the crawler's rear. "I'm in, sir, if you'll have me."

Rechs eyed them both.

And then Captain de Macha, whose tanks had all been destroyed, smiled and stepped forward as well. "I think I could come along and help."

A big black shaven-headed sergeant with burning eyes, a cav trooper whose LCE was open, and whose tag read *Greenhill*, coughed once. "I'm in too, sir."

"We won't quit on you, sir," said Sergeant Major Andres. "Even if you are Tyrus Rechs, we'll get this done."

"Yeah," said someone else. "We'll go all the way. Together."

And finally, behind all that, was a man in no kind of military uniform. Surplus fatigues, civilian pants, and old work boots. He was carrying a massive sniper rifle, cradling it like it was the most precious thing in the world.

He was horribly scarred.

He tried to talk, but nothing came out. Just a croak.

He hadn't spoken in a long time.

And for a moment, he felt her behind him. Watching him with baby on her hip.

He swallowed to get more saliva across his long-unused vocal cords.

Everyone eyed this stranger who was odd and out of place even among the haphazard mishmash of military organizations.

He tried to speak, and still nothing came out. He swallowed once more, hard, and said, finally... "Me."

It was all he could manage.

And then he felt her smile. Proud of him. And that was a good thing.

Do another one, babe.

45

They followed Tyrus Rechs—infamous war criminal, hero, or legend, depending on whom you asked—from the wan red glow of the emergency lighting beneath the *Chang's* rear cargo deck.

Sergeant Major Andres. Point man Martin. Sergeant Greenhill, late of the Three-Six Cav. Captain Ivy Davis, former commander of UW assault frigate *Raven.* Captain de Macha of the First Royal Espanian Armor. And a large, wild-haired, and scarred man carrying a massive sniper rifle. The kind that still fired bullets. Though this man's bullets were as big as the micro-rockets fired by some of the high-speed anti-armor systems that had been fielded of late.

"You look like a wild man," said Sergeant Major Andres of the civilian as they loaded into their transport. "You got a name?"

After a long moment the big man answered. Slowly. His voice rusty and tired like an old door unopened in years. "N-nno... Not—anymore," he said haltingly.

And the sergeant major, who had trained more men, led more men, and saved more men than anyone else he knew of, understood what kind of man he was dealing with. Someone broken. Someone lost.

Earlier he'd asked Tyrus Rechs, whom he kept addressing as "Colonel," as though "Colonel Marks" had been a real person all along and not a cover, and Rechs didn't bother to correct the error, "You sure that this civilian is good to go, sir? We're gonna need to count on everyone in there."

Rechs looked up from the industrial-sized repulsor pallet they were busy loading the trigger-nuke onto. Truthfully, Rechs had been impressed by the big sniper rifle the strange man carried. And he'd thought that someone, during all the hubbub of the battle for Triangle Square, and maybe even earlier, had been shooting a very powerful old-school heavy-caliber weapon in support of Coalition forces. Yes... playing back the images in his mind, he was convinced that some of their foes had been knocked down by old-school lead. In all the chaos of killing and trying not to get killed, it had been hard to catalog who and what was shooting with what and at whom. But now that he thought about it... he was sure that someone other than the Savages had been firing hard caliber.

"Pretty sure his skills are tight, Sergeant Major," Rechs responded. "And this is what we've got to work with."

He didn't really want to say what he felt. That he'd rather have gone it alone without any of them. Less risk. More control. But Rechs wasn't the kind of person to think too highly of himself. And if he failed, they might succeed. Which would mean one less Savage hulk. One step closer to making sure humanity remained viable in the galactic scheme of things. Had a chance to go on and not be annihilated by their ancestors.

And maybe…

Maybe this was what Sulla had been trying to push him toward in all those years he'd been out destroying Savages alone. Work with others. Because if, in the end, everyone was depending on one man to save the galaxy from the worst threat it had ever known…

Well.

That was a recipe for failure.

For sure.

Men died alone all the time.

Even Tyrus Rechs, Sulla once told him.

"If you're sure, Colonel," Andres said, keeping step with his notorious new commander.

"Yeah," Rechs said to the sergeant major. "He'll do."

And there was one more. One last late addition. A spider monkey of a shirtless man. Just battle dress pants and dirty engineer boots that had never seen a lick of polish.

"Also, sir," said Andres, "there's a Private Makaffie wants to come along. Says, and get this… he 'knows the ways of the universe.' But he seems pretty good with mechanical and tech. Kinda guy who knows too much and tells you about it all the time whether you want to hear it or not. Could be handy in a pinch. Also could make someone want to frag him. Your call."

Rechs indicated with a mere hand gesture that this too was okay. The more the merrier. If they wanted a chance to get killed, who was he to deny them their opportunity?

And when he thought about it that way, he realized that he wasn't liking the odds on this one.

Feeling a bit fatal, Tyrus? he heard some voice inside his head ask. But he didn't answer. He never answered. Just kept moving. Keep moving and try to avoid being hit—that was the only way forward.

The ideal method of transport to deliver Rechs's doomsday weapon was nothing less than Ogilvie's personal command vehicle. It sat abandoned, ripe for the picking: a low, flat, wicked-looking armored personnel carrier that ran on four ceramic balls shielded by armor plating. It carried one automated heavy pulse gun that could be controlled internally.

The case carrying the nuclear weapon just barely fit inside the vehicle's troop compartment. Everyone else was forced to either ride forward in the comm station, in the driver's compartment, or up top behind the heavy twin-barreled pulse gun.

When they were ready to go and carrying as much in the way of weaponry and reloads as they could, the admiral and his security detail saw them off from the deck of the *Chang*. The ship would lift off shortly, but a small group had volunteered to stay behind and try to hold the LZ. So that Tyrus Rechs, and anyone else who survived this mission, if anyone did, could be picked up. Whisked away. To live and fight another day.

Admiral Sulla called after Rechs, who was riding atop the APC. "I sent you when dusk is expected to come tomorrow night, in local time, Tyrus. Be here."

"Do my best, Cas," said the armored man, his head fully enclosed by a helmet, his voice coming forth in a mechanical growl.

And then they were off.

The APC moved a block into the shattered wastes of the industrial district surrounding the shot-to-hell stadium when the *Chang* lifted off, its massive struts retracting, its strobing landing lights suddenly switching off as it cleared the stadium bowl. Then max power to the engines and repulsors, and the ship rocketed for orbit and rendezvous with the surviving task force fleet.

"Why do you call the admiral 'Cas'?" asked Davis, using the direct comm link they'd set up for the op.

Rechs gave no reply.

46

The command APC had not only been designed to move silently, it was skinned in UW's latest battlefield stealth tech. Nothing was too good for the ancient republic's finest flag officers in close-combat situations. The same wasn't always true for the men those flag officers commanded.

Sergeant Greenhill was assigned as driver because he had the most experience with mechanized transport, being Cav. Captain Davis was serving as navigator since she knew the route into the subterranean labyrinth they were aiming for. Makaffie was aft with the weapon and the vehicle gun controls—partly because of his artillery experience, but also because he was small and could squirrel around inside the cramped APC.

The rest—Rechs, Sergeant Major Andres, Martin, de Macha, and "Wild Man," as the sergeant major had taken to calling the big stranger—rode up top behind the automated gun.

They worked their way west through the industrial district beyond the stadium and below the dark towers of Hilltop. Some of the fires up there were still out of control, raging through streets and skyscrapers; others had burned themselves out, leaving nothing but the skeletons of ruin.

"Kind of funny that these fires haven't spread," said Martin, watching the distant glow. "Been enough wind."

"Maybe the Savvies put 'em out," remarked the sergeant major forlornly.

The clock moved into the late hours.

Along some of the blocks traveled, all was just as it had been six weeks ago on the day before the Savages came down out of the sky in their ancient ship from Earth's past. Storefronts were untouched. Closed up, but not barricaded. As if only left for the night, until business opened up once more. Waiting for the streets to fill with the daily traffic of New Vega. And then at the next block they would find a crater taking up half the street and the buildings blown outward, beyond recognition, in stark contrast to the relative serenity they had just passed through.

As they reached the first streets in the lower part of Hilltop District, the power grid, which had come on to illuminate vast sections of the abandoned city, failed once more. And there was something about its sudden absence that seemed final.

"Switch to night vision," ordered Rechs.

Goggles were lowered into place, and almost by force of habit suppressors were checked along the tops of pulse rifles. Not normal-issue gear, but made available for this little excursion into the belly of the beast.

There would be no rest tonight, despite the weariness in their bones. They had only until dusk tomorrow to get in, drop the bomb, find the tech, and get back to the LZ. Otherwise they were going up with the trigger-nuke. The deadline was tight to say the least.

But this was the only option to stop the Savages from actually taking this planet. Right now, the biggest advantage the civilized galaxy had over the Savages was real estate. Planets. Land. The Savages had their big ships, but vast as they were, they paled in comparison to even the smallest planets, and they were closed ecosystems with limited resources. If they were to get a foothold on a habitable rock—especially one already developed by human colonists—they would not only have access to resources, they'd have a launching point from which to plan future attacks. Especially now that it was clear they were working together.

And if the Savages got their hands on the galaxy-changing tech like the hypercomm, or worse yet, shared it with other Savage ships they'd made alliances with... that would change everything. In a heartbeat.

Stopping them here was essential.

"Why'd they build the top of the city over an old colony ship?" Andres asked over comm.

Captain Davis answered the sergeant major. "New Vega was a rough world when the first colonists landed in a big colony ship they'd built out in the American wastelands that used to be... Ohio, I think. Their ship wasn't Savage large, but big enough. And, obviously, hyperdrive-capable. Back then this world had a vicious species called the *nuelithiri*. Highly intelligent tribalized raptor. Cross between a heron and a cottonmouth snake. They put the ship down on the flatlands next to the coast but kept getting killed when they tried to set up farms and villages nearby. So they just started building around the ship. It wasn't the type that would ever be able to take off again once it landed. The settlers created a whole structurally reinforced hill, lots of packed earth, concrete, bunkers, deep massive tunnel systems until they could wipe out the raptors. That took decades, and most trade ships wouldn't even call here because of the situation."

"You seem to know much of this," commented de Macha.

Davis nodded. "We were thoroughly briefed before our mission. To better understand the mind of the local populace."

De Macha nodded. "So after the... *aliens* were eliminated?"

"Right about the time they wiped out the apex predator, pirates were having their heyday, so even the aboveground city became a kind of medieval fortress. It wasn't until things quieted down and the pirates were cleared out that the city began to expand. That's when the government took over the old colony ship. They set up in there with their labs, bunkers, secret prisons, and everything else they wanted to keep from prying eyes. Sold the rest of the hill to commercial developers. The New Vega boom, they called it. For the most part, the residents forgot about Old Colony, as the underground space is called."

"And you been runnin' around down there for weeks?" asked the sergeant major.

"Yeah," she replied. And nothing more.

"Got something," said Greenhill from down in the driver's compartment beneath the ceramic-armored front of the vehicle.

Everyone had some kind of comm device to tap into. For most it was a mere headset. For Rechs it was managed by the advanced HUD inside his helmet.

"What is it?" asked Rechs.

There was a long pause as everyone hovered over the comm, waiting for Greenhill or Davis to tell them what they were seeing on the sensors. The vehicle had no windows, which meant they were reliant on a passive sensor system that imaged everything from night vision to thermal to allow the driver to visualize where he was driving. It even showed the surrounding streets at least three blocks beyond the current position.

It was Davis who answered. "Really not sure. I've seen this kind of activity during my time here, but nothing above the surface before. It's... some kind of construction crew a few streets over."

Rechs paused to consider this. "Can we bypass?"

No disbelief. No questions. No wondering why the Savages would be building anything in the middle of a battle. Because for all the Savages knew, the battle wasn't over. Even though it was. A normal adversary would be waiting to see if combat operations resumed at dawn.

There was never anything normal about the Savages.

"Negative," Davis replied. "We need to cross the intersection they're near. Just past that is a raised roadway into Hilltop, coming in from the suburbs, that'll put us a few streets away from the insertion access point for the underground system. It's our best route in without being detected."

Rechs thought through more silence.

"If we weren't under a time clock, we could take another route in…" Davis added. "But…"

"Yeah," said the sergeant major. "Time is a luxury we for sure don't have. The only bus off this rock is leaving tomorrow night."

Rechs made up his mind. "Those of us on top will dismount and work our way closer. Stand by to come forward on our signal."

"Affirmative," replied Davis.

Greenhill killed the whisper-quiet engine of the APC, and the dark street was utterly silent.

Rechs, Andres, Martin, de Macha, and Wild Man hopped down onto the street and checked weapons. Rechs pointed out the order of march and threw a knife hand toward the route they'd take—a narrow alley running along the back of some buildings.

With Martin on point, they threaded its tight quarters, checking corners and moving with stealth. The city was as quiet as a graveyard. Only if one listened closely could they hear the crackle and groan of fires along the eastern side of the hill. Wild Man barely made a sound as he brought up the rear with his massive rifle.

When Rechs judged they were behind a building located across the street from the Savage construction team, he knelt and handed his pulse rifle to the sergeant major and pulled a tool off his belt that looked like a flashlight. Martin watched one end of the alley while the Wild Man took the direction they'd come from. For apparently having no military experience, or at least none that he'd told them of, the big man knew his patrolling skills.

Rechs covered the building's rear door with his body and fitted the flashlight-tool into the lock.

The lock exploded.

"Fancy, Colonel. Mag-breaker. Illegal on a lot of worlds."

"So are a lot of things."

"Gotta get me one of those," said the sergeant major softly, holding out Rechs's pulse rifle.

Rechs took back his weapon and gently pushed the door open. He tapped Martin and let the man enter first. Then the rest followed.

From inside the coffee shop, for that was clearly what the place was, a coffee shop on the edge of Hilltop District, they could see the Savage crew across the street. Except these Savages were different from the marines they'd been facing in the battle for Triangle Square.

Very different.

A big shuttle, like something out of Earth's low-orbital commercial spaceflight days, was beside them. No repulsors were evident, meaning it must've used chemical rockets to put down after being dropped by one of the Savage hulks. Just like in the early, Neolithic era of space travel.

It was dirty and old, and strange words were written on it. Words that had no meaning to most anyone these days. Though they had once been vaguely familiar to Tyrus Rechs.

Android-Fiber Lifter.

In faded script.

A massive spotlight was thrown from the shuttle onto the Savage workers, and Rechs took a moment to study them.

Three figures moved out there beyond the bottom of the ship. They were emerald-skinned, and each had some kind of rebreather attached to its face. Their hair was long, albino-white almost. They had no weapons, and they worked like hunched monkeys. The trio kept busy at unloading something.

With them were three small yellow construction mechs with articulating legs, a pod canopy, and massive claws. The mechs were tearing apart the building across the street—breaking down materials and collecting them in neat piles.

As Rechs watched, three white-armored Savages walked down off the shuttle's ramp. They had the swagger of soldiers, and matching weapons that said as much. Their body armor—ceramic-molded chest plates that covered their much-larger frames—seemed to add to the sense of their powerful build. The Savages' skin was a vibrant red, their arms were long and huge, and their feet were... hooved. Their helmets were like something out of Earth's ancient past. Open-faced helms like those once worn by ancient gladiators.

Rechs used the tech in his helmet to iris in on the faces of the soldiers, both red and green. These new types lacked the post-human, alien feel of the Savage marines—floating brains behind inscrutable full helmets. In fact, they had rugged good looks. Almost model perfect. Just like the ship he'd been a slave on. These, he could tell, these too worshipped themselves.

"What are they doing?" whispered Sergeant Major Andres over the comm.

"Don't know," Rechs replied. Though the real question on his mind was a different one.

Who are they?

The truth was that all the Savages had once been someone. Somebodies. Groups that had come together in support of some common interest, some mutual philosophical objective, and who had refined that objective into a unity of purpose, one to be achieved by any means possible out there in the dark between worlds.

The Savages on the hulk Rechs and Sulla had been slaves on for fifteen years—before the crew of a United Nations starship, the precursor to United Worlds, found them—had been formed from some major digital tech company from the past that had been closely allied with the entertainment and news networks of the day. Movie stars, they'd once called themselves. But their time in the dark had convinced some of them that they were Greek gods, capable of doing whatever they pleased to whomever they pleased. Or that they were demons come in from the outer dark, a minor distinction, as that too made them capable of doing whatever they pleased to whomever they pleased. But unnatural longevity, advances in medicine, and a taste for bloodsport had made the floating society a nightmare circus of mind-control experiments and haunting slaughters.

You never really knew what the Savages had once been. And it didn't matter. What *did* matter was who they were now. What they had become. What new nightmare that would have to be dealt with.

"Uh, sir?" said the sergeant major in a hushed whisper. "Time's a-wastin', sir."

And yet Rechs still didn't move. He just watched the Savages like some frozen jungle predator patiently waiting for its perfect move at the perfect time.

To someone like Rechs, the entire galaxy was prey.

A moment later a figure with skin like pure gold came gliding down the ramp. A woman. Beautiful, austere, tall. She was followed by an almost equally tall figure whose skin was blue.

The reds and the greens knelt, though the gold seemed to be entirely unaware of their presence. The blue handed her an ancient holographic flexy, a smart device that could be rolled up and stowed like some ancient map. Tyrus Rechs had used those himself. Long ago.

The blue held it out for her to study, then with great ceremonial aplomb, she nodded and cast a long slender golden hand across the street.

"It's like they gettin' ready to build a house... or somethin'," whispered the sergeant major.

The mechs continued to tear apart the building they were working on, oblivious to the stately ordeal taking place behind them between the greens, the reds, the blue, and the gold. The greens rose and hustled an ancient industrial-sized 3D printer onto the street from beneath the belly of the old shuttle. They were ripping packing material away from its sides when Rechs finally raised his pulse rifle and steadied it on the table he'd been covering behind.

"That's all of them..." he whispered over the comm. "Smoke 'em. I got the reds."

"I'll take greens," said Martin.

"Blue for me," whispered Andres. "Wild Man, you got an angle on Goldie?"

The big silent man grunted once, and it sounded something like "Acquired."

De Macha was at the rear of the restaurant on security.

"Engage," whispered Rechs without ceremony.

He fired a single pulse at the first of the reds. The shot tore the Savage's chest armor apart and sent him spinning into the shuttle's landing gear. Rechs shifted his entire body to maintain the rifle's stability and landed the pulse rifle's scope on the next red, who was only just reacting to the damage sustained by his comrade. Rechs flipped to burst and spat five pulse shots at that one, because he knew the Savage was going to move. The rounds hit, and he was down but scrambling away, dropping his old assault rifle as he moved for cover. Rechs followed the Savage and added another burst that cut him down for good.

The echo of the boom from the Wild Man's rifle was the first thing that registered in everyone's consciousness. It was so loud and concussive that it seemed like it had come after Rechs's second burst, but in reality it had gone off in almost the same moment that Rechs had dropped the first red. The woman with gold skin was knocked over onto her butt and out of sight beyond the shuttle's dirty landing lights. The Wild Man's rifle's massive shell ejected and hit the floor of the six-week-silent coffee shop, ringing out like some great brass bell that had been dropped amid the madness of ambush.

Martin and the sergeant major were easily cleaning up the blue and greens.

The last red managed to fire into the shop's glass window. But he shot wild with no target acquisition. Distantly Rechs recognized that the Savage was using a next-generation version of the old SCAR-X. Matte-black. Drum mag. Tri-dot laser acquisition system dancing across the shattering glass and into the dark of the coffee house.

He was firing and not moving.

Mistake, thought Rechs as the storefront glass became pocked with bullet holes and shattered. He flipped back to single and blew the Savage's head off with one clean shot.

All that had taken less than ten seconds.

Ghost images of burst fire, tracers, and such faded on the retinas of the ambushers. And soon it was all dark once again. The big industrial shuttle looming out there in the dark on her three ancient gears. Dirty light falling across the dead bodies that were slowly fading in color as dark blood ran out and pooled in the street.

The little mechs continued their work unabated.

"Stand by..." said Rechs over the comm. "Watch for squirters."

But nothing moved. No one else came out of the old Earth shuttle.

"You want me to check it out?" asked Martin.

That's a point man's job, thought Rechs. But no one had the armor he wore.

"I got it." He stood with a small grunt, swapped in a new charge pack for the pulse rifle, and made his way out through the glass of the ruined store.

"What's your status?" asked Davis over the comm. They'd heard the sudden fire back at the APC.

"Target neutralized. Securing location," replied Rechs, adding no further details.

He checked all the tangos. They were dead. All bled red despite their augmentations. It leaked out onto the street, mixing with a stream of hydraulic fluid coming from the shuttle's gear. Maybe someone had hit a line. Or maybe the vessel was so ancient that it simply couldn't be kept in good repair anymore.

"Thing's pretty damn old," he whispered to himself. "What do you expect? Not everything and everyone doesn't age."

He'd stopped expecting anything lasting from the galaxy a long time ago.

No. That wasn't right. War was lasting. He could expect that much.

Finally he stood over the golden woman who wasn't gold anymore. The advanced imaging provided by his helmet's HUD told him what he was looking at, but he switched on the pulse rifle's flash to be sure.

The sniper, the Wild Man, had made a clean hit right in the upper chest. Probably got the heart with the size of the round. Her lungs and bone were blown out onto the sidewalk on the far side of the street.

Her surreal golden eyes gazed up at the night sky and the stars that had been her home for so long. Except as he watched, the eyes turned from gold to blue. The golden skin was fading like a dying ember. And beneath it, Tyrus saw the skin of an ancient mummy. Wrinkled and withered. Dried up to a husk. Bony hands and limbs.

He checked the others. Same. These were never young and vibrant. Never perfect. Some kind of reality augmentation had only made them *seem* eternally young. Some glimmer they'd learned out there in their long crawl. Longevity without the eternal youth possessed by the Savages Rechs had known back on the *Obsidia*.

But now that they were dead, the trick was dead too.

These had been living mummies.

And vampires. The Savage marines were seen feasting on the dead.

But then again… every Savage, in his experience, was a kind of vampire. Weren't they?

47

The APC crawled up the winding street. Massive skyscrapers, dark and looming, rose up in silence above the vehicle's late-night crawl. Off to the east the red glow of fires illuminated the smoke still boiling up and drifting out over the leaden sea. One of the moons faded into the ocean behind a front of distant clouds.

Sometimes they'd get an alert from the sensors that another Savage hulk was passing overhead. They'd dial down and switch off engines, sensors, and any electronic gear. And sometimes they'd see more units dropping down into the city. Old-school chemical engines flared for landing. They'd sink through the drifting smoke and disappear.

"Judging by these signatures," volunteered Makaffie, "all those hot burning blue flames, man—there's a wide variety of vehicles and assets dropping onto New Vega. Like the galaxy has brought so many things together for this one moment in time, you know?"

No one had asked for his opinion, but that didn't stop the little gnome of a gun bunny from constantly sharing them, along with his frequent observations and general chatter, as much as the situation and the quiet remonstrations of Rechs, Captain Davis, and Sergeant Major Andres would allow.

"That's the entrance to the forgotten Old Colony," Davis announced over comm. "The New Vega government disguised it as a parking garage."

"Let's not drive any closer," Rechs said.

The APC came to a halt, its twin-barreled gun swiveling on a low hydraulic note, scanning the area.

"Sensors?" asked Rechs over the comm as he studied the surrounding darkness.

"Nothing," said Greenhill.

Davis got down to the business of navigating the secret underground of the city. "Three levels down, there's a security door. I have the access codes. Beyond that is the main tunnel into the central warren. There's a quieter way on foot, but since time is of the essence and no one is around, I suggest we save ourselves the walk and drive as far as we can."

"Fair enough," grunted Rechs.

The low, flat vehicle started forward again slowly, weaving down into the garage. It moved past large, cylindrical concrete support beams. There were few vehicles present, allowing them to drive a straight line to a security door marked with local government warnings and off-limits signs. It was sealed tight.

"This is the place," Davis said.

The darkness of the garage had necessitated the use of the vehicle's running lights. Even the night vision was having trouble.

"How do we get in?" asked Rechs. "You got a remote code?"

"Manual entry," Davis replied. "So I'll need to dismount."

"I'll go forward with you. Rest of you, watch the shadows."

The blinding glare of the vehicle's lights made the surrounding darkness in the garage depths that much more impenetrable.

Rechs, pulse rifle at the ready, accompanied the naval captain out to the door set in the wall of the garage's lowest level. The captain deployed an access pad from a hidden panel next to the door and began typing her way through the digital locks.

"Five weeks on your own down here," said Rechs.

"Not on my own," she replied. "Not at first. There were twenty-four of us when we set down on New Vega. A week later it was just me. And yeah… then I was on my own. So four weeks."

"What was U-Dub planning to do with it once they stole it?"

"Don't know," she replied tersely as she neared the last lockdown screen. The blue of the terminal bathed her beautiful yet austere face with a ghostly glow. "Orders are orders. They told me to get it. That's what I'll do."

Rechs understood that. Doing something because it needed to be done. Mission first. Mission only. The galaxy had gone crazy with needing everyone to understand *why* everything needed to be done. Sometimes you just had to do it, whether you understood it or not.

Sometimes things had to be done even if whole sections of the population thought you were a war criminal for doing them.

Rechs took out the folded flexy he'd taken off the dead blue Savage and handed it to her. She stopped typing.

"Intel," he said. "Give it to your people. And if you can... keep me in the loop if we survive. On the other side of this, I'd like to know what they thought they were going to do with this place."

She took it, unzipped her jumpsuit, and tucked it inside. Then she was back to typing. "Might be hard to get you that info. You are Tyrus Rechs after all," she said with a bare smile. "Half the galaxy wants you dead. The other half wants you to solve all their problems with... let's just say... your preferred methods."

Rechs watched the surrounding darkness beyond the APC's lights. His helmet could image both low and direct light and show him a picture of everything despite the varying degrees of illumination. Handy against flashbangs when it was that type of situation.

A moment later the screen she was working her way through turned red. "Ready to open," she said softly. "Bring the APC forward just in case there's something on the other side."

"Greenhill, move up," ordered Rechs. The quiet vehicle hummed back to life. He looked at the captain. "What are we expecting on the other side?"

"On the other side? Probably nothing."

"But we're moving the APC forward for something. What?"

Davis sighed, not in annoyance, more out of a vague desperation. Perhaps a tiredness. "Last time I came through this side, the Savages were working a big project deep down to cut into the old colony ship. Of course it has tons of entrances, like all ships of its size, but they're all sealed and secured. The Savages are trying to get in near the top security entrance."

"How many decks?" asked Rechs.

"It goes down about twenty decks into the substrata."

Rechs gave a growling "hmm" before saying, "I thought this *was* the entrance to the ship."

Davis shook her head. "No. Just into the tunnel complex built *around* the ship. That's as far as my team made it and as far as the Savages made it—at least that I'm aware. Anything else?"

"Suppose not."

She hit the command function key on the hidden security panel and the security door that accessed the deep tunnels began to rise. Yellow hazard strobes whirled and tossed busy light across the entrance, then ceased when the door had risen fully open.

"You have a big decision to make now," she said, turning to look at Rechs.

"What's that?"

"Are you really going to help me get what I've come for, or was that all talk just to get in so you could blow everything sky high?"

She watched the man in armor turn and look at the yawning darkness beyond the security door. Then he turned back to her.

"I may be a lot of things... but I don't renege on deals. We'll get your party trick. Then we'll destroy the hulk."

A few minutes later they were all standing around the APC, studying a crude map Captain Davis had made on one of the command vehicle's abandoned battle boards.

"This will take us straight to the main access tunnel. Once we hit it, it's as wide as a freeway with nearly as many exits. We can drive this rig right out of a hole near the Nest the Savages have blown open into the tunnels and right up to the belly of their ship."

"And you're certain," said de Macha, "that such a hole is true. Not... speculation?"

"It's real," said Davis, nodding. "I've seen it. In my time down here, I've had eyes on just about every tunnel in the complex. I expect the first thing they did after landing was create that entrance right next to the Nest. We just have to hope it won't be too heavily guarded. It was only lightly guarded before, and my guess is they've figured out you guys are leaving, bugging out, so they'll be even less alert now."

"Problem with that, ma'am," interjected Greenhill, rifle in hand, pointing with the other toward the captain's map, "is that we won't be sneaking around on foot like you were. We'll be driving the trigger-nuke right up to their doorstep."

"Can't we set it on remote det?" asked Martin.

"Sure," answered Greenhill. "But someone's still got to drive it in there. And whoever that is probably ain't gettin' out."

Rechs held up a hand like he'd already solved that problem.

"First things first," he said, touching a gauntleted hand to the battle board, scrolling toward their first objective. The old colony ship buried in the hill. "The hypercomm device. Any thoughts on where in there the thing is located?"

When no one immediately answered, Rechs looked up.

"When the time comes, I'll drive the trigger-nuke. Now tell me about the device."

Davis highlighted a section of the battle board, drawing an oval with her fingertip. "It's in the labs of the colony ship itself. When we came in to snatch it, we found the colony ship shut tight. And it sure as hell wasn't anywhere in the tunnel complex around it—believe me, I looked thoroughly. Then we had other problems."

"What problems, ma'am?" asked Sergeant Major Andres.

"Savages. At first they were focused on the underground transportation routes, which aren't connected to anything where we are, but once they moved into the tunnel complex, they cleared it out thoroughly. Wasn't easy evading notice."

"You said there weren't many Savvies," said Andres, in a tone that suggested he wasn't entirely trusting of the UW officer.

"Not at the end. Once they cleared the tunnels, the marines went to work elsewhere. But a very big work crew is still here"—she pointed at a spot on the battle board—"or they were, trying to bore through the outer hull of the colony ship, coming in from above."

"That sounds like," began Makaffie, who seemed to be searching for the right phrase, "*entirely* too much work, man."

"Maybe," said Davis. "But it's easier than trying to get past these sealed security doors. Trust me."

"So the Savages are below us. That means we move here," said Rechs, pointing at a spot on the map. "Three floors above where the Savages are, or were, trying to tunnel in. We leave the APC, then move down to use the entrance the Savages have made for themselves—assuming they've succeeded—enter the ship, find the labs, and secure the asset. And then we'll finish the job."

"Go *through* the Savages?" said Davis. "I wasn't joking when I said there were heavy concentrations working on getting into the ship. It was like watching a swarm of hornets."

Rechs nodded. "We'll have the advantage of surprise."

"And what if the Savages haven't broken through?" asked de Macha. "Surely we cannot expect them to let us join in and help with the process of boring into the ship."

Davis nodded in agreement. "We could try a sealed entrance. We won't be able to break in, but if there are survivors locked inside the ship, and they see us—guns, Coalition military—they may let us in, hoping for rescue. It's been weeks..."

Rechs didn't share her assessment. "No. I'd rather force entry and control access. Plus, I doubt they're going to want to part with their toy when we get to that part. And this is not a rescue mission."

No one said anything.

"Begging the colonel's pardon, sir," began Sergeant Major Andres. "But... the survivors inside the ship... when we det that weapon, they goin' too, aren't they?"

"It would seem," de Macha said while stroking his chin, "that the ruthlessness of Tyrus Rechs is not just legend."

When Rechs didn't say anything, Captain Davis interjected.

"It's an old starship, Sergeant Major. Strong. I'm not saying it'll be pleasant, but we were led to believe during the mission briefs it's rated to withstand a direct hit from a nuclear weapon. Those people could survive for up to two years in there, minimum. Once the Savages are cleared out, the rescue teams can still come in and pull them out. There'd still be an exposure risk... but the starship would probably survive."

"Theoretically," said Sergeant Major Andres.

Captain Davis nodded. Barely. "Theoretically."

Makaffie grew excited. "I seen them trigger-nukes in training recorders. They trigger a chain reaction in every hydrogen molecule within the blast wave. The entire surface of the planet will be cooked. Just turned to glass. It'll be beautiful, man."

The scrawny private was starry-eyed, as though he was watching the trigger-nuke's blast with his mind's eye and loving the spectacle. He wasn't helping Davis's cause.

"But below ground," she said, "chances are, they'll be safe." She stopped and looked at Rechs. "That about right?"

Rechs locked eyes from behind the expressionless face of his helmet with each man watching him. "Just so we're clear: I came to blow up that Savage ship. I know that what

I'm about to say will seem... callous. And it probably is. But a few hundred dead, compared to what I've seen the Savages do to entire populations... is a drop in the bucket."

Most of the enlisted looked down.

Rechs continued.

"Those survivors are not my priority. I came here to kill Savages. Not save anyone. The people here are already dead. Whether they go up with the nuke, or live out a nightmare under the Savages, they're gone. Trust me. The best I will offer is that we'll tell any survivors we meet to head toward the evac LZ once we have the asset. If they can secure transportation, they might make it to the *Chang* before we detonate the weapon. If anyone has problems with that... I don't care. This isn't about New Vega. It's about humanity. The Savages have to be destroyed."

No one said anything until Makaffie, at the back, whistled low and slow. "Man, that's ice cold. You sure don't play around, T-Rex."

"No," said Rechs. "I do not. And neither should any of you."

48

"Stop here," Davis said as the APC slowly moved through one of the tunnel complex's thoroughfares. It was empty. And quiet. In a way that felt good, a sort of relief, but also ratcheted up tensions as the riders of the command vehicle waited with teeth set for Savages to suddenly appear and destroy their secluded calm.

Greenhill slowly braked to a halt, his hand hovering over the engine's kill switch. "This our last stop, or do you see something I don't?"

"This is," she said, giving a nod for Greenhill to go ahead and cut power. "Set up the sentry gun to protect the vehicle."

"Everybody up top best jump on down," Greenhill said over comm. "Guns are gonna start movin' now that we've reached our destination."

"Where to now?" asked Andres in reply.

"The only way to go now is by foot," Davis said as she moved to the APC's exit to join the ad hoc task force outside. "Stairs."

The team stacked outside of a stairwell door. It was unlocked, and after smoothly bursting inside, Martin and Rechs waved in the rest of the team.

Scaffolding metal stairs wound around a subterranean pillar that fell through the dark void of an immense artificial cavern. Visibility was minimal, with the NVGs barely finding enough light from the distantly glowing exit signs to give them any appreciable optics.

Rechs knew that despite his armor's heavy-duty ability to stand up to just about anything thrown at it, it enabled him to move with absolute stealth. As they began their slow descent, his feet made as much noise as a cat's paw. And his breathing was utterly silent, each exhalation masked behind his full-cover helmet, all noise kept away from outside ears.

But the others, Rechs could hear. They weren't being loud, but in so much stillness, so much empty dark silence, the only way to be completely quiet was to stop moving—or be Tyrus Rechs.

"Hold," Rechs said over the comm.

Everyone froze.

They'd gone down two levels and Rechs didn't know if anyone else could see what he'd seen. His HUD had picked up the heat signatures in the dark. And at the instant the team froze, so did whatever was in front of them.

"Eight of them," Rechs said. Wan light from sources still running off subterranean power illuminated some of the lower walkways, and Rechs's HUD fed him the data it acquired. "Reinforced neoprene suits—light armor. Armed."

"New Vega military operating down here?" whispered Sergeant Major Andres.

"Negative." Rechs had irised in with his armor's enhanced vision. "Savages."

"Then they're hunters," said Captain Davis. "A subspecies of the marines you faced on the surface. More like animals than humans. Guard dogs."

And indeed, the troop of eight started forward like a pack, cautiously, as though sensing the intruders' presence in the bare movement of air down here. They didn't walk like humans. They didn't walk at all. Instead they pulled themselves forward on arms and hands where their legs and feet should have been. Four arms in total. Two for locomotion, and two—the ones where you'd expect them to be—holding their rifles.

"What the..." began Makaffie as he stared hard into his NVGs. "They look like *morlocks.*" His voice seeming loud in the quiet silence of the cavern here at sub-level five.

And perhaps it *was* loud. Loud enough for the Savage beast-man-things in any case. Because the troop went suddenly wild. Hooting like monkeys and flinging themselves in all directions. It was clear they knew there was someone else in the dark with them.

The leader, bigger than the others, raised up, lengthening its spine in a way no human ever would, and scented the air. Then it howled in something that might have once been one of the many languages of mankind but which now sounded much more... animal. Holding its rifle in one hand, it pointed a necrotic white figure at the team on the stairs high above.

Wild Man reacted fast, firing a shot from his massive rifle that smashed into the beast and sent it tumbling. The boom in the confined space was deafening, and seemed to set the pack on edge, drowning out their howls until its noise dispersed up and down the stairwell in successive echoes.

The hunters came swarming up the stairs, eschewing the path meant for a sane and rational mind and climbing instead with the arms, all four of them, up along the railings and pylons like parasites in a feeding frenzy. Their rifles clattered and smacked against the steps, but it seemed the beasts had no interest in using them, intent instead on dispatching the intruders with tooth and claw.

From other unknown spaces within the vast tunnel complex the shrieking hoots of more of the beast-like Savages resounded against the deep concrete walls and descended into cyclopean darkness.

Greenhill engaged and dragged the pulse rife ahead of the closest leaping monkey-like post-human. He shot on target and the thing howled and fell over the guardrail and into the void.

"Fall back to the level above," ordered Rechs. "We'll fight from there."

Andres and Davis covered Greenhill and Makaffie as they retreated, slipping through the narrow portal that led out onto the level. Greenhill ejected the charge pack from his pulse rifle and slapped in another. Makaffie, humping a ruck that seemed three sizes too big for him, flung himself forward with heedless abandon, swearing all the way and apologizing for having drawn attention in the first place. No one responded. They were too busy firing at the closing hunters.

"Martin!" shouted Rechs. The point man was the farthest down the stairs and anchoring the base of return fire. On full auto he was dumping pulse fire in bursts. "Fall back now!"

The point man came to himself, ejected a pack, and ran up the stairs just as a Savage hunter pulled itself over the rail where he stood. Clawed hands reached out greedily to snag his ruck.

That was when Rechs got his first good look at the thing.

Its eyes were of a human taken by madness long ago. But its mouth was pure animal. Fangs, yellow and crook-ed, dripping bubbly foam. Its white skin took on an almost sickly green cast in the wan light of night vision.

Rechs pulled the trigger of his hand cannon and ex-ploded the thing's head at five meters. Martin dashed past him. More and more of things were climbing over the rails all around them.

Wild bullet fire chased Rechs up a couple of steps, striking some of the advancing hunters in the process and skipping along the metals steps on either side of Rechs. He barely had time to toss himself around the corner of the next landing to avoid being hit. Popping a frag, he dropped it down the steps below, then pushed Martin far-ther up. "Move!"

The long-nailed scrabbling of the Savages' hand-feet clickety-clacked up through the darkness. It sounded like they were many, many more than the initial eight spotted. And who knew? The place was a vast and winding laby-rinth. There could have been multiple patrols all within a short distance of one another, prepared to swarm any en-emy encountered.

The grenade exploded, blowing Savages and concrete and even some of the stair structure off and out into the void. A vast cavern Rechs couldn't even see the edges of.

"We're coming up!" Rechs shouted into his comm. They needed only to cover two more flights of stairs, but the fire from the targeted landing already sounded intense. He didn't want either of them to get hit coming in.

The swarm of Savage hunters, whatever they'd become, was intensifying. Greenhill, who'd slung a light automatic pulse rifle carried by squad heavy gunners, laid down suppressive fire in intervals as Rechs and Martin squeezed past the door onto the escape level.

Beyond the doorway was a long balcony that ran alongside an open reservoir of dark water. The water was black, the concrete floor gray, and a lone white light somewhere high above gave the whole place an atmosphere of a forsaken gloomy well.

An immense underground cistern.

The rest of the team was already halfway down the balcony's curving length, running for another security door.

"Fall back, cover fire, reload, and fall back," ordered Rechs, pointing at Greenhill and Martin. "I'll go first."

Greenhill jogged backward, swapping in a new drum charge for the heavier weapon, while Martin sprinted out ahead.

The Savages came swarming through the door, heedless of the automatic weapons they were carrying. Except they didn't come through the portal like a normal human might—they clutched the corners and pulled themselves around the sides. Rechs was back on his primary, burning pulse shots with economy, sometimes having to pull three more times just to get a particularly fast mover.

Rechs took aim at a hunter darting past the one he'd just dropped. The thing was climbing up the wall, howling like an insane gibbon as it raced along unseen handholds toward the ceiling. They were inhuman in that way, performing animal feats of agility that came from something far removed from their humanity. Rechs hit the thing with pulse fire.

Another Savage hunter took position in the doorway and began firing on full auto down the length of the balcony, forcing Rechs to throw himself into an alcove. Perhaps this one had kept more of its humanity than the others, and remembered the power of the tool in its hands. Bullets whistled past in the darkness. The ancient sound of brass dribbling out onto the dry gray concrete filled the air.

As Rechs swapped a charge pack, he saw Greenhill get grazed along his shoulder. Greenhill let go of his weapon, which dangled from a sling, grabbed at his wounded arm, and stumbled into the cover of another alcove.

Martin was just turning to fire from the top of the landing.

Someone is gonna catch it full on, thought Rechs.

The massive *BOOM* of the Wild Man's rifle echoed out over the underground cistern. The Savage firing from the doorway was flung back out of sight, probably right off the landing and into the void beyond.

That gave the rest of the team the time they needed to get their fire and movement coordinated, and moments later they were falling back under covering fire.

The Savages continued to pour through the entrance— raging, charging beasts—and the combined task force Rechs had brought into this complex met their charge with deadly cones of unrelenting pulse fire. Hunters tumbled back, went over the rail, or lay dead where they were hit only to be trampled by those behind them.

"Keep comin'!" shouted Andres, his rifle pausing only long enough for him to swap out charge packs.

The Savage charge failed as the last of them died. The hunters' high-water mark was halfway down the long curving balcony. The ensuing silence was ominous.

"Climbing past all those bodies," de Macha said, searching his webbing for a new charge pack, "will be difficult. We must take care not to slip and fall over the rail, my friends."

"Going back is still the only way?" Rechs asked Davis.

"It was the easy way—"

Greenhill laughed while Makaffie applied field dressings to his wounded arm.

"—but not the only way. We can follow a door on this level to an elevator that will take us close to where the Savages were doing their dig. But that means going through open spaces with lots of visual angles. Lots of exposure."

The sergeant major made a sound, a sort of grunt as he felt under his chest protection to feel the wounded pectoral he'd suffered earlier in the fighting. "If they're communicating, and they sure had time to, means we'll run into more. They'll be looking for us. Maybe waiting for us to keep on going the way we was starting before we ran into them. But we go this new way, we gonna cut ourselves off if they come up along our back trail."

"Or," added Greenhill, "they'll just cut the elevators off when we try and use 'em. Kill us all."

Andres nodded. "What's it gonna be, Colonel? Ain't no good choice I can see."

Rechs thought for a moment.

Martin watched their six with the Wild Man.

"Let's take the elevator ride and hope we get lost near the dig site," said Rechs. "Chances are they were watching the outer tunnels for infiltrators. We may have gotten through their initial defenses by knocking out their patrol and everything else that came running."

"Those things sure didn't *look* like they'd be using comms," said Martin over his shoulder. "I bet they were just responding to the howls and noise."

"I agree with Rechs," Davis said. "The elevators are the fastest option now that we've lost the element of surprise."

"All due respect, Colonel," said Sergeant Major Andres, "but all this is a lot of wishful thinking. Sir."

"Agree, Sergeant Major. But it's an option forward," Rechs replied. "And I damn sure ain't turning back."

The sergeant major nodded to himself as though that was all he needed. The chance to express his concerns and the indication that they had been noted.

Captain Davis led them to a door with a pop-out keyboard. "Through here and then we're on our way."

After a few swift keystrokes, they went through to the darkness on the other side.

49

They moved through a warren of corridors, past rooms both furnished and empty. Rooms that looked like they might once have served some specific purpose—disaster-event temporary housing, emergency medical, or just plain office space. Everything was clean and bare and silent. As though only waiting for someone to come along and refill the space after a sudden crisis.

They found the elevator, and took it down to its lowest level: sub-level seven. A thirty-second ride.

"Be ready to go when you hear the ding," said Rechs.

The elevator slowed and settled, but wasn't the type to give a chime. Its doors slid open silently to reveal an open floor space, cavernous like a warehouse but with no racks or shelves. Just... empty.

"This is underwhelming," said Martin.

"I'd rather that than more of those... things," replied de Macha.

"Morlocks," insisted Makaffie. "We should call them morlocks."

Rechs took a few steps forward. "You've been here before, Captain Davis?"

"Yes." She walked past Rechs, her guard down, as though the idea of encountering trouble was completely out of her mind. "This is what I'd call the last safe area. This place is sort of like two levels in one. It looks down on the level below, like the engineers wanted space for some big equipment to be in here when they were first building. I couldn't say."

She paused, several strides ahead of the main force. "You coming?"

Martin hustled forward and took point, creeping across the wide, abandoned warehouse-like floor of polished concrete.

They reached the edge together, and looked down at a vast space with its floor far below. But it was not an empty space, and the structure that filled it was both unexpected and alien. It was immediately clear that over the past few weeks, the Savages had been doing much more down here than simply trying to infiltrate the old colony ship.

They had been... building.

At first it was hard to tell what it was. It was like looking at a series of liquid-filled bubbles stacked in hives and clusters, one atop the other. Stacks and stacks and stacks, several stories high, extending in all directions.

"What... is all that?" asked Sergeant Greenhill. His voice hovered between awe... and something else.

Fear, Rechs thought.

It was one thing to fight the Savages. It was entirely something else to get a glimpse of what happened within their secluded communities. To see what they did when the galaxy wasn't watching.

No one seemed to have an answer for Greenhill until Makaffie spoke up. He'd almost begun to whistle, long and slow like he had before, but Rechs put his gauntleted hand up, signaling the man to remain quiet. Best not to bring another patrol down on them with no space to retreat into that wasn't secure.

So Makaffie spoke low and quiet, with quaking disbelief verging on a kind of horror. As though what they were seeing was something beyond the ken of sanity and order.

"It's… a freezer," he said. "See 'em inside?"

The task force put their eyes to the scopes of their weapons or looked through 'nocs at the bizarre Savage structure. It was like looking at the eyes of a fly. But magnified to the point that it seemed colossal.

Rechs had seen it too. Probably before Makaffie. His armor's imaging enhancement had picked up the heat signatures within each tiny bubble. "Not frozen," he said. "More like some kind of stasis. Dunno how."

"These more Savvies, Colonel?"

Rechs shook his head. "Humans. Thousands of them."

"The Savages," said Captain Davis, "are cannibals. At least the ones from the Nest. I don't know if the newer arrivals are, too, but the ones who first invaded, the advance force… they are."

"How do you know that?" asked Makaffie.

She turned sharply on him, but her face was emotionless and her eyes dead.

"I had a crew and complement of twenty-four when we set down here five weeks ago. Now it's just me. Trust me, grunt, I know."

"Just asking, lady," Makaffie said. "Y'know, confirmation of intel. Didn't expect to get my head bitten off for it."

And from the look on Davis's face, she was aware that what she'd tried to bottle up had suddenly slipped out despite her best efforts to bury it.

"Sorry..."

It was a word that didn't seem to come naturally to her.

"I didn't mean to offend you."

Makaffie smiled. "No offense taken, man. We're all surfin' the same wave through the cosmos."

"My theory," she said, turning away from the artillery man, her voice controlled and low now, all of them watching the bubbles of humans floating in some kind of greenish fluid over there along the wall, "is that they, the Savages in that ship on the side of Hilltop, had hab problems out there in the dark."

"All that time," said de Macha, "and something is bound to go wrong. We were lucky for our tanks to stay together from one battle to the next. Imagine a ship so large for so long..."

Davis nodded. "Maybe they had a population explosion they couldn't control. And their answer... their answer was to get rid of their bodies. Dial it back to the brains, feed those, and keep going on a minimum of nutrients and calories. So calories must be the driving force of their culture. Their biggest priority, once they finally set down on a planet, is to make sure they have calories to spare."

She nodded at the bubbles across the way.

"They... might not even be capable of understanding how wrong what they're doing is. Or that it's wrong at all, depending on how many generations we're looking at. Hell, they've probably already done this on other planets, to other species we've never encountered. They're eaters. They show up and they eat. To them, this was one big shopping trip. Now they're icing everyone they can get their hands on, for either the long haul to the next planet or whatever it is they're going to do here."

"Hey," Andres said, squeezing his pulse rifle with both hands. "You think some of the strike force is down there, too?"

"I wouldn't bet against it."

The team fell to silence as the words, and their meaning, sank in for the team.

"You knew about this?" asked Rechs.

"I did," she said.

50

According to Captain Davis, the biggest survival bunkers were in the lower decks of the sealed colony ship. That's what her handlers had told her before sending her team on this mission. An entire small city might be down there, just waiting for the end of the world to hurry up and get on with it. The New Vega government had been ready for anything. Apex predators. Pirates. All the other calamities that could befall an isolated colony.

But not Savages. No one was ever ready for them. Or at least that had been Rechs's experience. And the experience of a few dozen dead worlds.

"How do we get down to the ship?" Rechs asked.

Davis pointed to the far end of the expansive and empty floor, suggesting they go around the great open space that showed the Savages' work beneath them. "There's another elevator this way. It'll take us down to where they were drilling. I never went that far myself, though one of my team did. It was dangerous to get down there so close to where they were working."

They proceeded directly to the elevator, a much larger freight lift. It crawled downward slowly, sliding through some deep dark well.

"Expect anything," Davis said. "They may still be drilling. Guarding, patrolling—"

"Waiting to ambush us," offered Andres.

"Just be ready," said Rechs, checking over his weapon as they descended.

But when the lift stopped, it opened on silent, lifeless, utter darkness.

Proceeding cautiously, covering the exits and angles, they moved forward toward the great drilling operation. The Savages were no longer there.

They'd managed to blast their way into the ancient buried colony ship.

It had been called the *Stardust Zephyr* when it hauled itself away from Earth's cluttered orbit, bound for promises a scout sold high on. Leaping bravely into the shadowy frontiers of hyperspace. In those days, a ship had been just as likely to not come out of hyper at all as it was to finish its jump.

Eight hundred had been the original colony number. Give or take. Some would be born and some would die just in those first few months. Eight hundred colonists had flung themselves at this distant world in hopes of a better life than the one Earth offered.

War.

Poverty.

Disease.

On New Vega they exchanged the challenges of the old world for those of the new.

Storms.

A powerful apex predator.

And disease. Lots of those on new worlds. Med suites hadn't been invented yet to clear out all the nasty stuff strange new worlds offered.

But it was a chance to do something. Room to move around and discover. A place to have something of your own.

And now, they were a top-of-the-line civilization competing with the best of the post–Great Leap star nations that had started out from Earth long ago. A place that seemed on the verge of being able to turn up its nose at the stodgy worlds in the galactic core.

Stardust Zephyr, built to last the rigors of deep space, protected them during those early years. It became the castle they fought from, sallied forth from, and hid in. And thanks to its protection, as the years of the predators, and then the pirates, came and went, the colonists survived. And, finally, hard generations later, flourished. As their city literally grew up around the sides of the great starship, a new mountain formed in the landscape. Hilltop. And what was once all of the colony became merely... Old Colony.

But the *Stardust Zephyr* was always and ever at its heart.

A starship that had carried every conceivable thing the colonists could ever need, because it was a one-way trip. No return ticket.

Hyperdrive worked both ways back then, same as it did now. A ship could jump back to Earth again.

But there were no repulsors. Not for something that large.

So a planet landing... that was a one-time deal.

Now the team was moving forward over discarded drilling equipment and boxes packing Savage technological pieces that defied easy explanation to the mind of a modern-age human.

"They spent a lot of resources to get in," whispered Sergeant Major Andres over comm as they proceeded through the mess.

There were no dead bodies. Savage or human.

They reached a great round well right in the middle of the level's floor. It was easily thirty meters in diameter, and seemed to have been blasted and bored straight through. Impossibly thick layers of reinforced concrete and mammoth metal plates so thick that you'd think it was the colony ship's outer hull itself—had you not been able to see the ancient ship down below.

"Down the ramp," Rechs said, cutting through the awe that seemed to have settled on all the others.

They clambered down a spiraling ramp, large enough for their APC to have driven down in tight, winding loops, until they reached a sort of great bridge of concrete that spanned above the hull of the ancient ship. The Savage light fixtures had been left on, illuminating the ship as if it were a work of ancient art on display in a museum. The light kits resembled the skeletons of long-dead robots, their lamps giant sightless eyes casting adoration at the beached whale of interstellar travel.

"Proceed across the bridge," called out Rechs over the comm.

"Roger, Colonel. On your six," answered the sergeant major.

For every one of them it had seemed that most of their time in the tunnels below New Vega had been spent hoping not to run into more hunters—Makaffie's morlocks—or other Savage patrols. But now, crossing in front of the monolithic starship buried beneath the city, they were exposed. Very exposed. It felt as though if there were ever to be a Savage ambush, it would be now.

Yet all remained quiet. Desolate.

"Where'd everyone go?" asked Makaffie, who was in the rear. Next to the Wild Man.

"Maybe they got in, got what they came for, and left," suggested Martin.

And then no one said anything until Rechs threaded the inward blossoms of the breach into the ancient outer hull of the buried ship. The metal had been torn and blackened. "They got in, all right."

They passed through the thick outer hull to the inner hull, climbing down a simple scaffolding system the Savages had no doubt constructed to move in en masse. Systems between those two shells had long ago been removed, probably used for purposes of survival in the early days of the colony. Precious salvage during the lean years. Some kind of construction foam-crete had filled in the gaps and been capped off with ceramic mold. Some of the stuff was now broken loose on the deck, but most of it was blackened and blasted.

Once through, the team found itself in what looked like a high-end corporate lobby. In frosted glass were displayed the flags and symbols of office for the government of New Vega. Or at least, in the bits of frosted glass that hadn't shattered.

"Weird," said Makaffie.

"How's that?" asked Greenhill.

"I dunno, man. I just figured—mentally, y'know—that once we got inside, it would be like the outside. A time capsule. The same as it was when it landed. This is a trip."

"No," interjected Davis. "Everything inside the ship has been updated and retrofitted for years by the government. You'd have to visit a museum to see what this looked like on the inside when it first landed."

"I'll add that to my list of things to do on New Vega," quipped Martin.

"Keep moving," growled Rechs.

There was dried blood here, but no bodies. And the dried blood had pooled before turning to drag marks. Whoever had been wounded here, or killed, had been dragged away.

"Calories," de Macha whispered over the comm.

This was confirmed as they proceeded forward. The rust-colored drag streaks led to bubbles waiting along the walls.

Like a kind of pantry.

The ship's internal areas, once packed tightly with as much equipment as could be stuffed into the premium space of a starship, had long ago been cleared out, forming wide-open office vistas of white ceramic, stainless steel, and frosted glass. But all of it was now ruined by the pock-marks of bullet fire and trails of Savage destruction.

"Firefight here," noted Martin.

"Doesn't look like much of one," said Greenhill. "New Vegans switched over to blasters years ago, just like everybody else. Don't see no return fire, or blaster damage for that matter. So... ain't much of a fight. More like a turkey shoot from the look of it."

All was silent as they proceeded toward a central well that had once been the power core. The old power plants on ships of that generation always required the most space. It had since been turned into a central lift and atrium at the heart of the government-in-hiding.

Rechs checked the time. Five hours until dawn. Then a day. Sundown and it was over.

Not much time left to get everything done. And his men had been up and fighting for much of the last twenty-four hours. The longer things dragged out, the tireder they would be.

A sound echoed up from far below.

"We ain't alone in here," said Makaffie.

"That's for sharp as sure," muttered Andres.

Rechs peered down into the shadowy darkness. The space carved out for the old power core likely ran all the way from the very top to the very bottom of the old ship, with intermittent deck access throughout. "What level are the labs?"

"Almost all the way down as best we could gather," said Davis. "We knew the deepest levels were where the most secretive and important work was done."

Rechs shook his head. "It'll take too long for us all to get down there and get back up. I can go quicker alone if I use the armor's jump jets."

"You got rocket boosters on that thing?" Makaffie asked. "Man... I always wanted to fly, you know?"

Rechs ignored the artillery man. "How do I find the device?"

Davis bit her lip, something Rechs had never seen her do. He could see she was wondering if she could trust him. And if she should.

"Our intel said it was in a secure lab called Gray Watch. Second-to-last level. The project name is Telos."

Rechs nodded and moved to the railing that lined the vast space. "Hold here until I get back."

"Rechs," she said, holding out a hand as if to stay his jump into the darkness. "We were told there was some pretty heavy-duty security stuff down there. Something called a 'Troll System.'"

"What's it do?"

"I don't know. We only ever had the name of the system. But given what we know they *have* invented, it's safe to say it'll be formidable."

Rechs studied her for a second.

"All right then."

And then he was gone, over the railing and falling. Bringing in the armor's booster jets as he descended into the darkness of the ancient ship.

51

Rechs had to flare the armor's jump jets then bump them hard to vault onto the circular walkway that girded the central well along the level next to the bottom. He scanned the darkness using the armor's radar-assisted imaging system, currently interfacing with low-light vision to produce a grainy blue-and-white image inside his helmet's HUD.

Here and there lay the remains of supplies. Food wrappers. Medical supplies. Discarded survival packs. And spent ammunition casings.

The Savages had been here, looking to harvest the defenders, the survivors. Those men and women who had held out here for weeks, hoping to last until the other worlds could get their act together and rescue them.

Obviously they had not held long enough.

The Savages had broken in to continue their work of... calories. Which was what they'd been doing all across the planet. Shopping. Putting away food for their journey to the next planet.

But this deck still looked to be a mess. As though the Savages hadn't had the time yet to clean it up like they had at the breach site. That made Rechs feel like this deck was the last stand. The place the government survivors defended at all costs.

He ventured through a heavy blast door that had been blown inward. A crude map on the wall gave directions to the section he'd come seeking.

Gray Watch.

Security Access Omega Black Required, noted a warning in broad lettering.

Rechs moved on without hesitation. The Savages didn't have security access, so he'd either find the defenses defeated, or he'd find scores of dead Savages. Either way, he had to move forward.

But when he arrived at the entrance to Gray Watch, no security access was needed. The ceramic-forged vault door with a seam down the middle slid open automatically as he approached, its security panel torn off the wall and obviously hacked. Some device hung limply from a series of spliced cables and wires that had been hard-connected to the panel.

Rechs looked inside the room and froze, pulse rifle ready. Not because the door had opened so easily. But because of what lay beyond it.

Not just tens of Savages, but hundreds.

And all of them dead.

These Savages were the faceless cannibal marines he'd fought on the surface. Their machine bodies tangled and torn, riddled by hundreds of rounds per. Their brains—the only thing left of their biological roots—exposed in sliced-open helmets or sprayed in chunks on other dead marines and along the walls.

A horror show.

Rechs stepped gingerly through the field of ruined corpse machines, head on a swivel looking for signs of what had managed this slaughter. Inside his HUD, the targeting laser at the tip of pulse rifle danced out and ahead, covering the dark spaces and caressing the corners as he advanced into the New Vega technology *sanctum sanctorum*.

There were fewer dead bodies farther in, as though the main fight had gone down hardcore and in earnest back by the door. Those who had made it this far had died alone, or sometimes in small groups, but just as badly.

Rechs suspected that the unknown Troll System was responsible. The question was... was it still active?

The space opened up to a massive lab complex and office space subdivided by high-impact safety plastic. Dozens of small labs, operating rooms, and clean rooms. And all were riddled with the spiderwebs of impact and weapon strikes that had left snowflake-reminiscent impacts in the heavy-duty partitions.

It grew darker the farther into the lab Rechs moved, so much so that even with his helmet he was having a hard time seeing. Now he was down to radar, which had switched him over to digitally graphed green lines of everything. Not the best imaging software to engage targets with, but better than firing blind.

Keeping his weapon steady, he popped a dark flare that would emit electronic light, scratched the activation lid against the wall, and tossed it forward. The imaging software in his HUD re-calibrated with the added low-spectrum light source and switched over to better imaging. Still not the best. But good enough to hunt by.

Far away, in the distance behind him, he heard the distant crackle of pulse fire.

The Savages were engaging his team high up in the ship's central well.

But there was something else within the soundscape that the armor's listening devices were picking up. A secondary audio signature, down here and close to his position. He could see its audio line at the top of his HUD.

A mechanical hum. Activating suddenly—then stopping. Then a different one altogether. Something... almost robotic.

The sound of a drum whirring to life.

It sounded exactly like a ship-based point defense cannon.

Rechs threw himself to the ground as hundreds of electrical *snaps* went off almost all at once. Invisible bees smashed into the ruined safety partitions, spider-webbing them even further. At points breaking through and creating crystalline geysers erupting on the horizontal plane.

Maybe a thousand rounds in eight seconds.

Then nothing. Weapons fire ceasing as instantly as it had begun.

The sound of a drum whirring to life was exactly what any mounted anti-armor gun firing ball ammunition sounded like. Except there should have been the singular telltale *BRRRRAAAAAAAAAP* of those infamous and ancient weapons that still found their places in the militaries of today. If only because they were so good at what they did despite the production costs.

Instead of that groaning *brraaaap* there had been only that low symphony of electrical snaps.

There were few things that actually interested Rechs. Few things he took the time to know and understand, to study in depth and at length. And he'd lived a long time; much of what he knew faded over the years. Or became obsolete. He'd seen that happen many times over.

But weapons, and weapons systems, he always kept up on those. Because he'd faced them in the past, he would face them in the future, and he had to survive them if he was going to do what he'd set himself to do a long time ago.

Which was another story for another time.

Facedown in the piles of machine corpses along this lane of the smashed lab, surrounded by pieces of technology that looked eerily like bodies and body parts leaking mechanical fluids in slow drips, the remains of brains putrefying in and among them, Rechs searched his mind to identify the weapon system that had just snapped out a thousand shots at him in the blink of an eye. Only the armor's advanced audio detection system and his own memory of ancient weapons systems had saved him at the last second.

And now something was moving through the lab. Coming toward him.

Coming *for* him.

On tracks. Like a small tank.

He scanned memories of a thousand different weapons systems on a hundred different worlds.

Could it be...

... a Gauss gun? An electrical rail gun system that fired cyclically.

Whatever it was, it was coming toward him.

The Troll was on its way.

And now he saw it.

Thermal overlays within his HUD showed him a tall inverted triangle with two massive multi-barrel weapons forming armlike appendages. Working its way through the massive space inside the ancient starship to arrive at the target it had sensed within its designated patrol.

Rechs began high-crawling across the bodies of the Savages.

Another blur of low electrical *snaps* rang out, short, sharp, and hissing. More angry bees smashed into the ruined plastic partitions, even shattering some in great sheets that caved in across his path.

Rechs popped a frag and bounced it back in the direction from which he'd come. Not to hit the sentry system, but to get it to target and fire. Which it did. Both of its arms spun up with five heavy barrels apiece and decimated that section of the lab in a sudden blur of destruction. The air it was firing into shimmered as its very fabric was ripped apart from the effect of so many rounds passing through at relativistic speeds. Ricochets and stray rounds were rebounding and smacking into other smashed areas of the lab.

The grenade went off and Rechs popped up and dumped the whole pack from the pulse rifle into the automated sentry robot. The Troll. Watching as his fire was harmlessly deflected and sent off in other directions.

Without a pause in its firing, the robot swiveled on its creaky treads and waved its spitting destruction all across the area where Rechs was standing. He had no other option, no other cover, than to activate his armor's defensive bubble. A technology that had defied his ability to understand it. It survived everything, for sometimes upwards of forty-five seconds. And, once, even a nuclear blast.

But since then… it would also collapse without warning. So…

You never knew.

Rechs hoped it would handle whatever the death-spitting automated sentry was throwing at him. And if it did, that was only half the battle. He still had to figure out what to do after it disappeared—without warning, as always.

The wave of swarming death covered the ball of translucent defensive energy that suddenly erupted from Rechs's armor. He didn't waste time. He ran deeper into the lab, the death machine hissing out its litany of angry swarming bees after him, smashing to pieces everything that stood in their way. Desperate to catch up to their target.

Just as he passed out of view of the Troll, the bubble capriciously failed.

Ten seconds. If that.

Truth was, the devices inside his armor had been acting up more and more often as of late. Who knew how much longer the armor would even work? And in time, someone would invent something better.

He swapped in a new charge pack as he hugged wall, then let his pulse rifle fall on its sling carry. He pulled the hand cannon and moved deeper into the ruined lab as the thing came for him, smashing barriers with volcanoes of fire. Hopefully there wasn't a second Troll active farther in.

Project Telos.

The project title was stamped into a door. A vault door.

"Must be the place," muttered Rechs.

Several other such doors lined this wide, clean, vaulted section of the lab. Each had its own enigmatic project title. This must have been the hub for New Vega's most secret R&D. The big tech leaps and doomsday machines every civilization Rechs had ever known eventually got around to playing with.

The important stuff, or so they thought before they started using it to annihilate one another.

The machine was coming closer.

Rechs told the armor to call up an image off its feed of the bot. "Predict weak points. Last target," he growled into the armor's system commands.

A replay of the last action taken against the bot spun past his eyes in a corner of the HUD. Every shot against it was calculated and graphed. Sensor overlays swam across the bot. All this was automatic. Rechs had learned not to pay too much attention when the armor started its quantum voodoo. The lunatics who'd designed the thing had touched the various essence of the unknown and had come back with something that wasn't supposed to exist.

Go figure.

But then again, you probably shouldn't, because, as had been explained to him by a very smart woman once...

That way lies madness, Rechs.

She always called you Rechs.

Didn't she?

Reina.

He powered up the armor's cybernetic interface to full, knowing he'd blow twenty-five percent of his available power doing what needed to be done next. But there was no time left for anything else.

The killing machine was coming.

He grabbed the vault wheel, ignoring the security-code entry request flashing holographically on emergency reserve, and yanked with all the armor's might.

The door came off its massive bolted hinges. Just a bit. He shifted position, still holding the hand cannon, pushed into the bent section of the vault door, and folded it away from its titanium frame. When enough of an entrance had been forced, he squeezed through.

Target Analysis Complete, the HUD informed him.

The image of the bot expanded, showing Rechs where vulnerabilities in the Troll might exist.

Might.

Optical sensors.

Main power plant.

Both were tagged as possible targets.

No sooner had Rechs slipped inside than the Troll revealed itself to have a few surprises of its own. Twin rockets screamed toward the vault door without warning, blowing Rechs into the side wall of the pristine clean room for the Telos Project.

As Rechs was thrown through the air, he spotted what had to be the experimental hypercomm device on a backlit pedestal at the rear of the lab. Behind another safety partition. It had to be the device, because it was illuminated reverently, like some holy relic.

That was the thought he had as he smashed helmet-first into the wall, slamming hard to the ground and then rolling onto his back, leaning against the wall he'd just struck in a daze.

A moment later the massive form of the sentry bot, its triangular body the primal shape of all the dark devils that had ever plagued mankind, filled the now gaping vault doorway with its shadow.

In Rechs's HUD, the analyzed potentially vulnerable target areas were tagged.

Rechs raised his massive hand cannon and fired on full auto, the armor stabilizing his gauntleted aim. Powerful depleted-uranium fifty-caliber slugs smashed into the machine's power plant located at the bottom of the triangle.

The Troll exploded, sending shards of metal and fragments of circuitry in every direction, devastating a large section of the lab. And leaving a hot burning metal fragment in Rechs's thigh as a parting gift.

52

After Rechs went down the well inside the buried starship, Sergeant Major Andres had taken charge, setting up firing positions and getting everyone settled to wait for however long it took the "colonel" to come back up. Food and water were broken out and consumed in pairs, with one person watching and the other eating.

It was Martin, paired up with the sergeant major, and checking the dressing on his wound, who spotted movement in the green light of night vision. "Someone's coming," he whispered over comm.

"Where?" asked Greenhill.

"From the left... corridors leading off the office spaces we just came through."

The team hastily shifted position. Reorienting itself to the newly spotted threat and watching their flanks in case it was a feint.

"I don't see nothing," said Makaffie. "Just dark."

"There was some kind of electronic distortion. A blue flash of light for just a second..." Martin paused, searching around the exact location he'd seen movement. "Now more of 'em on the right. Two teams. Bounding overwatch."

"I see them now," said de Macha. "They do not seem to see us, though, no?"

What was coming, or rather who was coming, wasn't totally invisible. The team's NVGs could see the distortion of a human shape refracting light and bending it away from itself. Crouched low and moving like a soldier. Holding an assault rifle.

Martin nodded, though no one could have seen the motion. "Yeah. Looks like a scout from each side. Picking up more distortion to the rear, so there could be squads behind the points, following them in."

"Got 'em," said the sergeant major. "Coming right at us. Get ready and wait for the main body. Then open up on my fire."

He got confirm clicks as the Savages moved forward in teams of two like the shadowy images of forgotten ghosts.

"They're pros," observed Martin in a whisper. "That's for sure. And they move in twos like they were trained aboard ships. Fighting in tight quarters."

"They're Savages," said Davis. "All they've ever known are ships."

That was when the sergeant major opened up on them, steadying his rifle on a trash receptacle he'd turned over earlier for cover. Pulse fire raced out across the dark like hot streaks of lightning in the green wash of night vision. One of the shapes went down, and as it did, it suddenly materialized into full visibility. It was like... like a shrouded mummy augmented by a chassis of metal.

"Some sort of cybernetic interface rig!" shouted Davis as she cut loose with a burst on the team closing on the right. She thought she hit one, but she didn't get any solid knockdowns.

Captain de Macha fired, hit one, and yelled, "Got one!" As a tanker, he was used to communicating with a team when he fired. Davis, a navy captain, was much the same. The other soldiers worked their weapons in near silence, only speaking to alert their teammates that they were swapping out charge packs.

Makaffie fired a blaster pistol he'd picked up before leaving the *Chang*, swore something at the incoming wraiths, and flung a grenade he'd probably forgotten to pull the pin on. It hit one of them and bounced around without exploding. The one it hit stopped, examined what had been flung at it in the middle of the barrage of fire, and caught a full burst in the torso from Greenhill.

Nearby the Wild Man cracked off a shot at close range with his big cannon rifle. But down here, in almost pitch black, and with no NVG interface for his scope, the powerful weapon was all but useless.

They could hear the electronic chitter of some kind of comm system on ambient. It made the Savages sound like a swarm of angry dub-step locusts raging at one another about how they were going to kill their prey. But it also sounded almost human at moments. As though if you only could have slowed it down, you might have understood what was being communicated. If you'd once spoken every language Earth had ever known.

Captain de Macha got hit by return fire coming in from the Savages. He doubled over and croaked, "Hit..." in obvious pain.

Keeping low, the sergeant major left his weapon, pulled his sidearm, and fired back at the Savages as he and Makaffie moved quickly to de Macha's position.

"Got one in the leg!" shouted a hyper Makaffie. He switched from his pistol to the pulse rifle he'd been carrying and started firing back with psychotic abandon.

"Is it bad?" asked de Macha, who had rolled over onto his back.

"Nah," Andres said. "Got you in the meat of the quad. Bet it hurts like a bastard, though. Checkin' the artery now... it looks good, Captain."

Fire continued to come in hot and fast, ricocheting off the railing of the well they were covering in front of.

"Need a new pack!" shouted Makaffie as he ejected an empty. Evidently he'd spent all his. Or perhaps he simply didn't know where they were.

De Macha groaned, fished one out of the LCE on his chest, and handed it up as the sergeant major set to work on the wound. Above them the Wild Man stood tall, blazing away intermittently at any Savages that dared to come close. He may not have been able to aim, but the fearsome roar of the weapon alone was enough to keep them back for the moment needed to attend to de Macha's injuries.

"All right!" shouted Makaffie. "Yer good people, Cap'n!" Then he was cutting loose again.

The sergeant major worked a self-adhesive smart tourniquet over the wound and activated the system. Without asking, he injected the captain with some Chill. "You're good to go, sir. Stay on the ground and provide cover," he said, handing the captain his rifle.

The firefight had gone wild, and it was looking like they'd set up in a bad place. Nowhere to fall back, and backs against the well deep inside the ship. Greenhill and Davis on the right got rushed. Davis was firing toward center, chasing a mover who kept shifting from desk to desk back in the main room, when Greenhill burned through a heavy charge pack on a cluster getting ready to move up on them. In that same instant an explosive was tossed and rolled right at them.

"Grenade!" shouted Greenhill as he let go of the heavy rifle's sling, stepped forward, and kicked the fragger off in another direction. A near-unseen blur tackled him with all the force a truck, sending him crashing down hard, his weapon pinned between himself and the attacker. The two grappled for control.

It was like wrestling with an invisible man. And a strong one at that. Both of Greenhill's hands were controlled by the powerful figure, so he tried to slam his helmet into what he thought might be the invisible opponent's head. But he missed, and the figure slowly moved him back to the edge of the balcony and bent him backward over the void.

Greenhill felt his helmet slipping from the back of his head, felt his shoulders threatening to dip down as they inched away from the stabilizing balcony rail. It was a long fall to the bottom.

"Need help?" asked Davis as she engaged more. Still busy acquiring targets, not realizing how dire Greenhill's position was. The Savages were closing in groups, firing from cover but unable to get a good angle on the defenders because of all the obstacles and partitions in the div-vied-up office space.

"Grrggghhh!" grunted Greenhill as the invisible war-rior lifted him up into the air.

He knew in the next instant the Savage was going to throw him over the edge. He slammed his knee into the thing's midsection, hoping it had a groin. And though the Savage didn't so much as flinch, its stealth tech fad-ed slightly. Greenhill could for the first time make out the shape of his assailant.

Captain Davis let go of her primary, pulled her second-ary, and capped two rounds in the soldier's head. The first round splashed brain matter out over the dark void of the well and shut off the thing's stealth camo completely. The second round was for good measure.

The dead Savage let go of Greenhill, who tumbled over the balcony railing, screaming.

Davis only barely caught him by his LCE.

Still, Greenhill was much larger and heavier, and in the next instant they were both being pulled down by covet-ous gravity with the very real possibility of going over to-gether. Greenhill folded his legs at the same time that Davis kicked off from the balcony rail, and they both ended up rolling onto the floor in the middle of the hectic firefight.

Two Savages crouch-ran forward, light bending and refracting off their armor in the green of night vision. And then the barrel of a wicked subcompact machine gun was pressing against Greenhill's dark, sweaty cheek. Another was against Captain Davis's midsection.

One Savage chittered frenetically. Electronically. Like several languages saying the same word over and over.

"Kōfuku!"

"Uppgjöf!"

"Surrender!"

"Aistislam!"

"Kapituliacyja!"

And then something that sounded like a long string of ones and zeroes spat out a high speed.

More Savages rushed forward, charging through the gaps in the defenders' firing lines now that Greenhill and Davis were down and gathering themselves. They chittered electronically at one another in their strange mishmash of ancient languages. Their active camo was switching off, revealing Savages like the blue they'd put down beside the shuttle aboveground.

Martin swore, never ceasing to fire. "No surrender!"

Savages went down at point blank. Wild Man shot one in the gut, and it doubled over, its intestines blown away in a dark spray. Makaffie tore another to shreds by rushing forward and pulling the trigger on every shot in his charge pack until the thing was dead by multiple ventilations.

But those who had pushed through on the right flank aimed their weapons at Greenhill and Davis. The one covering Greenhill screamed for the team to put their weapons down. It spoke like no normal human spoke, and in twenty different languages, but its meaning was clear: some of them, or all of them, were coming back as prisoners, and continued fighting meant the deaths of Davis and Greenhill.

And then, from behind them, came a great roar. Rockets flaring, Rechs shot up from the depths of the well and hovered there, jump jets burning blue flame. He was holding a clamshell case and his hand cannon. And he was already firing at the Savages even as he hung in midair.

The first shot from the powerful sidearm vaped the head of the Savage covering Captain Davis. The next two smashed into the rising chest of the one covering Greenhill.

Rechs bumped his jets and landed on the floor, forward of the team, firing into the Savages, who were now fleeing into the darkness. Their rush to take prisoners had cost them too many casualties to stand up to this new wave, this one-man reinforcement.

The Savages switched on their stealth tech again, but their active camo didn't deceive Rechs's HUD. He could see them plain as day and didn't waste time putting rounds in every one he could draw a bead on. The fifty-caliber slugs shot straight through the flimsy office workspace obstacles they tried to cover behind. Only a few Savages made it out of there alive.

In the silence that followed, Rechs walked over to Captain Davis. She was lying on her back, breathing heavily, her face pale and sweaty.

Rechs pulled her to her feet. "You okay?"

She wasn't hit. His armor diagnostics could tell exactly who'd been wounded. But she looked pretty shaken.

Not many people survived close contact with the Savages. She seemed to have a more acute awareness of that fact than most.

She nodded quickly. "I'm fine. I'll be fine."

Rechs handed her the device they'd come for. Its clam-shell carrying case was marked with New Vega's highest security warnings. "Here."

She smiled, but it wasn't a real smile. It had cost her too much to finally hold the object that she'd been sent for. Twenty-three lives. Five nightmare weeks she'd probably never forget. Her command and ship.

Nor would hers be the last such price to be paid in the coming centuries-long war against the Savages.

Not by a long shot.

53

Captain de Macha was slowing the team down. Even with another dose of Chill—which seemed to make him incredibly happy—he was still only able to barely limp along. They didn't encounter more Savages, but as they worked their way back through the ruined ship, Martin and Rechs again took point, clearing the way in case the Savages had set some kind of ambush for their egress.

There was none of that either.

"Not a big fan of going back the same way we came in, sir," said the sergeant major when they made it back to the elevator to take them up level.

Rechs had removed his helmet and was drinking water. It seemed even quieter than before down here—as though some show had gone on hours ago, and now everything had faded into the post-chaos silence that followed such major events. "Know a better way out?"

"It's oh three hundred," said Davis. "And this is the fastest way out."

Rechs knew time was short. He also knew that he had three wounded, and they were running low on charge packs. That was always the case. You never brought enough even when you thought you had. He'd alleviated part of that by redistributing what packs they had and issuing scavenged Savage weapons. Many of them now carried their pulse rifles as well as matte-black assault rifles complete with integrated suppressor system and a bunch of 5.56 ammo. Rounds that he hadn't seen in general usage since Earth, and seldom after.

The bigger problem was a more basic one: the team was tired. Rechs could see it in the way they walked. They had been up too long and fought too much, and a crushing fatigue had settled over the group.

Rechs turned to Davis. "Do you know of a faster way back to the LZ?"

The captain bit her lip pensively, the second time Rechs had seen her do so. "Outside the ship, in the tunnel complex, there's subway access for the commuters who worked under Hilltop. Private line, but ultimately it has access to the main lines, and those crisscross just about everywhere under the city. We could get close to the stadium."

It was a way out. Not the same way they'd come in. Potentially faster than moving on foot above ground.

They could divide up. Rechs and them. He'd go back to the APC and take it down the main tunnel right up to the Savage Nest. Drive in and det. And the APC was rated to handle the effects of a strike, at least for a time. He could put some distance between him and the blast, and let the stars fall wherever they chose to shine.

Rechs told them the plan a split second after deciding. "We're splitting up. Davis, you lead the team down into those subway tunnels and make straight for the LZ. I'm driving the APC into the Savage hulk alone."

"No dice, sir," said the sergeant major plainly. Sweat was coming down his face; he hadn't done a shot of Chill since he'd been hit.

"Yeah," said Greenhill, who'd almost just been thrown to his death. "We in it to win it. Together. Brother and sister, Colonel."

De Macha laughed and waved it all off with a broad and generous sweep of his hand, never mind the gunshot wound in his thigh. He was a true Espanian Cavalier. "This, my friend... this is just a small scratch. I'm good to go, as the sergeant major says." He laughed. "I still have both my hands. Stick a knife in my teeth. I'm... how does UW say it... highly motivated."

"We say that on Spilursa too," said Martin. "But we came from the old Earth—a long time ago. And yeah... I'm in it to win it, sir. We go all the way together."

All the way.

Long time since you heard that, thought Rechs. And long ago. In another life not this one.

He looked to the others. The question plain. The decision theirs.

The Wild Man said nothing, but his coal-dark eyes urged that this killing go on forever and never end.

Makaffie was in too. "This is some weird, wild stuff... uh, sir. I'd like to just get real high and see how it all comes out," he said. He looked like a real killer now with a bando of spare charge packs, magazines, a pulse rifle on his hip, a blaster pistol tucked in his waistband, and a Savage assault rifle slung over his shoulder. And of course he was still shirtless and dirty.

"I got what I came for, Tyrus Rechs," said Captain Davis. "The only way U-Dub would be happier with me now is if I arrested you. Or shot you. They'd pin more medals than I have room for on my navy blues. But I said I'd see this out with you. And I'll take you there. So..."

No one said anything.

"There's still the subway after we drop the nuke," said Makaffie.

It was a chance to see the other side of all this. To maybe make the LZ in time to see the trigger-nuke go off from orbit. To see New Vega destroyed. A loss... but who really cared? The Savages had already taken the world. The survivors, if you could still call them that, were stored in bubble freeze. Doomed. Eventually—in the days, weeks, and years to come—to be unthawed.... and consumed.

Calories.

"Then let's get going," said Rechs.

54

They returned to the APC via the same route that had taken them into the old starship, always expecting a textbook ambush that never came. The hunters, assuming there were more of them, had apparently gone back to their business. The stealth-kitted Savages they had repulsed either hadn't reported contact or were off looking in another section of the massive complex. Or maybe they were still down in the ship.

And Makaffie was careful to keep his voice down.

To Captain de Macha's credit, he complained little, even though he was covered in a sheen of sweat by the time they made it back to the vehicle. "Sometimes when there is nothing left to do but fight..." he gasped as they loaded back in, "then of course... you must fight." But his pain-filled eyes showed that that fight was an excruciating one.

In the APC they were able to top off on charge packs and reload. De Macha was moved inside to the gunner's position, Davis drove, and the rest rode up top. If they had to dismount to clear obstacles or enemies, they would do so under cover of the APC's gun. The APC had a laser-sweep sensor system to augment local radar plus low-light imaging for driving, but for everyone else, it was night vision unless they were riding inside the red-lit interior.

Davis called out the route over the comm as they drove.

"Entering main access tunnel now."

They passed gaping entrances into broad storage chambers and side roads that climbed in spirals or twisted down into the lower levels. Signs indicating directions, warnings, and locations passed by, but all of them were meaningless now. According to Davis, they were looking for "Access Ramp Seven."

"Never woulda guessed all this was under that hill we was up dyin' on yesterday," Andres sighed into the comm.

"Should be just ahead," said Davis, slowing.

"Contact," said Martin, who was hanging off the passenger side. The man's vision was sharp, thought Rechs.

Sure enough, just ahead was a wedge patrol of Savage marines like the ones they'd fought on the surface. Faceless and decked out in combat armor.

"Looks like Original Recipe version," said Sergeant Major Andres. "Not these new boys been showin' up lately. Light 'em up, sir?"

Davis brought the low flat APC to a halt after turning it slightly to the right to provide better cover. The men on top moved around to the side, putting the APC between them and the enemy.

"Light 'em up," ordered Rechs.

De Macha unleashed a fearful barrage of pulse fire from the deadly twin-barreled gun atop the APC. The Savage patrol was cut to pieces within seconds. The barrels fell silent in the darkness of the tunnel a moment later.

"Proceed," said Rechs once the kills had been confirmed.

A few hundred meters on, Captain Davis found the ramp leading to the desired sub-level. It was narrow, the APC spilling out into the opposite lane as they moved farther in the darkness.

A lone overhead light flickered on and off halfway along the ramp. The effect was more unsettling than comforting. Its very existence posed a question that couldn't be answered. Why was it on when everything else was dark?

The path curved, and became almost too narrow because of the vehicle's length, but finally the APC emerged onto a wide subterranean road. The walls here were finished in pristine gray concrete, and all the lights down here were on.

"How come these lights are on?" asked Greenhill.

"Separate generators?" offered Makaffie.

There was no time to consider further.

The APC had just started down this new tunnel when one wall dropped away, revealing a sheer drop with no guard rail, filled with the same bubble storage hives. Thousands of them. At least.

And then Sergeant Major Andres swore. "Savvies!"

From down the road, they were covering in narrow alcoves on the wall opposite the hives. Two ambush teams had already fired man-portable anti-armor rounds. Both rockets jerked up and down as they streaked down the roadway toward the APC.

De Macha slammed his hand down on the APC's IR distracting flares, and they erupted from both front and rear of the APC and shot to the top of the tunnel, trailing burning phosphorous and smoke.

It was the right move to avoid being hit by smart missiles. Almost an instinctual move for the veteran tanker. But that burning phosphorous presented a serious problem for the men outside.

"Move for cover!" shouted Rechs over the comm. "Don't let that stuff fall on you!"

Rechs had seen that happen before. Seen the way it just burned and burned. Like it was trying to dig down to the very soul of the man the bright shining embers latched on to. And then burn all the way through to the other side.

Rechs didn't know whether Captain Davis heard him or not, but she floored it, sending the APC surging toward the Savages and taking the men out of danger of falling phosphorous before any of them had the opportunity to get off. Now he concentrated on hanging on to avoid being thrown.

"Going through!" shouted Davis over the comm. Half a second later the APC reached the far end of the bubble storage devices on the left, and once more the tunnel was enclosed on both sides. Two of the Savages ahead ran right out into the middle of the road, firing weapons on full auto. The APC smashed into one, crushing it beneath the forward right ceramic ball, and clipped the other viciously.

The other Savages stayed in their alcoves as they sprayed automatic gunfire wildly. Rounds struck the APC close enough that Rechs had to drop down behind its bulk to avoid getting hit. There was no opportunity to fire back.

It required everything of those on the outside to merely hold on as they passed rapidly through the shooting gallery.

But the turret controlled by de Macha did its part. The Espanian captain raked the firing Savages, the mounted gun doling out blistering death.

And then the vehicle was past the ambush. For that's what it had to have been: an ambush. The Savages had known they were coming.

"Holy shit," panted Greenhill. "Holy shit."

"Did we lose anybody?" asked Andres. "Anybody fall off?"

"We're good," Rechs said, his HUD accounting for the life signs of each man on the team. Miraculously, they had all survived the vicious gauntlet they'd just run.

"Holy shit," Greenhill said again.

"More ahead!" shouted Davis.

Another open gallery lay ahead, off to the left. And alcoves to the right.

Rechs wondered at the thought of two such successive ambushes. Surely the Savages weren't expecting something big enough and strong enough to punch through even the first one. Maybe it hadn't been an ambush after all. Maybe that had been an outer perimeter guard for what was happening here. Important work. The work of calories.

Floating in the middle of this second gallery was a large dirigible—an airship—made of a Mylar-like material, suspended underneath what looked like a field hospital. Utility trucks, probably commandeered from the New Vegans, were lined up and offloading racks of sedated survivors. Each rack was lined with cages holding the survivors—at least twenty per. They were being loaded onto a conveyor belt that was attached to the floating dirigible.

Giant mechanical mandibles, like something from a child's nightmare of monstrous insects, were working on storage bubbles on the far side of the gallery. Loading sedated humans into the packing chambers within the bubbles.

"Hold your fire!" shouted the sergeant major, sounding exasperated. "We got survivors!"

Savage marines disobeyed the sergeant major's orders and kept shooting from behind the cover of the delivery trucks.

"Do we help 'em?" asked de Macha, smiling at the sergeant major's gallows humor in the face of the enemy. Bullets plinked against the APC's outer hull.

The question required a split-second decision as Davis drove the APC at maximum speed, seeking to angle the vehicle so it took fire away from its outer riders, who were hanging on for dear life on the narrow sideboards.

"Negative," said Rechs over the comm, his voice low and gravelly. "Keep moving. Stay on mission."

A silence fell over the comm as the APC sped forward.

Nobody liked what they had to do.

Nobody liked any of it.

55

The Savages had jackknifed a semi to block their escape a few miles ahead. Or maybe it had simply been left there weeks before when some panicked driver turned hard on the wheel in a desperate attempt to get away from the Savage threat. However it got there, they weren't going to be able to drive through it. Davis applied all four brakes at once and the APC fishtailed across the subterranean road before coming to a halt.

"Sir," said Sergeant Major Andres, "Savvies have cut us off ahead. Count about twenty covering. They just waitin' for range and exposure."

"Sensors are picking up more Savages closing from the rear," de Macha announced from inside the APC. "Maybe from that last gallery or one of the other entrances—I don't know. But they're moving."

Rechs jumped down from the vehicle. "Martin, Greenhill, on me. Use the APC's gun to keep them off our backs while we clear the ones ahead."

The Wild Man went prone on top of the APC, deployed a small tripod, and fired his behemoth rifle at the distant Savages covering behind the semi. He immediately dropped two of the exposed marines and forced the rest behind the tractor trailer's bulk. He scanned for glimpses of legs in the thin space beneath the trailer, then blew out a Savage at the shin and finished it off with a rapid follow-up shot the moment the marine hit the ground.

"Nice work," said Rechs. Because it was nice work. Some of the best shooting he'd seen in his years on the battlefield.

The other men quickly dismounted. Above their heads, the twin-barreled turret began to fire to the rear. It sent long bursts to keep the enemy pinned. Or at least to slow them down. Charge for the turret gun wasn't a problem; as long as the vehicle had power, the gun would continue to operate. Makaffie assisted, firing short controlled bursts at closer targets beneath the turret's current range.

Rechs, Martin, and Greenhill fanned out into a wedge and approached the semi rapidly, covered by the Wild Man's impressive shots. Along the left wall was yet another gallery full of storage bubbles, all of them filled. Thousands of people floating in suspended amber waited for a nightmare in one of their tomorrows. Not yet in a deep freeze. Waiting to become... calories.

Rechs made a knife-edge gesture with his gauntlet for both Martin and Greenhill to sweep left. Then he bumped the jets on his armor and shot toward the right side of the semi. As he neared the rear lift gate, he opened fire.

He kept the hand cannon on auto fire and ran it across all the Savages on that side, hitting several, blowing off limbs and turning heads to gray mists of industrial fluid, brain, and helmet fragments. Return fire connected with his armor, bounced, and flung itself away into the tunnel dark. The blows were like jackhammer shots that forced

Rechs to cover back by the trailer's taillights. As tires blew and refilled with stabilizing emergency foam, he continued to the opposite side of the trailer, wanting to force any pursuing Savages out into the open.

He peeked back around the corner and saw the head of a pursuing Savage marine turn to mist. The Wild Man had landed a perfect shot at range on the newly exposed Savages.

A nasty shot pegged Rechs hard in the chest plate and he ducked back into cover and tried to catch his breath, sinking to a seated position. His armor plating sported a new dent and was still smoking. It would stand up to a lot, but it couldn't hold up against everything.

Martin and Greenhill started murdering the Savages from the other side almost the moment Rechs was hit, overrunning the sole Savage guarding the other marines' flanks before lighting up the rest of the exposed enemy. Greenhill unloaded with everything the heavy assault rifle could spit out, and Martin followed, cleaning up strays, double-tapping any Savages who hadn't yet dropped.

"Clear!" called Greenhill once the last Savage was down.

Rechs struggled to his feet. "Pull back and cover me."

He staggered up and into the vehicle's driver seat. The ignition card had been left in the start-up slot, and in moments Rechs had gunned the accelerator and sent the big semi toward the subterranean canyon at the side of the tunnel. He leapt out seconds before the cab went through a barrier and over the edge. The hitch and connectors snapped, and with a cry of wrenching metal, the

cargo container bent and teetered on the edge as the tractor idled into the abyss.

Rechs picked himself up from the road and stumbled
back to the APC with Martin and Greenhill.

"You all right?" asked Martin.

Rechs made a gesture indicating he was.

Makaffie was still holding position from behind the
APC door, and he and the turret were engaging targets to
the rear. Small bursts now. Nothing sustained. The Savages
were being kept back.

"I think I can push through the opening you made for
us," Davis said. "Hurry and get back on."

They hustled to the sideboards and unconsciously
sucked in their stomachs as Davis squeezed the wide APC
through the gap behind the dangling trailer now only par-
tially blocking the road.

As they continued on, they encountered still more
of the Savage storage racks on the left side. Pantries.
Refrigerators. Little rooms crowding the road, waiting to
be cross-loaded to the waiting hulk. And now the thousands of stored survivors were surely adding up to tens of
thousands.

"Ma'am," said Sergeant Major Andres. Everyone was
listening over the comm as the APC whipped through
the darkness of the tunnel. "How many of these... *rooms*
are there?"

She was silent for a moment. Only the bare hiss of
the comm and the low menacing hum of the vehicle's engines could be heard. She was concentrating on the road.
Driving into the darkness ahead and following the images

laid in front of her by the APC's sensors. When she spoke, it wasn't in her command voice. The voice she'd used to run a starship. And it wasn't in any other voice that she'd used among them yet. The voice that spoke was dead. Devoid of all emotion. Made lifeless by the horrors it had been forced to witness.

"I don't know," she said. "My guess is once they'd captured the major population centers, they started filling it from the bottom up. There may even be other storage sites in other smaller cities across New Vega. I'm not sure."

"They got the whole planet," Martin said, his voice hot. "Bastards took the entire populace."

56

Captain Davis brought the APC to a halt when the lights of another vehicle appeared far ahead, shooting out of the darkness of an intersecting tunnel.

"Kill everything," she ordered. "Go silent."

It was some kind of utility vehicle local to the New Vega military or police force. And right behind it followed a long line of civilian cargo and delivery trucks.

A convoy.

Savage marines rode on top of the cargo and delivery vehicles, at least two or three per, automatic weapons at the ready, scanning the darkness to the sides of the route as each vehicle crossed the tunnel and disappeared on the other side. If not for Captain Davis's quick reaction, pulling over and going dark the instant she saw the growing illumination of the lead vehicle's high beams, they would have been spotted for sure.

"Wonder what that's all about," said Sergeant Major Andres over the comm. Whispering in the darkness.

No one said anything because everyone had a pretty good idea what the convoy was all about. Who was in the vehicles and where they were being taken. But it was de Macha, still under the influence of painkillers and Chill, in high doses, who spoke for them all.

"More survivors. Headed to cold storage bubbles. Very sad for them."

A morose silence passed over the comm net as they waited for the convoy to pass by.

"Each of those trucks must have room for at least twenty... maybe forty of those bastards who lost at hide and seek with the Savvies," opined Makaffie.

"Losers get eaten," said Greenhill sullenly.

As they watched, one of the convoy vehicles pulled over to the side of the intersection and slowed to a stop. Other vehicles slowed too, but continued on around.

Two Savage marines were on top of the stopped vehicle, with a driver behind the wheel. A faceless Savage. The driver slid out and began to kick the front of the vehicle where the engine compartment was.

"Breakdown?" whispered Martin as he watched through his pulse rifle's scope from alongside the APC.

"Must be," said the sergeant major over the comm. "'Cept what would a Savage who's lived all his life in a big ship with all kinds of internal automated transport know about fixin' a ground vehicle?"

"Or how to even drive one?" offered Greenhill.

Now the Savage was tapping the various panels along the front of the truck. Based on the signage, the vehicle had once delivered bread.

In a way, it still did.

"Those ships are big enough to be worlds inside," said Rechs. "Towns and cities and even roads."

"Well, if they don't get it started again, we'll have to either take them out or find another way around," said Captain Davis.

Without a word the Wild Man hauled himself to the top of the APC and crawled along its flat roof, dragging his big weapon forward.

***

Before he'd been the Wild Man, before the years of wandering across the worlds and killing Savages wherever he could find them, before all that and all that would come...

He'd just been some man with a name he didn't want to hear anymore.

But he'd been *her* man.

And that was enough.

The night the Savages came to Stendahl's Bet, the local broadcasts were filled with strange reports of settlements going dark, off-line, incommunicado. Strange lights in the sky. Fires and wrecks. Shooting. Things that made no sense in those first few hours. Things that made all the sense in the world once the Wild Man had the endless hours to look back and replay each detail.

They—him, her, and baby—lived in a farming collective out on the edge of civilization. Or what passed for civilization on Stendahl. It was fall when the Savages came out of the sky. Late fall and winter coming on. Evening dark making the vast spaces of that world cold and quiet.

He often wondered if that was why the Savages had attacked then. In fall. When it was cold. Deep space was cold and lightless. Maybe that was what they were used to. Maybe that was what was best for them.

"We got to go into town, baby," she told him.

They'd been sitting by the sat-caster, listening all day for reports, the few that came through, and the long drone of music-on-demand that filled the in-between times. Waiting for information on what was happening. What could be done. What was true and what was known.

Later in the day, reports of fighting in the bigger cities around Stendahl came in. And then those reports just stopped. And they waited as a cold afternoon turned to early winter evening.

She made tea. Then soup. The baby played on the floor of their stead. They only had so much juice for the generator. The stove in the kitchen and the light from their lamps kept them warm. Or at least, he was warm. She kept folding her arms and saying she was cold. And when the sat-caster network went dead, he took down the big rifle and began to clean it on the kitchen table.

"We should go into town so we can talk to the others," she said. "Find out what in the world is going on."

The dark blue of twilight came through their lone kitchen window. He stood and stared out at the silhouette of rolling plains and the few dark shapes of scraggly trees down near the river. They looked like fingers clutching at the winter sky. But the world inside the kitchen was bright, warm, and everything that home was supposed to mean. Death and danger and darkness would never come here. Not pirates, not armies. And certainly not Savages.

This world, this tiny world, was the opposite of all that they were.

It was human.

"They'll want to make a plan for whatever's happening," she continued. "Maybe an invasion. One of them confederacies—United Worlds—trying to take us over. And you got skills from your time in the military, baby."

He'd never told her. She'd just known. And of course there were the scars. But he'd never told her how he got those either.

In this memory she's not the smoky, cool seductress of death that approves of his killing from high places. She is frightened. She worries her favorite dishtowel between her hands. Pulling it through porcelain fingers.

There is not the *Do another one, babe* siren of snipers in this real moment inside the kitchen on the edge of night.

Because it is the edge of night in more ways than are understood at this particular moment. A darkness is falling, not just across Stendahl, but across its chances. And across the galaxy. The Savages have finally come in from the outer dark between the stars.

"I wish you'd say something!"

From the floor of the kitchen, the baby gurgles and shakes one of his toys.

Her eyes fall to their child, and she looks back at him as he oils the bolt carrier assembly for the big weapon.

"We have to do *something*."

So they do. They dress in their warmest jackets. Fleece and leather. Gloves. The baby bundled in a blanket so cozy you'd think it was protected from all the horrors of the galaxy. And they walk into town. Him carrying the big rifle. Her watching the prairie and the trees. The baby laughing because he knows the world and the galaxy is only this. And that there are no Savages.

In town they hear nothing new. Nothing that hasn't already chewed at the back of their minds.

But old Varney tells them, "It's Savages more likely than less. Invaders from another government would've been telling us to be peaceable by now."

"What will we do?" someone asks.

"Fight," answers the head man all call Varney. "It's all we can do now. We're too far out for other worlds to make it in time. Fight together and we might last where others won't."

On the long late-night walk home through the dark, they see no strange lights in the distance—until they hear the roar of distant artillery out across the prairie. Or rocket strikes. The air is clear, and the altitude is just right, and so this might be happening hundreds of miles away to the north. Near Gallup, or even Crisco. Where the big mag-railyards are. Where the stock is driven in each season for off-world sale when the big lifters come in.

The night sky changes colors with sudden flashes. White and green mostly. Sometimes the flare of red or almost orange shimmering in waves like the Northern Lights. The Savages are using their strange weapons, and the end of everything has come to Stendahl.

At midnight they reach home and an emergency flash text comes through from the rarely used global network.

She's putting baby to bed on that last of all homely evenings. He's started a fire in the fireplace.

He stares at the text.

It's a notice telling him he's being recalled to active duty. Report to Paradise City out near Farthing. The army will force an engagement with the Savages and try to save the planet, or at least some of it, from the invaders.

He has never been a man of words. So he just shows her the text and watches as she begins to cry. She cries because he must go. Like Old Varney said, "Fight together." It's the only way.

They make love. He wonders if either of them really wants to. But they do.

Because it's the last time.

The last night.

The fire stocked and wood brought in so she won't have go out again until daybreak. The baby safe in his crib. This house on the edge of the world is the last safe place in a galaxy descending into madness.

After, her lying in his big arms, tracing the horrible scars he received the last time he was in the army, she says, "You won't let them take us."

"No," he murmurs. Fading. Dreaming of any world for them not this one. Feeling the closeness of her beautiful body.

No.

"You'll be safe here," he tells her. "And I won't let them take you."

He feels her take a breath. One breath. As if there is nothing more to the galaxy than that single, perfect breath, that says... *life*.

Live. You must.

She trusts him.

"Promise?" she asks him.

"I promise."

***

"I promised," he whispered to the big rifle with his chin and face in the usual place, eye two inches back from the scope. Then he breathed and pulled the trigger as he let go of the air.

One of the Savages atop the distant bread truck exploded from the sternum up. The massive twenty-millimeter round just ruined him. These were the Wild Man's most special loads. They disintegrated everything they hit as the round fractured inside the target and exploded in every direction at probably six to eight hundred miles per hour. There was no way to know, really. That was just his guess.

The concussive *BOOOOM* filled the subterranean tunnel. Echoing and reverberating across the deep and hollow spaces of the way down dark beneath the corpse of New Vega City.

Round ejected and everyone shouting over the comm. Shouting both "Who fired?" and an instant later, when their minds caught up with their mouths, "What's he doing?"

In the same horrible moment of everything going off the rails.

The reticles inside the Wild Man's scope found the other marine whose only move had been to stand now that his comrade had just disintegrated from the waist up. The Savage marine had just jerked his rifle up to start engaging targets it couldn't detect when the Wild Man fired his next round.

This one went low but still connected. It blew the leg off the marine at the hip, taking a good chunk of the groin with it. The Savage promptly went helmet forward and over the side of the truck. Landing on the road at the exact wrong angle if one didn't want to have a broken neck. Who knew what that did to these things? They didn't have necks to break.

But whatever had happened, it wasn't moving.

And that was good.

He ejected the shell.

The Savage driver in the cab was trying to make the engine turn. Maybe get away and warn the others? It didn't matter.

Shot three was a head shot. Blowing helmet and brain across the inside of the cab. The round had been moving so fast that the body didn't even move in one direction or another. The head disappeared, and the body of the Savage marine driver remained upright—as though the only thing wrong was that its head was missing.

"Did you give him the order to fire, sir?" shouted Andres, knowing damn well that no such order had been given. His tone was businesslike and military, ready to instill order into the developing chaos before it got completely out of hand.

"Negative," said Rechs, who was crawling on top of the APC. Crawling toward the big sniper to stop the firing. Scrabbling really, as fast as he could. Each shot was a potential "come and get me" cry to every Savage for kilometers and kilometers.

But the Wild Man was already sliding off the front end of the APC and running for the stalled delivery truck. Ejecting a shell and sliding in a new one as fast as you please. His long loping strides taking him forward quickly.

"What do we do, sir?" Andres asked.

But Rechs was already running. Not to catch the out-of-control giant. But to support him in case he ran into more Savages they hadn't seen. Yelling at himself because this wasn't the mission. Knowing he should have taken the trigger-nuke into the Nest by himself. It would have been much easier that way. Even if he hadn't survived. He could have detonated at any moment and probably ruined the ship. He *definitely* would have ruined the planet. For the Savages, and humanity.

The APC started forward, cruising up slowly to speed, pursuing the two running men. But Wild Man made it to the stranded truck first.

Rechs could hear the big man breathing heavily, gasping something. Words. At the time he didn't register it. He was too busy scanning the four directions of the intersection for any kind of Savage response to the shots.

The big man reached the back of the truck, smashed the lock with the butt of his rifle, and jerked open the cargo doors.

It was then that Rechs heard it. Heard what the sniper was mumbling almost incoherently.

"I promised."

"I promised."

"I promised."

Rechs turned and saw what lay beyond the open doors.

Survivors huddling in the dark of the cargo vehicle. Scared and dirty. Staring wildly at the big man who was crying and repeating that he'd promised.

57

Makaffie was working on the delivery truck's ignition cards. The little gnome had lifted the maintenance hood and was sticking butt-out and going on about it always being the "tarned ignition card!"

A moment later he had it out and was inspecting it, squinting behind his thick glasses at its surface. Then he spit on it, rubbed it along the leg of his dirty fatigues, and threw himself into the guts once more to reinstall it.

"We need to get off this road ASAP," said Andres with no small amount of urgency.

Davis had left the APC to plot their next move with them. Greenhill and Martin had taken up overwatch positions to guard the two avenues the Savages had used in their convoy. And the Wild Man was standing near the civilians, who were alternately thanking him and sobbing. Several had come forward to hug him, and he seemed to awkwardly endure these overtures, made all the more difficult because he was so large and because he would not let go of his rife.

The civilians' leader was a thin, almost emaciated woman. She came hesitantly over to Rechs, Andres, and Davis.

"I don't know who you are... but... I just want to say thank you. I thought we were done for. Thank you."

"You're safe now, ma'am," said Andres, trying to deal with her quickly and get things moving. He knew that they were anything but what he'd just promised.

"We... uh..." she continued, heedless of the NCO's desire to hustle. Swallowing hard and trying to find the words she needed. Her eyes were hollow and haunted. But there was a fire. Deep down and awakening. "We come from a sea-ag research center out on the Marguez Sea. We've been hiding from the Savages for weeks. In communication with the resistance until that collapsed about two weeks ago. We... we... had a pretty good idea what was..."

She stopped. Turned back to the others and waved her hand, sobbing silently, her bony shoulders heaving once. Then she caught herself.

"We know what's going on down here. We knew where they were taking us. I'll be honest..." Big tears filled her haunted eyes. "I didn't have much hope left. Not for our world. Not even for us."

Rechs stood there listening and running through the HUD's map functions. Truth be told, he was busy trying to find a way for them to drive themselves out of here. So that they could get back to the mission.

Then he heard the sergeant major say, "We'll get you outta here, ma'am."

"What about the rest?" she asked. "Half the planet's down here. That was the resistance's last estimate."

"Ah..." began the sergeant major. "We don't have a plan for that... at present, but... uh... we're going to do our best."

She nodded, thanked them again, and returned to the cluster of survivors.

"There's no way they have half the planetary population down here," said Captain Davis. "Not that it really matters how many—it's still far more than we can help. We couldn't rescue them if we tried."

"I know that, ma'am. But... what are we gonna say right now?" Andres kept his voice low so the survivors wouldn't overhear. "We got to move or we'll be joining them in those bubbles before long."

Rechs spoke.

"Sergeant Major, get the truck ready to move. I'll take Sergeant Greenhill and Specialist Martin in the APC. We'll go for the Nest. That should draw their fire. I want you and Captain Davis to get the survivors out of here. Access that private government subway the captain mentioned. Commandeer a train, drive the tracks, or make them all march and leave the stragglers. I don't care, but make it back to the LZ. We'll plant the nuke and join you by the time the *Chang* arrives."

The sergeant major seemed unsure about this sudden change of mission. Not unwilling. But unsure.

"Make it happen, Sergeant Major. You came here with the Twenty-Fifth to rescue the survivors. You can rescue these. And I came here to destroy that ship. I'll do that."

The sergeant major nodded slowly. Then he gave a "Roger" and went off to make it happen.

Captain Davis turned toward Rechs. But she didn't face him directly. She cleared her throat and looked off into the darkness of one of the tunnels.

"I'll say this once. And then you can do whatever it is that you're going to do. Which, because you're Tyrus Rechs... well, that means what it means. Doesn't it?"

Rechs said nothing.

"There are probably millions of survivors on this planet, right now, in various states. Not everyone died in the fighting, and if they didn't die, and they weren't captured, then they're alive. Somewhere. If you set off your trigger-nuke, and if what I know about those things is correct... then yes. You'll probably take out the Savage ship. Fine. But have you considered that this entire world, as every hydrogen molecule cascades into a chain nuclear reaction, will become lifeless within an hour?"

She stopped. Waiting for Rechs to say something. Or indicate some human gesture from behind his immobile armor. But he did nothing and said nothing.

"Are you really willing to kill so many innocent people in the process, Rechs? This isn't some backwater planet with just a few thousand from a colony ship still getting their footing. This is New Vega. You will kill millions. I'm sure of that, Tyrus. I'm one hundred percent positive. The only thing I'm asking is... and I've..."

She stopped and turned away from him, lowering her head and pinching her eyes. He heard her suppress some cry. Maybe.

"I think I've earned at least the right to ask what I'm going to ask next. I lost my crew. My ship. Here. Hell"—she laughed and threw out her arms—"probably even my career. And believe me, I feel shallow just saying that in light of the situation of the people that crazy man just rescued.

You'd have to have known me before the last five weeks to understand what it all meant to me. How far I was willing to go to do whatever it takes for one more pay grade. But... the last six weeks have changed me. *Life* has changed me. Every life is precious in a galaxy that does nothing but chew us up and spit us out. And we keep trying, Tyrus. We keep throwing ourselves into hyperspace to beat the odds. Running into hostile and strange worlds, deadly aliens, and even our nightmare selves. Why?"

She stopped. As though waiting for an answer. As though realizing how foolish it would be to expect one. Not from Tyrus Rechs. War criminal. Or savior. Depending on whom you asked.

"We almost beat them here. The Coalition did. We almost beat them. And I know there were mistakes made. But that's not the best of us. That was a bunch of rink-knocker glory hounds seeking to promote themselves. Everyone looking out for their own skin. We didn't send our best. Not by a long shot. And if we did... well, then maybe we need to get better. But nuking worlds into useless oblivion isn't the answer. The answer is we get good and beat the Savages *without* resorting to doomsday weapons, because one day, Tyrus... one day, we'll be down to one last world. Just like Earth once was before we seeded the galaxy. Is *that* when we start fighting? When there's almost nothing left to fight over?"

She stopped.

Made a face that said she was disgusted with herself and was about to walk away. But she didn't.

"I watched you lead," she said. "I watched these men, and myself, fight under you. I even heard them talking about you when they thought you were the colonel. Where the idiots who ran their little attack yesterday failed... you'd have won. If you had been in charge, things would have been different. So I'm asking you, Tyrus... no, I'm begging you... let's leave. I'll help you forge... an... a force. Even if the other governments won't support it. A foreign legion. And we'll come back here and beat the Savages on the ground and pull those people out of the storage bubbles. We save this world... then we can save the galaxy. Because, Tyrus Rechs... every life... every life is damn important. The galaxy has an edge, and it's always trying to kill us. Every day."

58

Davis stood back, watching for some change she'd effected in the armored man and known war criminal standing in front of her. Some sign that she'd... well, not necessarily changed the fate of the galaxy, or even of this planet... but that maybe, just maybe... she'd changed one man's heart.

And perhaps that was all the difference it actually took to change the galaxy.

Tyrus Rechs removed his battle-scratched and worn helmet. The face beneath it was just as stoic as the iron mask of death the helmet presented to every enemy the galaxy could throw at one person. What she saw was a man slightly into middle age. Normal almost to the point of being nondescript. A professional soldier. No more and no less than all the others who served in all the different military organizations throughout the hyperdrive-connected worlds. In that, he was like them all, and you would have been hard-pressed to pick out anything particularly remarkable about him.

Other than the eyes.

It was the gunfighter-blue eyes that made him different. Not because they were blue. No. Not that at all. But because they'd been everywhere there was to go. Seen everything there was to be seen. Even the things you didn't want to see and hoped you'd soon forget. In those eyes there was that, and all the rest of it too.

People always remembered the eyes of Tyrus Rechs when recalling some happenstance meeting in some unlikely combat backwater. They were like looking into a well of endless worlds you'd never know the deeps of.

And then he began to answer her. And each word he spoke was like a gunshot that slammed into her and made her realize how little she understood. Of him. The conflict. And the galaxy.

"Stark 247."

That's how he began. The words meant nothing to her. And probably no one else living in the galaxy at the current moment in its turn about the spiral understood their significance anymore.

"Fifty years after the destruction of Mars," continued Tyrus, "I was on a scout trader working security along the old Bandos Run. Big Denver-class Q-freighter. We were running first contact and survey out that way for the New Horizon Company. Captain was doing trade where he could. The ship's astrogator picked up a previously unsurveyed world that looked life-habitable. It was a short jump from our last destination, so the captain made for it. His name was Stark. It was the two hundred and forty-seventh world he'd surveyed."

Tyrus Rechs paused and looked away. Watched the others working on the wheeled vehicle truck as though he had little confidence they'd ever get it started. And with an apprehensive conviction that at any moment they'd get jumped by more Savages and everything would get just a little bit harder.

Without looking back at Davis, he began to speak again. Low and just between the two of them. But the words were powerful in their clarity and truth. They dispelled what was known and the fiction of history, because, as she'd come to understand... she was talking to an eyewitness. No slick reproduced entertainment manufactured by the winners. No agenda-driven scholarly tome that begged to be taken seriously just because of its price tag in the store.

"On all spectrums the planet looked dead. No signatures. But as we got close, we were seeing structures. No life, but structures. At first we thought... dead civilization that nuked itself out of existence. We'd seen that before. But this society was on par with Earth in her heyday. Still had operational satellites running in degrading orbits. Cities easily could have topped out at twenty million. Estimated global population of at least seven billion. And there wasn't a single living thing we could find.

"We flew the surface for about two weeks. Setting down inside cities that hadn't heard the sound of an engine in years. There'd been a fight of some sort in a few of the cities. Nothing major. No global nuclear exchange between factions. So we looked closer. Went in and checked out the buildings. Stark wanted to find out what had happened.

"From their art we could tell they'd been equine humanoids. Horse-men, we called them. Beautiful art. Advanced early-stage solar exploration. But no tech anywhere. From a simple circuit and wiring all the way up to their computer systems, it was all missing. Completely stripped and gone across the entire planet."

"How?" asked Davis, her voice tight with emotion, hanging on the story.

"It was a mystery. One we didn't think we'd solve because of a mandatory rendezvous window closing in on us. The captain made his report on our last orbital pass.

"And then... almost by accident, we spotted it." Rechs turned his head back to her, staring at her with those depthless blue eyes that had seen everything there was to see. Done everything that needed to be done when no one else was willing to do it.

"Out in the desert wastes we spotted the remains of a large camp, along with a rough cargo star port that had been built in a hurry. Something like that was well beyond this civilization's ability. Extra-planetary launch was still a big effort for them. It was out of place.

"So we set down and explored it. We found prison camps hundreds of miles wide. And cramped quarters even at that. There were anchor pads for micro-forge printers where raw materials could be broken down and packaged for long-term storage, like for stellar flight."

Davis rubbed her shoulders as if the tale was making her cold. "The Savages had that tech before they left Earth."

Rechs nodded. "Then we found the ovens. And the pits. Trenches, really. We put it all together after that: Savages had set down on that world and stripped it clean.

"We documented everything we could, then left. I followed the investigation for a long time afterwards. A scientist with a knack for history ran the planetary research for twenty-two years, just putting the pieces together."

Davis inclined her head and squinted at Rechs. She'd thought she misheard him when he mentioned the destruction of Mars. And she'd wondered why she'd never heard of Stark 247. She stood now wondering just how old the man before her was, but she didn't dare ask the question and break up his narrative. This was the most she'd ever heard Tyrus Rechs speak—by orders of magnitude.

"On the day when we stood there looking at all the cages that ran for those hundreds of miles, and listened to the wind moaning across the plain and through the tattered camps, as we looked down at rivers of bones... we didn't understand it all. But in the end we figured it out. It just took time.

"You see, about the time Earth hit Mars with a crust-buster to restore order to the home system, the Savages discovered Stark 247. They set down with a small flotilla of ships. At first they tried to convince the equii—that's the name the scientist gave them—that they were friends come from another world to help. The equii fell for it, and in time the Savages were worshipped as gods. Which was fine by them. They already think they're gods. It suited them. And for the next thirty years they played factions off one against the other until they controlled the entire planet through a complex overstate.

"Then they built the camps and said that anyone who didn't think like them was mentally ill and needed to be... reeducated. But really they were just death camps. And a little more: a factory of sorts, along with a shipping terminal. Large sections of the population over the course of many years began disappearing to the camps with the help of equii 'loyalists.' These loyalists worked a whole production queue set up to break down every technological material on-planet and package it for long-term storage during space flight. It was all shuttled up to the hulk in orbit until nothing was left.

"Probably not more than ten thousand Savages in that hulk. They made the equii turn on themselves and assist in their own genocide. And everyone thought they were doing it for the greater good. But the Savages couldn't have cared less about any of that."

"They needed supplies," said Davis, looking around as if expecting to see more Savage marines walking right into their midst. "Just like these."

"Yeah," said Rechs. "So they stopped over for thirty years to top off their inventory, like they were at some roadside market and power station."

"And the... equii? They never even resisted? Never fought back?"

Rechs checked his hand cannon. "By the time the equii came to their senses, it was too late. That scientist speculated that the last of them perished a good five years before the Savages finally pushed off for deep space again."

"I don't understand. They had a developed world. Why not just... make their little Utopia there?"

"You know why."

"No," said Davis, shaking her head. "I don't."

"The answer is easy and no one likes it because they want to think there's some other reasonable explanation to the madness... but there isn't. Trust me. I know better than anyone. The answer is because they're not human anymore. The Savages gave that up for whatever they've found out there in the dark. So they spent those last five years strip-mining on a scale we've never seen, and they poisoned every river and ocean doing it. We thought it was just the lay of the land when we were first circling. But it wasn't. They killed the equii, then killed all life on the planet. You can still go there. It's a dead world. It's ruined. But it's there. That's the Savages."

He paused and watched her. Like he was looking for something that wasn't disbelief because he didn't care whether she believed him or not. Like he was looking to see if she was someone who'd do something about what he was telling her. If she was one of the rare few who cared enough to wake up. Or if even now her mind was trying to find a way to go back to sleep and let someone else handle the Savage problem. Which was most people as far as Tyrus Rechs was concerned. He'd learned that from experience.

"They've progressed beyond all this." His voice was stone-cold truth. He spoke slowly, clearly. Making sure she was getting every word and that there was no mistake. Because this was the important part. This was the part she needed to hear.

"They cannot be given an inch, a moment, even a week to fester. If you find them, you destroy them as fast as possible, because they are masters of exploiting your weakness. I've seen it all. I've worked with others. I've watched people try to bargain with them, reason with them, deal with them. And in the end, it's the same. They're destroyed or they win. I've personally seen them ruin a dozen human worlds, three alien worlds, and four undiscovered species' worlds that were like stumbling into a graveyard where there should have been a town. The galaxy is a big place that doesn't talk a lot. Even among the Coalition worlds. Just imagine all the things they've done and gotten up to out there in the dark where we've never been. They've been out there a long time, and they risk destruction every time one of their hulks shows itself to strip all that tech and raw materials. What are they doing out there?"

Davis turned down her head, then looked back up at Rechs as he continued.

"What we remember about the time they left Earth is fuzzy at best. Things were falling apart. Keeping records wasn't a priority. Survival was. But most accept that there were over three thousand lighthugger-class colony vessels. Sure... some died out there. Found the wrong civilization to mess with. Hit a star. Wiped themselves out. But out of three thousand... that leaves plenty that have survived. And the one thing in common—the one thing—is complete insular belief. Total xenophobia. Even for other Savages. We aren't human to them. And they're not even human anymore."

"Until now."

"How's that?"

"Total xenophobia for other Savages... until now."

Rechs grunted. "Until now."

He rolled his shoulders, feeling the tightness in his muscles. "I'm going into the Savage hulk today, and I'm going to blow it sky-high. Because killing more Savages is the only way to save the galaxy. And if I die here... then I die doing everything I could. And maybe someone else will go through what I've been through and realize how important it is that we kill them as fast as possible wherever we find them. Whenever we meet them. However we can. Total annihilation, or the galaxy will never go forward. They'll always be there feeding on us and ruining worlds faster than I ever could. Because if we lose, think about it, if we lose and if they win and go out there and find the other big stellar civilizations we haven't, then all those other civilizations will ever know about Earth, and humanity, is that we are utter and complete monsters. Because it'll be the Savages standing in for us. Nightmares made real. If for no other reason, forget our survival, then we must stop them from eating the entire galaxy like the locusts they really are. They will never stop. They'll just go on doing every world just like they did Stark 247."

Rechs clamped his jaw shut and swallowed. He felt confused by all this. By his need to say it. To tell it to someone other than Sulla. It was a month's worth of talk for him babbled out in the span of a few minutes. But he needed the captain to know. To understand what he was doing.

Because, deep down, he knew this was his last ride.

Makaffie hopped down from the engine compartment and told Greenhill to "Give her a try!"

"Win, lose, or draw," finished Rechs, "my contribution to all this is that I deny these Savages the right to the galaxy, one nuked planet at a time. No one man can save the galaxy—that's a fool's dream. But a million of us committing a million small acts of defiance against the edge... that might do something. And until everyone catches up... here I stand. And that's enough for me. If I have to kill everyone on this planet just to kill them... then yeah, that's what I'll do."

Horror. That was what was on her face. Her eyes. Her lips barely parted. Nothing like a dramatic silent scream. But the stark raving horror of what she'd just been told was there because there was nothing made up about anything he'd told her. No hyperbole. The near emotionless voice of Tyrus Rechs was pure truth. No more, no less. Like some needle that pointed toward true galactic north no matter what you did to it.

She put her slender hand to her mouth, then lowered it just as quickly. She tried to compose herself.

"How were you on a ship fifty years after Mars?" she asked, not knowing how to address anything else but the long years this war criminal was claiming to have lived. "That was hundreds of years ago."

Tyrus Rechs stepped close so that no one could hear what was said between them. He could see that she thought he was insane. A madman babbling about time machines and secret conversations with God. His eyes were blazing with fury. Fury at her. Fury at the galaxy. Fury for the Savages and what they'd done to everything.

"A sect of Savages did things to me—things that gave me the same long life they had. Back when I was a Ranger with the old US military. When they made me their slave on a lighthugger called the *Obsidia*."

59

Two lone headlights appeared from down the tunnel. At first it seemed, at least to Captain de Macha, who was pulling some quick primary maintenance on the APC's turret, that it was a lone ground vehicle approaching. Just two headlights. But when the headlight on the right split off from the one on the left, it became clear that it was some sort of motorcycle pair streaking toward them at high speed.

Greenhill and Makaffie had just gotten the delivery truck started when Savage gunfire erupted from the bikes. Both of them streaked in at incredible speed, firing at the rescued survivors who hovered near the vehicle's cargo door. The wounded and dead fell to the ground; others screamed or froze in horror at this new assault right at the moment they thought they'd been rescued.

Rechs returned fire, helmet in one hand, hand cannon in the other. The two bikes raced directly toward the crowd as if planning to drive right through them, full bursts opening up from mounted submachine guns on the fronts of their squat and long cycles.

Captain de Macha jumped down to get the survivors out of the way, wincing through the Chill at the jarring pain this sent into his leg. A burst of gunfire caught him and sent him sprawling along the dark subterranean road. But it also diverted the speeding attacker, who had to maneuver to miss him.

"Macha!" shouted Andres. "Macha! Damn it."

De Macha's last action had saved most of the survivors from being hit directly by gunfire and then run down as an afterthought.

A second later both bikes were red taillights moving into the darkness of the tunnel.

But more were coming in fast.

"Get them loaded now!" shouted Rechs at the soldiers and civilians as he slammed his helmet over his head. Pneumatic seals cleared and engaged. Internal HUD was active and showing targeting data. Behind them, the two initial attackers were turning back for another pass. A sort of tightening of the noose.

"Switch places!" Greenhill shouted to Makaffie.

Instead of listening to the clear, concise commands that would save their lives, the panicked survivors scattered everywhere while Greenhill and Martin did their best to cover and corral them. Makaffie gunned the delivery truck's engine.

Rechs tried to fire at the two closing bikers, Savage marines in light scout armor and faceless mirrored helmets, but survivors ran across his line of sight blocking any kind of effective engagement picture. So instead he kicked one biker as the scout Savage passed by and sent the rider careening into a wall. The bike exploded in a fireball behind him, causing the survivors to scream even more than they already were.

"He's dead, sir!" shouted Andres, who had dashed through the chaos to assist the downed Captain de Macha.

The second wave of bikes was now streaking in at full speed, firing wild and indiscriminately at both vehicles, the road, and any targets running in the tunnel black.

Rechs made his way to the APC, firing where he could get shots off and assessing the situation. Their quiet yet tense repairs inside the tunnel of just a minute before had now turned into a carnival of chaos and explosions punctuated by gunfire. Rechs had no idea what anyone's status was or where they were. He found himself wishing he'd skipped the long talk and just gotten them all moving.

"Sound off!" he ordered over the comm as he covered behind the door of the APC, firing barking bursts at passing riders.

"Covering at the truck," said Martin breathlessly. Automatic pulse fire reverberated in both real-time and over the comm feed. "Engaging!" he gasped.

A second later Greenhill added a terse, "Same here, Colonel!"

"Behind the wheel and ready to roll!" shouted Makaffie enthusiastically. If he was afraid, it didn't show in the slightest. In fact his voice indicated he somehow believed that an epic road trip to a fabled rock concert was about to begin.

"Andres!" shouted Rechs, knocking down a Savage rider with a brutal burst from the hand cannon at extremely close range. Several rounds struck the mounted marine, and the bike went down as the rider went tumbling across the pavement.

"Loading survivors in!" said Andres. Then, breathlessly—"We good to go, sir!"

"Get them out of here!" ordered Rechs.

He ducked inside to check the APC. Captain Davis had gone forward toward the driver's controls. His mind ran through who was left, and for some reason he couldn't think of who he was missing... until Wild Man fired with a cacophonic boom that echoed down the tunnel, racing off into dark and hidden spaces like the bellow of some ancient monster.

The fuel tank of a closing bike erupted in explosive fire, spraying hot fuel across road and rider. Incredibly the burning bike kept rolling even as its rider, full aflame, tried to dismount, flames crawling greedily across his armor.

Another bike zoomed in at the big sniper. Wild Man merely smacked the attacker in the helmet with the butt of his rifle, and the rider crashed a short distance later.

"We're leaving!" Rechs shouted.

But the big sniper seemed to have his own plan. He jogged toward the bike he'd just unmanned, picked it up, and stomped the starter, firing it up. He slung his rifle and gave Rechs a thumbs-up.

Good enough, thought Rechs, and sealed the APC.

"Get us out of here!" Rechs said to Davis at the controls.

A moment later the vehicle throttled up and lurched forward. Automatic gunfire ricocheted off its hull.

Rechs squeezed past the nuclear doomsday weapon and toward the turret control station.

"Where're we going, Tyrus?" Davis asked, as though giving him another chance to spare the planet and the frozen population from a self-propagating thermonuclear annihilation. Daring Rechs to be hard enough to actually make the call she knew he'd already made.

Rechs was still busy moving into the gunnery station, no easy feat in armor, when he noticed two little twin girls, dirty and shaking. He'd seen them in the crowd of survivors. In the chaos of the attack they must have fled into the APC, seeking safety in any cubbyhole they could find as the monsters that had devoured their family, friends, and everyone they'd ever known came howling out of the darkness.

And now they were headed with him on a one-way mission to deliver a trigger-nuke into the belly of his sworn enemies.

One screamed and buried her face in her sister's dirty jacket, mistaking Rechs for one of the Savages. The other stared at Rechs, hard and cold, daring him to hurt her sister. Forcing her fear to the side in one last act to save the last person she had left.

Aw hell, thought Rechs.

And then, over comm...

"I said where are we headed, Rechs?"

The war criminal looked at the face of the defiant girl from behind his enclosed helmet—or bucket, as he liked to think of it.

"Continue on mission, Captain Davis," Rechs sighed. Resolute. Unchanging in a galaxy that seemed to want to change with every second. "We're still hitting the Savages."

60

Comm faded quickly as the two vehicles headed off in different directions. The last thing Rechs heard was Makaffie swearing exuberantly as Greenhill and Martin engaged pursuing targets from their tenuous positions on the delivery truck turned evac cattle wagon. The screams of the rescued survivors competed with the weapons fire in the background.

But the APC had problems of its own. It was impossible to tell how many of the Savage bikers had broken off to follow them—Rechs wasn't even sure how many were out there to begin with—but it was clear that it was a *lot* of them, and they were swarming. Perhaps Savage sensors were attuned to detect the chemical and energy signatures of the trigger-nuke. That would explain the response and pursuit.

"Forty meters to a hard right!" shouted Davis over the comm. "Hang on!"

Rechs was having a hard time acquiring targets on the guns' control screen because the Wild Man on the bike was mixed in and firing at Savages with a blaster pistol he'd picked up somewhere. Maybe from the bike's former rider. And when he wasn't doing that, he was turning high-speed cycle racing into a contact sport as the pursuit shot through half-illuminated tunnels beneath the battle-ravaged city above.

Rechs got a clear field for half a second along the portside aft arc of the fleeing APC. He opened up with both barrels blazing. Bright fire smashed into three Savage scout riders, riddling them with high-energy pulse shots and igniting their bikes. Parts and wheels went flying away and behind the APC, falling all over the tunnel back trail and filling the tunnel with black smoke, and for a moment Rechs wondered if he hadn't jammed the Wild Man's game. But then the clear and distinctive outline of the big sniper filled the IR overlay, shooting through the smoke and flames in his commandeered cycle.

And if anything, it seemed they now had even more Savage scout riders in pursuit.

"They've probably figured out we're carrying the ball!" shouted Davis over the howl of the of the APC's straining twin turbines.

Rechs knew navy rats liked to call the big nuclear firecrackers "balls." And she was probably right. The Savages had to know it would eventually come to this. If they were working together, as it now seemed they were, then they would know how he'd dealt with their kind in the past.

Not for the first time did Rechs wish he'd just faded during the retreat after the initial battle and set out to do this all on his own. The opportunity for mission success had been highest at that pivotal moment—whether he'd lived or died.

The APC pulled three gees and turned on a dime as all four ball-wheels heaved the vehicle in a new direction at top speed. Inertial gravity decking took some of the load, but the sudden drag on facial muscles made it decidedly evident that hard gees were being pulled.

One of the girls—the one he assumed was younger, because the angry one was clearly the dominant—tried to scream at the sudden shift in direction, but the breath was yanked from her chest. The angry one clearly felt it too, and she glared bloody murder at Rechs, indicting him as a stand-in for all the wrongs of the last six weeks that had befallen her and her sister.

Rechs understood that.

And he liked her for it.

She'd fight the galaxy hard for what was hers. And that was precisely how humanity had to behave if they were going to make it out of all this. The galaxy was loaded with civilization-enders. Ignoring them didn't make them go away. Fighting them did.

And in the end, if it, the big it, was going to take you... then make it pay. Always.

Despite the pull, Rechs nodded at the defiant little girl who refused to die, making eye contact. Willing her to know they wouldn't die in this moment of something they'd probably never experienced before in their entirely too-short lives. That there would be a next moment, and that he would buy those moments for them until he was no longer able.

Her gaze didn't soften, but the look in her eye as the gees reached their peak, trying to crush them all, indicated that she'd accepted his contract.

He could make no promises for any of the moments that lay beyond the next desperate ones. But that seemed to be enough for her. Or maybe not. Rechs wasn't particularly good with kids.

Though Captain Davis was probably used to flying starships as opposed to driving ground combat vehicles, she was still a pro. And just as the hard-turn moment seemed like it might last forever, like all the worst fears of the little girls would come true and the black well forming at the edges of their vision might just grow and swallow them forever... the moment passed.

The vehicle shot forward along a narrow circular tunnel. Accelerating hard to outrun the monsters that came for them.

Rechs dragged his mind away from consuming unconsciousness and scanned the mounted gun's targeting screen for the signature of the Wild Man. Nothing appeared.

He watched the circular tunnel disappearing in banded illuminated lengths behind them.

Still nothing...

And then the Wild Man raced into the tunnel and right up onto the curving wall. Four Savage scout riders followed while others missed the turn or made it badly, spilling from their bikes amid showers of sparks like bright fireworks with chemical ignition trails.

"This is a venting access," announced Davis over the comm. "Gate controls are down. Brace for impact!"

Rechs hadn't strapped in, and neither had the little girls. And there was no time. He grabbed them both, one with each gauntlet, and jammed his legs against the gunnery bulkhead. The vehicle surged forward and smashed through something amid two shrieking screams and a groan of rending metal. The sound of a witch's brittle fingernails raked the outer hull of the vehicle that protected them.

"Damn it!" Rechs swore as the girls' high-pitched shrieks flared across his helmet. He swore not because the sound hurt his ears, but because they were here, and they had no place in this horrible moment.

And then the APC was weightless. Falling.

Sudden uncertainty once more.

Because who knows how far it will fall, he thought.

It crashed onto a new surface and continued forward.

"Sorry!" said Davis from the controls. "Unavoidable. But now it's a straight run ahead to the Nest. Let's hope they left a light on!"

Rechs was still clutching the two girls to him. Both had stopped screaming, but their eyes were squeezed tight shut. Then the youngest, the one he'd assumed was the most timid, looked up at him, her big dark eyes filled with tears.

"Don't be mad at us!"

"What?" asked Rechs.

"We just came looking for our brother," said the older. "He's all we have left."

And he knew in that moment that they'd faced fear and real monsters to find the last of their own. That they'd been brave enough to try. Even though there was fear. Which is what bravery is.

"I'm not," said Rechs, letting them go and moving them over to the troop seats. "I'm not mad. Strap in."

He looked back at the targeting screen. There was no sign of the Wild Man.

61

The Wild Man wasn't thinking about her smile when he plowed into the four remaining cycle scouts as he came down the side of the curving tunnel after the hard turn.

All he saw was red murder.

And here was the chance to get four for one even if it cost him everything.

Fair enough. A good trade on any given day.

Someone had once told him, some trader or storekeeper when they'd figured out what his Savage hunting game was, they'd told him vengeance made you blind. Because in the end, that's all you saw and everything was about that. Even when it wasn't.

Like that's a bad thing, he thought now as he slammed the bike into all four Savages. He flung himself from the bike moments before impact, having braked just enough to manage a non-fatal rolling landing. It wasn't that he wanted to save himself—he just wanted to end a few more enemies in the last of whatever remained to him.

That was enough. Fair trade.

Two Savages were dead. Wrecked all over the long tubular passage. Ruined by their speeding bikes that had suddenly lost control. And two were down and slowly getting up.

For a big man he moved fast, like a bear suddenly coming to life to chase and hunt you down no matter how swiftly you ran. He was like that as the fight began. No longer a wild man. Now a wild animal.

His first instinct was to go for the one on his right. He pulled his rifle off his back with no time to spare as the Savage rose to one knee and pulled a sidearm. Wild Man fired from the hip and blew the Savage marine in half. And then the second Savage slammed into him, knocking him to the floor. Which was a big mistake for the marine. Like some liquid snake that had only ever known wrestling reversals, the big man was on top of the armored marine almost instantly, both paws grabbing at the Savage's helmet, slamming it into the hard gray concrete. Again and again and again...

"See that, darlin'?"

I see it, babe.

The Wild Man watched his own image in the dull reflective sheen of the faceless helmet. Watched himself go from far away to up close as he raised the marine's head off the concrete floor, then suddenly rush away as he slammed the helmet down with a brutal shove.

And again...

And again...

His eyes were like a mad demon's.

And when he'd finished, the helmet had just come to pieces. As had the brain inside.

He came to himself and stood. His body suddenly breaking out into a cold sweat as he returned to the reality of the chase through the tunnel system and the realization that the APC had gone on without him. Certain that he was dead. Already he could hear more cycles coming down the tunnels after him. Picking up the trail their brothers had been intent on.

They would come here, he told himself, grabbing the big rifle off the floor. They would come here right to him and he could...

Do them all, babe.

He went down on the floor of the tunnel and used a wrecked bike as a firing position. The next wave of bikes was coming fast. Throttling up and roaring as their riders electronically scented the prey they'd been ordered to hunt down and destroy. The APC. The people who'd been kind enough to take him along and make him one of their own. Coalition soldiers.

That had been nice. It had been a long time since he'd had anyone else in his life. And they'd been good to him. Talked to him even when he gave them so little in return.

Words had never been easy for him. Even before...

The least he could do was give them more space to do what needed to be done. What they'd come to do.

Rifle stabilized, he sighted in on the distant leader of the next Savage scout team.

"How 'bout him, darlin'?"

That's the one, babe.

"Yes, ma'am."

And then she would smile. Smile so big that all the bad things just didn't matter anymore.

That would be good here at the end of himself.

The rifle was roaring out in steady booms as his mind worked the shots and his fingers did that reloading trick he didn't even think about. Smoke and cordite filled the tunnel as he shot them down, one by one.

And still they came on.

62

The APC didn't sound too good. Something had gone wrong in the undercarriage or the drive train, and it was growing worse by the second.

"I'd stop, but I'd have no idea what to look for or what to do about it," said Davis over the comm.

"Keep moving," said Rechs in reply. "How much longer until we reach the hulk?"

"Ten minutes down this road and we'll be right near one of her cargo hatches." She paused. "Then what, Rechs?"

Silence followed her question for a long minute.

"Then we shove the weapon out the back, arm the trigger for detonation, and try to make it back to the *Chang* in time to dust off."

"What if the Savages try to disable it?"

"Thought about that. Was worried they might. I worked something out back here so that any attempt to tamper will activate the ignition sequence. There is no way to disarm it except via my armor's authenticating system."

"What if they try to dump it and just lift off?"

"It's geo-trapped. Moving it will cause it to detonate."

"It looks like you've got this all figured out then," she said with contempt. Clearly she was frustrated that no amount of reason or logic would dissuade him from ruining this world forever.

"Not my first time."

But she wasn't done. She tried again.

"And if they do tamper... because they either don't care, or don't understand the markings, then we get cooked too?"

"Affirmative," answered Rechs.

They entered an eight-lane highway along the subsurface of Hilltop District. They passed the occasional abandoned vehicle, but it was wide open and devoid of Savage assets or patrols.

"They probably didn't think anyone would get this close," said Davis as she called out distance and location markers.

Rechs bent forward over the gunner station screen and then looked over into the troop compartment where the two twin girls were securely strapped in.

"It's gonna get rough for a few minutes..." he began awkwardly. "So..."

He was going to tell them that they needed to be brave, but then he remembered that they'd come into the city looking for their brother on their own during the middle of a Savage invasion. So they already had bravery covered.

"I need you to stay strapped in. Let me do the work I need to do and then we're going to get out of here. I'll get you to a ship that's going to rescue you, okay?"

The two girls looked at each other. Then the older one spoke.

"What about Austin?"

Rechs said nothing.

It seemed they took this for confusion on his part. Not understanding who they were asking after.

The younger one clarified.

"He's our brother. The one we came looking for. He's—"

"All you have, right," said Rechs. "I remember. Just stay strapped in," he added, and turned back to the gunnery station. Not knowing what else he could say to them that would be of any comfort.

A moment later the massive entrance back into the daylight of Hilltop District appeared down the distant length of the tunnel. It was full daylight now on the surface. Rechs checked the time. Just barely afternoon. He felt suddenly tired as sunlight filtered through the opening, revealing swirling dust motes and falling ash in the forward view feed.

It had been a long time since he'd slept.

But he drove that thought from his mind and charged up the APC's defensive gun. "I thought you said we'd come up underneath the hulk."

"Eventually," Davis replied. "Gotta spend some time up top and then make sure of a pass-over."

The vehicle started taking fire as it neared the exit. The Savages *did* have a checkpoint set up. But not a great one. It didn't even slow them down. Captain Davis smashed right through the improvised barrier and the two marines who refused to move. It seemed they'd been optimistic about stopping the intruding vehicle with automatic fire. Instead they were crushed beneath its massive ceramic ball-wheels.

The APC took the off-ramp and emerged midway up a street that ran from the base of Hilltop to its highest point. This area had been shelled badly by the Coalition. Here was where the stories-tall walking mech had finally been found and destroyed by Coalition artillery. Resulting in extensive collateral damage. But even the rubble and smashed ruin of the once-grand buildings of New Vega, a sight that should have been apocalyptically awe-inspiring, was dwarfed by what drew the eye and demanded that attention be paid.

The Nest. Here, near and close, the kilometers-long colony ship loomed like the end of the world.

The road passed beneath some sort of massive wing section, and beneath this wing, which was easily twenty stories over their heads, towers jutted down from the underside. Construction cranes and loading gantries raced up to meet these structures. At first they looked to be manned by repair crews, on an epic scale.

At first.

"They're not repairing it..." said Captain Davis. Her voice was frantic, almost on the verge of hysteria as she drove hard to avoid hitting the ground structures. "They're *dismantling* it! They're staying!"

Rechs had seen Savage hulks from far closer than most humans had ever cared to. Their gargantuan scale didn't take away his breath like it did to others. Didn't impress him. Didn't make him question his place in the galaxy. The Savages weren't gods. They were monsters. And monsters had to be slain.

He existed only for that. And he'd accepted that fate a long time ago.

Besides, he'd seen and destroyed far bigger ships than this one. If anything, this one was more like an escort for some of the more massive lighthuggers from the last days of Earth's darkest hours. When the supposed best and brightest had fled the ruin they'd created. Telling everyone with such extreme certainty that they'd been right despite the lessons of history. The failure to properly execute their extreme thinking could be blamed on those they were leaving behind. But they would try again, out there in the dark, safe within their floating science experiments.

Just like Stark 247. Just like Dachau and Buchenwald and every other camp that most of humanity had forgotten. Man's inhumanity to man. Out here. Even out here.

"They're not human anymore," muttered Rechs through gritted teeth at the grounded Savage hulk looming over them.

The Savages were still collecting survivors. Still organizing the captured. Storing up calories for the winter like insects. Tearing apart their own ship to make a new, terrible, and twisted home.

They'd get it right despite the lessons of history.

If only because they were so certain this time.

Just like they'd been every other time.

"Colonel..." The transmission came in broken and distorted. It was Sergeant Major Andres. "Do you read..."

There was pulse fire in the background.

"In case you're still operational, sir ... proceeding on foot ... government transit ..."

Rechs tried to get something through, but they weren't receiving. They were too far down and, from the sound of it, engaged in a running gunfight on foot.

They were still beneath Hilltop and on foot. They'd never make it in time to meet the *Chang*'s departure.

The APC drove off the road, cut onto another one, and entered a tunnel. When it burst out the other side, it turned hard beneath an overpass, jumped the barrier, and shot up a very steep grade. Everything inside that wasn't bolted down slid backward.

"Hang on back there!" Rechs called out to the girls.

Davis kept the engines roaring at maximum capacity as the APC zoomed up the hill and exploded forth, all wheels in the air, before landing hard on a hilly paddock. The vehicle rocked and threatened to fishtail from the rapid application of brakes, but at last it came to a halt in front a grand cargo ramp leading down from the Savage hulk onto the shattered streets of New Vega. There were dozens more doors erupting from the ship all down its length.

Rechs scanned the surroundings through the up-top weapons screen. There were no Savages in their immediate vicinity, just the gently drifting grass that carpeted the edge of some park.

"Can you get us inside through that ramp?" he asked Davis.

But the captain had other ideas.

"They'll never make it, Rechs. You heard Andres's transmission. Not on foot. Not down there and engaged. We've got to go back for them."

Rechs growled and then popped the hatch to exit the APC. He pointed a finger at the girls, growled, "Stay here," then dashed back to the cargo hatch and accessed the lift control. A moment later the cargo deck was exposed, and so was the repulsor-palletized trigger-nuke.

The wind continued to sweep the heights of Hilltop, and Rechs monitored his HUD displays for signs of oncoming trouble. But he saw nothing. No threats, no movement. This Savage colony seemed to be the type that thought so highly of itself and its occupation that the prospect of trouble coming to its front doorstep was unthinkable. They had thrown everything into holding New Vega when the Coalition forces attacked, but their overwhelming success had apparently caused them to overextend their perimeter.

And now Rechs was but a few yards away. Close enough that he could inspect every pockmark on the hull, see every telltale sign of travel through the deepest and darkest of space.

"Rechs?"

"I'm pulling out the trigger-nuke. They made their choice when they left the *Chang* with me, same as you. Keep an eye out for Savages. They'll pick up the signature soon enough."

He disconnected the nuke from the travel locks and pulled it from the cargo deck. It came toward him as easily as a cloud drifts across the sky, and he let it wander out onto the dark and ruined street that climbed skyward beside this beached whale of an old starship. This Savage dream of a new world long ago on Earth. Now a nightmare unfolding on this world.

"Here they come!" shouted Davis. "Whatever it is you're doing, do it fast, Rechs. We got Savvie responders moving in on foot!"

She knew what he was doing. But even now she was distancing herself from the act, the weapon, the solution to the Savage crisis... even if she didn't realize it. She knew the people on this planet—those trapped in the storage bubbles below the surface, those awaiting transfer to that gruesome fate, and those who had fought along with them to reach this apocalyptic end-all—would pay the price. And she couldn't live with that. So she'd begun to distance herself. To find some way of living with what was going to happen in the next few hours.

As Rechs popped the shell on the trigger-nuke, the first rounds zipped through the artificial night the giant ship created beneath its bulk. Tracer fire from some heavy automatic tried to range the APC.

Rechs entered a code and unlocked the arming display. Nothing fancy. He enabled geo-trap and set the timer for eighteen hundred local.

And as he turned away, he heard a distant noise—a voice. So faint that at first he thought he'd imagined it.

"Help us!"

He heard it more clearly that time. Perhaps amplified by the wonderment that was his helmet's tech. Someone was screaming from... somewhere.

Rechs took a few steps toward the edge of an embankment, and looked down.

He saw hundreds of people pressed up against a wire fence, their haunted eyes suddenly hopeful. Their skeletal arms straining through the wire. An internment camp.

He looked back. The United Worlds emblem was proudly painted on the side of the APC near the twin guns, and was likely just visible to the camp over the crest of the hill. It was that emblem that caused the prisoners to scream for help.

And scream they did. A myriad of tired, frantic, and pitifully hopeful voices, all pleading for the same thing.

Help. Help us.

Heavy machine gun bullets zipped wildly above Rechs—sent by the approaching Savage marines. For now, they were still too far away to be a threat. But that would change soon enough.

Static came over the comm. It was Specialist Martin. "Be advised: Any surviving assets on New Vega. We are engaged near the underground subway access at the bottom level of the Hilltop subterranean complex. We are on foot with civilian survivors. Sergeant Major Andres is down. Colonel... if you're out there... we need help, sir. We're not gonna make it."

Help us.

They all needed it—demanded it—of Tyrus Rechs. And he was helping in the way he knew best.

Rechs ran back into the APC. The trigger-nuke was armed, ready to blow if the Savages messed with it in any way. Then it would be all over. He'd done what he'd come to do despite everyone and everything.

That was the way it had to be in the galaxy. The winner got all the marbles. So it was best to play for keeps.

"Help us!" shouted the mass of prisoners, their shouting growing in fervor and pitch as Rechs disappeared from view.

Now he would do what he could for the soldiers who had followed him—who had volunteered to see it through even after humanity's best effort to contain their worst enemy had met with overwhelming defeat.

"Do we just leave them?" asked Davis.

She was talking about the scarecrows behind the wire.

Savage weapons fire was growing in accuracy. It pinged against the hull and kicked up the dirt around Rechs's feet. But it seemed to Rechs that they were firing tentatively—perhaps aware of what he had delivered and not wanting to set it off with an errant shot, were such a thing possible.

"There's thousands just in this section, Captain. We can't rescue them." His voice was plain. His words matter-of-fact. And she hated him for it. And hated herself because he was right.

"We could at least set them free," she offered, and heard herself begging. Trying to make a deal where none could be made. "At least give them a chance!"

A pair of Savage marines ran down the ramp, reaching the APC before the first wave of attackers Davis had spotted farther out were close enough to engage. They sent a storm of hurried shots, all of which danced alongside their target, hitting only dirt, road, and APC.

The Savages had reason to be excited. Tyrus Rechs had come to settle up for what they'd done.

Rechs aimed his hand cannon and, with a sweeping motion, shattered their helmets and pulped their brains, leaving them to collapse and roll down the ramp. More would be coming from the same direction. It was time to move.

Rechs climbed into the APC and moved toward the gunnery station. "They've never had a chance, Captain. When the trigger-nuke goes, the whole planet gets cooked. Now get us back into the tunnels. We're going to go down there and try to get ours out."

The Savages were only now responding to the new threat that had arrived at their very doors. Their business and focus had no doubt been elsewhere. Out along the lines. Down in the tunnel complex. Rechs and Davis had had the area to themselves for a time, but that time was clearly coming to a close—quickly. More small arms fire pinged against their vehicle's outer hull.

And soon, larger munitions would be used.

The APC howled to life and spun a hard turn back the way they came, traveling over rough and ruined streets, leaving its precious gift behind.

"Oh..." Davis began, the start of a cry that just choked away as she stared at the instrument panel.

Rechs could see it too from his gunnery station. The hornets' nest—the Savage Nest—had awoken. A solid mass of hostile targets were in pursuit now. Savage marines of every size and type, big hulking fighters, what looked like mechs—just about everything the Savvies had. And all coming right after them.

From the troop compartment Rechs could feel the eyes of the two little girls watching him. He'd heard it said that children saw and heard everything. They always did.

And they understood far more than adults ever gave them credit for.

63

The bread truck loaded down with liberated captives hadn't quite made it to the lift that would take them down through the various levels of Old Colony's outer complex before it gave out again—the result of constant Savage attacks. Martin and Greenhill had managed to put the attackers down, but not before the tires and engine compartment were ruined.

"Everybody off the truck!" Sergeant Major Andres ordered. He pulled the survivors off the smoking vehicle and hustled them forward down the big tunnel they'd been traversing.

More Savages appeared, dismounting from the back of a civilian pickup truck and firing on the stationary bread truck moments after the last of the former prisoners had jumped off. Greenhill and Martin laid down a base of interlocking fire from both sides of the tunnel, and despite the poor physical condition of the refugees, they moved with haste.

Bullets skipped up into the path of a straggling clump of survivors, narrowly missing Greenhill. "Martin! Time to drop back!" He ran to an alcove, turned, and set up a steady stream of pulse fire with his heavy assault rifle while Martin in turn fell back.

The rest of the team moved forward, trying to outrun the din of blaster fire that seemed to haunt their steps. A din that grew louder as Martin and Greenhill added their own steady pulse fire into the pursuing elements.

As soon as they had all reached the lift—a disc the size of a carrier's bridge—Andres activated it. Everyone with a blaster rifle fired until the large doors shut behind them and the lift began to descend.

"They must've used this to move heavy construction equipment and bulk cargo down into the lower tunnels," announced Makaffie, still panting from the running firefight.

But no one else cared what the government had used it for before the entire world was ruined by the Savage invasion. They only cared about surviving. And the only hope any of them had was the high-speed rail that might take them back to the LZ—if they could reach it in time.

The *Chang* was due back in less than three hours.

The disc moved slowly, groaning mechanically and occasionally echoing out with loud titanic booms as locks at various levels slipped in and out of place. The survivors huddled along one edge of the disc while Martin, Greenhill, and the sergeant major scanned the darkness of the abandoned levels they passed through, watching for more Savages to come at them in some fresh new assault.

Time and charge packs were running out.

They'd lost three survivors in the running fight to reach the disc. People who'd been hit and bled out alone because there was no time for the soldiers to give them aid and no way to carry them along. The other ragged and dirty survivors, those without weapons and nothing else to do, had tried to help them, but to no avail. In two cases, the wounds didn't even seem all that bad. Didn't seem like they should have been fatal. But they were. Like maybe those poor souls had simply been through too much already over the last six weeks. Their time in the galaxy was done.

At the bottom of the well, they arrived into a vast underground domed vault from which several tunnels, guarded by impressive vault doors two and three stories high, led off in different directions.

"Last stop," announced Andres, and ordered everyone off the lift.

"Should be that way, guys!" said Makaffie. He was using a battle board on which Davis had sketched a rudimentary map, and so far her sketches were proving more or less accurate.

"No kidding," said Greenhill. He pointed up at an overhead sign showing the way to the transit tunnel trains.

Makaffie put the board away. "Well. We didn't know those signs would be there, man."

That was when the morlocks announced their presence once more. They couldn't yet be seen, but their howls warbled and whooped out across the dark caverns.

Andres cursed the all-too-familiar sound and attempted to hush the screaming survivors. "Not so loud!" the sergeant major called out. "Damn it, be quiet!"

At his urging, the panicked survivors hustled forward and bunched up to get onto the frozen escalator.

"Moving up," said Martin. He bounded down the escalator, pushing through the survivors. "They sound like they're still a ways off yet. Maybe not even on this level."

"Greenhill," Andres called out, "you stay back with me. Don' want nothin' sneaking up on us. 'Kaffie—keep with the locals."

Makaffie was being used as a sort of ad hoc military/ civilian interface liaison. Listening to their grievances, agreeing with them, and then at the same time trying to explain why the military did the things it did, the way that it did them. Which, it seemed, he usually didn't agree with. And then explaining to them the mysteries of the cosmos, and how it could be understood by looking through the fourth eye of the mind, but only when you "unlocked the potentiality of spiritual vision hidden inside us all. Man."

All of a sudden bright government lighting, dull and soulless, filled the terminal. The power had come back on. The escalator lurched to life, jostling the already panicked survivors. Some screamed, others cried or moaned. A few fell and were in danger of being trampled in the rush to get away to any place other than the one they had come from.

And yet no place seemed safe anymore.

Martin, out of sight down below, opened fire.

"Contact!"

"Get down!" shouted the sergeant major at the civilians. "Get your heads down and *stay* down until I tell you otherwise!"

The sergeant major moved through the huddled press as best he could to reach the bottom of the long escalator. Citizens crouched and cowered around him. Greenhill was left to cover the rear on his own. And now the sound of the big cav sergeant's heavy fire echoed out over the transportation hub too, sounding harsh and brutal to the ears.

Enemies up front and in the rear.

Surrounded.

On the subway platform below, the Savage morlocks had made the mistake of charging across open ground with no cover, likely enticed by the screams of the prisoners. They'd entered the area from another platform across the tracks, and Martin, covering behind a directory board that now read ERROR for every point in the line and DELAYED for every time, cut down three before they even left the platform, catching them in a sweep of burst fire, then dropped four more as they crossed the wide canyon of the tracks. But five made it far enough to get cover as they disappeared below platform level.

If they're smart, Martin thought as he went to pull a frag off his carrying system, *they'll stay down there, hold their automatic slug-throwing rifles over the lip of the platform, and just pray and spray.*

But he'd seen before that these hunters had traded smarts for bloodthirsty aggression. And the constant noise of pulse fire and frantic survivors was whipping them into a frenzy.

The sergeant major raced forward, blazing away with his weapon until he was literally at the edge of the platform shooting down into the Savage hunters. He'd rushed them, and they hadn't expected that. After six weeks of being the new alpha predator on New Vega, they were used to being the hunter and not the hunted.

Martin cooked the spool on the grenade and yelled, "Frag out! Hit the deck, Sergeant Major!"

Andres jumped back as the grenade bounced onto the tracks and went off a second later. Any Savages that had survived his shooting spree were now a bloody mess— and Martin came forward and made good and sure of it. But up above, Greenhill was firing in longer bursts.

"No rail cars, Sergeant Major," said Specialist Martin matter-of-factly.

Andres was bent over, catching his breath. He waved at Martin. "Get 'em moving down the tracks on foot. That's all we can do now. I'm gonna go back up and help Greenhill."

***

Soon the bulk of the survivors were moving again, almost running for their lives down the long, dark subway tunnel. But the Savage hunters still had the scent, and they would not give up the chase no matter how many were mowed down by Greenhill and the sergeant major. Martin was ahead, scouting the tunnel and hoping some rail train didn't bear down out of the darkness and slaughter them all.

After what seemed at least a kilometer of moving, the sounds of the hunters faded.

"Think they're gone?" Greenhill asked, taking the opportunity to check his charge packs. "Shit. I'm almost spent."

"Not much better." Andres looked around. "We definitely movin' out of the hillside, though. I wonder..."

He activated his comm. "This is Sergeant Major Andres. Colonel—Tyrus Rechs—do you read me?"

He paused and looked to Greenhill. "Not gettin' a response."

"Let's get going, Sergeant Major."

Andres held up a finger. "One more try. This is Sergeant Major Andres. Colonel, do you read me?"

And then pulse fire erupted from farther down the tunnel. Either the hunters remembered their weapons, or Savage marines had joined the hunt.

"Gotta go!" shouted Greenhill, answering with his pulse rifle.

"In case you're still operational, sir, we're proceeding on foot in the government transit tube."

Bullets snapped and hissed around Andres. Close. They were close.

The sergeant major ran, catching up to Greenhill, then turned and added his own fire to the mix.

"Contact rear!" Greenhill yelled into his comm.

"You need me to come back or send 'Kaffie?" asked Martin.

"Negative!" growled Andres. "Keep that column moving!"

Greenhill took a knee to better fire at the sporadic muzzle flashes erupting in the tunnel's distant darkness.

Andres sat down right next to him. It was an odd way to set up and fire. And then Greenhill realized that Andres's pulse rifle wasn't firing. He looked over and saw the sergeant major clutching his stomach. His uniform was already dark and wet with blood.

Greenhill didn't give aid to the sergeant major—he couldn't. Instead he kept up a steady stream of covering fire and activated his comm. "Sergeant Major is hit! I need someone back here to pull him back!"

"I'm on it!" shouted Makaffie. He came sprinting back with a few of the more capable survivors to carry the gut-shot NCO farther down the tunnel.

Martin continued firing, skipping backward as he shot, moving as fast as he could while keeping eyes on the enemy. This was going from bad to worse. And the only way he could see out of it was to try once more to reach the man they'd known as the colonel. Hoping he was still the kind of man who would get them out of there, even if Tyrus Rechs was not.

"Be advised: Any surviving assets on New Vega. We are engaged near the underground subway access at the bottom level of the Hilltop subterranean complex. We are on foot with civilian survivors. Sergeant Major Andres is down."

But the specialist got no answer over the static-distorted comm down in the clutching close darkness of that deep tunnel leading off into the unknown. Behind them, the Savages were closing in once more.

"Colonel... if you're out there... we need help, sir. We're not gonna make it."

64

They'd lobbed an explosive at the Wild Man covering behind his improvised fighting position of ruined Savage scout cycles. He'd felt it go over his head in the darkness. That was the last thing he remembered. Remembered that silence between his shots and their return fire. Remembered the sound of the grenade bouncing on the tunnel floor.

How many? she asked.

Twenty.

He always knew the number.

He always knew... because he knew any number of dead Savages made her happy. And so he kept track. Because her happiness meant everything to him. Nothing else in the galaxy really mattered anymore.

Twenty.

I killed twenty for you.

She was saying what she always said when he felt the grenade go flying over his head in the dark. Heard it bounce around.

And in that moment he'd had a choice.

Scramble for it and get it away from him. Or...

Go ahead and kill one more with the seconds that remained of the sometimes dream and sometimes nightmare of his life.

His mind had done the math. A flung grenade had already cooked for at least three seconds. Who knew how long the Savages ran their fuses, but five or six was standard for most militaries. Finding it and then getting it away from him with little more than a hurl just to get it down tunnel... in the dark... no, three seconds wasn't much. And he'd already just burned one on the math. The fatal math. So much of life and death was math. Cold, relentless math.

Maybe that was why miracles were miracles. Because they defied the math. And maybe her voice was its own kind of miracle. After all, it had made a dead man want to live a little longer, if only just for vengeance.

Do another one...

He pulled the trigger one last time.

... babe.

Boooom.

Lights out and waiting to feel your flesh torn to shreds by hundreds of pieces of shrapnel... or needles, like some frags used. And then... maybe then... maybe... well, just maybe she'd be waiting for him on the other side of whatever. Smiling. Glad that he'd finally caught up with them in the place of miracles. Holding out their baby for him to dandle on his knee and exchange coos with.

That's not so bad, he thought as his mind was suddenly scrambled. There was a bang. Lights flashed, and it felt like he was going to have a stroke. Or rather... it felt like reality had just stuttered. Like the game had frozen. Or the signal had locked on an image. Or the sun had refused to go down.

Yeah. That's what it felt like. Reality had just stuttered. Skipped a beat. Missed a groove. Taken a bad step.

He couldn't move and he couldn't see. Couldn't hear either. Except he could. He could do all those things. He could do them where he was at now because he was no longer in the tunnel where he'd been shooting down Savages. No one-shot-and-gone. It had been a gallery back in the tunnel. A shooting gallery like the star carnies sometimes set up when they made planetside on Stendahl.

Shoot the ducks! Win a prize for your lady, hoss!

Do another one, babe. She'd said that that summer night when the stars were close. Red hair and that green dress. And those eyes.

He was back on their stead now in this place where reality had just stuttered. And he was smiling the biggest dopey grin he could smile. It was so big and dumb even he could feel it. And here's how it felt.

Remember the best day you ever had. The day when everything was perfect, and only good times were ever had. And everyone you ever truly loved was there with you. Safe and happy at home. Remember that day when the future seemed like a good thing you weren't always so constantly afraid of. Remember that simple day of good things you took for granted. When darkness and evil had not touched you. When the love in your heart had not grown cold. Remember that.

That was how he felt at that moment. He could feel how unreasonably happy he was. Like every bone in his body was turned to jelly and every pain that had been there, the scars both real and emotional—those were all just gone now. And it was afternoon turning to evening at the end of a long week.

He was finishing up organizing some rope out along the corral in front of their old stead. Getting it set up for a horse that he'd need to break come first of the next week. A beautiful horse that half of him wanted to just turn loose and let go to run the plains of Stendahl forever. One of the mustang stock brought up with the first colonists and let go to run the planet and go where they would. He wanted to let that horse go. But he needed it. So he'd break it.

But part of him just wanted to let the beautiful creature go.

Later she came out onto the front porch, and he was struck dumb by how beautiful she was in that moment of every good thing you want to take with you forever. And he had to stop and wonder why she'd ever wanted him.

Picked him.

"Don't ask silly questions," an old hand had once told him. "Because the answers often aren't."

The galaxy skipped into that moment, and he was helpless with the joy of vision of her. She was... she was his treasure.

Treasure.

He'd never known quite how to phrase it. But she was that. His treasure. And all he'd ever been doing since... was just killing Savages to get back what they'd taken from him. Wasn't that true?

That ol' pardner who told him not to ask silly questions said that. Leaning one boot up against the fence and watching that mustang toss her head and throw up dust in the corral. Like she knew her wild and free days were over for good.

"Weren't that true?" the old hand asked inside that stuttering reality. He was just a drifter who worked from ranch to ranch, never putting down roots. Helping where help was needed. "You just wanted your treasure back, didn't ya?"

He nodded that this was true, and when he did, he felt big wet tears fall from his eyes.

"You never loved her," said the old poke as he uncoiled a lasso and sent it about him, right around the big man's chest, as easy a trick as there ever was. "You just didn't like having something taken from ya. That's all, hoss."

He sat on the ground, smiling like a dope and crying at the same time. Watching her on the porch. She was coming out to tell him the chicken was fried and cooling. Dinner soon.

That's home to me, he thought as the cowpoke tightened the lasso around him. He began to crawl across the hard-packed dirt of the yard. If he could just reach the porch, reach her... then he'd be home now.

But the old cowpoke was on him. Tying him up like a hog.

"She's just a thing to you," said the old trail hand. He was thin and rangy and he had a wolf's teeth and eyes.

"No... no... no..." he was telling the cowboy while smiling, laughing, and crying and crawling all at once. "No!" he shouted. "You're a liar! She was my treasure!"

He couldn't move. He was just feet from her.

She stood there on the porch in that dress, smiling her smile.

"You're all done now," said the ol' poke. "Might as well go ahead and just give up."

He struggled. But even he knew it was useless now. Cowboys tie knots better than a preacher, as the old saying goes.

"You're all done now," she said from the porch of their old stead, echoing the poke who'd trussed him up.

Sadness washed over him.

And then darkness as he felt himself carried along the tunnel. Blind and helpless. His hearing coming back. He could hear their digital speech. High-speed bursts between them, low and sinister. They had him. The Savage scout team had immobilized him with some kind of sensory scrambling explosive. And now they had him and were taking him to the coolers, the bubbles, where all the other survivors had ended up. Until it was their turn to become calories.

He was crying. Just like in the dream. Sad that he'd never *do another one, babe* for her ever again. Sad that he would never see her smile again. Sad that he'd somehow failed.

65

Admiral Sulla was at the forward bridge of the *Chang* after leaving command of the *Defiant* to a subordinate officer. It was important for him to personally assume command of the assault frigate for the rescue effort. Because Tyrus Rechs was his responsibility. And his oldest friend. He'd introduced him into the operation for better or for worse. That their little plan was going to be found out and that there would be serious repercussions with UW Navy was also a fact.

There was a reckoning coming and there was no denying that.

And it was nearing go time for *Chang*'s micro-jump back to the rendezvous with the trigger-nuke team on New Vega.

But Sulla had been an admiral for a long time, much longer than most suspected, and he'd made a lot of allies during that time. He knew a lot of secrets. He knew where the actual bodies were buried. So he had some cards to play. And if things didn't swing his way... well, then he could always start over. He had before. It's just that he'd never been so close to accomplishing the one way he saw to deal with the Savage threat as had been with the formation of the Coalition. He, like Rechs, knew personally why the threat had to be dealt with before humanity could assume its place among the stars. The Coalition had been the first step toward a formal galactic government that oversaw the worlds and fielded a unified military capable of dealing with external threats.

The Savages were considered an external threat. They'd left humanity long ago. Hyperdrive-connected humanity had more in common with the alien species they'd encountered via jumps through hyperspace than they had with their sociopathic ancestors crawling around at sublight speed between the worlds like ancient Viking invaders come to set some colony back for a few more hundred years of galactic dark age.

In the day and half since the assault frigate *Chang* had lifted off from the stadium LZ as New Vega burned and Coalition ground forces retreated en masse, once the micro-jump back to the fleet had been completed, a massive rearmament program had taken place aboard the sturdy ship.

All the missile stores the *Chang* could handle had been transferred from the rest of the surviving ships of Task Force Wrath. So had secondary shield generators from two other ships. Jury-rigged and patched into the defensive network, they were unreliable at best. But Sulla had thought it best to take everything he could to what was sure to be an all-out junkyard dogfight. They'd even transferred the one multi-warhead nuke the *Defiant* carried and set it up for a fast load off the cargo deck if they needed to fire it in anger.

Using a ship-based multi-warhead nuke wasn't nearly as bad as lighting the fuse on a trigger-nuke... but it wouldn't be pretty.

Sulla finished briefing the *Chang*'s skeleton bridge crew he was carrying. Other than a full engineering complement to keep the power on and handle damage control, he'd transferred as many personnel off the assault frigate as he could before the rest of the fleet jumped out of the system.

Because you don't think you're going to make it back out of this one? he'd asked himself as he watched the quiet hum of activity that precipitated a ship getting underway for combat ops. Or rather heard some voice asking him.

After all, he had to admit to himself, one assault frigate against four Savage hulks was hardly good odds on a great day with surprise in the mix.

No, he answered himself and slid behind the flight controls of the frigate. He didn't trust anyone to fly this one but himself. And the fewer people aboard, the fewer casualties they were going to take when they came out the other side of what was about to happen. And they were going to take casualties. That was for sure. Even if not coming out the other side wasn't.

"Jump plot locked in?" he asked the captain who was now flying left seat on the frigate.

"Locked and green across the board. Standing by to jump at your command, sir."

Sulla finished strapping in and donned his flight helmet. Then he moved his chair forward and took the stick.

"I have the stick," he said formally announcing that he was in command of flight for the *Chang*. "Sound the bells for battle stations and give me engines to max. Executing jump in five... four... three... two..."

66

The Savages were pursuing the APC into the tunnels as if they were some hive mind that had only just now reacted to the imminent threat within the vastness of underground complex. As the APC powered through the midnight dark, two armored mechs moved fast on articulating walkers to cut off the vehicle before it could reach the lift down to level twenty-two. Both Savage war machines were spooling out heavy doses of lead ammunition. Rechs directed a burst of aimed pulse fire from the APC's guns into one of the mechs' insectile pilot's canopies and smashed glass and melted internal systems. A second later Davis clipped the other mech's extending walker at high speed, shearing it off and collapsing the mech.

The collision caused Davis to lose control of the APC. It spun off, slammed into a wall, and fishtailed before she finally regained control and they were racing through the dark once more.

"Sure you can find that lift without the battle board?" Rechs called.

"I drew the map, didn't I?"

Rechs didn't answer. He didn't like sarcasm when it wasn't coming from him.

"The lift should be close now," offered Davis.

The emergency lighting within the APC flickered on and off. Its power system had been damaged by the concussive impact of the two mechs' heavy weapons fire. In its flickering flashes Rechs got glimpses of the two little girls staring at him. One radiating cold anger. The other uncertain fear. Both were a kind of indictment against him that for some reason he couldn't shake off.

"Hang on!" shouted Davis over the comm. "Lift's not here!"

All four balls of the vehicle locked and extended their braking treads, and the vehicle skidded toward the yawning well where the lift should have been. With just meters to spare, they came to a halt.

Rechs popped the main hatch. His helmet's audio picked up the distant sound of more Savage cycle teams inbound on their location. The awesome well that descended into darkness also rose up toward the smashed and ruined surface, from which distant shards of waning daylight fell down and died in the gloom. He scanned the utilitarian maintenance areas and cargo off-loading decks that surrounded the well. All of the blisters, pipes, and bulges conspired to look like the bizarre hieroglyphics of some lost alien civilization.

"There's a smaller lift over there," he said over the comm. "Your nine o'clock, Davis. Does it go down to the same place?"

"Only one way to find out."

Rechs vaulted from the vehicle and Davis followed, letting the low growl of the engines pull the APC forward.

Reaching the lift control, Rechs flipped open the safety cover and accessed the gate. Then he slammed his gauntleted fist onto the lift call button. The platform was currently three levels below.

Seconds later, the first of four speeding Savage cycles tore into the empty area of the well. He drew his hand cannon and engaged, dropping the weaving riders as they tried to rake him with strafing fire in their quick passes.

"Radar reads more contacts coming in from multiple directions!" Davis said. Her voice was controlled, but Rechs could tell the veteran starship captain was nearing some limit.

And so was he.

Bullets smacked into the gate, and one nailed him solidly on his left arm. It was like being hit by a rocket-fired hammer even with the armor he wore.

He stumbled for the cover of the APC. The armor ran a diagnostic medical check and indicated a possible fracture. Armor integrity tightened up the area to immobilize the break and still allow some mobility. Then it hit the screaming nerve endings with some anesthesia and calming drugs.

"You all right?" asked Davis. She'd been watching him on the driver's screens. She'd seen him take fire and move for cover.

He shot her a thumbs-up in the cam feed, threw his back against the APC, and fired at another passing Savage, dropping the rider and sending his bike skidding off the lip of the well and down into the distant darkness below.

The platform had almost arrived when two Savages activated their high beams and swooped in head-on at him, intent on running him down. The histrionic blare of their mounted submachine guns crackled to life.

The lift gate was down, and the platform arrived on their level.

"Move!" shouted Rechs.

And then he took two steps toward the bikers and hit the armor's jets, vaulting above them in a sudden flare of energy-assisted lift. He was hoping to draw their attention off the broadside of the APC, whose armor seemed on the verge of giving up all integrity. If even one round breached the hull it would ricochet around inside and eventually hit Davis or the girls.

Davis drove the APC onto the lift platform as Rechs pivoted in midair and followed the targeting tags on the two bikers. Two shots. High-powered fifty-caliber depleted-uranium slugs.

Both bikes kept moving, their riders most likely dead, or at least dying. They too shot off the lip of the central well and were swallowed by the darkness.

And then Rechs had his boots on the ground and was sprinting for the lift. Savage ground troops were flooding the chamber from access hatches and maintenance tunnels. A heavy weapons team opened up, attempting to range him as he crossed the distance.

Rechs closed the gate and sent the APC down to the complex's deepest level.

67

"Run!" shouted Martin, his voice hoarse, his breathing ragged. He'd grabbed the dying sergeant major from Makaffie and the two survivors who'd been carrying the wounded man. All three looked out of even the energy to move themselves to safety.

"Pack out!" shouted Greenhill over the comm. And then announced, "Last one."

With the limp sergeant major dangling from his shoulders, Martin turned and sprayed the shadows behind with his pulse rifle, buying time for Greenhill to get his last charge pack loaded into the heavy. The Savages returned fire, but it was wild and erratic.

"We gon' die here, Specialist!" murmured the sergeant major. His eyes were closed and his blood was soaking Martin's back and shoulders. "Last pack now... we down to knives and insults." The old NCO thought that was funny and laughed. But it sounded like a death rattle.

"Keep running!" shouted Martin at the survivors.

Only darkness lay ahead, and the civilians didn't seem too keen to disappear into that all on their own, without weapons, but their pursuers were surging from the rear, and neither Greenhill nor Martin could be spared to take point.

And now both soldiers were low on charge packs.

"Put me down, Special-list," coughed the sergeant major. "This here... good as any place... to die."

"Negative, Sergeant Major. We're gonna make it."

Martin hustled up the tunnel as Greenhill laid down more fire from the heavy he carried. At least they still had sidearms. And after that... combat knives.

"Ain't over yet, Special-list... Ah, I like that!" coughed the sergeant major. Martin could feel the man shaking on his back.

Behind him, the cav sergeant's heavy pulse rifle suddenly went wild and cacophonic, like he was firing without pause at everything in every direction. And then it went silent. Its missing strobe-like flash plunged the tunnel into complete darkness.

Greenhill was down for sure.

Keep moving, Martin told himself. Not really thinking about the odds, or the situation, just thinking ten steps more at a time. And then if he made that, maybe another ten.

Life was down to just ten steps.

Imagine that, said some distant part of his mind, and then he pushed that thought away and hustled on because he didn't need that right now. It didn't do him any good here at this last of moments. He understood that now. He'd passed some limit, and payday was coming due.

***

"Can't shoot fer—" grunted Greenhill, and then one of the Savages kicked him in the gut with an armored combat boot, driving the air out of him. Out of the corner of his eye he saw one of them drag his heavy away from the circle of punishment that was forming all about him, all of them chittering in their insane high-pitched digital eruptions.

A circle of punishment. Or a circle of death.

Because that was the way it looked right now.

Another boot connected with his head. Stars and light erupted across his skull. *This must be like what it feels like to get a pulse rifle shot right in the head*, he thought distantly. When you got double-tapped, and then another in the head. The last one. Dull and distant.

Well, he'd done that enough on Kimshana to others. That was for sure. So maybe his turn had just come up.

Then the gloved iron fists were raining down on him. Kicks, too. Beating him like he was a piece of meat.

They jes' tenderizing the meat, another part of him thought from far away.

He tried to shout at them, to call them what they were—not just Savages, but cannibals. The opposite of human. Animals. But nothing came out because his jaw had been broken.

He tried to call them that all the same. Because he was down to just insults now.

Knives and…

No.

Sidearms and…

And he was aware in that moment that he was certainly going to die in the next.

He reached for his pistol. It was supposed to be on his thigh, and he hadn't felt them pull it off. Maybe they didn't know. Or didn't understand sidearms, or really anything that used to be human and the way humans did things. These Savages were little better than animals now. So maybe there was a chance he could pull it and go to Fiddler's Green. Just like the old cav poem that was part of every unit since...

Another mailed fist hit him in the back, driving him to the dusty concrete of the rail tunnel floor.

Put your pistol to your lips and go...

It was there. His sidearm was there. His hand was broken, but he never no-minded the pain and got it out of its holster.

In one last act of defiance, as the Savage marines stepped away from him, laughing histrionically like dig-itized demons in some dance party song, he got on his knees and pulled the sidearm, his arm making it go wild as he tried to get it to his lips.

And then a distant cannon was roaring, blazing away with angelic fury. Like some summer storm in the morning on the highlands of the Kimshana mountains when every-thing was gold and silver and diffused light. Terrible and beautiful all at once. Like that.

He remembered those days on that hard world.

The Savages were dying in sudden explosive sprays, or scrambling away only to be torn apart by sharp barks of automatic gunfire up close, too close, and far too personal.

Maybe I'm next, thought Greenhill. And he didn't mind too much. He'd done his best to see it through. But your best didn't always mean it was enough.

His mama had tried to tell him that when she'd tried to teach him religion.

And then he fell over and passed into unconsciousness for at least thirty seconds.

When he came to, Tyrus Rechs was dragging him into the APC. And Sergeant Greenhill wondered if he might just live a few minutes longer.

68

There was no argument about what would happen next. Survivors were quickly loaded into the heavily damaged and shot-to-hell APC, occupying a space that had belonged to a trigger-nuke that would end everyone else they ever hoped could still be alive in short order. It was still going to be a tight fit. Both Greenhill and the sergeant major were no longer combat effective. And truth be told the sergeant major was in far worse shape than that. There were meds and a stabilization kit on board, but it didn't look good for the senior NCO.

As Davis supervised the loading of the civilians, the ragged and desperate survivors squeezing in next to the two twin girls in the troop compartment, Makaffie took Rechs aside. Martin was on rear guard, waiting for more Savage assets to catch up. Waiting for them to appear out of the darkness and come swarming in for the attack. For now, things were awfully quiet. But rather than soothing everyone, the absence of battle-rattle, incoming fire, return fire, and swarming and chittering Savages seemed to put everyone on edge and even more ill at ease. The silence was more ominous than the battles that had been fought. If such a thing was possible.

"Hey-a there, Tyrus, old buddy," said the scrappy artillery private. He spoke to the galaxy's most wanted war criminal with a familiarity that hadn't been established by any prior conversation Rechs could remember having with the man. "Heads up... but ah... Wild Man is still active. He's still out there. He's alive is what I'm tryin' to say."

Rechs turned his head, but his emotions were hidden behind his battered and battle-scratched helmet.

"Yeah," continued Makaffie, running his grimy hand through a dirty-blond shock of barely military-cut hair. "He had a comm device on him and I folded it into our net when we joined up. Comm also came with a locator and vitals authenticator. So it must've been military and not civilian. Anyway, I just checked to see if he was still alive and he is... but his vitals are low."

The scrawny man didn't wait for Rechs to get a word in. He just kept talking. "He was in one place for a while just after we split up and them cycle teams was after us. Then he was on the move to sub-level eight. And that's where he is now."

Captain Davis had finished loading the APC and was now hovering over their conversation.

"There's no time, Tyrus," she said almost immediately. "We're less than two hours from the *Chang*'s dustoff back at the LZ. Not to mention the weapon you've set to detonate moments after departure. I'm sorry... but..."

She looked away suddenly, realizing what she was saying.

"It's a hard choice. I get that..." she continued. "But we have to leave him behind. There's not enough time."

Rechs could tell that half of her was hoping he'd re-mote-disarm the nuke. To give them more time. But that wasn't going to happen. Not at all.

"I'll get him," said Rechs. "Get these people to the dus-toff. If we're not there before departure, then tell Sulla it's gears up and emergency takeoff, because that weapon will go off at eighteen hundred local."

"Hold on a minute, Tyrus," said Captain Davis, put-ting up one knife-edged hand. "Just hold on a minute. I'm telling you right now, I've lived down in these tunnels for six weeks..."

She bent over and studied the map on Makaffie's battle board. She pointed a finger at a blip that identified Wild Man's locator-transponder. Makaffie had even changed the tag inside the comm roster to read "Wild Man."

"... and you will not make it up to that level and back to the LZ in time," she continued. "No way. No how. I guaran-tee it, Tyrus. It cannot be done, and you will die down here."

"Feed me his loc and identifier signature so I can track him," said Rechs to Makaffie, ignoring the protestations of the captain.

"You got it. Want me to go with?" asked the private with a maniacal grin that indicated he was up for just about anything.

"Negative. Captain Davis needs you and Martin to get these people off-planet. Make it happen."

Makaffie saluted—badly—and scrambled into the APC. Maybe he hadn't been as up for going back into the nightmare tunnel network as his initial enthusiasm had suggested. Getting out had seemed impossible at various points during this little jaunt into the Savage stronghold. Now there was the real possibility that they might make it. And that was not a chance to be thrown away lightly.

But Rechs had always resolved himself to expect a one-way mission. That was his way. Every time. That way you played your hardest to be wrong about the outcome.

Because if you were already dead, then what did you have to lose?

Captain Davis stepped close and stared into the face of Rechs's soulless helmet.

"Clarify something for me, please, because I don't understand this. You've accomplished your mission. The weapon is armed and will go off at just a few minutes after eighteen hundred local. Job done. The entire remaining population, captured or not, hiding out somewhere in the hills or whatever, is going to die when this planet starts to cook. And that's fine by you. And now, with a straight shot to get to an inbound ship that's got a chance of getting us off this doomed rock... you're going back for just one man."

Rechs had grabbed a tactical ruck from the loadout and was busy stuffing it full of spare charge packs for the heavy, plus all the remaining fraggers.

"Yeah," he said as he closed the ruck and strapped it on. "That's about it."

"That makes no sense, Tyrus! Not in any equation in this whole messed-up mess does that make even the slightest bit of sense. Then... why not shut down the timer on the trigger-nuke and just save everyone?"

"Can't."

"*Why?*"

"Because they're already dead. The Savages will either turn them into resources, or they'll turn them into more of themselves. This planet was dead the moment those Savages set down. I've seen it too many times for it to be any other way, Captain. I can't save them."

"So you'll just let them all die?" she practically shrieked. "No... that's not even right! You'll actually be the one *killing* them, because that's *your* device that's about to do all the dirty work. It'll be *you* who does them, Tyrus Rechs. Just like every other world you've tried to 'save.'" She looked up and dropped her head back down, shaking it with her hands gripping her hips. "What a colossal joke. Both it and you."

She slammed her palm into the side of the APC as though she were finished.

But she wasn't. She was just opening her mouth to say more when Rechs spoke again, getting right in her face.

"Or maybe I'm trying to spare them from a living nightmare that might last for hundreds, if not thousands, of years. Or, since these here on New Vega have gone cannibal, which is a new low I've never encountered before, some of these survivors might wake up out of one these frozen bubbles to be next week's Sunday dinner. No, I don't think so, Captain. What I'm doing may make me look like a monster to you and all the rest of the galaxy who want to always choose the path of least resistance. But I don't care what all of you think. I never did. You and the rest get to have your pretty starships and snow globe civilizations because there are men, and women frankly, who are willing to do the hard things that need to be done when that's the only way forward. We slaughter the cattle so you can eat steak. Spare me your moralizing. And I'll spell it out for you so you get it in your head, and maybe if I don't make it back, after you've learned your lesson watching planet after planet get annihilated by these monsters, you'll get it and figure out what needs to be done. Here it is:

"There can't be two of us. It's either a galaxy full of Savages, or we humans get a chance. But we cannot co-exist. It's us or them. Because according to them, we have to be eliminated for them to go forward. We're the part of the gene tree that didn't make the evolutionary cut as far as they're concerned. We're the Cro-Mags. The dodo. Their first mission is to destroy us or turn us into them. Both options have about the same mortality rate. Trust me on that one. They want us dead. The quicker people getting around to believing an enemy that tells you time and time again that it wants you dead... the faster something can be done about it in which you *don't* end up dead."

Through it all Davis just stood there, arms crossed. Eyes smoldering. And for a moment Rechs wondered why he was doing it again. Why it was suddenly so damn important to make her understand his point of view. It didn't matter. She wasn't going to stop him. And yet he went on, more worked up than he could remember in a long, long time.

"And us... we have to, repeat *have* to, clear them before we can find out what's out there. We can't have these monsters they've made themselves into constantly tearing down everything we've built the farther out we expand. New Vega's dead. This is all we could save," he said, waving one gauntlet at the APC and everyone within. "This, and one more. I'm going to go get the last one."

She tilted her head after he finished, looking in no way convinced. "Why?"

Rechs stared at her from behind his helmet for a long moment, saying nothing. He clenched his fists.

"Because he said he would follow me. For that reason and that reason alone. In that, including you, we all became brothers. If just for now. If just for this battle. You fight together, you survive together. We're something more than just the rest of the population. We're family now. And to the best of my ability, if there's a chance, I'll bring my brother back alive. I have to take that chance. I wouldn't be me if I didn't."

"Tyrus Rechs." She said his name like it was a dirty word.

"Yeah," replied Rechs dismissively. "Whoever that is."

She stared at him. Hard. Just like the twin girls.

"I'm going now," he said in the silence that followed. "Listen to me and get off this planet, Captain."

And then he was gone. Down tunnel. Trotting off into the darkness with several kilometers to cross. His pace looked too slow for the two hours that remained of the planet's life. Too slow if he was going to accomplish what he'd set out to accomplish. Not enough in a time when so much would be required to merely go on drawing breath.

But there are some who run toward the fire, despite the odds.

She knew that much as she watched him disappear into the tunnel dark.

69

There were abandoned scout cycles all along the way. Most had been destroyed, either exploding against a tunnel wall or riddled so badly with pulse fire that they were now inoperable. But eventually Rechs found one still in working order, its rider shot down by one of his volunteers from Strike Team Ranger, and he got it started.

Inside his HUD he had a good tag on the strange and enigmatic sniper that had just folded himself into their little ad hoc fellowship with barely a word. And he'd been one of the best snipers that Tyrus had ever fought alongside.

That some horrific tragedy had befallen him prior to the battle was evident. That he'd once been a soldier was evident too. That he'd been horribly wounded was plain to see by anyone with functioning eyes.

Rechs had met many such men in his travels across the stars.

But this Wild Man, like all of them, had agreed to see it through no matter what. And Rechs had promised to do his best to get them all back.

He owed them that.

Now it was time to honor his end of the commitment. No one gets left behind.

He set out along the tunnel riding fast. He was carrying Greenhill's heavy along with his own hand cannon. He killed the high beam and relied on his helmet's IR, low-imaging overlays, along with the bare emergency lighting, to see his way forward as he thundered along.

And what he saw was a swarm of cycles approaching fast. With something bigger behind their speeding cluster. A mech even larger than the two they'd collided with in the APC. In fact, it was barely able to fit inside the tunnel.

Rechs met the oncoming cycles like a comet headed into an asteroid field.

Whether the approaching Savage scout marine riders thought he was one of their own—a survivor with a malfunctioning comm returning with intel—or another Savage unit from a different vessel, was unclear. But the riders parted to make way, and he shot through their midst and underneath the massive legs and gears of the following walker.

Only at the last second did they realize he wasn't a friendly.

Rechs knew more about the Savages than any living soul. Even more than Sulla. And as frightening as this new alliance of Savages from different hulks was, he knew the chances were good that there was some miscommunication going on between them. The various sides might not yet be married up and cohesive. Everyone using the same playbook, the same codes and phrases. The arrogant nature of the average Savage culture was probably still on full xenophobic overdrive against any other culture, even other Savage cultures, that didn't think exactly like they did. There was even a decent chance they'd start fighting one another again soon. As some old politician had once suggested... maybe the answer is to have two enemies so that they would kill each other.

But right now, that was probably too much to ask for.

His armor's local radar showed that some of the Savage scouts had broken off from their pack and were heading back after him. Seconds later incoming rounds were streaking across his HUD. The armor kicked in, computing bullet-fire trajectories and anticipated cones of engagement. He had a good head start. They wouldn't catch him unless they were packing something bigger in the engine department.

The rest of the Savages continued on, no doubt in pursuit of the APC. But as long as the armored vehicle's engines held, it would make it to the LZ. And then they'd be safe. Unless the Savages were planning on mounting another assault—and Rechs thought that unlikely. Despite their reinforcements, the Savages had taken a beating just as badly as the Coalition forces had. It would take time for them to regroup.

Which meant this was the exploitable moment for Rechs and the others. Move about in the confusion between xenophobic cultures and try to get off-planet before the trigger-nuke detonated and cooked off every hydrogen molecule it could chain-react with.

He'd seen a trigger-nuke crack a planet's core before.

It was horrible.

Ahead, Rechs saw the wan half-light over a terminal platform. There was no way to get the bike up on the platform—at least, not quickly enough to stay ahead of his pursuers—so he ditched it and ran for an escalator, dragging the heavy from around his back and looking for a good ambush site. He found one at the top of the escalator with a good field of fire on the platform below.

Unlike Rechs, the pursuing Savages did take the time to stop their bikes and drag them up onto the platform.

A mistake.

When they were all in view, some gunning their engines while others worked their bikes up off the tracks, Rechs opened up with the heavy.

They were grouped together tightly. Whether they had no real military training or had merely gotten lazy after driving the Coalition off-planet, he couldn't say. But it was bad soldiering, and they paid the price. Heavy pulse fire, on high-cycle automatic, spat out hundreds of shots.

A normal squad heavy gunner would have had a hard time stabilizing weapon crawl on high-cycle automatic fire. The powerful rifle tended to jump and squirm at the blur of heavy automatic fire spraying from the barrel. But the armor's cybernetic stabilization system, coupled with the advanced targeting in Rechs's HUD, stabilized the heavy and kept it on target working the tangos until they were good and down.

All dead in fifteen seconds.

Rechs stood from his concealed position at the top of the escalators and swapped in a new charge pack, letting the old one clatter to the floor. Smoke rose from the barrel of the heavy pulse gun.

Then he turned and set off through the field of dead Savages his team had shot during their flight not long before.

70

Wherever Rechs went, there were more dead Savages. Both the hunters and the cannibal marines with the dull-finished mirrored helmets. Martin, Greenhill, and Andres had made the Savages pay all along the way. Mixed in was the occasional human—one of the New Vegan citizens who'd gotten hit in the crossfire. But there were many more dead Savages.

There was no sense in picking up the Wild Man's back trail; Rechs had a clear ping on his current location. And he had a pretty good idea what the Savages had in mind for the big sniper.

Storage.

He found a small passenger elevator, away from the big central transportation disc. Using the big lift would probably bring him into contact with more Savage elements. This smaller one didn't go up as high as he needed to go to reach the Wild Man, but it was close enough, and more importantly... less deadly.

He leaned back against the hard wire mesh of the small cage as he passed several unlit levels. He was tired, and any bit of rest, what he could get of it, was welcome. Some part of his mind asked him how much more he had left. He ignored it, as he always did. The moment you decided how far you'd go… that was exactly how far you would go. Too bad if you needed to go farther.

Tyrus Rechs wasn't a thinker. Never had been. Or at least, no one would have ever accused him of such. He seemed a man of constant action and determined purpose. But the galaxy was vast, and there had been many hours, days, accumulated years in hyperspace… to just sit and merely think. And because he'd lived longer than most—and was quite unsure exactly how long he had yet to live, thanks to the Savage experiments aboard the *Obsidia*—everyone he'd ever known, everyone he ever *would* know as the years progressed, had died or would die long before he did.

And so he spent a lot of time thinking things forward. Never looking back unless he was tactically assessing some situation from the past with the intent of figuring out some problem of the present or the impending future.

Right now he was thinking about Captain Davis and her hard words. And Sulla, who'd said pretty much all the same things to him over the years about finally getting humanity together to deal with the Savage problem instead of emulating Tyrus Rechs and employing the most extreme of measures.

But it *took* extreme measures. Because, when you thought it all the way forward, that was all that one man could do. He couldn't fight a battle on his own. But he *could* wage a one-man war. And trigger-nukes evened the playing field when it was one against upwards of forty thousand combat troops at a go, not to mention all the high-tech surprises the Savages brought to the battlefield—always an unknown variable.

Not even Tyrus Rechs could beat those odds. No soldier could. It would take an army. A collection of warriors with a unity of purpose.

And in lieu of that... trigger-nukes.

They were a necessity. So he had said, many times. And he had been right.

They were a necessity because he'd been fighting alone. Forced to wage the war that no one else would.

Forced there by the indifference, unwillingness, or shortsightedness of others.

One soldier against a thousand armies.

You're not a soldier anymore, he told himself.

At first he wanted to say it was Sulla's voice that had stung him, reminding him that he was no longer what he'd once thought only of. It might have even been the voice of the pretty yet austere starship captain telling him that he hadn't been a soldier for a long time. But in the end, as the lift slowly crawled up through the half-lit shadows, he had to admit it was his own voice.

His own voice telling him the truth.

"You're not a soldier anymore," he whispered. "You're just an assassin."

The small ramshackle cage shuddered to a halt, and the security gate swung open.

As Tyrus Rechs stepped out into the darkness of a multi-level warehouse, IR signatures flared to life in his HUD.

There were hundreds of Savages waiting here in ambush.

As though they'd known he'd come this way all along.

71

The *Chang* came in hot through New Vega's atmosphere. She was burning up O$_2$ through reentry effect when they fell out of micro-jump at almost full cruising speed.

The ship's captain, who was now acting as co-pilot to Admiral Sulla, called out the bow angle and altitude. Overspeed indicators moved to alarm, direly warning of impending impact with the ground below.

Sulla, who had his hand on the throttle, pulled back all four levers connecting to the main four engines. "Bring in inertial reversers!" he commanded.

For the first few seconds, flying reentry was all the crew could do. Micro-jumps with a destination exit inside an atmosphere were the trickiest of feats to pull off when it came to jump navigation. It took everything you had, and a little bit of blind luck, not to leave a crater in some world's face. The ship was shaking violently, and automated damage-control reports flared across the digital HUD along the forward window of the cockpit.

Radar and sensors called out from the CIC at the rear of *Chang*'s bridge. "Contact! We got a hulk in the air, Admiral!"

"Find the LZ!" ordered Sulla. He sat up in his chair, straining to see the ground over the controls and instruments in front of him. Atmosphere howled and whistled beyond the fuselage.

"Multiple lock-ons detected!" shouted another tech from back in CIC.

"I have it," said the *Chang*'s captain from the co-pilot seat. "Our two o'clock."

Sulla spotted it and heeled the ship over to pick up the course track.

"PDCs warming up," announced the weapons officer prophetically while at the same moment the radar and sensor tech shouted that the Savage hulk had sent missiles incoming.

A moment later the belch of the *Chang*'s PDCs erupted across the hull as the defensive weapons system tried to fill the air between the ship and the incoming missiles with hundreds of thousands of tiny projectiles. Any hit would detonate a ship's missile.

"Multiple splashes," called out a tech operating the PDC assessment grid, indicating the weapons were doing their job of keeping the incoming missiles at bay.

"Hulk leaving the battlespace!" cried out the navigation officer. "Their intercept was all wrong."

There's a break, thought Sulla.

He flew the course toward the LZ, dropping the ship down through the billowing black smoke and the scud of atmospheric layers.

"We got lucky!" said the captain, and laughed nervously.

Sulla's eyes went wide as right behind the man, out the co-pilot's window, Savage interceptors swooped out of the smoke-filled afternoon. Hot bright lines of incoming fire raked the *Chang*'s hull with just three kilometers to the LZ.

"Weapons hot on all turrets!" announced the CIC's tactical officer. "Engaging!"

72

There was no retreat. No safe place to fall back to. Tyrus Rechs knew the only way through... was through.

He bumped his jets in the instant before the Savages began to fire at him, crossing the floor to a pyramid of stacked supply freight containers each the size of a rail car.

That quick movement instantly denied a firing solution to at least seventy-five percent of the Savages involved in the ambush. Or so Rechs's helmet told him.

His back pinned to a container, Rechs raised the heavy rifle and cut loose with a blur of fire on a team of Savages to his right. Within seconds he'd pulsed them to shreds.

But the Savages were reacting quickly. They swarmed the container from all sides to get at the crevice he'd found. He shot three with quick bursts and bumped his jets once to hit the next level as he let the heavy dangle from its sling.

He'd used those jump jets a lot. Like the defense bubble, they couldn't go on forever without a recharge. And neither could he.

He popped a fragger and dropped it where he'd been, then ran along the side of the container.

Farther back and higher up in the darkened warehouse, the Savage version of squad-designated marksmen had taken up support positions for the close-infantry assault teams. Now these snipers fired crack shots from old-school weapon systems that reminded Rechs of the ancient Barrett rifle of his earliest days. Any one of those rounds would do a serious number on his armor—and the body beneath. That was the thing about the Savages: it was their anachronistic tech in this bright brilliant modern age of the galaxy, an age of energy-efficient blasters and older-model pulse rifles, that made them so vicious. Old-school chemical firearms were still the most violent thing the galaxy could produce. They went beyond simply killing—like a blaster or pulse rifle—and inflicted maximum damage.

Huge holes appeared in the cargo container Rechs ran along as the snipers sent down shots from the upper reaches of the warehouse. Rechs popped more grenades, bumped his jets, and tried to stay a moving target. There was neither room nor time to bring the heavy into play.

Explosions ripped through the warehouse as his grenades detonated. Small sprays of shredded metal were turned into projectiles with their own terminal velocity as Savages were ripped apart.

All was chaos and madness within the subterranean cave of the storage facility.

Rechs hunkered low, raised the heavy, and sprayed the area where a sniper was shooting from. Vicious pulse fire ripped through the atmosphere of the warehouse and the Savage working the old Barrett-like rifle.

Charge pack out, Rechs swapped in a new one and shifted position. A squad of Savages tried to block his escape route, but he was guns up on them as they almost collided into one another in the tight quarters. At point-blank range he dumped the whole charge pack on high-cycle fire and ventilated the entire squad because there was no room in all the chaos for precision or economy.

There was no room for anything but *extreme* violence.

Just how you like it, Tyrus.

He wasn't sure whose voice that was. But it was right.

Another charge pack out, and Rechs had no time to swap in a new one before an additional team came at him from another quarter, honing in on the carnage of the seconds before. He pulled the hand cannon and auto-fired it into the surging mass. Heavy-caliber slugs tore through the Savages' armor. Rechs's fifty-caliber rounds disintegrated systems and brains, sending misty metallic sprays from the helmets of the Savage marines and the skulls of the morlock attackers. Their demise was brutal and without mercy.

If only because there was no other way.

For a moment Rechs caught a break, but not enough of one to load in a new charge pack. The armor was picking up the sound of more boots and creating an overlay of where everyone might be in the battlespace. Which was, to put it simply, everywhere.

His only way out was straight up.

He chain-ripped a bando of fraggers and left them right where he'd been as he rocketed skyward with what remained of his jump juice—and there was precious little of it left.

The swift jump brought him to the top of the pyramid stack of containers just as the bando exploded, devastating the two swarms of Savage infantry who'd tried to close in on his last known position in a coordinated effort.

From up here he could get better a look at the squad-designated marksmen teams. The armor tagged them, and Rechs burned the last of his jump juice to reach a crane balcony where a team was operating. Hand cannon ready, he started putting rounds into snipers up here in the heights. They couldn't react fast enough to his sudden proximity and died on their bellies.

Moving along the gantry beneath the ceiling of the warehouse, taking badly aimed fire from scrambling sniper teams at the far end, he returned fire with the hand cannon. Switching back to single fire and doling out head and upper torso shots with the armor's targeting assist. He shot them down mercilessly as he climbed up through the shaky network of catwalks that formed the support walkways for the loading tractor that supervised this bay.

Not all of the Savages were dead by the time he reached the main control room at the top and climbed a ladder up through its ceiling into silent darkness. But the Savage ambush had been effectively ruined, and for the most part they were doing little more than laying down covering fire in order to pull their wounded off the deck.

Which seemed odd to Rechs. Because why should they care about the wounded? He put the unbidden thought away—he didn't need to humanize these post-human monsters. Not now. Not ever.

He crouched down behind a control panel and checked his charge packs. He was down to half, and just a few grenades. Ammo for the hand cannon was solid. Zero jump juice.

And three more levels to reach the Wild Man.

An hour and twenty-seven minutes until official sunset.

A lot of ground to cover and a short time to do it in.

73

The Wild Man came to while they were immersing him. Just before, in fact. The Savages had their hard, cold metal gauntlets all over him. And for a moment as he came out of that terrible nightmare of the old place where he had lived with her, he thought they were rescuing him.

The Savages were again humans—just like him—in those first unclear seconds as he struggled to breathe while they drowned him. Not the galactic boogeymen that parents used in order to frighten their children into good behavior, leveraging tales of abduction and slavery if vegetables weren't eaten and studies not performed.

Clean off your plate or the Savages will come and snatch you straight out of bed, I promise you that.

In hindsight, years later, every parent knows they shouldn't have done that. But in the exasperation and fatigue of constantly trying to make some little version of yourself into something better than you'd become in order to survive a galaxy with an appetite for destruction... well, sometimes you used all the cards. Even the bad ones. Even the nuclear ones.

You can feel guilty later, when they're safe.

Like Tyrus Rechs, thought the Wild Man as he came up from the sickly sour-sweet maple syrup pool gasping for a new lungful of air before they managed to plunge him back down. Like Tyrus Rechs using nukes to save the galaxy when no one else, except him and his rifle, would do anything to stop another family from disappearing.

Do another one, babe.

In that moment they, the Savages, seemed just as human as he was. Or even like the angels some talked of.

But then his mind came to full alertness and he realized they weren't angels.

They were demons from the outer dark.

He'd kill them all, except he couldn't move. There were too many hands. Cold, metal hands. Everywhere.

They'd taken him to a subterranean road much like the ones he and Tyrus Rechs's soldiers had traveled through during that seemingly endless night and day. The ones that ran alongside the vast walls of bubble-stored New Vega civilians.

Maybe it was the same road, he thought, as they forced his head and limbs beneath the gel. For good this time. No coming back up. They held on too tight and were too strong.

And in the moment before his eyes went under, his head and neck straining to the last in this vat shaped like a sarcophagus, he saw the floating dirigible and the loading gantry. And the wall of bubbles. A wall of humans. Waiting to be eaten by eaters who were once human.

He tried to move. Tried to fight them in some way.

Fight back, babe! Do something. You have to do something!

But the body would not listen. And all he could do was watch helplessly as he was drowned in their gel-solution. Their horrible gauntlets holding him beneath its goopy surface. His body completely restrained—not only from the hands, but from the gel itself. It was grabbing hold of him. Pulling him down. His mind screaming as his lungs filled up with gel. And those soulless faces, alien things no human mind could have ever conceived of, stared down at him with no pity, remorse, mercy... or even grace. The sound of their harsh electronic barking carried through the gel, and it was like they were laughing at him as they did their drowning work. Laughing along with one another like bullies having their fun with some stray child they'd caught to torment. Out beyond the edge of town where no one can save you.

In the late afternoon turning to evening dark. The feeling that you'll never see home, or your family, again.

Helplessness filled him. He knew he was drowning... dying... but not just yet. It would take a horrible long time for him to die. The gel had a narcotic effect that overwhelmed every sense... taking him away from that horrible place to a promised future of a thousand unending nightmare lifetimes.

A future of bleak hopelessness and unending torture without end. Waking up from one nightmare only to find yourself in one even worse.

"It's an endless well!" his drug-ravaged mind screamed as he got a look at it.

And then words he could not contain struggled up out of him and into the dense gel. Sounding nothing like words but needing to be cried out, if only for the horror of what was happening.

"It's forever in here..." he screamed to no one.

74

The twin-barreled defensive gun of the APC was literally smoking by the time they made the end of the rail line at the stadium terminal, and the vehicle's drive train was a mess of hard clanks and reeking, burning lubricants.

But they'd made it. Wave after wave of Savages had sought to overtake them, and had been beaten back on the strength of their up-top weapon's devastating effect in the enclosed tunnels they escaped through.

They'd made it.

There was no longer any pursuit. In the course of fighting off the last wave of Savages, Martin, operating the turret, had over-cycled just to smash to pieces a lumbering mech that looked like some great mechanical troll thundering after them on hands and knees while lobbing missile salvos the APC's onboard defensive ECM system barely managed to scramble. The tunnel had been ripped to shreds by the missile strikes and collapsed in sections behind the fleeing APC. Blocking further pursuit.

For now.

"Everybody out!" shouted Captain Davis.

Makaffie, who'd been wedged into the boarding well, popped the hatch and rolled out onto the high-speed magnetic tracks beneath the platform. Carrying details were quickly organized for Greenhill, who was tranqed out, and for Sergeant Major Andres, who'd turned gray and was barely breathing. Neither man was conscious.

"He don't look so good," commented Makaffie as they hoisted the senior NCO up onto the platform.

"Sergeant major's tough. Don't mind him," said Martin. "He's gonna make it all right." He was covering the retreat with the only two remaining sidearms that had charge packs. All charge packs for the rifles had been expended.

The soldiers and civilians made their way up through the still-pristine levels the Savages had apparently not tried to breach during their initial counterassault against Objective Rio. That was, until they reached the last set of protected escalators that led up from the secure government access to the stadium and the high-profile dignitary seating. The security had been state-of-the-art for the Galaxy Games that had captured the collective galactic worlds' attention just two years back. New Vega had been the place to be that glittering summer.

Now, below that final set of escalators, they came across Savages who had died by the score. Ruined corpses and shattered armor littered the scorch-marked and carbon-scored marble flooring.

"Halt and identify!" came an enhanced voice from up at the top of the long escalator system. Temporary quick-deploy barricades had been erected up there, and it was clear several heavy-pulse muzzles were now centering on the ragtag group of soldiers and the wounded, desperate civilians who'd just shown up in their kill zone.

"It's Captain Davis of United Worlds Navy, special sections. Admiral Sulla knows we're coming through!"

For a long moment they were greeted by a tense silence. Someone up there was making a decision either to open fire or to take the time to check out the navy captain's story.

"Where's Tyrus Rechs?" came the reply. "Admiral wants to know."

"I'll tell him myself," she shouted up. "Please let us through. We have wounded."

Another long pause.

Some of the civilians began to whimper at this final obstacle when they had made it so far and come so close. The two twins had taken to sticking to close to Davis, and she heard the stronger one, the older one, whisper as her younger sister began to cry.

"Don't worry," the older one said. "They're soldiers. Not monsters. And all soldiers are good. Just like Austin."

In that moment of waiting, hearing the little girl express faith in a thing that wasn't always true in Captain Davis's experience, she wished for a better galaxy than the one she was handing off to the next generation. If there would even be a next generation.

She moved to both of the girls and took their hands in hers. Feeling their tininess as she covered them. Vowing to change things as best she could with what time remained to her.

"It'll be okay," she whispered as she continued to watch the barrels of the rifles of the sentries poking out from their fighting positions high above. Pointing at them. Pointing at the girls.

The voice shouted down once more. "Admiral says you're clear. Come up one at a time. We'll need to search you. Send the wounded up first—we have medics on the way."

And then Captain Davis began to breathe, realizing she had not in those long moments between life and death when she'd wished for a better galaxy.

75

There was one charge pack for the heavy left. Ammunition for the hand cannon was depleted by a little less than fifty percent. A couple of fraggers. One tactical machete.

Tyrus Rechs had fought his way through the checkpoints and quick reaction forces that had responded to his journey through the levels surrounding the old colony ship. Leading the Savage teams along a running battle through an interconnected series of subterranean ventilation systems to keep the whole complex fed with oxygen, he'd decimated their forces by fractions as they dared to follow.

That they were aware he was still running around inside their complex was clear. They were *very* aware. The last wave to come at him was a group of heavy infantry Savages with much better armor, servo-assisted light machine guns, and some sort of energy shields. Rechs had led them into a narrow ventilation feed, climbed upward through the blades of a giant fan that fed into surface air chambers, and then shot them down as they pursued, falling back each time they attempted to dislodge him with grenades. In the end they'd paid a heavy price and pulled back due to losses.

He'd survived, but it had taken time. Time that was running out. And he'd purposefully taken a roundabout path, trying to stay away from his target destination so that they wouldn't fortify there or send more reinforcements.

But now, with the Savage heavy assault teams pulling back until they could come at him from another angle, it was time to make his move. Time to rescue the big sniper. Less than an hour until the *Chang* departed and the whole planet got cooked.

No part of his mind doing the math told him he wasn't going to make it despite the overwhelming evidence that he wasn't going to. He had a plan, if Sulla was game. A way of maybe bringing about what the admiral—and Captain Davis—seemed to think would win the war. Not trigger-nukes, but a unified fighting force. But the plan was no good if he didn't get the big sniper out of the deep freeze.

But that's not true either, is it? his mind told him as he raced along a maintenance passage to get to a spot overlooking the last known position of the Wild Man's transponder. Its signal had gone offline an hour ago.

You could just leave him, continued that other voice. *Because you don't need him for this plan. Not really. You can still make the rendezvous at the LZ. Or you can make it to Plan B. You don't have to rescue him. Why throw yourself away?*

He switched off that other part of his mind that always offered the easy way out. He'd learned to ignore it a long time ago. Even when it told him the truth.

He had said he'd do his best. Which meant if there was a chance... then he'd do everything he could.

A few minutes later he was in position near the last known ping. He'd come out above the roadway that ran alongside the massive vault of bubbles that were seemingly glued to one wall of the storage well. If you didn't look closely, they just looked like a big expensive corporate office art decoration to make some company that was like all the rest seem somehow different. *Individuals working together* might have been the message.

But the armor didn't tell lies.

Inside his HUD he was getting tags on the thousands of suspended lives floating in crystal-clear amber, as it were. They were barely alive in there. Hovering between life and death.

The transponder was still not pinging.

Rechs, who'd had to crawl the last hundred meters once the maintenance access turned to little more than a large air duct, ran through the armor's functions. He called up an image of the one they'd all just called the Wild Man. Then he accessed the armor's recognition algo. Something he'd used a lot during the frontier days of the galaxy—after the Savages had taken him and before they began to show up in earnest—when he worked as a bounty hunter and law enforcer for hire. When he'd grown tired of soldiering for generals who seemed indifferent to anything other than making sure their troops were good and killed in skirmishes between planets seeking domination the way nations and continents once did. Days long gone once the galaxy got civilized.

The armor, a thing that had come from the Savages, in a place they'd found inside the galaxy that didn't exist in space-time—the Quantum Library, they'd called it—ran the search, using the HUD to examine the faces of the thousands of men, women, and children trapped inside the bubbles along the far wall. Searching every face for that of the Wild Man.

Within three seconds it had a match. A filled bubble halfway up the wall in a tiered cluster was the one the Wild Man had been stored within.

The processing dirigible was still floating along the tier, loading more survivors taken from a multi-wheeled cargo hauler. Seven Savages stood around the vehicle, but there was no other defensive force.

Rechs ran through his plan.

More than likely, once he extracted the sniper, he'd have to carry him. Couldn't count on him to be of much help for the short term. So best to use the heavy now, because he'd need less weight when it came time to exfil. And he'd gone this way before. Within the tunnel leading past the storage well there was an access door that accessed a stairwell, a long one.

Davis had mentioned, as they passed it the first time, that it led right up to street level. A fire exit route up from the lower levels. Which hadn't done them any good when they had an APC and a trigger-nuke to cart around. But now, it would do just fine.

A small sign outside the stairwell read *Emergency Exit: Do Not Use Except in Case of Emergency*. If ever there was one... now would qualify.

That was the best he could do to get them both out of here. If he could get them above ground, then maybe there was a chance the comms would work and… something. Rechs hadn't figured that part out yet.

He smashed out the cover of the air duct and dropped down onto the dark subterranean roadway across from the canyon of bubbles. Walking quickly toward the Savages surrounding the cargo truck, he raised the heavy on its sling and began to fire from the hip, his targeting HUD helping him to send rounds just as accurately as shoulder fire.

The first thing that happened was several Savages dropped, surprised, in death. Then those not initially hit by pulse fire scrambled for cover.

This was fine for Rechs's purposes.

Now they would try to assess the situation by popping out for a look, or engaging to pin him down while a flanking team closed the distance from another angle. Standard tactics. Useful for what they were.

He unloaded a brutal burst on the first Savage to pop from around the truck. Pulse fire tore the head and torso to shreds at the same moment that three Savages on the opposite side of the cargo hauler began to fire from underneath. Hot rounds skipped off the pavement; their fire was wide and bad. He'd rattled them. But they'd recover.

If he gave them time. Which he wasn't going to.

With barely a pause he bent over, lowered the heavy pulse gun, and swept the street beneath the truck. Pulse fire smashed into faceless helmets leaving horrible gaping holes in the dirty glass of the twitching bodies.

The rest of the team was spooled up and charged from behind the vehicle. Rechs merely stood, pivoted, and dumped the entire charge into over-cycle fire, cutting them all down before they even got five meters. The felled Savages were armored, so most weren't killed outright, but they were all knocked down by the relativistic effects of the pulse gun, and most were left with smoking holes in their various systems.

Without slowing his pace, Rechs unclipped the empty heavy and dropped it onto the roadway. He pulled the hand cannon and put a single round in the helmet of each still-moving Savage. Then he rounded the truck and made for the gantry leading out to the processing dirigible.

Gunfire streamed down from a sentry team stationed onboard the dirigible. They had seen the carnage that had been done to their rear guard. But the shots missed, merely smashing the wide windows of the cargo hauler between Rechs and them.

Rechs waited for his armor to tag every armed Savage inside the dirigible. Then he scrambled up the gantry and used burst fire from his hand cannon to make sure that each defender had been cut down. He was burning through what precious little ammo he had left, but it was necessary.

He boarded the airship and pulled the tactical machete with its carbon-forged blade with his off hand. A Savage medical tech, who'd been processing the drugged-out citizens of New Vega, attacked him with two old-school metal scalpels, swinging them in wide vicious arcs as he advanced. The first one struck Rechs's armor and snapped. The second one never made contact as a sudden slash from the machete brought the assault to an immediate halt. The

Savage, unarmored, and wearing only some sort of biomechanical carapace, howled like a wounded dishwasher and went stumbling through pristine racks and trays.

There was one other tech remaining. This Savage came at Rechs with a spinning bone saw.

Rechs raised the hand cannon and blew the tech's head off at point-blank range.

All resistance had been dealt with.

Time for extraction.

Sixty seconds later he'd used the dirigible's rudimentary joystick controls to center the floating ship's extraction portal with the bubble where the Wild Man was stored. He moved from the controls to the extraction portal and studied the bubble's surface, aware that klaxons were reverberating throughout the tunnels. They were definitely on to his scent once more. It was one thing to wipe out their front-line troops in the running game of tag-with-weapons they'd been playing for the last few hours. It was quite another to go after their food source.

That was sure to trigger the direst of alarms.

The Savages didn't mind taking, but they hated to be taken from.

Tells you volumes about what monsters they've become, that other voice told him. But he wasn't interested. They were less than human to Tyrus Rechs, and he'd stopped trying to figure them out beyond tactical advantages he might use to kill them. He felt nothing when killing Savages. Even less than when he'd killed animals for survival or protection.

They were less than.

The bubble in front of him had a connecting hose, apparently for draining the gel in which the Wild Man was stored.

Rechs didn't have time for that.

He smashed the machete into the glass. It was heavy glass, but the machete could cut ceramic armor like it was made of butter. Two more strikes and the glass collapsed into sheets of spider-webbing debris. As the gel flooded out in amber goopy waterfalls, he reached his gauntleted hand into the mess.

Over some PA system a Savage voice bellowed in its peculiar electronic shriek. It sounded like an old arcade game speaking twenty different languages at once and it went on and on about something.

He figured it boiled down to... *Protect the Nest. All must respond.*

But repeated a thousand times a minute and said with a frantic neuroticism.

The HUD identified dangerous narcotic compounds within the gel flooding out from the bubble that could have harmed him were the armor not protecting him. It was already suggesting a drug suite it could manufacture just in case there was an integrity breach in the armor.

No time for that either.

He sheathed his machete and pulled the Wild Man out through the bubble's smashed front, clearing away as much fractured glass as he could, knowing there'd be some cuts.

For a moment Tyrus Rechs thought he'd caught a break. The big sniper's eyes opened, wild and rolling, and he focused on Rechs as he coughed and retched and spewed out thick, viscous gel. And then, gel mixing with spittle on his chin and dripping from his nostrils, eyes, and ears, the Wild Man croaked, "It's forever in there!"

Then he collapsed into unconsciousness once more.

Using the armor's servo assist, Rechs got the bigger man over one shoulder in a fireman's carry. He moved for the gantry to exit the madhouse floating hospital, or morgue, that was the dirigible, and drew his hand cannon. Best to have it ready. He was sure to meet more Savages soon.

Already he could hear Savage scout cycle teams streaking down the midnight black tunnels. Coming for him. And other things too. Big lumbering mechs that must be brimming with missiles and all kinds of weapons he'd didn't have a tactical answer to right at this moment.

He only had one plan now.

Run.

Fast.

That was the best he could do.

76

Admiral Sulla met Captain Davis in the triage station that had been set up on the aft cargo deck of the *Chang*.

"Where is he?" asked Sulla.

A medic was treating a bad cut she'd sustained somewhere along the way and hadn't even noticed.

"He went back in after one of our..." she began.

What were they? What had they been—that little fellowship of soldiers and a navy captain who'd suddenly formed up after the battle to complete one last denial-of-service mission? To deliver a doomsday weapon like no other weapon mankind had conceived of in all its years of turning things, forces, and concepts into weapons. A weapon that burned a planet up within hours.

A brotherhood, Rechs had called it. Brothers. Even her.

Thinking about each of them, the ones she'd journeyed with for the last night and a day, down there in the tunnels... it seemed like she'd always known them. Known them better than the crew she'd lost here. Or lovers she'd once known. Or family she'd left behind.

"One of us," she finally finished. "He went back after the sniper who got captured."

"Tyrus," said Sulla, saying the name as if it were a curse. His cool, calm, and at times stern admiral's exterior was now gone. There was nothing but concern here.

The concern of one best friend for the other.

Who would've thought? Tyrus Rechs, galactic war criminal... and a senior ranking admiral in the United Worlds Navy.

Best friends.

"I don't know what happened after that," she said, wishing she could provide some relief or comfort to the now very human admiral standing before her. "He turned off comm after he left us. I don't know why."

Sulla made a face. A face that said something not pleasant. And best left unsaid.

"The sniper?" he asked.

She nodded, because there wasn't anything else to say. Tyrus Rechs had gone back after one man who probably wasn't even Coalition-attached.

And what about the doomsday weapon that's about to go boom? That's what you should really be asking about, Admiral.

"And the trigger-nuke?" asked Admiral Sulla.

She nodded tiredly and waved one dried blood-covered hand.

"It's armed. Geo-trapped, too. It's going to go off in... twenty minutes and thirty-three seconds. I wouldn't expect anything else."

Sulla nodded. But his eyes and his thoughts were far away.

"I probably don't know him," she said, "as well as you do, sir. But... I'd bank on that weapon detonating. From... well... he's a hard man. A good man. Definitely not the war criminal the governments make him out to be with the help of the media. I know that... now. But he's a hard one. He'll let the trigger detonate because killing Savages seems to be what he lives for—besides the thing that sent him back after one... of us. Even if he has to die to do it. He'll cook the planet to kill as many Savages as he can. That's his end game, and it might as well be today."

Sulla turned toward her. Staring at her. And she knew from the look in his eyes that she had correctly diagnosed his oldest and best friend. That the admiral had learned these things long ago.

Then he nodded. Once, and more to himself than to her.

"You're probably right, Captain. But I'll still do everything I can to rescue him. I owe him that."

And then the admiral was off, heading back to the bridge of the *Chang*.

But Davis called out after him. She felt a burning desire to know more of the man she'd just fought with, and something told her the admiral might be her last opportunity to know it. "Admiral!"

Sulla paused and looked over his shoulder.

"He said he was... hundreds of years old. Is he... is he mad?"

Sulla nodded curtly. "Absolutely."

77

Even inside the environmentally controlled armor, Rechs was sweating loads. In order to save the armor's charge, he had cut off nonessential functions and dialed back the cyber strength enhancements, which meant he was largely on his own as he carried the giant sniper up flight after flight of stairs to reach the surface of New Vega. He might need that power later. If things were close at the end.

He gasped for breath, and sweat ran down into his eyes. But he could hear the Savages below him on the stairs, coming up after him, and he pushed himself to move faster. Stair after stair. Flight after flight. It was a race to the top now. They knew he was going this way, and surely they'd try to cut him off ahead. He'd deal with that when he came to it.

He pushed himself up another flight with the dead weight of the giant on his back, and he was glad he'd trained without the armor powered on. Like an ancient knight in a glimmering metallic suit. The armor was the greatest piece of military equipment he'd ever encountered in all his long years. But if relied on, it could make a man weak with dependence. And so he'd trained just like back in the army. Just like in selection for the...

He couldn't remember what he was being selected for as he humped his way up another level. There was still far to go, and it seemed by the sound of the Savages' boots that they were gaining on him.

Still far below, but gaining.

He couldn't remember the name of that course after Ranger school. Either because of how long ago it was, or because he was so tired.

"Long day," he gasped and pulled himself upward. "Long one."

The giant sniper on his back was dead to the world. But the armor assured Rechs that the man was alive, even though he wouldn't be coming around any time soon.

At this moment Rechs was actually glad the sniper had lost his terrific large-caliber rifle somewhere along the way. That thing had probably been sixty pounds alone.

"Q Course," he huffed as he hit the topmost level. "That was it."

He banged through a security door and exited out onto a red daylit street between two crumbling office buildings that were still on fire and raining down ash. Glass littered the sidewalk, and the dead bodies of Coalition forces and Savages lay thrown about like the forgotten rag dolls of careless giant children who had tired of playing war.

His armor told him he had incoming messages from the *Chang*.

He also knew from the map, range, and time, that he'd never make the LZ in time.

Over the city streets, doomsday sirens wailed. It was hard to tell if the sun was setting, but through the inky wash of great billowing fronts of oily smoke, he could see enough of the sky to tell that dusk would be here soon.

And then... *booom*. No more New Vega once the trigger-nuke detonated.

He started off down the block toward a wide intersection, telling the armor to scan and see which buildings still had emergency power. He needed to know that before he contacted the *Chang*.

There were Savages moving in on his position. The armor's radar tagged incoming groups. And it identified a massive tower that was still running on an emergency backup generator. It was just across the intersection, in the middle of which lay a smoking Coalition tank. The crew had been burned alive trying to get out.

He was halfway across and hustling for all he was worth, practically bent double and stumbling, when a Savage point man spotted him and opened fire. Rechs had already caught sight of him out of the corner of his eye and was running for cover by the melted tank. He could hear the Savage calling out to others as it slapped a new mag in and readied to engage.

Rechs paused only briefly behind the tank before bursting forth, firing as he did, and running for the building. The hand cannon roared, its recoil sending Rechs's un-powered arm jumping as the Savage scout dropped on the sidewalk, its body twisting and turning.

More were coming at him from both sides of the intersection, firing wild.

He made the smashed glass darkness of the tower and the interior beyond, and he activated the comm link with the *Chang.*

Sulla was there at once in his ear.

"Tyrus, what's your loc?"

Rechs lowered the sniper next to the elevator bank, slammed his hand for the elevator call, and ran back toward the lobby. He needed to keep them back for a moment.

"Suit's ping is coming through now, Cas. But you're not the only one who's gonna be able to see it."

He fired at two Savages storming the lobby as fast as they could, turning themselves into a cartwheel of limbs and arms. Two brutal bursts smashed into the chest of one, spinning the Savage back and away to die on corporate furniture. For the other Rechs had to overcorrect, because they were both moving at each so other swiftly—Rechs striding and the Savage spinning. He shot the Savage's legs out from under him, and the thing flopped to the polished floor.

Rechs put two bullets in the Savage thing's skull-helmet almost as an afterthought.

He covered as the rest of the mop-up platoon opened fire from the street outside. Sections of giant windows that hadn't been fully destroyed in the madness of the previous day's battle collapsed inward on the lobby, sending fragments everywhere. Luxurious corporate furniture exploded in tufts of synthetic stuffing as hundreds of rounds were thrown at wherever they thought Rechs might be. They were taking no chances. They wanted him dead.

"I read you at Fifth and Horizon," said Sulla over the comm. "You're never going to make it back to the LZ in time. Suggest you—"

"Negative, Sulla," said Rechs. "I'm making for the roof. Bring the *Chang* in and pull us off this tower. Or get out now. But that weapon goes off in..."

Rechs checked the countdown in the lower corner of his HUD.

"... thirteen minutes."

Rechs couldn't even chance return fire. Everything was exploding around him. Expensive woods splintered into the air. Rare leathers received gaping bullet holes. He crawled, shifting position for new cover, and employed his last two fraggers, ones he'd held back instead of leaving for the pursuers back on the stairs, just in case something like right now happened. Just to keep them from storming the lobby.

"I'm coming in for you, Tyrus," said Sulla over the comm. "Be there."

"Will do," he responded and cut the feed.

Rechs raced back to the big sniper and dragged him into the elevator. An automated voice was telling him that elevator access was currently restricted due to an emergency situation.

"Come on," huffed Rechs, pulling the fiberwire connector off his helmet.

Savages were storming the lobby now. Their own version of frags and flashbangs were being lobbed in, followed by hurricane fronts of gunfire as they advanced.

"They're coming..." slurred the Wild Man from the floor. He raised one hand to point, forming a gun with thumb and index finger. "Boom."

Then his hand flopped down. His eyes rolled wildly.

"Don't worry about them," said Rechs. Once he was hard-connected into the building AI, he released an algo-worm that covered the building's emergency restrictions.

He could see the Savages now, entering the lobby amid smoke and ruin, targeting lasers sweeping.

Sweeping for him.

And then the doors closed and they were on their way to the top.

Seventy-five floors to go.

***

Sulla already had the *Chang* ready for a hot departure. Crew were in position. Weapons online and engines at departure idle.

Moments after losing comm with Rechs, he had the gears up, and the last of the Coalition presence was lifting off from the ruins of New Vega.

"Two hulks on an intercept course," said the captain from the co-pilot's seat. "They're going to try to take us before we make jump."

"This is going to be close," said Sulla as he ran through the systems, flicking off everything they wouldn't need. Then he brought in the deflectors and sent as much power as he could to the forward screens.

"Sir," the captain said. "I have jump coordinates pre-loaded and ready."

"We're not going to jump yet, Captain. We have the opportunity to make an additional pickup that the Coalition cannot afford to miss."

"Admiral, we'll be lucky to get out at all once the Savvies reach us. You saw what those hulks did to the fleet on arrival, sir."

The engines were whining toward takeoff power. The sun had begun its final descent behind the sea to the west, obscured by floating drifts of black and gray smoke. Sulla added power and set course for Fifth and Horizon. Rooftop of InterSystem Capital.

"I didn't get to be admiral by playing the odds, Captain."

78

The elevator was the opposite of everything involved in the battle of the past few days. Whereas it seemed everything else had been shot, burned, exploded, or torn to pieces, nothing unmarred by the tremendous battle between both sides, the interior of the swiftly rising elevator was untouched by all the wrongs that had occurred at the end of New Vega City. It even played a corporate soundtrack of instrumental recordings of various pop songs.

The Wild Man hadn't lost consciousness again, though he was still lying on the floor and murmuring incoherently. Conscious but not necessarily lucid.

Tyrus listened and held his hand cannon. Readying himself for whatever they were going to find on the rooftop. There were eight minutes left before the trigger-nuke entered its cascade sequence and detonated.

"Sorry, babe," said the big sniper on the floor. "I was gonna kill 'em all for you, but... but... they got me."

And then the man began to sob.

"I'm not enough," cried the Wild Man. And then he was looking at Rechs. "Nothing is ever enough to bring 'em back, y'know."

Rechs did.

He also knew this man was suffering over some personal loss—that was why he'd been out here hunting Savages. Fighting his own one-man war. Thinking that was somehow doing something. That was how the Wild Man had ended up in the biggest fight between human and Savage there'd ever been.

And perhaps that was *really* why Rechs had gone after him. Because this wild man, he was Tyrus Rechs on a smaller scale. Doing what Rechs did with trigger-nukes, just one bullet at a time. Each waging a one-man war.

Chances were... this was the shape of the galaxy going forward. This was what it would be like for hundreds of years to come.

Could be longer. And humanity... could lose.

That was what Tyrus Rechs was thinking when the Wild Man said the same thing, clarity growing in his eyes.

"Now that they're working together, I won't ever be enough to stop them. Thought I was. But I wasn't. And they..."

The elevator was nearing the top floor now. Rechs readied himself as the door slid open. Maybe they'd already have teams up here. Maybe there'd be Savage spotters or snipers up here. Or the spot had been zeroed in for a Savage artillery strike or interceptor strafing run. Maybe the roof would be on fire and there'd be no way to board the *Chang*. And maybe Rechs and the sniper would be forced to just watch as the ship throttled up and went for jump.

But he had to try.

The elevator door slid open...

... and they were greeted by an empty rooftop.

The sky beyond was gorgeous in its apocalyptic destruction. Storm fronts of black smoke covered the ruined city. Buildings burned, fires on many levels. And two big Savage hulks were closing in on the approaching *Chang*. He couldn't see the smaller Coalition ship, but he knew she was there; he could hear her straining engines.

And then the two hulks fired missile salvos at him. Or in his direction. Smoke trails of sidewinder snakes erupted across the impending night and drove in straight toward the rooftop. In that moment Rechs knew they were done for.

He tapped the omni-defensive bubble on his arm controls.

Nothing.

It wouldn't work. Sometimes it did. Sometimes it didn't.

This was one of those *didn't* times.

So. They were going to die here. If not from the blast of the missiles... then when the building fell.

Some old soldier had once told him that. It ain't the bullet... it's the fall.

But there was no fall.

Not today.

At the last second the *Chang* hovered into view and her PDCs exploded the missiles, causing a daisy-chain that cleared the sky and sent shockwaves to be absorbed by her deflectors. The air split with a sudden outrage of explosive thunder.

"C'mon..." said Rechs, picking up the big sniper once more, using the armor's servo-assist. Thankful he'd saved that extra power. "Here's our ride, soldier."

"One man ain't enough, darlin'," moaned the drugged-out madman on Rechs's back. "All the wives and babies gonna die now unless someone comes to help me kill, Rechs. Too much, babe. Savages too much now that they're all one and together. I thought I might find you someday... but now I..."

Rechs grunted and shuffled across the rooftop. It was right then the armor ran out of power. Came to its end. And he, too, was at an end. The end of himself. He'd never felt so much like just stopping right there and letting what would happen... happen. Regardless of the consequences. His legs were on fire and they felt incapable of moving any farther. This was how he trained. In a powerless suit. But never after having already endured so much. Gone so far.

Everyone has a limit.

"Wish we could be together," moaned the Wild Man at the *darling* he was talking to. "Like they is. I'd kill 'em all for you, darlin'. But one man ain't enough against the galaxy... is it, Tyrus? Tell her. One man ain't enough! Damn it! I hate you all!" screamed the Wild Man at all the Savages there ever were. And at the galaxy that had taken away the two he had loved most.

Rechs's strength failed as he neared the hovering *Chang*. Another missile strike from the hulks slammed into the ship, the impact knocking the *Chang*'s lowest deck into the side of the tower, sending glass and steel cascading down into the Savage-overrun streets below. The tower groaned titanically.

Sulla had put a portside cargo door onto the roof of the building while the ship's massive repulsors held her aloft, impossibly adept flying for a ship so large.

Drones were screaming across the rooftop. Ignoring Rechs and slamming into the *Chang*.

Door gunners appeared in the cargo hold. And they opened up on him as he struggled to take another step. No... not on him. Behind him.

The Savages must have finally gained the roof. But there was no time to look back. Just to stumble forward. The building shook. It was going to collapse.

The armor's HUD warned him that another drone strike was inbound. The helmet—Rechs's bucket—was always the last thing to power down. And now it was telling him that the original hulk that had grounded on the capital of New Vega was sending more drones, giving everything it had to put down the last remnants of the Coalition on New Vega.

Rechs willed his legs to move forward toward the open cargo bay. Crew chiefs beckoned him forward from within while the door gunners continued to pour fire out onto the rooftop. The building swayed violently, steel crying out and then snapping somewhere in the deep levels below. Sheets of concrete slid down from the faces as the *Chang* hovered and maneuvered to get in closer. Rechs stumbled sideways and it felt like he was going to go down with the big sniper on his back. He could see Davis hanging onto a cargo strap within the hold. Calling out to him. Willing for them to make it.

Above all this the looming Savage hulks closed the distance.

Legs are fried, some part of Rechs's mind told him as he continued to stumble forward. Moving slowly. A step at a time. One after the other.

Just put him down and save yourself, said that other voice we all have. The one that tells us to live no matter the cost to others.

He saw the trigger-nuke's weapon clock in the corner of his HUD.

Three minutes.

If the *Chang* was still in atmo when it went off, she'd burn too.

His mind told him he couldn't go another step.

He stood there, hovering between falling over and just freezing, legs locked and useless as bullets raced past him and the building collapsed beneath him.

Yeah... Rechs told himself. *Fine. Legs are fried. So what. You'll rest some other day.*

And then he began to lumber forward for the last of the distance, the weight of the man on his back crushing him.

But he didn't care now.

Not anymore.

He was too tired to care. All he had left he gave to moving forward.

A swarm of drones darted through the PDC fire and slammed into one of the *Chang*'s four main engines. It exploded, sending hull plating and fragments out across the skyline.

Chang didn't need four engines to get out. But losing any more would be pushing it.

Rechs stumbled into the cargo bay. The crew chiefs caught the big sniper as Rechs crashed onto the deck. They were dragging him forward and he was blacking out as the cargo door sealed. Bullets slapping into the hull.

And damage-control sirens.

Internals across all decks.

One minute until detonation.

No idea if the *Chang* would make it.

Medics were loading both him and the Wild Man onto stretchers regardless of the fact that the *Chang* was under fire and was most likely about to go up with three hulks and an entire city within the next sixty seconds.

Through his back he could feel the *Chang* straining to reach jump altitude. Maybe the nav comp was having to replot because of the two hulks on an intercept course.

Maybe…

Maybe they'd make it.

Maybe they wouldn't.

It was out of his hands now.

And there was a peace in that. In things being out of your hands. Being out of your control.

But that wasn't a peace that belonged to Tyrus Rechs. It didn't suit him.

It wasn't who he was.

Never had been.

And there was still one thing he could do. A thing *only* he could do.

A decision only he could make.

He brought up the trigger-nuke's menu and watched as the clock hit thirty seconds.

Then he selected... *ABORT*.

He looked over at the Wild Man. They had fresh oxygen pumping through a mask over the big sniper's face. His chest was rising. His eyes were closed and fluttering.

Rechs gave him a thumbs-up anyway.

No man is an island, he would think days later when he thought about this moment. Tried to figure out why. He would know after he talked to the little girl. The angry twin.

But in that moment he just raised one thumb of his gauntlet and said, his voice a harsh croak within his own helmet...

"We'll come back. We'll do it together."

And then he passed out, and somewhere along the way, under fire, the *Chang* jumped free of New Vega. Leaving behind a world that hadn't been trigger-nuked, and was under Savage control.

For the time being.

Epilogue

Three days later, ship time, Tyrus Rechs was released from medical holding. He stood without assistance and wandered the decks of the assault cruiser on his own.

When he passed the civilians in their bays, they thanked him and cried. Grateful that they, of all those on New Vega, had been spared. But in their eyes, despite the gratitude, he could see the haunted survivors' guilt. The knowing that they were the few, out of the many.

And yet still they thanked him.

Tyrus nodded. And murmured things he couldn't remember. Because what can you say to someone who's just lost their everything, city, livelihood, planet... loved ones. All of the above.

What can you say?

Nothing.

So he didn't.

Later he saw Greenhill in medical. He was still under sedation. But the big black cav sergeant had fought like a tiger. And so Rechs just sat there listening to the machines work. A doctor came in and told Rechs that everything would be fine. That Greenhill would make a full recovery.

Rechs nodded.

Everything would be fine.

And yet the doctor, like everyone, knew that the Savages were now working together. And that there would be no treaties, no peace agreements. There would be only war. War unending. And it would be either us, or them. He saw that in the doctor's face when Tyrus was told that Greenhill would make a full recovery back on Spilursa. Saw that there was really no safe place left in all the galaxy now that all the Savages were one.

He saw the doctor smile in that way that doctors smile when they know the prognosis is grim. But the best doctors are like soldiers in that they're willing to fight the good fight as long as the patient is willing to be the battlefield. The smile of yes, things are rough. But there are some treatments we can still try. There is always hope, until there is none.

Though Rechs might be near immortal, barring violent death, he'd seen enough death to know that smile.

The smile that said... well, we're not done just yet.

Sergeant Major Andres was going through another surgery. Rechs waited some more. Having coffee. And when it was time to see the NCO, he went into the recovery suite.

The sergeant major was conscious but still on narcotics.

"I'm alrrrrigght, sir," he slurred slowly.

Rechs nodded and listened. They talked for a while, which mainly consisted of Andres asking after everyone. Making sure they'd all made it back.

That's what good NCOs do.

"Captain de Macha got killed before me, sir," said the sergeant major. "He was a real good officer, sir."

"Yeah. He was."

Both men looked away when a tear ran down the NCO's cheek. Every death is a failure for an NCO. Or at least... the good ones. The best ones. The ones charged with bringing back the galaxy's children from all the worlds and wars they're sent to.

"You put him in for an award, sir?" Andres asked.

"I was never really a colonel in the Spilursan military, Sergeant Major," said Rechs after a moment. "So... I don't know if I can. But I'll ask Admiral Sulla to do what he can."

The NCO made a comically hurt face. But maybe that was just the meds. Maybe he meant that hurt face.

"Aw, nah, sir. You was my colonel. That's for sure. Wherever you end up, I'll come make sure the grass is cut and the flag is hung right every morning, okay. You just let me know. You be the colonel and I'll be sergeant major..."

The tranqs the nurse had given him were taking effect, and his eyes fluttered. But before he drifted off, one last time, he said it again. As though from some place far away and better than all this.

"You my colonel, sir. You... you all right..."

And then he was asleep.

On his way to meet Sulla for more coffee—he'd slept enough over the last three days—Rechs ran into Captain Davis. She didn't say anything. Just looked at him.

Both of them thinking about the trigger-nuke.

"How come?" she asked.

Just that.

How come you didn't cook the whole planet... Tyrus Rechs?

"I don't know," Rechs said. And paused. "I just knew..." He scratched his stubble and leaned against a bulkhead. "I just knew it was the right thing to do. This time."

She thought about this, and when she'd made it all make sense in her mind she said, "It was, Tyrus. That it was."

He nodded, and they just stood there for a while.

"When you go back... to rescue them," she said, "I want in."

And then she turned and walked away because she was afraid of what he might say.

In the officers' mess, which was quiet and between meals, he sat with the admiral and had coffee.

The two of them saying little.

And then Sulla spoke.

"If you want," he began, leaning in like the old conspirators they'd been for so long, "there's a small ship on the flag deck. I keep it around for... emergencies. When we exit jump, you can take it and get away. They've already let me know I either place you under arrest or I face a court-martial."

"And?" asked Rechs.

Sulla smiled. "I'm a little more powerful than they suspect. I have a lot of connections, Tyrus. I don't know if you know this, but... I've been around for quite a while."

They both laughed at this inside joke.

But it wasn't much beyond a chuckle.

"But there's another option, Tyrus," continued Sulla seriously. "I've talked with most of my crew. Everyone agrees something needs to be done about the Savages... and that the Coalition had their chance."

Rechs raised his eyebrows but said nothing. Instead he took another sip of the coffee. And listened.

"You were right, Tyrus. Stitching all those militaries together isn't going to cut it if we're going to deal with the Savages effectively. We'll just get opportunistic peacocks like Ogilvie. We'll get hamstrung, and hampered, and we'll never be allowed to win. You and I have seen it in every other conflict we've ever been in. I get it now. So... I want to do it your way."

"My way?" said Rechs quietly with no small amount of disbelief. He looked around. "Nukes?"

Sulla laughed again and then leaned in to explain.

They were whispering. Because most people didn't need to hear, nor would they even understand nine tenths of what was spoken between two near immortal ex-slaves who'd become fierce warriors over the course of centuries. Fierce warriors who'd taken on the mission of saving humanity from itself. Or rather... from the Savages.

"That's not your way, Tyrus. Your way is to fight. You want to kill them first before they kill us. You were just using the nukes because one man can only do so much."

Rechs remembered the things the Wild Man had been saying in the elevator. Things that made sense then, and more now. Maybe that was why he'd aborted the nuke. To be honest, he still didn't really know why. Maybe it was to save the *Chang* from burning up in the atmosphere.

Or maybe it was because of who was inside the bubbles. All of them. And what the Wild Man had said when he'd brought him out.

It's forever in there.

No one should know that for the last of their existence. And he had a pretty good idea what the Savages had been playing with to make that possible. All that quantum voodoo they liked to get up to.

"What if there was someone to fight alongside you, Tyrus? Someones. A bunch of us. What if we formed our own fighting force? Our own army to find and destroy the Savages, and it was independent of any government body? What if we did that, Tyrus?"

"Like a..." But he couldn't think of the term. It was there. And it wasn't. He was getting old. He didn't look it, but he was.

"A foreign legion," said Sulla. "We could be that."

"How?"

"Like I said, I have connections. A lot of groups, corporations, and people would finance this just to stop the Savages from destroying the fledgling galactic economy."

Rechs looked at his oldest friend. A man he'd known since Earth. Since the *Obsidia*. And all the years in between.

"I don't know. Outside interests and all, Cas. There's a way it needs to be done and... I don't want to sound arrogant, but I see it. And I don't want someone controlling me for their own agenda. But I'll keep fighting. You know I'll do that. And one day the Savages will run out of ships. One day I'll get the last one."

Sulla gave him a look that said... *You think so?*

And Rechs nodded.

Despite the years.

Despite the new Savage alliance.

Despite everything the galaxy could throw at him.

One day he'd kill them all.

Or die trying.

And what if you do? What if you die trying? that other voice asked him. *What if you die and no one else takes your place and the Savages end up the dominant life form in the galaxy?*

What if that, Tyrus Rechs?

He thought about that dark alien thing from another reality that they'd met on the *Obsidia*—the Dark Wanderer. A being from beyond the galaxy that had already worked with the Savages at least once before. And the results had been supernaturally terrifying. Things that shouldn't have been done... had been.

What if the Dark Wanderer finds this new Savage alliance?

"I'll think about it," said Rechs—with every intention, at that moment, of just going on killing them with trigger-nukes wherever he could find them.

Later, most of him was leaning toward being on that small freighter when they fell out of jump. Then he could get on with the business of handling the Savages on his terms. The best way he knew how.

The only way, in light of a more compelling argument.

With just hours to go until that decision moment, he ran into the angry little girl. The dominant twin.

"My sister says I should say thank you now."

She stood there like she was confronting him. Or some monster, or stray dog that needed to be dealt with. That was how she held herself in all her smallness compared to the vastness of his age, skill, and size.

She stood there, *confronting* him.

She looked at the floor, stared at it hard, forcing herself to do something she didn't want to even because she knew it was the right thing to do. Doing it because her sister had made her. And in the end she wanted to be more like her sister than herself.

"Don't," said Tyrus, standing above her in the quiet of the passage they'd found themselves in.

"I don't want to," she whispered suddenly. And Tyrus saw tears fall onto the deck even though he could not see her face.

"It's okay," he said softly. "You're mad at the galaxy. Mad at the Savages. Mad at everything. I get that. You don't need to thank me."

"Why?" she whispered. Her shoulders were shaking as she tried to hold back the tears that were flowing freely now.

Tyrus sighed and looked off.

"Because you're not ready yet to be thankful. You don't... feel like you have anything to be thankful for. And so it burns in your mouth to say it. And... that's okay for now."

"It is?" Her voice small and uncertain. Afraid. Then he heard her moan softly. Still trying not to cry. Thinking of all that was gone and would never come back.

Of *who* was gone.

Who.

"You've lost everyone," said Rechs. "You're alone and you feel like you're on an island. But you're not. And someday... well, you'll see that you aren't as alone as you feel. But maybe not for a long time."

She wiped her face with the sleeve of some crew uniform someone had tried to fit her with. It was much too large.

"How do you know that?" she asked.

He bent down and looked her in the eyes. They were coal dark and burning. But they were looking for help. Any help, any port in this storm of vulnerability and emotion. Looking for some light in the storm by which to find a safe harbor.

"Because I've been there," Rechs said. "On that island. For a long time."

She stared at him. Daring him. Testing him to see if he was a liar who told lies to little girls.

Then...

She saw that he was not.

"Austin was studying poetry. Before the Savages came and..."

Rechs remembered that they, the two little twin girls, had been looking for their brother. Austin.

"... he used to teach us about them. About being alone. Because... our mom and dad were killed before the Savages. In an accident. And it was just the three of us after that. Alone. And then... it was just us."

Rechs said nothing. Because what can you say? that would make anything better?

So often he'd found the only answer had been... nothing.

"He always read us this one about no one being an island. That even though we were alone... we really weren't. He always... read us that one."

Her eyes began to run with tears, but she did not sob. Instead she continued staring straight into Tyrus Rechs. Soldier. Bounty hunter. War criminal. Killer of monsters.

Just one man.

"Is that still true?" she asked.

He pulled her to his shoulder and held her close. Because it was the right thing to do. The only thing he could do at that moment. And she began to cry in full, sobbing for all the wrongs that had been done to her. Sobbing as though there would never be a day not filled with the sorrow of what had happened.

He hated the Savages. Hated them for doing this to countless numbers of little children. He hated unjust death. And those that caused it.

He always had.

And he knew he was just one man who thought he was an island in the universe. An island that could change the course of the galactic ocean. And he knew that he was no longer enough.

He knew that now.

He would work with whoever would do it his way, to stop the Savages once and for all. They would form Sulla's foreign legion and... maybe... maybe... they could save those who couldn't save themselves.

Maybe they could beat the Savages, and stop the tears of little girls. And everyone else. Maybe the galaxy would know humanity for its... humanity. Instead of the monsters the Savages had become.

Maybe.

This wasn't the end.

It was the beginning of the Savage Wars.

And...

The Legion.

THE STORY CONTINUES IN SAVAGE WARS BOOK TWO: GODS & LEGIONNAIRES

"No Man Is an Island"

No man is an island entire of itself; every man is a piece of the continent, a part of the main; if a clod be washed away by the sea, the world is the less, as well as if a promontory were, as well as any manner of thy friends or of thine own were; any man's death diminishes me, because I am involved in mankind.
And therefore never send to know for whom the bell tolls; it tolls for thee.
—John Donne

JOIN THE LEGION

You can find art, t-shirts, signed books and other merchandise on our website.

We also have a fantastic Facebook group called the Galaxy's Edge Fan Club that was created for readers and listeners of *Galaxy's Edge* to get together and share their lives, discuss the series, and have an avenue to talk directly with Jason Anspach and Nick Cole. Please check it out and say hello once you get there!

For updates about new releases, exclusive promotions, and sales, visit inthelegion.com and sign up for our VIP mailing list. Grab a spot in the nearest combat sled and get over there to receive your free copy of "Tin Man," a Galaxy's Edge short story available only to mailing list subscribers.

INTHELEGION.COM

GALAXYS
EDGE
TIN MAN

ANSPACH COLE

GET A
FREE,
EXCLUSIVE
SHORT STORY

THE GALAXY
IS A DUMPSTER
FIRE...

OTHER GALAXY'S EDGE BOOKS

Galaxy's Edge Season One:
- Legionnaire
- Galactic Outlaws
- Kill Team
- Attack of Shadows
- Sword of the Legion
- Prisoners of Darkness
- Turning Point
- Message for the Dead
- Retribution

Galaxy's Edge Season Two:
- Takeover

Tyrus Rechs: Contracts & Terminations:
- Requiem for Medusa
- Chasing the Dragon
- Madame Guillotine

Stand-Alone Books:
- Imperator

Order of the Centurion:
- Order of the Centurion
- Iron Wolves
- Through the Nether
- The Reservist
- Stryker's War

ABOUT THE AUTHORS

Jason Anspach and Nick Cole are a pair of west coast authors teaming up to write their science fiction dream series, Galaxy's Edge.

Jason Anspach is a best-selling author living in Puyallup, Washington with his wife and their own legionnaire squad of seven (not a typo) children. Raised in a military family (Go Army!), he spent his formative years around Joint Base Lewis-McChord and is active in several pro-veteran charities. Jason enjoys hiking and camping throughout the beautiful Pacific Northwest. He remains undefeated at arm wrestling against his entire family.

Nick Cole is a Dragon Award winning author best known for *The Old Man and the Wasteland, CTRL ALT Revolt!,* and the Wyrd Saga. After serving in the United States Army, Nick moved to Hollywood to pursue a career in acting and writing. He resides with his wife, a professional opera singer, south of Los Angeles, California.

Honor Roll

We would like to give our most sincere thanks and recognition to those who helped make *Galaxy's Edge: Savage Wars* possible by subscribing to GalacticOutlaws.com

Jonathan Clews

Beau Clifton

Alex Collins-Gauweiler

Garrett Comerford

James Connolly

James Conyers

Jonathan Copley

Robert Cosler

Andrew Craig

Adam Craig

Phil Culpepper

Ben Curcio

Thomas Cutler

Alister Davidson

Peter Davies

Ivy Davis

Nathan Davis

Ron Deage

Tod Delaricheliere

Ryan Denniston

Christopher DiNote

Matthew Dippel

Ellis Dobbins

Ray Duck

Cami Dutton

Virgil Dwyer

William Ely

Stephane Escrig

Hunter Ferguson

Ashley Finnigan

Steve Forrester

Skyla Forster

Timothy Foster

Bryant Fox

Mark Franceschini

David Gaither

Christopher Gallo

Richard Gallo

Kyle Gannon

Michael Gardner

Nick Gerlach

John Giorgis

Justin Godfrey

Luis Gomez

Gerald Granada

Gordon Green

Tim Green

Shawn Greene

Erik Hansen

Greg Hanson

Jason Harris

Jordan Harris

Matthew Hartmann

Adam Hartswick

Ronald Haulman

Joshua Hayes

Jason Henderson

Jason Henderson

Kyle Hetzer

Aaron Holden

Joshua Hopkins

Tyson Hopkins

Christopher Hopper

Ian House

Ken Houseal
Nathan Housley
Jeff Howard
Mike Hull
Bradley Huntoon
Carl Hutchens
Wendy Jacobson
Paul Jarman
James Jeffers
Tedman Jess
James Johnson
Randolph Johnson
Tyler Jones
John Josendale
Wyatt Justice
Ron Karroll
Cody Keaton
Noah Kelly
Caleb Kenner
Daniel Kimm
Zachary Kinsman
Rhet Klaahsen
Jesse Klein
Travis Knight
Ethan Koska
Evan Kowalski
Byl Kravetz
Brian Lambert
Clay Lambert
Grant Lambert
Jeremy Lambert
Dave Lawrence

Alexander Le
Paul Lizer
Richard Long
Oliver Longchamps
Brooke Lyons
John M
Patrick Maclary
Richard Maier
Brian Mansur
Robet Marchi
Deven Marincovich
Cory Marko
Lucas Martin
Pawel Martin
Trevor Martin
Tao Mason
Mark Maurice
Simon Mayeski
Kyle McCarley
Quinn McCusker
Alan McDonald
Caleb McDonald
Hans McIlveen
Rachel McIntosh
Joshua McMaster
Christopher Menkhaus
Jim Mern
Dylon Merrell
Robert Mertz
Pete Micale
Mike Mieszcak
Brandon Mikula

Ted Milker

Mitchell Moore

William Morris

Alex Morstadt

Nicholas Mukanos

Vinesh Narayan

Bennett Nickels

Andrew Niesent

Greg Nugent

Christina Nymeyer

Colin O'neill

Ryan O'neill

Tyler Ornelas

James Owens

David Parker

Eric Pastorek

Carl Patrick

Dupres Pina

Pete Plum

Paul Polanski

Matthew Pommerening

Jeremiah Popp

Chancey Porter

Brian Potts

Chris Pourteau

Chris Prats

Joshua Purvis

Nick Quinn

Eric Ritenour

Walt Robillard

Joshua Robinson

Daniel Robitaille

Thomas Roman

Joyce Roth

David Sanford

Jaysn Schaener

Landon Schaule

Shayne Schettler

Andrew Schmidt

Brian Schmidt

William Schweisthal

Aaron Seaman

Phillip Seek

Christopher Shaw

Charles Sheehan

Wendell Shelton

Brett Shilton

Vernetta Shipley

Glenn Shotton

Joshua Sipin

Scott Sloan

Daniel Smith

Michael Smith

Sharroll Smith

Tyler Smith

John Spears

Peter Spitzer

Dustin Sprick

Graham Stanton

Paul Starck

Maggie Stewart-Grant

John Stockley

Rob Strachan

William Strickler

Shayla Striffler
Kevin Summers
Ernest Sumner
Carol Szpara
Travis TadeWaldt
Daniel Tanner
Lawrence Tate
Tim Taylor
Mark Teets
Steven Thompson
William Joseph Thorpe
Beverly Tierney
Matthew Titus
Jameson Trauger
Scott Tucker
Eric Turnbull
Brandon Turton
Jalen Underwood
Paul Van Dop

Paden VanBuskirk
Jose Vazquez
Anthony Wagnon
Christopher Walker
David Wall
Andrew Ward
Scot Washam
John Watson
James Wells
Ben Wheeler
Scott Winters
Jason Wright
Brandt Zeeh
Nathan Zoss

Made in the USA
Coppell, TX
18 April 2020